GET YOUR FREE FANTASY NOVELLA

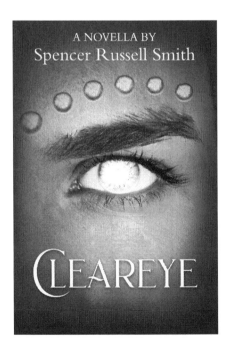

To sign up for my author newsletter and get your free copy of *Cleareye*, visit www.spencerrussellsmith.com/freenovella

BY SPENCER RUSSELL SMITH

Awakening The Lightforged
Throne of Darkness
Sanctuary
The Shattering
The Last Knight
Awakening the Lightforged (The Complete Trilogy)

Tales of Efruumani
Another Way (short story)
Music of the Lights (short story)
Cleareye (novella)

Get a FREE novella set in the world of this series—*Cleareye*— by signing up to my mailing list at: www.spencerrussellsmith.com/freenovella or scan the QR code below:

There is a map included in this book, but if you want to see a full-color, high resolution version to follow along with, you can find one on my website at: https://www.spencerrussellsmith.com/art

SANCTUARY

AWAKENING THE LIGHTFORGED
BOOK 2

SPENCER RUSSELL SMITH

This is a work of fiction. All names, characters, places and events are a product of the author's imagination and are used fictitiously. Any resemblance to real people, alive or dead, or to businesses, companies, events, institutions, or locales is purely coincidental.

Sanctuary
Awakening the Lightforged:
Book II

Copyright © 2022 by Spencer Russell Smith
Illustrations © 2022 by Spencer Russell Smith

First Edition: October 2022
The right of Spencer Russell Smith
All rights reserved.

No part of this book may be reproduced, transmitted, or stored in a retrieval system in any form or by any means without permission in writing from the copyright owner, not otherwise circulated in any form of binding or cover other than that in which it is published and without a similar condition being imposed on the subsequent purchaser.

www.spencerrussellsmith.com

Cover Design by: Stuart Bache
Map by: Spencer Russell Smith

CONTENTS

Content Warnings	xiii
A Brief Glossary of Auroramancy	xvii
Prologue: Muuzuuri	1
1. Unmasked	9
2. Monsters	17
3. Storm	30
4. The Hope In Their Eyes	39
5. Phantom	49
6. Do You Want to Fight?	57
7. Visions and Spies	67
8. The Silver City	73
9. The Silent Forest	88
10. Makala	95
11. To Fight Again	105
12. What Now?	113
13. The Right Course	121
14. The Workings of the Stars	127
15. Mshauuri	141
16. Protected No Longer	146
17. Tower Six	156
18. A Different World	164
19. Fundamentals	185
20. Diwani	194
21. Preparation	218
22. Make it Work	224
23. Healing	229
24. A King's Anger	237
25. Sleepers	248
26. Exploring Scars	256
27. Power Begets Conflict	277
28. A City Asleep	289
29. Personal Research	312
30. Among the Stars	322
31. Music of Aioa	331

32. Secrets	334
33. Coward	345
34. Something Incredibly Stupid	352
35. Understanding	365
36. Arrogance	370
37. Professor Modibodjara	376
38. The Gift of the Vale	380
39. Failure	388
40. I Hope You Remember	391
Epilogue I: Bykome	397
Epilogue II: Alajos	403
Epilogue III: Araana	409
Epilogue IV: Matsanga	412
THE END	419
Thank you so much! Please keep Reading!	421
The Shattering Sale Page	423
About the Author	425
Acknowledgments	427
Notes on Pronunciation	429
Introduction to Aikwe Arna's History of the Buuekwenani	431
The Fiddler in the Night	443

CONTINUE READING FOR AN EXCLUSIVE LOOK AT "THE LAST KNIGHT"

1. The Last Day	449
2. Move Out	457
3. To Know Each Other Again	463

GLOSSARY

Gemcrests	471
The Auroras and Lightlessness	473
Auroraborn, Fireborn, Iceborn, and Genetics	475
Origins of the Powers and Legends	477
Individual Abilities Basic Mechanics	479
Substances of Interest	489
The Redeemed	493

Mom,
Thank you for always believing in me.

CONTENT WARNINGS

This story contains some difficult material. I do not put these in for shock value, and try my best to approach these thoughtfully, but I encourage you to take care when reading if any of the below is something you hard for you to read.

This is a non-exhaustive list of content warnings:

Graphic
Violence, death, dead bodies, blood, loss of limb, death of a spouse, concentration camp, death of a child (off screen), death of family (off screen), forced migration (off screen)

Moderate
Suicide, imprisonment, enhanced interrogation/torture (implied), suicidal thoughts (implied), drug use, alcohol use, authoritarian regime, cursing, fade-to-black seduction and intimacy.

Minor
Injury details, innuendo

Note:

I am lucky enough that I have rarely needed content warnings when consuming media except in the case of graphic horror (just can't do it), so if there is anything in this book that I have missed listing above that causes you distress, please accept my sincerest apologies, and if you wouldn't mind, please let me know so that I can add it to the list in this book and on my website to prevent others from having a similar experience.

The Efruumani System

Myrskaan

Efruumani Atjakuu

A Brief Glossary of Auroramantic Abilities

Samjati Abilities

Violetnodes: sap heat from the air or produce ice
Aquanodes: manipulate existing ice or water
Greennodes: push and pull ice and water
Greynodes: enhance strength and durability
Clearnodes: enhance sensory perception
Opalnodes: flare other abilities
Orangenodes: see into the past
Yellownodes: manipulate luck, chance, coincidence
Rednodes: produce and manipulate darklight
Bluenodes: steal auroralight from others
Ambernodes: limited precognition
Blacknodes: hide uses of auroramancy

Natari Abilities

Violetnodes: produce heat, fire, and lightning
Aquanodes: manipulate existing fire or lava
Greennodes: push and pull volcanic rock and lava
Greynodes: enhance stamina and agility
Clearnodes: enhance sensory perception
Opalnodes: flare other abilities
Orangenodes: see into the past
Yellownodes: manipulate luck, chance, coincidence
Rednodes: produce and manipulate hardlight
Bluenodes: transfer auroralight to others
Ambernodes: limited precognition
Blacknodes: detect uses of auroramancy

Pre-Destruction Efruumani

Note: Globular Projection.

Yrnnuthal's Grave

Darkside
- -
Lightside

Mjatafa Mwonga
and
Booathal

Planetary System Notes:

Satellite research of the Beyond has provided immesurable context for the Efruumani System. Our red-orange, volatile star ranks low in temperature and lifespan.

In this Projection, Accuracy is Sacrificed for Artistic License. Spacing Between Objects at the Horizon Line and Poles is Distorted.

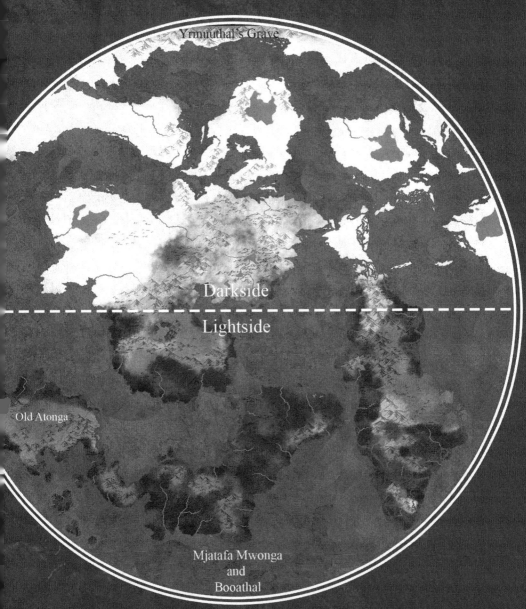

Efruumani appears to be a habitable moon of the gas giant, Myrskaan, rather than a planet in its own right. We were surprised to learn that Efruumani's tidally locked position in Myrskaan's Lagrange Point is unusual, and should be much less stable than it has been throughout our history. The Destruction of Yrmuunthal has made this painfully evident, and has spurred Mjatafa Mwonga's construction and the race to find a suitable home among the Beyond.

Prologue

Muuzuuri

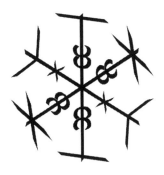

Exodus countdown: 19 days, 3 hours, 3 minutes

The ringing, rhythmic scrape of a spinning coin on wood combined with the scratching of charcoal against paper, the occasional shuffle of a card or tin cup being moved, and the near constant soft chewing, to lend a rhythm to the small room Muuzuuri and her companions lounged in. If it could be called that. Lounging implied luxury, and this modest room with its mix of scavenged furniture was far from luxury even by Remnant standards. Even here at Gold Base, the former home of the Stormswind faction, and the second smallest of the Remnant's remaining bases. Yet the familiarity and company provided a sense of comfort.

Well, usually.

Muuzuuri sat at one of the room's two tables—a taller wooden one near the wall with a rough surface. Sometimes they ate or drank at it, but its primary function was as a stand for the commdisc. Muuzuuri's coin would waver or fall every now and then when it encountered a rough patch or part of a splinter. She just kept spinning it, occasionally glancing at her companions and taking a bite—a small one—of her rations. The room was tense with the commdisc's silence and the air of waiting—waiting for anything since the go-ahead two days past—though they all tried to ignore it.

Muuzuuri's coin fell again. Heads. It was an old coin. One side displayed the bust of Sana Maaryna, an old Juusanaritii queen known for her progressive policies. The other displayed a twelve-pointed snowflake symbolizing Kweshrima's Knights, sometimes called the Knights Reborn in recent years. She glanced about the room as she spun it again.

Jaran, bearing the light blue complexion and wide, shovel-like antlers typical of the Kysuuri, sat in the room's far corner in a squat canvas chair, eyes downcast. He sipped at his small tin cup, his second since they'd all come in today. Jaran's other hand gripped the bottle of lakka that Oka'ada had broken out for. No one said anything. Jaran had a right to his sadness. They all did, but him most of all.

Oka'ada sat across from Adisa at the room's main table—a large, squat thing of wood and metal. They played Balance, an old game that had been played by high society types and nobles to train their children for lives of strategy and political maneuvering and to keep the adults' sense sharp. Now that all the noble houses and aristocracies were no more, it was just a fun game to play in times where enjoyment was often hard to come by.

Oka'ada held the dark cards, black stripes highlighting the muscles of his thick arms—thick for a Natari, at least—while Adisa held the light in fingers of a dark blue-violet. The object of the game was to try and play off your opponent's cards to match what they laid down, then be the first to run out of cards. Both nibbled at their rations in time with drawing and placing cards—a strategy of stretching rations that Oka'ada and Muuzuuri had come up with some time ago. It wasn't that they had a food shortage, but most of their food supplies consisted of military rations. While nutritious, they were not tasty, and taking very small bites periodically helped. A bit.

Kjatirna sat over in the corner curled up in an old wooden chair with a high back and armrests, one blanket draped over the seat and armrests beneath her, and another piled up behind her. She had her sketch board out and seemed to be working quite intently, golden eyes trained on the page before her, slender antlers bobbing slightly as she worked. Occasionally, she'd smooth a lock of silvery-white hair behind her ear or out of her face.

Paper was in short supply since they no longer had the resources or the infrastructure to produce it—mostly they had to scavenge for it now —yet Kjatirna always seemed to have paper or something to work her magic on. Everyone in Gold Base slipped her whatever they could find, and Muuzuuri could remember when someone—Koruuksi, maybe; that would be like him—had sent over a large stack from Remnant One. Kjatirna had been incredulous at that, not knowing what to think. Muuzuuri and the others had smiled and told her the truth. Her sketches were one of the few things gave people hope, nowadays, whether they were portraits or more imaginative sketches of what the world had once looked like before...

Muuzuuri sighed, spinning her coin again. She didn't like to think about that. No one did.

"What do we do once we hear something?" Oka'ada said absently as he placed a few cards on his side of the board, then placed one in the discard pile.

Adisa shrugged, drawing her cards as she did at the beginning of each turn, "However it turns out, Estingai will think of something. I met her once when visiting Remnant One. I don't think there's much out there that can stop that woman once she has her mind set on a target."

Oka'ada didn't respond, instead just placing his discard. No one responded.

Muuzuuri agreed with Adisa's assessment of Estingai—the woman had an iron will—yet Estingai's will alone would not be enough to defeat the Imaia.

It might be enough to save us, though. If everything goes exactly as planned.

Muuzuuri almost laughed. How long had it been since that happened?

Footsteps from the hall outside caught Muuzuuri's attention. She looked toward the room's entryway to find Sergeant Ekorna peeking past the thick dark blue curtain that gave the room a semblance of privacy and helped dampen noise from either side.

"News, Sergeant?" Muuzuuri asked as everyone else in the room perked up, even Kjatirna.

"We received a distress signal from Edendo's fighter on the encrypted channel," the sergeant said, shifting so that he stood entirely in the room, "Wolfden Base is closest, so Koruuksi himself is leading the rescue team to recover Edendo and the fighter."

Muuzuuri felt herself smile. Koruuksi was one of their best, and had been personally trained by the Knights Reborn. She noticed a few other smiles around the room, but then her gaze settled on Jaran. The man just stared down at his cup of dark liquid.

"Any report of the others?" She asked.

Ekorna frowned, shaking his head, "I'm afraid not." He glanced at Jaran and lines of sympathy entered his expression, "I'll let you know, though."

The officer disappeared back through the curtain and the room fell silent. No sketching, no moving cards, no spinning coin.

Oka'ada broke the silence, "Jaran, I'm sure Edendo—"

The loud crunch of folding metal cut Oka'ada off, followed by the splatter of lakka as it sloshed out of the crushed tin cup over Jaran's hand and onto the floor.

Kjatirna rose from her position, "Jaran, let me—"

"Don't," he snapped, voice low, but tight. He gripped the neck of the bottle with white knuckles for a moment, then relaxed, "And don't say anything about Edendo either. We all knew it was a suicide mission. When he volunteered, he and I said our goodbyes, and that's the end of it. My husband died knowing I love him and knowing that his actions would help all of us. That was enough for him, and it's enough for me. I don't need your sympathy."

Kjatirna sank back into her seat, expression deflated. Muuzuuri frowned, spinning her coin again.

Jaran had spoken correctly. All of them were pilots, and they had trained for the mission together. Edendo had been the only one among them the spies had deemed able to infiltrate the Imaia well enough to pull this off, however.

They hadn't wanted to admit to it, but they all felt the pain of their friend's loss.

Muuzuuri shuddered that what her friend must be feeling, causing her coin to spin unsuccessfully and fall to the table with a clatter that was deafening in the room's silence.

To lose not just a friend, but a lover...

The thought of being that open and vulnerable with someone, of letting herself care that deeply, terrified Muuzuuri under normal circumstances. The idea of doing so in a world that was ending, where lives could just snuff out any day without warning? Jaran and Edendo were both much braver than she.

Muuzuuri prayed—though she wasn't sure what good any of their prayers did anymore—for Edendo's safety, for Jaran. She didn't let herself hope, though.

She went back to spinning her coin, and the shuffle of cards and scratch of Kjatirna's pencil started up a few moments later. Muuzuuri watched the card game.

"Your move," Adisa said softly a few moments later, discarding.

The two played back and forth for a bit, neither making any big moves.

"Why do we play with multiple suits?" Oka'ada murmured. Muuzuuri grinned, perking up, "Well, you see—"

"Balancing actually started among the noble houses of the Nimikadeka," Kjatirna said, affecting a scholarly tone, "It was originally known as 'The Game of Houses,' with a suit assigned to each house, and was used to teach the sons and daughters of the houses how to maneuver against one another."

"Over time," Oka'ada continued, affecting the same tone, "Additions and adaptations were made to include the Kysuuri and Juusanariti'i, and eventually even the Narati peoples."

"And as certain systems of government changed and died out," Adisa said, taking it up, "It simply became a game to play at parties, in taverns, or as a subtle way for merchants and those with power to test one another in political skill."

Muuzuuri glared at them, then sniffed. It wasn't her fault that none of them were as interested in history as she was; she *had* tried to make it more interesting for them.

Wemba would appreciate that if she was here.

"You all now know the game's history now, though, don't you?"

Kjatirna giggled. Oka'ada and Adisa just shared a grin before returning to their game.

"We all knew that, Muuzuuri," Oka'ada continued, "I just meant why do we *still* use all the suits instead of just two?"

"To keep them from fading."

Jaran's words drew Muuzuuri's eyes along with everyone else's. "The Imaia only uses the two suits when they play," he continued, eyes toward the floor, "They don't want people to think about the past or the freedom that allowed the old powers to maneuver against each other, no matter how pointless that maneuvering often was. They don't outright forbid learning about them, but they make sure people only see the negatives. Keeping their memory alive even in such a small way is the least we can do to resist them."

Muuzuuri and the rest nodded solemnly. Her studies told of enough small acts of resistance leading to success in the past. As those nations and governments had risen and fallen, however, the Imaia had continued, untouched. As far as history was concerned, they had seemed immune to such things.

As the relative silence stretched, the card game continued. Kjatirna continued to sketch, Jaran continued to sip from the cup he'd half-successfully uncrushed, and Muuzuuri continued to spin her coin, watching it all.

At one point, Kjatirna rose from her chair, catching Muuzuuri's attention. She crept over to Jaran, kneeling down beside the chair and handed him her sketch. Jaran stiffened, then set down both cup and bottle. He took the small piece of paper almost reverently.

From her angle, Muuzuuri couldn't see it in detail, but she thought Kjatirna had sketched part of one of the fighters with someone in the cockpit. The tear that rolled down Jaran's cheek told her it was Edendo.

Muuzuuri couldn't hear Jaran's words as he thanked Kjatirna, but she saw her friend's hands shake as he squeezed Kjatirna's hand, gazing up at her.

Muuzuuri felt a hot tear roll down her own cheek and glanced back at her spinning coin as she wiped her eye.

The sound of hurried footsteps coming down the hall sent everyone to their feet, though Muuzuuri caught Jaran carefully folding the sketch before tucking it into his coat.

Akajaa, one of the runners, flung open the curtain. Muuzuuri blinked at the broad smile on her face. The girl was young—six or seven cycles. She should have been playing and joking with friends rather than running messages for soldiers.

She's not even that much younger than Kjatirna or myself. In a different time, we probably would have been looking for husbands or wives instead of thinking of ways to escape a dying world.

"Akajaa," Jaran asked as the young woman caught her breath, "What is it?"

"Word from Remnant Base," she panted, "They captured the Deathknight."

"What?" Muuzuuri breathed, mouth dry. That was impossible. No one had ever survived an encounter with the Deathknight and lived.

Except...

"Koruuksi found her when he went to find Edendo's ship," the girl continued, "She apparently made a deal with him to get us off Efruumani and away from the Imaia. Commander Aaden wants everyone in the briefing room now to get their orders."

As the young girl ran off to corral the rest of the soldiers in the modest base, Muuzuuri found eyes hot, shivers and goosebumps washing over her body. At some point, she'd started laughing. Maybe crying. So had everyone else.

As they made their way down the hall at a trot, wiping at their eyes and trying to contain themselves, Akajaa's words echoed in Muuzuuri's mind.

Off Efruumani and away from the Imaia.

And above that, they had Othaashle—the Deathknight, the Imaia's champion. Muuzuuri didn't know how that could have been possible.

At the moment, she found she didn't care. Whatever plan would get them all off Efruumani and away from the Imaia would likely be the most insane thing she had ever heard. Muuzuuri was willing to do whatever she was asked, and she didn't think any of her friends or fellow soldiers would hesitate either.

After all, what did they have to lose?

1

Unmasked

Though culturally, our people were of the Nambaatuu, being ruled by the Atonga made no difference. When Ezanga defeated Ketshande in the duel and our lands were suddenly under their yoke, others fled, but we stayed and welcomed the tax man. We were allowed to continue worshiping Oshuunta as long as we made the proper offerings to Anyawuu and acknowledged him as a powerful deity. Our Auroramancers, however, we kept secret from the budding empire, sending only those who wished to see new lands and serve as offerings to make the Atonga believe Auroramancers uncommon among us, and so consider us unimportant.

Exodus countdown: 19 days, 2 hours

Skadaatha rolled her shoulders as the Auroramantic senses allowed her by her brightened Natari onyxnodes picked up the agreed upon pattern of Symen, brightening and dimming his clearnodes. She turned to her companions, "He's found them."

Skadaatha flexed her fingers as her companions checked

weapons, straps, and armor. Looking north toward the source of that signal, she took a deep breath to center herself.

Today I finally kill her and end the Remnant. And I might even find the Throne.

Skadaatha tried not to dwell on that second one. If the Throne was nearby, she should be able to sense it from here. Then again, the Iceborn ability to shroud one's Auroramancy came from the Throne itself. If Ynuukwidas's power manifested as a beacon, then it would only make sense that its opposite remain hidden from one's Auroramantic senses.

Skadaatha's brightened clearnodes enhanced her perception of the world around her, so she was the first to hear Symen approach their sheltered hiding spot. Skadaatha noticed Mnene perk up a few seconds before the others. He was Auroraborn, but his abilities weren't as potent as Skadaatha's. Only Lightforged could match her in that respect.

Symen stepped around the rocky outcrop that hid them from eyes to the north. He, like the rest of them, wore garments of different shades of greys and pales greens to blend in with the landscape, yet his bore extra flaps and fringes that made him nearly invisible unless he wished it, even to a cleareye.

"I found tracks leading to an abandoned mine up ahead. I found no sentries, but there appear to be eight guards armed with rifles and sidearms. They kept to the shadows of the entrance."

Skadaatha nodded, then turned to the rest of her elites.

"This will be harder in a cave, but the plan is the same. We go in silent and kill all Remnant personnel that we find, picking them off in groups. Ljamyla will try to pin down Kojatere, but if that fails, we draw her out, letting her think we're retreating, and Symen will take her out."

"Pardon me, Vizier," Symen said, "but shouldn't we make sure that the Mestari has indeed been compromised before eliminating her?"

Skadaatha swallowed a sigh and met the eyes of each of her companions. The conflict she saw mirrored her own.

With Kojatere finally eliminated, everything would turn around for Skadaatha. Even without the Throne she would be more powerful than anyone else in the Imaia save Ynuukwidas, she would have avenged her son, and she would be able to focus on Vysla again and fix their problems.

But is eliminating her best for the Imaia?

"You're correct, Symen," she said, "we go in as though this is a rescue mission."

Skadaatha paused, forcing the next few words out. "Hopefully, that is all it will amount to. But we should be ready just in case."

The gathered elites nodded.

"And the Throne?" Mnene asked. Skadaatha had revealed her suspicions to them on the way here.

"We save that for once we're done or try to beat Kojatere to it if she runs deeper into the caverns. I doubt she knows it is there, but we—"

Skadaatha cut off as she picked up a power signature. Fireborn greynodes and clearnodes. They were getting closer. A moment later, Mnene tensed.

Skadaatha whirled and brightened her greynodes before leaping to the top of the outcrop that hid them, the rest of her biogems primed. She gritted her teeth.

Kojatere sped toward her. She—

Skadaatha's eyes widened a moment before Symen hissed, voice tense, "Vizier, she's—"

She's not wearing a mask.

"What is it?" Mnene asked.

A grin tugged at Skadaatha's mouth.

This will be even easier than I thought.

"Othaashle—Kojatere is…" Ljamyla stopped for a moment before turning to the rest of them. "She has her mask off. She doesn't care if we know."

Skadaatha frowned as her elites tensed, gemcrests primed, hands going to weapons. Othaashle wasn't that stupid. Neither was Kojatere. She was doing this for a reason.

Taking a few steps forward, Skadaatha tried to appear calm, even relieved, despite the tension pulling at her shoulders, as her elites assembled behind her. As Kojatere approached, Skadaatha realized just how much power the woman held. It radiated from Kojatere despite using only her clear and grey biogems.

Skadaatha checked the urge to look back at her elites. They'd all worn heavy braces of biogems, but Skadaatha was no longer as confident as she'd been. Kojatere did not wield the power of a goddess, but something more than a mere Lightforged. This wasn't completely hopeless, yet...

A thought crept into Skadaatha's mind, but she crushed it. The woman had been able to draw power seemingly from nowhere when they'd fought before. This was likely just a similar ploy to try and intimidate her. She drew in a deep breath and stepped forward, rolling her shoulders again.

"What do we do, Vizier?" Kwaasa asked.

Her plan was null, now.

"Back me up."

She heard her elites form up behind her as Kojatere closed. Kojatere came to a halt a few paces before her and looked over Skadaatha and her companions.

"Vizier," Kojatere said, fixing her gaze on Skadaatha. "I'm not entirely surprised to find you here—you seem to enjoy interfering in my work, lately."

Skadaatha frowned, clenching her teeth.

"You need to leave," Kojatere said. "Now."

Skadaatha forced down her anger. "You—"

"You really don't know when to stop, do you, Skadaatha?" Kojatere said, cutting her off, "I almost have the Remnant entirely in my grasp. I thought I made it clear last time that you should run back to Mjatafa Mwonga and stay there."

She gestured to Skadaatha's companions.

"Did you bring them after realizing that you can't hope to defeat me on your own? Mnene, I thought you more loyal to the Imaia than this."

Skadaatha resisted glancing back at the man as he spoke.

"I am loyal to the Imaia, Mestari," he said, slowly. "That is why I came. Skadaatha has shared disturbing news with us. She claims you attacked her when she came to your aid on Adjunct Yndlova's request."

Kojatere shrugged. "I did. I needed to ingratiate myself with the Remnant somehow. At the very least, I needed one alive to interrogate after she slaughtered the rest of the base."

Skadaatha gritted her teeth as her elites shifted behind her.

"I have them entirely in my grasp, Skadaatha," Kojatere continued. "Leave now, before you ruin that."

"Why do you need them alive?" Skadaatha almost called the woman 'Kojatere' but bit it back. Not yet. "Why didn't you simply slaughter them all as I did? Old sympathies slipping through, perhaps? Old loyalties?

Skadaatha's blood boiled as Kojatere shook her head. "This is not their only base, and therefore not their only cell. The spies we've captured may not be the only ones within Mjatafa Mwonga. They have some interesting technology that the Imaia could use as well as powerful Auroramancers that would make excellent Redeemed."

"Lord Ynuukwidas has not Redeemed anyone in years."

"Then I'll just have to keep them alive until Exodus is complete." Skadaatha opened her mouth, then clamped it shut, glad for her

helm's cover.

Burn her for giving solid reasons. And Lightforged can't lie.

Skadaatha blinked.

She can't lie.

Skadaatha tried to keep her grin from her voice. "And what, exactly do you plan to do with the Remnant if I leave?"

"Convince them that I will return to Mjatafa Mwonga and acquire a capital ship for them to escape on and orchestrate a distraction that will allow a small team to steal it, bringing it back to their bases to evacuate their people and round them all up in a single location. That ship will of course have Redeemed lying in wait."

Skadaatha tensed as Kojatere stretched out her hand, motes of fire and ice flashing around it.

"Of course, in order to do that, I will need to prove myself by getting rid of you. One way or another."

"Is that a threat?" Skadaatha growled, eyeing Ilkwalerva as it coalesced in Kojatere's hand, its massive, silver-and-gold blade shining in Lightside's perpetual sunlight. She extended her own hand, fingers splayed.

"Vizier," Mnene started. Skadaatha cut him off with a gesture.

She's made them uncertain.

Skadaatha would not be able to kill Kojatere by herself. Admitting that made her taste bile, but she knew it was true.

Kojatere cocked her head. "Was that not clear? Let me try again. You can either leave, or I will kill you, Skadaatha. None of your companions need to die—none of them tried to kill me."

She paused, looking over all of them. "If not, I'm sure the Remnant would be very convinced of my allegiance if I brought them your heads."

"And what of the Throne, Kojate—"

"Do *not* disrespect the taboos of the Redeemed, Skadaatha."

"So, you do remember."

Kojatere hesitated, gazing at her. Skadaatha took the opportunity. "How much do you remember, *Othaashle*?" Skadaatha snarled the last word. "Someone like you doesn't set aside their convictions lightly. You served two gods. How can we be sure you still serve ours?"

Kojatere was silent, face unchanging.

"The Vizier makes a point, Mestari," Aarnal said. "The Redeemed are a mystery to us as it is."

Skadaatha grinned.

Kojatere looked past Skadaatha now. They both knew her elites would be the deciding factor in this. Skadaatha held herself ready, just in case the woman decide to kill them outright.

She can't do that without leaving herself open to me.

"I was unable to find my mask after the Vizier attacked me. A few in the Remnant seemed to recognize me, so I thought I would use that, and went without my mask. The different reactions I received have been... interesting. One of them seemed as though she wanted to kill me almost as much as you do."

"And the Throne?" Skadaatha asked, gauntlets creaking as she clenched her fists.

The smirk on Kojatere's face was almost enough to make Skadaatha attempt to ram a spear of ice through the woman's throat.

"I destroyed it."

Spikes of ice needled Skadaatha's chest.

"You what?" she hissed.

"I destroyed the Throne of Darkness," Kojatere said, voice and expression betraying nothing. "And Kweshrima along with it. Her power is now my own."

Skadaatha gaped beneath her helmet. She'd known it was possible. The Thrones were nothing more than concentrated power given shape and definition by the collective thoughts of the world or region. Even for a Redeemed, however—

Ilkwalerva caught the light, drawing Skadaatha's gaze, and her eyes grew wide.

That blade.

Skadaatha knew it somehow granted Kojatere the power to chain the souls of those she killed so Ynuukwidas could make them into Lightforged, but for it to be able to destroy a Throne and absorb its power...

Could that work on Ynuukwidas?

Would the God King have given such a weapon to Kojatere on purpose, knowing who she had been—who she was? Did he even know it had such capability?

Of course, he does. And he probably inserted some block into Kojatere's soul to prevent her from using it against him, just as he made his Lightforged incapable of lying.

"She didn't have much after all these years," Kojatere continued, "after what she did, but it will suffice for my purposes."

Skadaatha wanted to erupt with rage, to throw every last scrap of power she could muster at Kojatere. With her elites, she might have been able to kill the woman, even with Ilkwalerva. With Kojatere holding the power of a Throne, however...

That power should have been mine!

A plan was forming in her mind. She could still take that power. But that would take time. As much as she wanted that power, Skadaatha wanted Kojatere dead far more.

She killed my son.

Skadaatha had one last card to play.

"And what of the visions?" she asked, "the ones that make you, one of the Redeemed, fall unconscious. Helpless."

Kojatere's pale grey face darkened, golden eyes flashing.

"Those visions led me here," Kojatere said slowly, voice low. "Without them, I would not have been able to trick the Remnant into leading me to the Throne."

She paused, head swiveling as she looked over Skadaatha and her elites.

Kojatere raised Ilkwalerva. "Leave now, Skadaatha, or I will reconsider my decision to spare your life."

Skadaatha almost took a step forward. She just barely managed to hold herself back.

Glaring at Kojatere, Skadaatha searched for something, anything else that could throw the woman off balance; something that would give her a chance at victory. She found nothing.

This isn't the end. I haven't failed. Just a strategic retreat.

Skadaatha sighed. "We return to Mjatafa Mwonga."

Her elites shifted behind her.

"Vizier?" Mnene asked.

Skadaatha blinked. She wouldn't have thought Mnene would remain the most loyal.

She raised her voice. "We will leave Othaashle here to continue with her plan to eliminate the Remnant for good. If she betrays the Imaia by aiding them, we will kill them all, and Othaashle with them. The Throne's power will not protect her."

I will have that power, and I will see you dead for killing my son.

The bitch grinned at her.

2
Monsters

Because we kept our Auroramancers hidden and trained them differently than the monks of Atonga, we knew of the danger of Tombara long before anyone else. We prepared our ships, and our families and tried to warn our neighbors. Some listened. Others accused us of heresy and went to the Atonga. That was the first time we had to fight and defend ourselves. If the mountain's eruption had not covered our flight to the sea, our people likely would have been captured and persecuted for hiding our Auroramancers and worshipping the god that saved us, rather than those that destroyed their worshipers.

Exodus countdown: 19 days, 1 hour, 51 minutes

"I'm surprised you let her go."

Estingai eyed Koruuksi.

The young man whose family had taken her in long ago lounged against one of the display desks, antlers still dusty and grimy from his journey here, as were his clothes. He gazed off at nothing, golden eyes contemplative, cup of water held at his side.

As always, Estingai took a deep breath to help disperse the complex whirl of emotions she felt whenever she looked at Koruuksi.

He looks so much like—

Estingai shoved those thoughts away. They hurt too much. She'd had trouble keeping them at bay since Kojatere arrived.

"What was I supposed to do? You said it yourself—she's the only one of us that has any chance against Skadaatha. Either she's with us and fights her off or she's against us and we're dead one way or another."

Koruuksi raised an eyebrow. "I'm surprised you managed to admit that without swearing or crushing your cup."

Estingai frowned, glancing down at the small metal cup in her hand to make sure she hadn't dented it. She hadn't.

"And I didn't mean then."

Estingai looked back up at Koruuksi.

"I meant before," he continued, "when she asked to see the commanders. You just took her there."

She glanced over at the commanders, Uuldina, Paiz, Miek'ka, and Marjatla, standing on the other side of the War Room, talking quietly among each other. They'd ordered everyone out of the room after the proximity sensors had been tripped and Kojatere left to face Skadaatha, leaving all of the normally bright and colorful displays that lined the walls and divided the space of the open, otherwise stark room dark. They didn't have the power to keep them running if no one was monitoring them.

"I knew they wouldn't trust her," Estingai said, taking another sip from her cup, "and I wanted their perspective on her plan and her in general."

Estingai looked over at the commanders again. Marjatla had been essentially a glorified assistant, and Paiz, the daughter of a faction leader, when—Estingai took a deep breath, steadying herself—when she'd formed the Remnant. Now, they were the best officers the Remnant had, and the best any of them had been able to do was follow through on a half-baked plan her husband had come up with the night he died.

Murdered.

Koruuksi sighed. "So you're gonna do that?"

Estingai took a deep breath, forcing away the memories of that night, but didn't bother to play dumb, instead holding her little brother's gaze.

Not so little anymore. Not for a long time.

Just because he wasn't a kid anymore didn't mean he no longer needed her protection, however.

Now more than ever.

Koruuksi had tried to play it off, but she'd seen the way he'd looked at the creature wearing Kojatere's face. He wanted a mother again. She couldn't blame him.

Don't you? Don't you want the woman who took you in and loved her like her own to come back and save everyone so you don't have to?

Estingai gritted her teeth. Of course, she wanted Kojatere back. But Estingai refused to believe as easily as Koruuksi did.

"She's not our mother, no matter what she says," Estingai said, surprised at the half-growl that came out. "She's been that *thing* for fourteen years. Who knows what she is, now."

Estingai regretted the words only somewhat. The way Koruuksi's jaw bunched pained her, as did the hardness in his eyes, but she needed to make sure he didn't hang all his hopes on an unknown.

"Is there anything that would actually make you trust her?" Koruuksi asked, tension fading from his face.

"Do you?"

Koruuksi gazed at her for a moment, then sighed. "I want to. When I saw her face...For now, I trust her as much as I trust you or Uuchantuu."

He paused, studying her, "It's more than just that, isn't it? That you don't trust her."

Estingai gritted her teeth. She gave him a slow nod. "I could barely stand even being near that monster."

"Is it—"

"It is."

Estingai didn't want to think about that.

Koruuksi just sighed.

"Is there anything... good left in you, Estingai?"

Estingai blinked, then narrowed her eyes at Koruuksi.

"That came out wrong," he said, holding up a hand before she could say anything.

His lips drew to a thin line as he thought for a moment, then he sighed, running a hand through his hair.

"Sometimes, it just seems like you're either angry, hurt, or waiting for a reason to feel either of those. If she really is Kojatere, then *she* didn't kill him. Svemakuu would understand that."

Estingai gritted her teeth. That excuse didn't work for her, and she did *not* agree that her husband would have seen things differently than she. Estingai knew she wouldn't get anywhere with Koruuksi on that line of conversation, however. She sighed. "We can't all be like him."

Koruuksi shrugged. "You're right. Is it really that hard to try, though? If I don't, then what will I do if we're finally able to end this fight and escape one day? What will you do when you don't have anyone to attack or throw your anger at?"

Estingai found she had no response to that. He was right, of course. All she had left was the pain the Imaia had caused her, and anger at them for doing so. She clung to those emotions to keep fighting, but worried that if she tried to feel more, it would break her. She didn't have to worry about what came after the fighting, because she didn't see herself making it that far. She'd made her peace with that, as long as whatever sacrifice she made would allow Koruuksi and Uuchantuu—and the Remnant, ideally—to get off this dying rock.

She couldn't bring herself to admit that to either of them.

He sighed. "I'm just worried that you'll be too reckless and do something stupid because you don't think you have anything left to hope for."

Estingai heard the pain in Koruuksi's words. He'd tried to hide it, but she knew him too well.

She immediately felt guilty at her previous thoughts. Koruuksi was the only bit of hope Estingai had left that her actions could matter for anything good, but Estingai knew that if she ever de-compartmentalized their relationship, she would break every time Koruuksi was in danger. Especially if she couldn't be there to protect him herself.

Instead, I've become so single-minded over the last seven years that made him think I don't care about anything. Even him. Auroras, Uuchantuu probably thinks the same thing.

"Koruuksi," she began, "I—"

Estingai stopped, straightening as Koruuksi looked toward the opening War Room doors. They revealed Uuchantuu, who rushed in, barely pausing to salute the generals before speaking. The short, pretty Natari woman's cheeks were dark from sprinting. She, like Estingai, wore her uniform. The sight of the pan handle fitted with georaural framework sticking out from behind her hip made Estingai grip the similar one she wore at her waist.

"Kojatere is back." Uuchantuu said. "Skadaatha is gone. Sensor equipment shows her and the others she brought leaving."

"Is she heading here?" Estingai asked, tense.

Uuchantuu shook her head, her braids of silver, white, and black swishing with the movement, "The main hangar. She asked the guards who let her back in where our largest chamber was in here, and then told them to have everyone gather there."

"Everyone?"

Uuchantuu nodded.

Estingai looked to Koruuksi, then the generals. They nodded, and together they followed Uuchantuu at a trot toward the hangar.

As they walked, Estingai found herself glancing toward Uuchantuu. She thought of the young woman like a sister, and missed the closeness they'd once shared. She wanted that still, but Uuchantuu's skills in tactics and georaural tech, along with her closeness with Koruuksi, had taken her away from Remnant One recently, and after Svemakuu's death and all the people they had both lost, Estingai felt like she'd failed the young woman.

Again.

Estingai still missed Uuchantuu's sister, Uukojana, dearly despite only have known her a few months.

But Uuchantu has volunteered for every mission I've needed someone like her on.

Estingai didn't know what to say. So she said nothing.

By the time they made their way through the rivers of people heading for the hangar, it seemed as though the entirety of the Remnant was already there. At last count, they numbered at around forty-two hundred, with around three thousand at this base and the rest spread throughout their four other bases, and over half their number was family and support.

Three other bases, now, if everyone at Stormswind really is dead.

Estingai clenched her fists. They hadn't even been able to send a recovery team there yet.

Marjatla is barely holding it together with Aaden assumed dead.

Even with so many people gathered here, the hangar was nowhere near full. The massive obsidian room held the sixty-one fighters they'd stolen and salvaged over the past seven years, a few sitting in the repair bays, their eight transport ships, and the capital shipped they had hoped to escape on. Many bore the insignias of the old Remnant factions or other decorations to distinguish and remove them from those of Imaia design.

Estingai was proud of that, at least. They'd managed to assemble a decent fleet and repair the cruiser such that, theoretically, it would be able to fly at low altitude with little issue. Getting it through the atmosphere was the problem. Repulsor georaurals could only lift something so far off the ground. Their engineers had learned from the stolen and salvaged fighters that the Imaia used a type of palladium reactor to power their aircraft. Even with everything they'd salvaged so far, they didn't have the necessary parts and resources to build one large enough to power a capital ship. They'd hoped to acquire those in their recent raid, but most of what they'd managed to steal, their team had brought to Stormswind. If Kojatere were to be believed, she and Skadaatha had damaged or destroyed much of that during their fight.

The Deathknight herself—Estingai didn't believe true change could happen so quickly no matter what the woman said—stood atop one of the 4-Tails they'd stolen from Mjatafa Mwonga during their raid on the city. She wore the same rough coat and trousers she'd arrived in and peered down at something in her hands. Estingai brightened her clearnodes.

The faint odor of grease, sweat, and ozone from the chamber's machinery filled Estingai's nostrils, accompanied by the mixture of different body odors from over a thousand people who bathed by wiping themselves down with wet, soapy rags. Estingai became more aware of her clothing; the scratch of the rough wool and cotton, the weight of her harness and weapons. The low murmur of the gathered crowd grew loud and clear enough for Estingai to pick out words and conversations. Years of practice allowed Estingai to tune out all of the extra sensory input in a few seconds. Though the power of her clearnodes enhanced all of her senses, at the moment, she just needed the enhanced vision and sharp details it allowed her to pick out at a distance.

Kojatere held something—papers, maybe—a puzzled look on her pale grey features as she gazed at it. The woman glanced to the side, and Estingai followed her gaze just in time to see an antlered figure disappear into the gathered crowd. She searched but couldn't find anyone that stood out to her.

Estingai looked to Koruuksi and Uuchantuu. The two had taken up seats atop supply containers against the back wall, Koruuksi had brightened his own clearnodes. After hesitating a moment, Estingai followed them, taking up a seat nearby, keeping her clearnodes brightened.

Closing her eyes, Estingai allowed herself to listen to the conversations of those around her.

Most were confused. Others—those who recognized Kojatere and the markings of a Lightforged—were wary. Some expressed the same anger she felt in quiet, tense whispers.

"Who is that?"

"That looks like one of the Lightforged. It can't be, can it?"

"Why were we called here?"

"Is that the one who attacked us? What is she doing up there?"

Kojatere held up a hand, the movement catching Estingai's attention, and within a few minutes, the hum of conversation faded.

"Most of you know me as Othaashle," she said, voice loud and clear, echoing slightly in the stone chamber. "Kifrytari. The Deathknight. Some of you, however, remember who I once was. After he took me, Ynuukwidas twisted my soul in a way that made me forget who I was and gave him control over my thoughts and actions. But now, thanks to a final sacrifice by Kweshrima, I remember who I was. I wish to be that person—your Champion—once more."

Her words brought forth a mixture of panicked murmurs and loud, angry objections from the crowd. Estingai was surprised not to find herself among those calling for Kojatere to leave. Instead, she was intrigued. Estingai's adoptive mother had always been good with speeches, but she'd also been arrogant to a fault. This woman had some of that, but not enough. Estingai found within herself a perverse desire to see what other discrepancies she could discover.

One voice rose louder than the others.

"We should finish her here!"

Estingai thought she recognized the voice, but a cheer of agreement distracted her.

No. If they attack...

Kojatere wouldn't just let them have her. Maybe she wouldn't slaughter them, but—

"Finish her, Mboro?"

Estingai blinked, glancing over at Koruuksi as most of those nearby fell silent and did the same.

"The only thing you've ever finished on your own is the lakka rations you manage to swindle your 'friends' out of," Koruuksi continued, voice loud enough to carry through the stone chamber. "She kicked my ass, and I'd be happy kick yours again if you don't shut up and let her talk."

The objections did not rise again, and for a moment, silence held the large chamber once more.

"I understand your anger," Kojatere said. "I am not asking you to forgive me or the Imaia for what they have done to you."

Estingai frowned at the slight waver in the woman's voice—one she only detected due to her enhanced hearing—and looked to Koruuksi. He met her eyes wearing a similar expression.

"I am telling you that this is the only option you have left," Kojatere continued, "I can go to Mjatafa Mwonga and procure a ship for you—one that you can escape this dying world in—or you can wait here to die. I was able to deter Skadaatha and the squad of elites she brought to eliminate you, but if I don't return to Mjatafa Mwonga and follow through with that plan, the Imaia will come here in force."

Kojatere paused briefly, eyes widening for a moment as her gaze fixed on a specific spot in the crowd, but she continued speaking before Estingai could follow her gaze to figure out what she had been looking at.

Something to do with whatever she's holding?

Her hands hid most of it, but it looked like a small bundle of papers with snowscript writing. She'd crumpled them, but it didn't look intentional.

Looking back to her face, Estingai blinked.

Is she actually nervous? Or is that just a façade?

Kojatere did a good job of playing it off, and at a distance, the shining gold accents on her face likely distracted from her actual expression. With her enhanced vision, however, Estingai picked out the slight creases and lines of tension.

What is her game?

Still dressed in the plain padded coat and trousers she'd worn under her armor, no impressive weapons or shining iron, she didn't look much like a champion.

Kojatere had never needed the right clothes, either.

But Kojatere had loved showing off her beauty and hard-earned figure with beautiful clothing. She hadn't been the slave to fashion her brother Suule had been, but...

Estingai's jaw bunched as she let out a low growl of frustration.

"The plan that I proposed to your leaders," Kojatere said,

"involved using a distraction to procure an older capital ship stocked with supplies and large enough to safely transport you all off this world. I would have told the Imaia that it was a trap—a trick to gather you all in one place."

The gathered crowd began buzzing with murmurs again, but Kojatere continued.

"That plan will no longer be enough. I... who I was, has enemies within the Imaia that will work against me. We will need to plan for the possibility of a need to attack Mjatafa Mwonga in force and defend your base and the capital ship while everyone boards it."

A few cheers and whoops rose at that, the crowd's buzz growing even louder, yet rather than looking pleased, Kojatere appeared disheartened.

Though she wanted to, Estingai found she could take no pleasure in that. Any satisfaction from Kojatere's discomfort was outweighed by the shame of how many people seemed more excited by the prospect of hurting the Imaia than of saving themselves.

And I'm the one that made them think it's okay to think that way.

It had been necessary, but that didn't make it right.

More than that, however, Estingai wanted Kojatere's plan to work. Even if the woman was likely setting a trap for them, Estingai wanted whatever she proposed to come true.

"This would not be a direct attack on the Imaia," Kojatere continued over the voices, "just a distraction, attacking Mjatafa Mwonga itself in a way that would hurt the Imaia's ability to pursue you or produce more weapons of war in the near future. Maybe even steal some more equipment or ships to make it more credible."

The buzz of conversation grew louder, more conflicted this time, but a few calls stood out, one echoing Estingai's own thoughts: "We should ground the city!"

Estingai looked to Kojatere just in time to see the woman's silver and gold eyes flash. Her expression grew dark.

"Would you so callously condemn hundreds of million people to the same death you seek to escape?" she asked, tone surprisingly neutral, with just a hint of the venom Estingai saw in her eyes.

The question silenced the room for a few moments, and Estingai felt its weight. She could not carry out a sentence like that, despite her hate, despite all the Imaia had taken from her. She wanted to say she could—to argue that every person in that city was culpable for giving in to the Imaia in exchange for its protection. Yet she could not blame refugees for fleeing to the one place left on this world that provided sanctuary and stability.

Still, Estingai believed the Imaia's leadership or its war machine needed to suffer. An attack that was simply a distraction might be too little.

"You want us to spare them?" a voice called.

Another: "You're still on their side, aren't you?"

"We deserve retribution."

"How do we know this isn't just a trap?"

"She's still with the Imaia!"

"They need to answer for what they've done to us!"

Estingai frowned as she watched the frustration on Kojatere's face go cold. As people jeered and accused her of cowardice and called for her to leave, she stood unmoving, mouth drawn to a thin line. Tense, Estingai looked to Koruuksi. He didn't glance over at her, but the lines on his face told her he was ready to move if needed.

Eventually, the room grew silent as others noticed Kojatere's stolid demeanor and grew discomforted by it.

"Do you know what the people of Mjatafa Mwonga think of you?"

Kojatere's words were quiet and cold, yet they cut through the entire chamber. Estingai noticed a few people lean forward.

The woman let her words hang in the air for a while, eyes scanning the crowd, before she continued.

"You are the monsters they tell their children to fear."

KORUUKSI WINCED AT THAT, eyes darting to Estingai, then Uuchantuu. His friend's eyes were downcast, jaw tense. Her hand clutched at her opposite wrist just beneath the bracelet she'd worn since leaving her home.

He put an arm around her shoulders. Once she leaned into him and squeezed his hand, Koruuksi returned his attention to Kojatere.

His mother's gaze had shifted from the crowd to where the leadership stood in a clump off to the side.

"Did your spies tell you that?"

The commanders gave away nothing, but Koruuksi knew they had. Leadership just hadn't shared that information with the rest of the Remnant.

"Do you want to prove to them that you are the terrorists the Imaia's propaganda paints you as?" she continued, turning back to the crowd. "The common people of the Imaia are little different than you. They felt betrayed, desperate, or like they had no other options. Most of them flocked to Mjatafa Mwonga because of the safety and stability it offers. They had no home left, so they fled to the one place that promised to keep them fed, clothed, and housed. The Imaia keeps its darker atrocities carefully hidden from them, so they don't feel they are doing anything wrong by living there."

She paused, scanning the crowd again.

"By attacking them, you feed into the Imaia narrative that you are the fanatical followers of a goddess who destroyed the world."

Koruuksi's jaw tightened at that. Uuchantuu tensed beside him, leaning into him more. He squeezed her hand, and allowed himself a faint smile when she smiled up at him, relaxing just a bit.

"We need to attack Mjatafa Mwonga to create the distraction necessary to steal the capital ship," Kojatere continued, voice a bit louder, less cold, "but we will focus on military installations only."

"How can we trust you?"

Koruuksi scanned the crowd for the source of the voice as a few sympathetic murmurs rose. When he couldn't find the speaker, he looked back to Kojatere.

"You don't really have any other options, do you?"

The entire chamber fell silent at that. Koruuksi allowed himself a glance at Estingai, and watched long enough to see those words sink in.

If she had no response to that, no one else in the Remnant would either.

Kojatere waited, scanning the crowd. Her shining eyes passed over Koruuksi and Estingai at one point, and he thought he saw a bit of relief in them.

Apparently satisfied, Kojatere looked to the gathered commanders.

"We need to work over logistics and assemble two teams to help with the assault," she said, then turned back to the crowd, "the rest of you... prepare to leave Efruumani."

Koruuksi looked first to Estingai, who sighed as she hopped off the supplies and strode toward Kojatere and the Remnant leadership.

Koruuksi made to follow but looked to Uuchantuu.

"You alright?"

Uuchantuu raised an eyebrow.

"Right. Stupid question."

"I will be, though," she said, "once we get through this. I take it we're going to be on one of those teams?"

Koruuksi cocked his head. "Would you have it any other way?"

Uuchantuu smiled. "I'll gather the team and prep them."

Returning the smile, Koruuksi hugged his friend, then hopped down from the supplies.

"I'm going to go speak with the commanders," he said, looking up at her. "Be back as soon as I can."

She nodded, features strained again, and Koruuksi hesitated for a moment before turning away and weaving through the dispersing crowd, braids of silver, white, and black swishing as she went.

She'll talk about it when she's ready.

3

Storm

The seas were hostile in the days following the mountain's eruption. Massive waves buried groups of ships beneath the waves, and dark clouds blotted out the sky, hiding the auroras. Every one of our people became lightless, and for a while, all hope seemed lost. When we found land, however, though the sky had not cleared and the seas were still troubled, our people flourished in an untouched paradise. When the auroras returned, we celebrated for an entire week. From then on, Auroradays became holy. Times for celebration and hope for the future, and remembrance of the past and pain of lightlessness.

Exodus countdown: 18 days, 38 hours, 2 minutes

Vysla stood from his place at the table as Skadaatha entered their home. He wore a simple robe, wide eyes tired as he gazed at her. Skadaatha glanced at the table and breathed in the warm scent of spiced kaffa just as she registered the mug next to Vysla's datapad.

Right... it's early morning.

"You're back," Vysla breathed.

Skadaatha nodded. She didn't remove her helmet. She could see the questions in her husband's eyes but didn't trust herself to speak. She didn't want to snap at him.

Her hands still shook, though at this point she hoped it was from running all the way home from the edge of the city rather than the rage that still seethed within her.

Mountains do not bend.

Yet she'd done just that. It was a temporary retreat, but still. The weight of the temporary failure, she could bear. The pointlessness of her attack and the thought that she may have even *helped* Kojatere with her plans made Skadaatha want to scream.

I'm the only one left. We failed Ezthyl once. I cannot do so again.

Turning toward the bedroom, Skadaatha took a step toward it only to suddenly find Vysla before her, arms encircling her even in her cold, unfeeling armor.

The gesture made her chest clench around her heart even as warmth flowed through her.

I can't do this.

Skadaatha gently returned her husband's gesture.

"Skadaatha," Vysla said, his soft voice a balm to her burning anger, "we need to talk."

Skadaatha let out a ragged breath she'd held in for hours.

"You're right," she said, voice thick, though she managed to keep it level.

Vysla's squeezed her waist a bit tighter.

Doesn't he find that uncomfortable?

Skadaatha didn't voice the thought, however. She needed his arms around her.

"I take it you were unsuccessful."

Skadaatha took a deep breath.

"Wildly. She already wields the Throne's power. It isn't enough to rival Ynuukwidas or even what my own power once was, but enough that even the seven of us had no chance of arresting her, much less killing her. I need..."

Skadaatha paused as her voice wavered, trying to collect herself.

"I—"

I can't even put myself together long enough to utter a single syllable.

But she didn't need to with Vysla. She didn't need to be a goddess or even a Vizier for him.

Just a woman. A wife.

Knowing that didn't make remembering to do so any easier.

"I need to remember how to be myself again," she forced out, closing her eyes, voice ragged. "I need to be the woman you fell in love with. Not the Imaia's raging bitch of a Vizier."

"Well, you weren't Vizier yet when we met, but..."

Skadaatha barked a laugh, then turned and wrapped her arms tight around the husband.

Vysla didn't respond. Instead, he withdrew his arms from around her. Skadaatha nearly gasped at the sudden loss of contact, but his hand took hers a moment later as he stood before her. Skadaatha met his eyes through her helmet.

He reached forward and gently took it off her, smiling as he revealed her face. He took the helmet under one arm, bringing his other hand up to brush his knuckles against her cheek.

The simple touch sent a much-needed, comforting warmth through her entire body.

"You're still the same intelligent, passionate, enigmatic goddess that I fell in love with," he said, cupping her cheek now. "You've just been through a lot. We both have."

Skadaatha took a deep breath as shivers ran through her at the word 'goddess.' From Ynuukwidas or Makahaba, the word mocked her. From her own mouth, it was a reminder of what she'd lost. From Vysla's...Skadaatha had never been worshiped. She'd never asked to be. But if this was what it felt like, she could see why Kweshrima and Ynuukwidas had sought it.

"Let's get you out of this," Vysla said, taking her hand again and tugging her down the hall toward their bedroom.

Skadaatha followed. Her instinct was to remain silent, but...

"I've grown too emotional."

The admission was more to herself than to him. She'd known it, but she'd thought of it as more of a passing phase, not something that had changed within her.

Skadaatha couldn't help but glance at their son's room as they passed. A deep, shuddering breath calmed her.

"I miss him, too," Vysla said.

What father doesn't miss his child?

The words made her feel less alone in her grief, though. They kept Aiolo alive, even if in only a small way.

Once they were in the bedroom, Vysla took the padded lining out of her helmet and tossed it into the basket next to the armor stand before setting her helm at its place at the top.

He turned to her then, eyes warm and loving as his hands went to the straps of her gorget. For a time, they let silence cover them, him removing her armor, piece by piece, her standing still as he did so.

"You and Aiolo were the only ones that ever made me... *feel*," she said after Vysla had removed both of her arm harnesses. Her voice was ragged with grief and rage. "And then she took him. She took our boy."

Vysla remained silent as his hands continued to work at the various straps of her armor and padding. Most of the latter was damp and dark with sweat.

"When Ynuukwidas let me break her," she continued, "I thought it would be done with. But then he brought her back. The woman who took my son from me was allowed to cheat death, yet my son had no such chance."

Skadaatha knew that Ynuukwidas likely would have been able to bring her son back had he possessed the necessary knowledge at the time. She knew that she likely wouldn't have even needed to ask, though she would have prostrated herself at the God King's feet and begged if that had been his price. It still infuriated her.

And that's the problem.

"She took his place," Skadaatha breathed.

Vysla looked up and met her gaze, eyebrow raised.

"I think that's why I'm this... not myself," she explained. "You and Aiolo were the only two that were supposed to make me feel such emotion. Now he is gone, and it's you and Kojatere that spark that emotion in me. That's why I'm not myself when I deal with her. She torments me by taking a place in my head she has no right to."

Vysla raised a hand to her face again, cupping her cheek. Skadaatha let a smile tug at her lips as she gazed at her husband. He grasped the buttons at the collar of her sweat-soaked undershirt with his other hand, deftly undoing the first one.

"Let's get you out of this and into the shower," he said, smiling. It morphed into a grin. "You smell."

A laugh pushed past Skadaatha's lips at that, and she found herself smiling with her husband.

Vysla helped her out of her clothes and toss them into a basket beside the one he'd tossed her padding into. Her clothes could be machine-washed, but the padding needed a more hands-on approach.

Vysla took her hand again—he in his robe, she nude—and led her to the shower, turning on the water to just the right heat before she stepped in under the spray.

Skadaatha had thought Vysla would just lean against the counter and talk with her from outside the shower while she cleaned herself, as he'd done last time, but she glanced over just in time to see him shrug out of his robe and hang it on the back of the door before joining her.

Skadaatha smiled at her husband, meeting him in a deep kiss. She hadn't realized just how much she needed that. Feeling his lips on hers, their bodies pressed together under the hot, steamy water, made Skadaatha want to do much more than simply clean herself off.

She knew she had a bit more to do first, however.

Skadaatha enjoyed the kiss until Vysla pulled back. She drank in the love and desire in his tired eyes, drawing strength from them.

"You didn't sleep well, did you?" she asked, stepping back to grab the shampoo.

Vysla beat her to it, and they shared a smile as their hands touched on the bottle. He moved her gently out of the spray and she turned, presenting her back to him. She realized then that he'd undone her braid. Her heart swelled at that even as she wondered how she hadn't noticed until now.

"You know I never sleep well when you're gone," Vysla said, tangling his fingers in her hair. "Especially when there's the possibility you might not return."

Skadaatha frowned at that even as her body reacted to Vysla massaging the shampoo into her scalp, occasionally using his nails to dig through her thick locks of hair.

"I'm sorry. For that...for not being myself lately. I've been too reactive, letting others dictate my actions and moods."

She shifted, interrupting his wonderful massage so she could look over her shoulder and meet his eyes. "Even with you."

Vysla gave her a quick smile, withdrawing his hands from her hair as he moved aside so she could rinse her hair. "Thank you. You know that isn't all of it, though."

Skadaatha nodded, stepping under the water. "I know. You deserve better than that, but..." She sighed. "Right now, I can only take this one step at a time."

He smiled at her again, then let the spray wash the shampoo off his hands. "I'm okay with that. As long as you let me help you."

"I will. I promise."

Vysla smiled. Skadaatha took the opportunity to look him up and down as she cleaned her hair of the shampoo and smiled to herself. When she was finished, Vysla gestured for her to switch spots with him as he reached for the conditioner. Skadaatha did so, enjoying the steamy confines of the shower as she waited for Vysla's fingers to return to her scalp. She gasped when he surprised her with a kiss where her neck met her shoulder before tangling his fingers in her hair again.

"I found another use of the metals," he said, fingers working wonders on her scalp. "One that I believe will be a bit more practical than the weapon I made for you, if less... flashy."

Skadaatha had to shake herself out of her massage-induced trance to process Vysla's words.

"Can you work on both?" she asked, nearly laughing when she

heard the laziness in her voice. "Repairing the weapon and your other project, I mean. You can requisition the materials for both under a classified research order."

His hands hesitated for a moment, then continued. "Of course, but why?"

"The Lightforged have their symbols," Skadaatha said. "It's time I had my own again. I'd like you to look into a power siphon on the weapon, as well."

Skadaatha nodded, reluctantly reaching for the soap and moving her head out of Vysla's reach. When she straightened, careful to keep her head out of the water, Vysla snatched that out of her hands, too. He met her gaze with a smirk that made Skadaatha's blood run hot and sent her eyes roving down his body.

He began to lather her up, his touch making her shiver despite the hot water.

"I'm guessing you're thinking of something beyond a standard bluenode georaural?" he asked.

Skadaatha nodded. "Ideally something that can siphon more than just Auroralight."

Vysla stopped his ministrations, peering up at her with a bit of hesitation. "This isn't about the Throne, is it?"

Skadaatha shook her head. "Not in the way you're thinking, at least. I plan on going after Kojatere as soon as Mnene and the others have had some time to rest. I'm going to approach this way I once would have done things—the way I should have gone after her from the beginning—but if it comes to a confrontation between the two of us, I want to have something I can use to level the playing field."

Vysla gazed at her for a moment, then nodded, soapy hands continuing their half-cleaning, half-exploration of her body. "I can help with that."

He was silent for a bit as he washed her, and Skadaatha leaned in closer in the comfortable quiet, enjoying the sensation of his warm, slender hands sliding across her soapy skin. When Vysla lingered on her arms, tracing their shape back and forth, she looked up. "What is it?"

His eyes lingered on her arms for a while longer before drinking in her body again, then meeting hers. "I was just wondering... will we really meet other peoples out there? Ones like you?"

Skadaatha arched an eyebrow. "I'd imagine there are very few people like me in Aioa."

Vysla rolled his eyes. "You know what I mean."

He held his arm out next to hers. They were roughly the same width, but his limbs seemed longer, more wiry, and hers more bulky. Skadaatha maintained the athletic form she'd been given, but she had nowhere near the muscle mass of a body builder. While Natari generally had leaner builds than Samjati, both appeared long-limbed and willowy when compared to her physique.

Skadaatha met his eyes and shrugged. "Depends on the gravity of the inhabited worlds we find. If it's heavier, they could be shorter and even more compact than my form. If it's lighter, they could be thirty centimeters taller than Natari on average, though they might have weaker bones."

Vysla let out a long breath, shaking his head. "It's still hard to believe sometimes."

Skadaatha raised an eyebrow. "The science is—"

"Not the science. The existence of other life—not just life, but *sentient* life."

Skadaatha smiled. She had always known that varied forms of life would exist within Aioa. She had only seen those of two worlds, and barely remembered much of the first, but for the people of Efruumani that revelation had sparked myriad reactions. Vysla's main reaction, of course, was curiosity. One of the many reasons she'd fallen in love with him.

"It's a good thing the Ministries of Science and Culture are both under my administration," she said. "I'll make certain you have every opportunity to learn about the new worlds we find and the new peoples and forms of life we encounter."

Vysla smiled. Then he leaned in, nuzzling his forehead against hers before kissing her.

Skadaatha pressed herself against him, deepening the kiss.

When they pulled apart, Vysla gave her a quizzical look. "Did you leave them on their own at the edge of the city?"

Skadaatha was glad her cheeks were already hot from Vysla's touch, though her voice gave away her embarrassment anyway. "Yes."

Vysla snorted, shaking his head.

"I needed to think," Skadaatha said. "I didn't want to be around anyone at the time, and couldn't answer their questions."

"I noticed," Vysla said, a bit of mirth still in his voice. "It's a good thing you're Vizier. I've heard quite a few stories about what soldiers will do to commanding officers that pulls something like that. You told me about half of them, if I recall."

Skadaatha sighed. She would need to find a way to make it up to them. Friendship wasn't a concept she'd entirely figured out for herself yet, but Mnene and the rest were the closest thing she had to true friends.

"What do you plan on doing until they return?" Vysla asked, turning her so he could get at her back. "Is there anything I can do to help today, or do you need to plan with them first?"

Skadaatha let out a satisfied moan as Vysla pressed his fingers along the side of her spine, kneading the muscles there, then gathered her thoughts. She would do things differently this time—the right way. She would bring down Kojatere the same way she'd brought down Matsanga so many years ago, through cunning and careful planning.

But that can wait until tomorrow.

She turned around, interrupting the wonderful massage, and pulled Vysla against her into a kiss.

When she pulled back, she grinned at the desire in her husband's eyes.

"I want to spend the day alone with my husband."

4

The Hope in their Eyes

It was not to last, however, as others fled in the aftermath of Tombara's eruption and the devastation left in its wake. They came looking for succor, and some were grateful when we gave it. Others were jealous and angry of our prosperity in the wake of the dark times. Some were simply covetous and driven by greed. Once again, our Auroramancers were driven to violence. Our people were safe, but our peaceful way of life was disrupted, and our people lived in fear for the first time in memory.

Exodus countdown: 18 days, 17 hours, 53 minutes

At the sound of his name from a voice that was both familiar and unfamiliar, Koruuksi looked up from checking his kit for the fourth time to find Kojatere, his mother, striding toward him out of the bustling rivers of people that snaked through the hangar.

She still wore no mask, so Koruuksi was able to read her emotions. She projected confidence, but as she approached, Koruuksi could tell that it was forced. For some reason, it became more obvious to him the closer she came.

Is she nervous? About me?

Koruuksi's throat threatened to close up. At his mother's expression—he *had* to believe she was his mother, despite Estingai's worries—at his own emotions that welled up when looking upon someone he'd thought lost. He forced a smile, though, for her sake.

It's what Svemakuu would have done.

He wasn't his brother. but he could still emulate the best parts of him.

"Thank you for taking the time to meet me," Kojatere said as she stopped a pace away from him. The tight smile she offered made Koruuksi blink, smile slipping.

She is *nervous, but...*

That line of thought dissipated as Koruuksi brightened his expression. He didn't know exactly how to speak with her.

And she doesn't know how to do that with me, either.

It hurt, but more than that, it was just strange. He'd always been so close with his mother. They'd been able to talk about anything, but fourteen years apart was a lot of time apart, even without factoring in the end of the world.

How much of her is really still in there?

"Of course," he said. "Is this regarding the mission, or did you just wish to talk?"

Kojatere's expression relaxed just a bit. "Both. I have more to tell you and Estingai regarding the tasks I gave to you and your teams, but..." She paused for a second, taking a deep breath, then smiled again. "I'd hoped to be able to speak with my children before I leave to return to Mjatafa Mwonga."

The way her voice caught at 'children' and grew distant at the mention of the Imaia city made Koruuksi's chest tighten, cementing his belief. The cement wasn't completely dry yet, but it made his smile a bit more genuine. The loneliness and restraint he sensed in her tugged at something Koruuksi hadn't felt since he's last seen her, bringing up memories that likely would have been lost to time if not for his orangenodes.

"Koj—Mother," he began. "I—"

Heavy, booted footsteps from off to the side made Koruuksi falter, and he couldn't help but frown as Estingai strode toward them. Her expression bordered on a scowl, and she seemed to specifically look anywhere but at their mother.

"I'm here," Estingai said, coming to a stop a pace away from Kojatere. "What's so important?"

Estingai ran a hand through her blue-black hair and oriented herself so that she faced the woman, standing slightly between her and Koruuksi. Anyone passing by probably wouldn't notice it, but Koruuksi had grown used to Estingai's over-protectiveness of him over the years.

He held in his sigh.

"Thank you for coming, Estingai," Kojatere said, voice a bit more authoritative than it had been with him. Koruuksi smirked at that.

"As I told you earlier," his mother continued, "while the main challenges of our escape will be organizing everyone to evacuate when the time comes and my task of procuring the capital ship and a distraction, your tasks are equally, if not more important."

She paused, glancing around the massive hangar, then moved closer and lowered her voice. She didn't seem to notice the way Estingai stiffened at that.

"There are a few details about your assignments," Kojatere whispered, "that I can trust only the two of you with, and I would ask you to only reveal to your teams once you are in the air and well on your way."

Koruuksi nodded, then rolled his eyes at Estingai's cold gaze.

"What are they?"

Kojatere looked between the two of them, then settled her gaze on Koruuksi. "Your team's destination is E Kwekuue."

Koruuksi blinked.

Estingai growled, hand going to her sidearm. "Do you really think we're that stupid? A child would know that's a trap."

Kojatere shook her head. "I recently learned of their likely location. I don't believe the Imaia even knows of it."

"And how is he supposed to find it if the Imaia couldn't?"

She turned her gaze back to Koruuksi. "You've heard of the

warriors that fought with the Uumgwefili during the war? The ones most wrote off as mercenaries of the jungle tribes?"

Koruuksi exchanged a glance with Estingai, then studied his mother.

"I thought those were just legends," he said slowly, "Like the ancient Apebiti people that were supposed to have lived longer and been stronger and more beautiful than any other peoples."

"E Kwekuue is real," Kojatere continued with a pointed look at Estingai. "Kweshrima searched for their people while she recovered. She believed they were hidden somewhere near the coordinates I gave you. The knowledge I gained from her makes me believe that their people will not only provide us with reinforcements, but something that will help us find a new home once we escape this world."

"You expect him to uproot an entire population?" Estingai asked, not bothering to hide the venom in her voice. "You made it sound like you just knew of a hidden cell that could help us."

Instead of responding to Estingai, Kojatere looked to Koruuksi. "I didn't say it would be easy, but I trust you."

Koruuksi knew it probably shouldn't have, but the statement made him straighten and square his shoulders a bit.

"If you do find E Kwekuue," Kojatere continued, "save as many as you can, but discovering what has kept them hidden and finding a way to bring some piece of it back to the Remnant is the more important part of your task. The systems available to us once we leave this world contain habitable worlds, but they will be harsh and unfamiliar, and we will need to use the Imaia's starmaps, so they will not be entirely safe from discovery."

Koruuksi nodded. "I will do my best."

An entire population? Darkness, I'll need to move fast to get them organized in time.

At least they would likely be grateful for a way off the dying world and not need too much convincing. And hopefully, a hidden city would barely even have enough people to match the Remnant's numbers.

Estingai snorted. "I still think both of us should stay and help prep everyone to leave. Is that why you called me here, too? Am I off to find some mythical lost city instead of hermit Auroraborn? Maybe a flight of draakon that managed to stay hidden from the Imaia's conservation teams?"

Kojatere shook her head, then looked to Estingai. "Your team is still looking for the Union's former leaders and surviving Knights, if they've managed to survive this long. The set of coordinates I gave you should lead to Matsanga."

Koruuksi winced, and glanced over at Estingai in time to see genuine shock on his sister's face. It quickly turned to scorn.

"Why would you send me after that coward? He abandoned us," Estingai growled.

"Don't let your anger make you so quick to judge, Estingai," Kojatere said, and edge to her voice. "Matsanga is no coward, and his return would provide much-needed leadership and morale to the Remnant."

"A leader that abandoned us when we needed him most," Estingai spat back.

"Yes," Kojatere said, "*exactly* when you needed him most. After an encounter with...with Othaashle where she broke him. So you can take my word when I say that you have no right to judge him."

Koruuksi blinked at the thread of pain in Kojatere's voice, though his sister didn't seem to notice.

"Your word?" Estingai snarled. "Your word means nothing when you won't even admit to being the one to break him. Get out of here. Go back to your golden city and get us a ship. If you're not just leading us all into a trap."

Kojatere opened her mouth, but Estingai cut her off. "Leave. Now."

Koruuksi watched as Kojatere looked between the two of them, seeming to deflate, then straightened and walked off toward the main tunnel that connected the hangar to the rest of the compound.

Once she was out of earshot, he turned on Estingai, grabbing her arm roughly. "What in darkness is wrong with you?"

Estingai actually managed to look taken aback, golden eyes wide. "You're mad at *me*?"

"Yes," Koruuksi said, "she just wanted to talk with us before she leaves again, but you had to blow up, as usual."

Estingai yanked her arm away. "She's not our mother, Koruuksi. And how do you plan on evacuating an entire city?"

"A capital ship will certainly help with that."

"Even if it will, you won't have time."

Koruuksi gritted his teeth. "I'll make it work, Estingai. Don't take this away from me, and don't change the subject. You're blaming her for things she had no control over, things she never would have done if she hadn't been compelled to do so."

"But she did them, which means she is not Kojatere."

"She was," Koruuksi protested, despite his own reservations. "And it seems like she is again. If she's still only Othaashle, why hasn't she just slaughtered us all? She's more than capable of it. Especially if she'd let Skadaatha join her."

Estingai started to protest, but Koruuksi pressed before she could get another word out.

"No, Estingai," he said, "I'm not arguing about this with you. You'll just get even angrier like you always do. There's no winning with you as it is, but it's even worse when you get like this."

He closed his kit and hefted it over one shoulder. "I'm going to find and save these people. I don't care how hard it is—I will make it happen so I can finally do something with my life that I know is objectively good. Tell Matsanga I miss him if you find him, and tell him you missed him, too."

Koruuksi stalked off toward where his team waited, fuming. He ignored Estingai's calls for him to stop, angry at her and angry at himself for letting her get to him.

Make it back safe, Estingai. Stars guide your way.

∼

"Koruuksi. Koruuksi!"

Estingai took a step after her brother, about to call again, but took a deep breath and dropped her hand, turning away. Koruuksi didn't often get angry, but when he did, there wasn't any getting through to him until he worked things out for himself.

She decided to find Uuchantuu.

It took her a while, threading her way through the Remnant soldiers and support that worked prepping their ships and supplies even though they would not move for another three weeks. Hope of escape from what they'd believed an unavoidable sentence had breathed new life into them, it seemed. That made a smile tug at the corners of Estingai's lips.

Until her anger and suspicion rose to quash it.

She couldn't let herself get caught up in Kojatere's promise having any truth. The way Estingai saw things, the most they could hope for was being baited to a capital ship that the Imaia set up as a trap for them. She intended to see that the Remnant captured that ship no matter what, but she knew that she had little hope of escaping with the rest of her people if it came to a fight.

And only three weeks to make that happen.

A week and a half maximum for both her and Koruuksi to accomplish their tasks, then return for any last-minute logistics and planning.

At the very least, I'll get to see Koruuksi again.

She could give him a proper good-bye then.

Eventually, Estingai found Uuchantuu next to some of the supply caches near the edge of the hangar. She was by herself.

Estingai approached, about to ask after Koruuksi, when she noticed Uuchantuu's posture. The young woman seemed... smaller than usual, more drawn in.

"Uuchantuu?" Estingai asked. "Are you alright?"

Uuchantuu turned to Estingai, golden-brown eyes tired, expression tight.

Estingai watched as she tried to force a smile for a moment, only to sigh. The younger woman clutched at her wrist, just beneath a familiar bracelet. Even after all these years, seeing it made Estingai's chest grow tight.

"I miss her, too," Estingai said, voice suddenly raw.

"Do you think we actually have a chance?" Uuchantuu asked, forcing a tight smile. "It isn't just wishful thinking?"

Estingai bit her tongue. She wanted to speak with Uuchantuu about her doubts, to be vindicated in her anger and suspicion. Instead, she found herself setting a hand on Uuchantuu's shoulder and meeting the young woman's amber gaze.

"It isn't just wishful thinking," she assured Koruuksi's friend. "Even if Kojatere does end up betraying us, I will see this through to the end. I will get you and Koruuksi and the others off this dying world. Somewhere you can just live, rather than needing to fight to simply survive."

Uuchantuu blinked, then cracked a smile. "I've gotta say, I didn't expect that from you."

Estingai shrugged. "I've been told that I've become a bit too bitter and pessimistic lately."

Uuchantuu snorted. "That sounds like something Koruuksi would tell you. Let me guess, you fought again? He stalked off before you could make up?"

Estingai sighed. "Are we really that bad?"

Uuchantuu shrugged. "Only because I know you so well."

Estingai snorted. That was all Koruuksi. She'd been supposed to take care of him and Uuchantuu after Kojatere and Aiteperit and Suulehep had died. She'd tried, but...thankfully, Svemakuu had somehow picked up most of the slack. Once he was gone...

I could have at least tried to keep our family dinners going.

Estingai drew in a shaky breath, trying to push back the tightness in her chest. "I'm... sorry for being so distant."

Uuchantuu blinked, then took Estingai's hand. "It's okay. I'd rather things were better, but..."

She trailed off, then shrugged, giving Estingai a tight smile. "Everyone looks to you, now. Not just Koruuksi and I. You need someone who would just help you with whatever was on your plate and that was it. Without giving you all the shit Koruuksi does."

Estingai smiled. "Thank you. And thank you for always looking out for him. That's part of why I wanted to find you. Apparently your team might be able to save a lot of people, and Koruuksi seems set on getting that done. I just don't want him getting in over his head."

Uuchantuu smiled, nodding as she zipped up her back and set the strap on her shoulder, "Of course. Take care of yourself, too. I know Koruuksi always tries to keep people's spirits up like his brother, but neither of them would've been able to do that if anything happened to you. Stars guide your way."

Estingai returned the farewell as Uuchantuu headed off at a trot toward her and Koruuksi's team. She watched after the woman for a moment, wanting to say something. Uuchantuu was like a sister to Koruuksi, and had once felt like that to Estingai. Lately, though, Estingai felt like she'd failed the woman. They spent enough time together that they should be closer, but...

Loosing Koruuksi would be hard enough.

With a sigh, Estingai turned from Uuchantuu to head toward her own team.

She found them ready and waiting near their shuttle

Estingai felt her step quicken as she looked toward the ship, her mood growing a bit lighter. The modified Imaia shuttle was nothing special as far as aircraft went—beat up and rough like most of what they'd stolen or salvaged.

But it was a ship nonetheless, a vessel to take her above the clouds and beyond.

Her team snapped salutes as she approached, shouldering their packs and waiting for her to enter the ship before filing in after her.

As she stepped into the shuttle's main hold, a warmth spread through Estingai. The discordant mix of fresh oil and cleaner nearly made her laugh at the absurdity of how welcome she found the scents as she drew in a deep breath. She stepped past the row of collapsible seats in the middle of the main hold and stepped down into the cockpit, gazing out through the viewport at the bustling hangar, framed by the blinking lights of controls and relays. As she took her seat in lead position, the lumpy nylon had never felt so amazing. The hum of the ship's electronics transported her to another world. One where she had some measure of control, and the weight on her shoulders seemed lighter. She'd helped with upgrades and repaired all their vehicles, but this one was *hers*.

A genuine smile tugged at her mouth as the others took their seats, with Araana, an attractive Natari woman, taking her seat next to Estingai in the cockpit. A warmth spread through Estingai, her heart beating a bit faster in anticipation.

At the hiss of the transport's door closing and sealing behind her, Estingai looked over her shoulder at her team. "Everyone ready?"

Each person called out or nodded in turn with Araana, Estingai's second, checking a few of the controls on her side of the cockpit before saluting.

Estingai turned her gaze back out of the cockpit into the hangar. She was about to open up the comm to check with the traffic control, when her gaze fell upon Koruuksi's team. She brightened her clearnodes just enough to see the group smiling, talking and laughing as they loaded the last of their gear into the ship. That seemed to make the utter silence from behind her even more deafening.

How long has it been since I laughed like that with my own team?

She knew exactly how long it had been. Seven years, two months, and thirty-four days. Almost four full cycles. Ever since the Imaia had taken her husband from her. Since—

Stop.

Estingai took a deep breath.

Plenty of time for that later. Don't let her ruin flying for you.

It took more than just a deep breath to get her anger over Svemakuu's death out of her mind, however. It showed in her voice when she cleared her take-off with Traffic Control.

Koruuksi probably has a point about my anger issues.

Adding Matsanga to the mix didn't help.

As she maneuvered the transport to the end of the hangar and out of the massive cave's hidden exits, however, the thrill of flying took over, managing to quell Estingai's anger for the time being.

Once they'd been in the air for almost an hour, Estingai composed herself and delivered Kojatere's news to her team.

The hope in their eyes was worth the effort.

5

Phantom

When the Iron Empire came and offered protection in exchange for wood from our forests, iron from our mountains, and a shipyard in one of our sheltered bays, our people rejoiced. We wanted nothing more than to resume lives of peace, living off the sea and the coast, with our Auroramancers serving their people instead of giving their lives to protect them. The Empire was so impressed by our Auroramancers, they allowed them to do as they wished, and ask only that our Auroramancers teach their own.

Exodus countdown: 18 days, 10 hours, 44 minutes

Yndlova tried not to fidget as she watched Othaashle exit the Vale and stride toward her and Itese. She'd been told already that the champion wore no mask, and to bring one to her immediately, but actually seeing her without one was...

Taking a deep breath, Yndlova exchanged a look with Itese. She couldn't see the Redeemed's face, of course, but the woman's posture said she was as shocked as Yndlova.

Neither had seen their commander's face before, of course, but there was no mistaking that confident, purposeful stride, even had she not borne the pale grey skin and golden markings of a Redeemed.

Yndlova tried to keep her fingers from drumming on her datapad or the spare mask she held for Othaashle. She didn't know where to look in this situation, and apparently didn't know what to do with her hands, either. She knew that for a Redeemed, being without one's mask was like being naked in some of the Imaia's more conservative cultures. It was probably even worse, given Redeemed removed their masks only to eat. The thought of being *that* exposed made Yndlova shiver.

Taking a deep breath, Yndlova looked to Itese again. "You don't have to—"

Itese cut her off with a raised hand. "Forget about it. Just show the commander she can trust you. She'll realize you were only looking out for her."

"Thank you."

Itese wobbled her head a bit, making her braid and the hair of her mane swish back and forth—the Redeemed's version of a smile. "We like you too much to let her do anything too bad to you. Janitorial duty might fit, though."

That make Yndlova crack a smile. For the moment, the tension in her shoulders faded. True friends like Itese were rare this high up in the military.

Then Yndlova returned her gaze to Othaashle, who had covered half the distance between the pair of them and the ornate open gate leading to the Vale. Taking a deep breath, she tried to look at the woman's armor rather than her face.

Though Yndlova hoped Othaashle would allow her to apologize and make things right, she was entirely prepared to be disciplined and even stripped of her rank and position if that was what it came to. She hoped it wouldn't—that would throw away years of hard work and make pursuing her personal research project much more difficult. If it came to that, however, Yndlova would not try to escape the consequences of her actions. She'd disobeyed orders and betrayed her superior's trust by telling Skadaatha about the visions. She deserved whatever judgement Othaashle decided to dole out.

As her commander came closer, Yndlova couldn't help but look up. The contemplative expression on Othaashle's face as she covered the last of the distance between them kept Yndlova from relaxing. She wasn't used to being able to read her superior's expression, and her mind raced to the worst possibilities of what Othaashle could be thinking about.

"Your mask, Mestari," Yndlova forced out once Othaashle came close enough. She held out the spare.

Othaashle blinked, looking at her, then the mask. She gazed at the latter for a moment before taking it and donning it.

"Thank you, Yndlova."

Yndlova snapped a crisp salute, as Itese had already done beside her. "Commander, I wish to apologize for disobeying your orders. I told Skadaatha—"

"So you did," Othaashle said, cutting her off as she started past them at a brisk walk. Yndlova turned on heel and took a few quick steps to catch up and keep pace with the woman, as did Itese.

"I'd hoped it was you," Othaashle continued after a moment. "If it hadn't been, I would be worried Skadaatha had a spy in our ranks or some way of listening in on my conversations without being present."

"Sir?" Yndlova ventured. "I disobeyed your orders."

"Yes," Othaashle confirmed, and Yndlova's shoulders sagged, "which ended up working out quite nicely for me. Skadaatha's attempts to kill me made infiltrating the Remnant much easier."

Yndlova blinked. It took her a moment to realize she was gaping and had stopped walking. She glanced over at Itese, who had also come to a stop.

They both had to jog to catch up to Othaashle this time. She appeared to be headed for the Isle of the Redeemed.

"Skadaatha tried to kill you?" Yndlova asked.

"Attempts?" Itese added, "She tried more than once?"

Othaashle looked to both of them, cocking her head. "You think I would joke about that?"

Yndlova's cheeks grew hot, and not for the first time, she wished she had the luxury of wearing a mask that would conceal her emotions.

"No," she answered, "but... shouldn't we issue a warrant for her arrest? That's—"

Othaashle held up a hand. "We came to an agreement. Though I would appreciate it if you could task a few personnel from different departments to keep an eye on her and her team." She looked to Yndlova. "I should have heeded your earlier suggestion." Othaashle turned to Itese. "Redeemed tailing her team would be too obvious, but have everyone keep an eye out for them when off the Isle."

"Of course, Mestari," Itese said.

"I will take care of it immediately, Sir," Yndlova said.

"No need for that just yet," Othaashle said. "I would like the two of you to assist me with some research and planning for how to deal with the Remnant."

"Of course, sir," Yndlova said.

"Should we start with the spies we managed to round up?" Itese asked. "We've attempted to question them a few times, but I expect you might wish to do so yourself. Especially since Skadaatha had asked for permission to interrogate them during your absence. Now that you've returned, she will likely come asking again."

Othaashle stopped, nearly causing Yndlova to trip over her own feet as she came to an abrupt halt beside her. They stood just before the bridge to the Isle of the Redeemed.

"Yes," she said after a moment, resuming her pace forward and venturing onto the bridge. "Do you have their names?"

"Yes, Mestari, I can pull them up."

"Do so."

"Sir," Yndlova ventured, "what exactly happened with the Remnant? What is the plan going forward?"

Instead of responding to her, Othaashle turned to Itese as they passed through the shining gates to the Isle of the Redeemed. "Has Yndlova brought you up to speed on my visions yet?"

Itese hesitated. "No, Mestari."

Othaashle nodded, head swiveling for a moment before she lowered her voice. "The important parts are that I started having visions of who I was before Lord Ynuukwidas remade me: Kojatere, Kweshrima's champion. That information led me to the Throne and gave me the knowledge I needed to infiltrate the Remnant. I seized the Throne from Kweshrima, ending her in the process, and though its power is not what it once was, it is enough that even Skadaatha and her elites could not stand against me. It has also put a stop to the visions."

She glanced between the two of them, raising a hand to a few Redeemed nearby that noticed and saluted her. "I would appreciate it if you two keep that information close to the chest for now. Skadaatha knows, as do her elites, but I don't believe she will try to use it against me for now unless the trail back to her is non-existent."

Yndlova nodded.

Any further conversation was cut short as they entered the center of the Village of Light and came into contact with an increasing number of Redeemed. Othaashle greeted many as they passed through the lush, ever-white plaza, but continued her pace through the square toward the Spear.

They passed a group of four guards as they descended into the interrogation hall, but did not resume conversation until both thick, iron doors had closed behind them. Yndlova had never gotten used to that.

"To answer your earlier question, Yndlova," Othaashle said, "I succeeded in convincing the Remnant that I am Kojatere returned to them, and that I plan on helping them escape Efruumani by providing an older capital ship with a starmap and a distraction to cover them stealing it from the city. I have yet to decide whether it would be most advantageous to capture the ship and those on it once they have their entire population on board, destroy the ship, or insert spies into their number to give us their location once they establish themselves on a new world. The God King approves of this plan and has decided to leave the details up to me."

Yndlova nodded, mind racing with ideas. "The last option seems like the most advantageous. The Remnant would do all the hard work for us. We could either invade when the time is right or wait long enough for a new generation to come to power that would not show us as much hostility."

Othaashle nodded. "My thoughts exactly. Don't speak of this to anyone else, though. I did not have the time or the trust when with the Remnant to discover if they have any active spies besides those we rounded up after their attack."

She stopped, turning to Itese as they reached Interrogation, where the spies were being held in separate rooms. Taizak and Katamori—two very personable Redeemed who acted the most like true family of any Yndlova had encountered so far—waited here, tasked with maintaining the prisoners while they waited. Both snapped a salute once they noticed Othaashle. They numbered among the youngest of the Redeemed, but their charming dispositions made their presence felt on the Isle despite their short time on it.

"Champion."

Othaashle stopped and looked between the two of them. "Do you two ever find it ironic when you're put on guard duty?"

"Not at all, Champion," Taizak said.

"Takes troublemakers to know how to watch them, sir," Katamori echoed.

Yndlova rolled her eyes as Othaashle shook her head.

The commander gestured back toward the entrance. "Go join the others. I don't want anyone else coming down here."

"Sir."

As the two Redeemed trotted off, Othaashle watched them for a moment, then turned to Itese. "Do you have the list of names up?"

Itese nodded, holding the datapad up to Othaashle. She gazed at the screen, then raised a finger to it.

"Phantom," she breathed.

"Mestari?" Itese asked.

"This man, Torni Hyhainen," Othaashle said, angling the screen toward Itese. Yndlova held back a frown at being unable to see it. "Where was he hiding? How did you find him?"

Yndlova shared a look with Itese. She couldn't see the other woman's face, of course, but she'd been around Redeemed long enough to know read their body language. Itese shared her confusion.

"He was in logistics, the domestic office, under the name Vaino Lapla," Yndlova said slowly. "We only found him because the orders to move the stolen craft to the more easily-accessible point they were at during the attack came from his office."

Othaashle sighed. "That sounds like him."

Yndlova frowned. Othaashle sounded almost amused.

"Sir?" she ventured.

Othaashle looked to Yndlova, then Itese. "I shared this with Yndlova already. The visions showed me that I was a part of Symuuna Team when I was Kojatere. This man, known to me then as 'Phantom', directed our missions." She snorted. "I'm actually the one that gave him the scar and the need for a new eye."

Yndlova blinked, mind reeling. Othaashle was Champion for a reason, even without Ilkwalerva or the powers of a Redeemed to make her more dangerous, but Phantom...she'd heard the name in myths and tales used to frighten children long before Kweshrima had broken the world.

If he directed an operation like Symuuna Team...this man is probably the same one.

That didn't track entirely with how long the legends had been around, but still...

"How? Why?"

Othaashle hesitated. When she spoke, there was a dark tension to her voice. "He got a few of my men killed and didn't even pretend to care."

"Sir, are you alright?"

Othaashle turned her masked face on Yndlova, then sighed. "Even though they fought against the Imaia, those men he got killed were still *my* men, good soldiers. Good soldiers follow orders. Giving orders in bad faith like he did is unacceptable."

She paused for a moment, then squared her shoulders, handing the datapad back to Itese, who showed it to Yndlova.

"He should be the only one I need to speak to," Othaashle said, heading toward the prisoner's interrogation cell, "He'll be the hardest to break, but his information should be the most valuable."

She stopped with a hand on the door's electronic panel, then looked to Yndlova and Itese, "While I'm in there, discuss the logistics of creating a distraction for when the Remnant attacks and getting a capital ship somewhere easily accessible to the Remnant without it looking like bait or raising flags for our people. I don't want it to seem too easy for the enemy, but I want as little damage to Mjatafa Mwonga and our people as possible."

Yndlova nodded, then frowned. "Won't you want one of us in the other room monitoring the interrogation?"

Othaashle shook her head. "I only want you in there long enough to turn off the recording equipment. I' going to remove my mask to see if I can fool Phantom the same way I did the Remnant, and I don't want Skadaatha to have any possible way of leveraging that against me."

Yndlova nodded, "Of course, sir."

Othaashle entered the room, and Yndlova followed Itese to do as instructed.

6

Do You Want to Fight?

Our joy did not last. We had exchanged a handful of hyenas nipping at our haunches for an Iron Draakon that loomed over us. Game became scarce as the forests were turned into ships. Fish fled as the increasing ships in the bay disrupted their patterns. The iron mines led to sickness for anyone who ventured too close, attracted rough, foreign workers, and stole many of our own people. In time, even our Auroramancers were drafted into the Iron Empire's service. They had trained their own oppressors. When currency came and enslaved our people it bore the hammer of the Iron Empire on one side, and the sun of Atonga on the other.

Exodus countdown: 18 days, 2 hours, 5 minutes

Forests on Lightside had always unsettled Koruuksi—not that he'd had the chance to visit too many in his life. There were too many bright, shining colors. Most of them were teal or maroon; every single tree in this forest seemed to possess leaves of pure white. The caves at least possessed the beautiful strata: wondrous patterns of color of varying hues caused by layers of stone pressed together over the ages. The overwhelming brightness of the forest made even the various shades of greys, browns and reds of the trunks and branches seem out of place. The bright glare from the constant sunlight—even through the shaded lenses of his mask—didn't help either. He found himself unable to keep his clearnodes brightened for more than a few seconds at a time unless he closed his eyes and decided to just rely on his own senses. Though they weren't as keen as a cleareye's would be even without Auroralight, they were better than most.

Koruuksi glanced around at the thick foliage that surrounded them. It was incredible, despite his own feelings.

After so long in sterile caves and barren deserts, being surrounded by so much life seemed unreal, as though he'd stepped into another world.

I could do without feeling like I'm wading through soup with every step.

It made him feel a bit of guilt when he carved a small cross into the trunk of a nearby tree, as it had the seven other times since they'd hidden their ships near the coast and ventured into the dense, glaring forest.

Suspicion tempered that guilt, however. While lush foliage surrounded them in abundance, Koruuksi had yet to see any wildlife larger than some insects, and few of those at that. From his few visits to Lightside before the end of the world, he knew forests like this should be teeming with all sorts of annoying little insects. He had to stop himself from reaching toward the phantom itch between his shoulder blades.

It didn't help that the heat made his clothing stick to him like a second skin.

"Why couldn't E Kwekuue have been on Darkside?" he grumbled, pulling at his clothing where his body armor didn't hold it down. "Or at least somewhere in the twilight band?"

"I'd rather be able to feel my toes and fingertips, thank you," Wemba shot back.

Like Uuchantuu, Wemba was Natari. Her red skin—the darkest shade Koruuksi had seen—didn't burn easily under Lightside's sun, so she didn't have to carefully cover every bit of her skin. She still wore the same black outfit and body armor that the rest of them did, but her helmet hung at her hip rather than suffocating her.

Koruuksi glared at her. "That's because you don't have to cover every inch of your skin to avoid severe burns."

"I know. It's great."

Wemba's grin made Koruuksi want to trip her. Instead, he turned his attention back to the forest. When the Imaia had scoured the lands for resources, they had leveled most forests, even uprooting the stumps of the trees they'd harvested. Yet here in what had once been northwest Nilobanta near the ruins of Uumgwefilo, it seemed the forests had been given time to regrow.

Or maybe the Imaia had simply never touched this forest to begin with.

The way it had seemingly come out of nowhere once they'd gotten close enough was eerie at the least. They'd hidden the ships as close to the coast as they could while still keeping them somewhat out of sight.

He'd pointedly avoided flying anywhere they might be able to see Uumgwefilo's ruins—if the Imaia had left even that; they'd taken anything and everything that could be reused when building their massive city-ship—Koruuksi had been to Uumgwefilo a few times. He'd liked it there. He didn't want to see what had become of it.

Koruuksi caught Uuchantuu's gaze. As much as he could in his helmet, at least.

"Do you know any stories about E Kwekuue that mention the forest surrounding just appearing out of nowhere?"

Uuchantuu rolled her eyes. "Don't you think I would have mentioned them if I did?"

Koruuksi sighed, then glanced around at his companions. He caught Wemba's gaze and motioned for her to approach. She hurried over.

"What is it?" she asked in a hushed voice as she crouched next to him. "Contacts?"

Koruuksi nearly laughed at the absurdity of Wemba crouching. She was the tallest on their twelve-person team unless Koruuksi counted his antlers, and her slender build exaggerated the effect. He shook his head and she relaxed a bit, thick, full lips curling into a smile.

"I was wondering if you knew any stories about E Kwekuue since you're always studying history," he said. "Specifically any that mention a forest just appearing out of nowhere."

Wemba's nose crinkled as she thought. After a few moments, she shook her head. "Most of what I've heard mentions the city itself—concealed in a fertile valley—or its warriors fighting alongside various peoples against the Imaia and the Imaia's failed attempts to find them. Nothing about the area around E Kwekuue." She paused, then grinned. "I was actually surprised when we headed here—I'd guessed the city would be on an entirely different continent, not right next to Uumgwefilo's—where it used to be."

Koruuksi nodded. "It still might be. Hopefully it isn't though." He met her eyes and smiled. "Thank you, Wemba. Tell the others to keep their eyes open."

She saluted and fell back, and Koruuksi shared a rueful look and a shrug with Uuchantuu before continuing on in silence.

Lysanda came up beside him a quarter of an hour later. Wemba's opposite, she was short and stocky, and her blue skin required her to cover herself up just as much as Koruuksi. Like him, she wore a hood over her helmet, gloves, a balaclava, and clothing that covered her completely in addition to her armor and equipment.

"What is it, Lysanda?" he asked as she saluted.

She hesitated for a moment before speaking. "I was wondering if she should split up into pairs. Just in case Estingai is right and this is an Imaia trap."

Koruuksi sighed. He couldn't rule out that possibility. Searching in pairs would be a better way to cover ground than a big group, and it would mitigate some of the threat if one group walked into a potential trap, but...

Koruuksi looked around at the forest, then shook his head.

"I don't want us separated in a place like this. We'll have a hard time finding our way back to the ships as it is even with our markings on the trees."

Lysanda nodded and fell back. Only a few seconds passed before Kakengo's voice reached his ears.

"He worried about this place?"

Koruuksi rolled his eyes and raised his voice just enough to be heard, "I can't be the only one creeped out by this forest."

Kakengo just laughed. "You need to relax, Koruuksi. Stop worrying and just think about all the grateful women who will want to thank us for coming to their aid."

"*And* men," Koruuksi added, shooting Uuchantuu a grin.

She just shook her head.

A few of the others laughed.

"More fun for the two of us, right Koruuksi?" Ilona called.

"Probably just for Koruuksi," Akseli said. "Shouldn't they all be Natari?"

"What's your point?" Ilona said.

"Natari *men* are usually the more open ones," Muuzuuri said, "not their women. You might be willing to jump into bed with them, but I doubt many of them will feel the same."

Even Koruuksi laughed as Ilona sighed. "Why do you have to ruin my fantasies?"

Koruuksi glanced over at Uuchantuu. As he expected, a dark blush graced her cheeks. He still didn't entirely understand that. In some ways, Uuchantuu was a prude—her coat remained buttoned up when the other Natari in their group had undone theirs to deal with the heat, and she grew embarrassed whenever anyone talked about sex—yet she had no problem washing with the rest of them in the communal showers back at base. She'd also never judged Koruuksi for the many men and women he'd slept with. Unless he was being an idiot or an asshole, of course.

"You realize that most of these people will be part of families, right?" Luuhuuta said. "Not just a bunch of young single men and women waiting to be swept off their feet?"

Koruuksi laughed at the chorus of groans at Luuhuuta's comment. He was about to respond when he glanced over at Uuchantuu and frowned as they continued through the forest.

Telling her about the true nature of their mission had bolstered her mood initially—as it had for the rest of the team—but she'd seemed more subdued since they'd landed. At first, he'd thought it just her hyper vigilance combined with the eerie emptiness of the forest. Now, though...

"You alright?" he asked in a low voice, moving closer to her as they continued through the forest. The others' banter faded into the background.

"Fine," she said, "why wouldn't I be?"

Koruuksi rolled his eyes. "You're gonna do that with me?"

"You want to talk about it *now*?"

"Why not?"

Uuchantuu was silent for a moment, the sighed. "Fine. This mission... it just seems too good to be true. Even if it wasn't E Kwekuue we were trying to find—another group of people resisting the Imaia that we've never heard of? What if Estingai and Lysanda are right? What if it is a trap?"

"Do you really believe that?"

Uuchantuu glanced over at him, then sighed, shaking her head. "No. I want to believe Kojatere as much as you do. But what if this isn't as easy or straightforward as we hope?" She hefted her rifle. "What if we actually need to use these?"

Koruuksi frowned. "This is about what Kojatere said, isn't it? About what the Imaia think about us?"

Uuchantuu tensed, then nodded slowly.

"I don't want to fight anyone that isn't the Imaia," she said in a small voice. "I barely even want to fight them anymore sometimes."

Koruuksi sighed. "I don't either. I think that alone is enough to show that we're not the monsters they think we are. Helping these people will prove that."

Uuchantuu gave him a weak half-smile. "Yeah, I guess you're right."

"Of course I am."

Uuchantuu snorted, punching him half-heartedly in the arm.

Koruuksi grinned at that but turned his attention back to his surroundings.

"Shut it," Uuchantuu hissed over her shoulder. Koruuksi blinked—he'd tuned out their team's banter more than he'd realized. Probably out of habit.

Koruuksi marked another tree—one every sixty paces—as they crept through the forest in silence. They tried to keep as straight a path as possible over the tangle of roots and underbrush.

Auroras, I hope there aren't any brilliant white snakes hiding here.

That would be just his luck.

Koruuksi tried to banish the thought but scanned his surroundings with even more scrutiny as they continued deeper into the forest.

Koruuksi almost missed a step when he noticed the bone. The white leaves of the plants around it had turned it nearly invisible. He couldn't tell if it was human or not, and didn't stop to check, but it was the first indication that there was any life larger than an insect in this forest aside from them.

He didn't stop, but instead tapped Uuchantuu and gestured to it as they passed, then held a finger to his lips.

"I think we're getting close."

Uuchantuu nodded and signaled those behind them. A moment later, shuffling from behind them indicated the rest of their team checking and readying their weapons. Koruuksi checked his own. It was a standard semi-automatic mid-range weapon with a sixty-round magazine and a wooden stock to brace against. He'd affixed a bayonet to the front, and the georaural he'd added under the barrel allowed it to function as a short-range flamethrower if needed.

As they ventured deeper, he and Uuchantuu picked out a few more discomforting signs—pieces of discarded Imaia armor and weaponry that it seemed the forest had claimed and worked to eliminate. That probably meant this wasn't an Imaia trap, but it didn't make him feel any better.

With each new detail, the shining white forest seemed to grow darker. With each step, Koruuksi's itch—the feeling that he was being watched—grew stronger.

When leaves shuffled off to the side, Koruuksi primed his gemcrest and barked orders without a second thought. It took all of twelve seconds for his team to form a porcupine with rifles pointed out at their surroundings, gemcrests primed.

"Show yourself!" Koruuksi demanded, brightening his ambernodes to save them from any surprise attacks, "or we *will* fire."

For a moment that seemed to stretch into hours, silence and stillness dominated the forest. So much so that Koruuksi nearly jumped when a group of white-clad figures armed with spears and bows stepped into view. He saw it a few moments ahead of his teammates, but just because he could process the information faster and sooner didn't make it any less surprising. Even with their weapons, their clothing and the white backdrop of the forest made them difficult to track. Antlers would have helped, but it looked like they were all Natari. If they decided to run or lunge, Koruuksi expected that tracking their movements would be nearly impossible without his ambernodes. He was already down to half of his Auroralight in those from holding them brightened for so long.

They didn't appear to wear much armor unless it was under the white tunics, trousers and head wraps they all wore. Koruuksi counted at least thirty as he looked around—a few had come out from the forest behind them as well.

Nice to know I wasn't just being paranoid.

"If you and I shield the team at the right time, I think we can take them," Uuchantuu whispered.

With firearms against bows and spears, she wasn't wrong. Not at first glance, at least.

As Koruuksi locked eyes with one of the warriors, however—the one part of their bodies they left uncovered—he reconsidered. This one stood back behind the rest—a woman, Koruuksi thought, or a young man with *very* shapely hips. She held a spear, but something about her posture and the way some of the other warriors positioned themselves around her, implied that she was their commander, or someone of value to them at the very least.

Those eyes.

Koruuksi hadn't often felt such fierce intensity from a mere look. *She could put Estingai to shame in that respect.*

He imagined the two would either be the best of friends or try to kill each other within seconds.

As the already thick, muggy air thickened between the two parties, Koruuksi flexed his fingers around the heavy stock of his rifle. A shot from the massive handheld railgun would probably make them scatter, even if he only hit one.

They must have Fireborn among them.

Unfortunately, their white clothing was thick and bright enough that it obscured the color of any gemcrests shining underneath.

Koruuksi clenched his teeth, meeting that woman's eyes again, then glancing at Uuchantuu.

She met his eyes.

"Do you want to fight them?" he whispered.

Uuchantuu gave a slight shake of her head.

Koruuksi looked back to the white-clad woman.

"Stand down."

He lowered his rifle, then adjusted it so it hung from the strap properly, and held his hands up in the air.

His team hesitated but followed suit a few moments later.

"We aren't here to hurt anyone," Koruuksi said, raising his voice for any other hidden warriors to hear. He held the woman's gaze. "We want to talk."

The woman's eyes took on a curious light for a moment, then narrowed.

He blinked. "Can you understand me?"

The woman's expression didn't change.

"I need to speak to whoever is in charge," he continued, shrugging out of his rifle strap and placing the heavy weapon on the ground. "Please, we are here to help."

Koruuksi waited as the rest of his team followed his lead, placing their weapons on the forest floor before them.

That itch between his shoulder blades nagged at him again. It had almost become impossible to ignore, when the woman tapped the arm of one of her companions and said something too quiet for Koruuksi to understand.

The other warrior—a man much taller than the woman—seemed to hesitate for a moment, then turned back toward Koruuksi and lowered his spear. He fished a dark strip of cloth out of a pouch at his waist and started forward. A few others did the same.

Koruuksi sighed.

Of course, they're blindfolding us.

That made it much more likely that these people were from E Kwekuue. Given the current situation, however, that didn't do much to comfort Koruuksi.

"Just go with it," Koruuksi said, sensing his team's nervousness.

As the tall warrior stepped up to Koruuksi, however, he reached for Koruuksi's mask.

Koruuksi flinched backward and held up a hand, causing everyone on both sides to tense.

"I can't take this off," he said, tapping the mask and shaking his head. He looked to the tall warrior, then the woman. "Neither can my friends. You can put the blindfold over my mask, but it will hurt me if you take it off."

Normally, he only had to worry about direct sunlight. In this forest, though, the cover the trees provided wasn't much given how reflective their leaves were.

Koruuksi tensed as the warrior looked to the woman. She looked between the two of them, then nodded. Koruuksi let the man blindfold them.

"Koruuksi?" Uuchantuu said.

"Yeah?"

"If we get thrown in some sort of dungeon because of this, I'm going to kill you."

Koruuksi sighed, then put on his best grin as the man led him forward.

He tripped over his rifle and nearly fell on his face.

"Please bring those with you. They're very valuable."

7

Visions and Spies

Yet our gods of sea and storm had not abandoned us. When it seemed as though our people might fade into obscurity, lost to history, a savior emerged wielding the hammer and flame of a blacksmith of the Empire. In secret, he armed our people and secured ships for flight. He was betrayed by an unknown ally, yet he led us from bondage, and dealt a great blow to the Empire with the theft of their ships.

Exodus countdown: 18 days, 10 hours, 6 minutes

What if we moved one of the older ships to the hangars on the outer wall? We could say we need to use it as a drydock to do some minor repairs on the ship and that the shipyard will need space for any newer ships that need repairing after or during Exodus."

Itese frowned, eyes downcast, unfocused as she thought.

"Itese?"

A hand on her shoulder broke her away from her thoughts. Itese started, giving herself a shake as she looked to Yndlova. The woman wore a concerned expression.

They were in the interrogation hall, a lower level with stark hallways and floors. The only hint of decoration were the hexagonal ceiling tiles. If not for the bright lights every few tiles, the underground space would have made Itese claustrophobic.

"Sorry," Itese said, glad that her mask hid her blush.

Even after ten years, she hadn't gotten over how strange it was that most of the Imaia's people had no problem bearing their faces and emotions to anyone who would look.

And none of them seem to find it inconvenient.

"What were we talking about?"

Yndlova raised any eyebrow. "Logistics for Othaashle's plan. Like she asked."

The Natari woman peered at Itese, removing her hand from her shoulder. "Are you sure you're alright? You're not normally this... jumpy."

Itese sighed. She couldn't lie, but that didn't mean she couldn't deflect.

"It's just a bit much to take in," she said, "Othaashle's visions, that she used to be the enemy's Champion."

She sighed again as Yndlova nodded.

"It does explain a lot, though."

Itese nodded. "It does."

Othaashle had always been even more powerful and adept with her powers than any of the other Lightforged. Some thought it was due to Ilkwalerva and the power it bestowed upon her, but Itese knew it was more than that. The God King wouldn't have given such a powerful weapon to just anyone. Knowing now that she'd not only been one of Kweshrima's Knights, but their Champion...it somehow made Itese even more proud to serve under her, even as it troubled her.

Before either of them could say anything more, the door to the interrogation cell they guarded hissed. Othaashle burst through the opening a moment later, expression dazed and frantic, mask in her hand instead of on her face. Without a word, she bounded across the hall to one of the empty rooms, its door already open, and closed the door behind her.

"What—" Itese began. Her words fell away when she saw Yndlova's expression. The woman's mouth had drawn to a thin line, jaw clenched. Her entire posture was tense, coiled. Itese's own body tensed in response.

"What was that?" she asked.

"I've only seen the commander look like that right before she has one of her visions," Yndlova said, moving over to stand in front of the room Othaashle had disappeared into. The woman took a deep breath, then looked to Itese. "Are you alright?"

"Is it always like that?" Itese asked.

Yndlova nodded. "From what she's told me, she starts to see flashes of the vision—or memory, I guess—and quickly falls unconscious. Occasionally, she will move around or mumble something related to the vision while she's out. After that, it takes her a few minutes to get her head back on straight."

"Why?"

Yndlova shrugged. "Disorientation? She didn't tell me."

Her expression softened then, and she put a hand on Itese's arm.

"I don't think it's anything you would need to worry about for you or any of the others, though. Othaashle is certain this only happened because of her interaction with the Aathal."

Itese found herself relieved at that. Yet also troubled. A part of her—a secret part of her she'd told no one about—wanted to know who she'd been before the God King remade her. If for no other reason than to know if she'd deserved this second chance. She—

Shouting from the end of the hall cut her thoughts short. She recognized the voices of the Redeemed guarding the entryway, but the other was less familiar. Still...

Itese groaned as she looked to Yndlova.

Skadaatha.

~

"Vizier, please. The supreme commander ordered us not to let anyone down here."

Skadaatha ignored the two Lightforged guards that trailed her with their protestations as she made her way through the hallways toward interrogation. They'd proven up above that they wouldn't touch her, and she was above reasoning with them.

I may have had my power stolen from me, but I am still a goddess born of Aia's First Melody.

Power was only an illusion of perception to most, after all.

When Skadaatha rounded the final corner, she found Kojatere's two pets waiting for her, as expected.

Each stood angled toward her with their backs to a door. The tension in their postures intrigued Skadaatha.

Something to hide?

Of course, that could also mean Kojatere told the adjuncts about her attack. She took a deep breath.

Just be pleasant.

"What brings you here, Vizier?" Itese asked, stepping toward her, a bit of bite to her tone. Yndlova stayed where she was. "Commander Othaashle forbid access to this area until she said otherwise. Or did Taizak and Katamori not make that clear?"

The two Lightforged behind her—Taizak and Katamori—came to a stop just behind her, "Sorry, Adjunct. We—"

They cut off when Itese raised a hand.

"I'm here to assist Supreme Commander Othaashle in any way necessary, as we discussed," Skadaatha said, trying her best at a natural smile and pleasant tone, "I figured I would start with the interrogations, as that was left unfinished."

The two adjuncts gazed at her for a moment—well, Yndlova did, at least. She could only assume with Itese due to the mask—then exchanged a look with each other.

"We can handle things from here, Taizak, Katamori," Itese called, "return to your posts."

The snap of crisp, twin salutes reached Skadaatha's ears from behind her.

"Yes, Adjunct."

A moment later, their footsteps echoed through the hall as they retreated.

Skadaatha studied Yndlova and Itese, then frowned.

She told them.

"If Othaashle is with one of the prisoners, I can take on another to make things go more quickly."

"That won't be necessary, Vizier," Yndlova said, "the Commander wished to interrogate each of the spies personally."

"Then I will observe. Which room is she in?"

"The Mestari asked not to be disturbed," Itese said.

Skadaatha flexed her fingers. Her mind began searching for an excuse to strike one of them.

No. Don't let them goad you. You are above negotiating with them. If they won't be accommodating, just choose a room and go inside.

The only problem was that Itese blocked the door to room holding the only prisoner that seemed like he knew anything of use.

What is Yndlova hiding?

Skadaatha didn't remember that room holding anyone before she'd left.

She took half-a step toward one of the nearby, unguarded doors, when the door behind Yndlova hissed open.

Kojatere stepped into the hall.

Unfortunately, she'd donned one of the Lightforged masks again, keeping Skadaatha from reading her emotions, though her posture seemed a bit uncertain as she looked around before focusing on Skadaatha.

"Vizier," Kojatere said. "What are you doing here?"

"Leaving," Itese half-growled.

"I came to assist, as we discussed," Skadaatha said, ignoring the Lightforged. She nodded to the door Kojatere had just exited. "Did you have any success with the prisoner?"

Kojatere cocked her head, then glanced toward the room. "No one is in there. I needed a moment to think upon what I'd learned."

Skadaatha said nothing. Something strange was going on here, but she couldn't get a read on just what.

Not yet, at least.

"Would you like some assistance breaking Torni, then?" Skadaatha asked after a moment, "I didn't have much time with him before... our meeting outside the city, but he seemed like he needed some special attention."

Kojatere barked a laugh. "I know who these spies are now, Skadaatha. That one is likely the most useful one, but he isn't likely to break."

I broke you. You just can't remember it.

Still, Skadaatha swallowed her anger and tried to be pleasant. "Well, maybe together—"

"That won't be necessary, Skadaatha," Kojatere said. "I've determined that time in Makala will make them more eager to divulge what information they hold. Itese will be assisting me with the transport. If you insist on helping, you can accompany Yndlova to the archives. We will need some explosives for my distraction—they need to be something that either the Remnant could produce or easily steal so that our investigators don't grow suspicious after the fact—as well as a place we can set them off where we won't be at risk of damaging any expensive or essential infrastructure."

Skadaatha blinked. Sending the spies to that prison...would she really do that to her own people?

Yes. Othaashle may have been a more tempered version of Kojatere, but Kojatere always fought to win. If she thinks she can win and get them free, consigning them to a few more weeks of lightlessness is just a necessary sacrifice.

"I would also appreciate it if you could assist Yndlova with a project I assigned to her before the Remnant attack," Kojatere added, voice pleasant enough to make Skadaatha want to grind her teeth, "concerning security and safety measures regarding the refugees and Samjati in particular."

Forcing a smile, Skadaatha nodded.

"It would be my pleasure, Mestari."

8

The Silver City

Some wanted to let the sea guide us, as it had given us our salvation. Others wanted to travel as far from the Empire as possible, even suggesting the supposed sunless lands, where Auroras alone lit the skies.

Exodus countdown: 17 days, 39 hours, 17 minutes

"So, how much longer is this going to take?" Koruuksi asked as the texture under his feet changed from hard stone to something softer. "Are we still walking through a giant maze?"

He knew they'd left the forest a short while ago, the heat from the sun had grown more intense, and the air had somehow grown less stuffy, despite an increased humidity. Now the air was cool. Something sheltered them from the sun's heat. Koruuksi tried not to think about Uuchantuu's suggestion of being locked in some sort of dungeon out of a story.

We're in a place that only existed in stories until a few hours ago, though.

"You must find people wandering in your forest pretty often,"

Koruuksi said. "Otherwise you all probably wouldn't just have blindfolds on hand."

The cloth was thick and well-cut, letting no light in. They must have made it specifically for this purpose.

"Or do you just kill time by playing hide and seek with blindfolds on in the forest?"

"Shut it, Koruuksi."

Someone nearby—one of their escorts, Koruuksi thought—grunted in what seemed like agreement.

Koruuksi sighed and focused on keeping his mouth shut. It wasn't his fault. Not entirely, at least. Boredom made him talkative. So did nervousness. The long, blindfolded walk combined both. Before they'd exited the jungle, at least. Tripping over roots every six steps wasn't fun, but it definitely wasn't boring.

He tried to recall details about the warriors escorting them as he continued forward, turning when prodded. Something that might give him an edge should this turn poorly. Each time he tried, though, Koruuksi found his thoughts pulled back to that woman with the intense eyes. She hadn't been the only woman in the group, and most of the warriors had gazed at them with suspicion, but she'd been the only one whose gaze had been almost palpable.

Koruuksi sighed.

If things go poorly, we can just try to get her for leverage. Hopefully these people like keeping their commanders alive.

Hopefully they would understand him. At the very least, Koruuksi hoped they would have some sort of translator wherever they were leading them. He was almost certain that they'd understood him earlier—the woman with the eyes had, at least—but he hadn't heard a word out of any of them since then.

Finally, someone grasped Koruuksi's shoulder and stilled him. A moment later, his blindfold loosened and fell away.

Koruuksi found himself in a throne room, a concept he'd thought lost to legends.

Blue, teal, white and silver dominated the chamber almost a third the size of Remnant One's hangar, colors that seemed more vivid and lush than Koruuksi thought possible.

Maybe I've just spent too much time in a utilitarian cave surrounded by barren desert.

Men and women in colorful clothing—some guards, from the ornate armor and weapons—stood behind arched galleries that lined the edges. Stones of all different shapes and sizes formed the walls, with some carved in the likeness of Natari or animal faces, and others fitted together to make intricate designs. All of the stone appeared to be some form of marble, displaying the beauty of the mineral's natural veins and swirls of color. Stone columns lined a carpeted path from the entrance behind Koruuksi, to the dais and the two thrones before him. The throne itself seemed made entirely of some silvery metal—aluminum, Koruuksi assumed—with plush cushions for those who sat upon them.

Only one of those was occupied at the moment, and the man sitting in it had to be the largest Natari Koruuksi had ever seen. His dark red skin, full lips, and broad nose reminded Koruuksi of Muuzuuri, and this man had to be at least as tall as her, if not taller. Unlike Muuzuuri, however, this man was anything but slender, sporting thick, powerful muscles displayed by the colorful wrap he wore that covered him only from the waist down. His dark red skin also bore a collection of dark stripes on his arms, shoulders, and sides of his torso. His rainbow gemcrest shone bright just above an enameled necklace of a winged sun. A simple thin circlet with the same design in the front sat atop his brow and crimped, jet-black hair that looked pulled back into a bun or horsetail. Koruuksi met the man's dark eyes and found himself more relaxed than he had been a moment ago. This man was a king—or something equivalent—but he did not wear his crown or throne as much as they wore him.

A glance to the man's right made Koruuksi blink.

Those eyes.

As Koruuksi took in the rest of the woman, his eyes bulged, and his cheeks grew hot.

How did I not notice that?

This woman was definitely the same one they'd encountered in the forest, and the thin silver circlet on her head said that she was likely a princess. Even without that, her features were similar enough to the man on the throne—yet more delicate—that Koruuksi would have made the connection. She'd changed clothes since then, however, or simply shed some. Like the man in the throne, she wore a wrap of white, silver, teal, and blue that looked striking against her dark red skin and covered her from her waist to her calves, where intricate sandals covered her feet. A thin silver chain loosely encircled her neck before dipping down over her rainbow gemcrest and between her breasts, splitting in two at her sternum before flaring out to the side and disappearing beneath the hem of her wrap. That was *all* she wore on her upper body—she hadn't even arranged her long, crimped, jet black hair to strategically cover anything. Koruuksi swallowed, and a quick glance around the room made his face grow even hotter. None of the women—or men for that matter, save the guard—wore anything over their chests. He'd read that Natari cultures had favored clothing that showed off their gemcrests, and their spies within Mjatafa Mwonga had noted the same, but he didn't remember reading anything about cultures that decided not to cover their upper bodies at all. Not anymore, at least.

These people likely didn't interact with the rest of the world much, though, and I wouldn't mind wearing less clothing in this heat.

Koruuksi looked back to the princess and frowned when he noticed the troubled look on her face and realized she was looking near him, but not *at* him. He followed her gaze to Uuchantuu and nearly cursed. Uuchantuu, while not gaping, started at the princess with eyes wide, mouth open just enough to be noticeable.

Koruuksi elbowed her in the ribs.

Uuchantuu glared at him, but her dark cheeks told him she knew she'd deserved it.

As he looked back to the king, Koruuksi found himself suddenly unsure of what to do. As the man upon the throne looked over him and his companions with a warm, yet considering gaze, Koruuksi went to one knee, taking his mask off. None of the natural light was directly on him. Still, he dimmed his clearnodes to help with the brightness. Shuffling behind him a few moments later told him his team had done the same.

The man on the throne—the king, Koruuksi guessed—seemed almost amused by that.

He stood and took a few steps forward, spreading his arms. "Welcome, travelers. I am told you wished to speak to the person in charge?"

His voice, rich and deep, but with a hint of gravel to it, boomed throughout the chamber as he spoke.

Koruuksi nodded. "That is correct. Uh... Your Highness."

The king grinned this time. "I am King Kuula'ande of E Kwekuue. You may rise—I've heard kneeling like that is a bit hard on the joints."

As he stood, rolling his shoulders, Koruuksi found himself both reassured and off-put by the man's jovial attitude. On the one hand, it spoke well for their mission. On the other, it seemed a bit too easy.

"You must tell me how you found my city," Kuula'ande continued, "and what your intentions are here. We find refugees wandering on our borders every now and then, but given your outfitting and your weaponry, I doubt you fled here seeking sanctuary."

Koruuksi forced himself to take a moment and think before he spoke.

"I am Koruuksi, the son of Kojatere, Champion of the Knights Reborn. We are refugees just as much as any others you've found, Your Highness, just a bigger group. You are correct in that we have not come to your city seeking sanctuary. We were told where to find this place by... the successor to Kweshrima, who seeks to right the wrongs of her predecessor." He paused then. "How is it you speak Atongo so well?"

Kuula'ande raised an eyebrow. "We have not been completely isolated from the world since the early days after we found our paradise. Most still speak our own language of Buuekwenani, but trade through Uumgwefilo taught many of us to speak your common tongue."

Something about that tugged at Koruuksi. There were academics within the Remnant that sought to preserve the language and culture of peoples that existed now in memory only, but necessity required that everyone speak Atongo as the common tongue.

The king , shoulders sagging as his jovial demeanor slipped just for a moment. "Before Uumgwefilo fell, that is."

Koruuksi brightened his clearnodes and looked around the room again, nodding. High windows illuminated the room with natural light, and sconces on the wall holding gemstones added Auroralight to the mix. Something seemed strange about the former, however—something he couldn't place. Intricate designs of metalwork soon caught his attention, especially their strategic placement on a few of these sconces, the thrones, and the clothing of the king and princess and some of the guards.

"I can see that."

"Lightoruu!"

Koruuksi blinked, whirling on Uuchantuu. Her eyes shone with unshed tears as she gazed up toward the high, unadorned windows. Koruuksi followed her gaze and found his chest tighten. Sparkling motes of reddish light, just large enough to be seen, floated aimlessly around where the light entering the room was brightest.

Auroras, it can't be.

Koruuksi blinked, yet the sight remained. His own eyes started to grow hot.

He blinked away his tears, turning his attention back to the king.

"Apologies, Your Majesty, we..."

His words fell away when he noticed the troubled expression on Kuula'ande's and the princess's faces, becoming acutely aware of the tension in the room.

"Are there no lightoruu where you come from?" the king asked slowly.

Koruuksi shook his head. "None, Your Majesty. Though there used to be. I haven't seen oruu of any kind in over ten years."

Murmurs broke out at the edges of the room and even from the guards flanking them as Kuula'ande shared a look with his daughter.

Koruuksi frowned, then glanced back up at the windows where—

He blinked.

They're still there.

That was almost as unusual as seeing the oruu at all. When they appeared, they did so for a minute at most before returning to their own realm.

I wonder.

Koruuksi gazed at the lightoruu and thought about how long the spirits had lingered there.

He looked around, but no oruu appeared, confusing him even more.

Is it just the lightoruu that survived, then? How does that—

A violet spirit in the form of a wisp leisurely floated out from one of the galleries along the side of the room. The timeoruu stopped near Koruuksi, then its form shifted to display two characters that marked the time.

Koruuksi gaped at the spirit.

"That's impossible," he breathed.

He looked to Kuula'ande about to ask if oruu always lingered like this, but then shook his head.

That's not what you're here for.

Not the main thing, at least. The lingering oruu made him think of stories he'd heard. Stories that could be the key to finding the secret Kojatere had tasked him to find.

Drawing himself up, Koruuksi returned his attention to Kuula'ande. "In answer to your question, Your Highness, we are here to talk. The weapons were just a precaution, as we didn't know what we would find here."

Kuula'ande nodded slowly. "You said Kweshrima's successor sent you. A new goddess of Darkness?"

"She sent us here to ask for any help you could give in a final engagement against the Imaia," Koruuksi said, nodding. "She also sent us to save you and your people from this dying world."

Kuula'ande frowned. "Dying world?"

Koruuksi blinked, stomach sinking. "Surely those you've taken in have spoken about the world outside your boundaries?"

Kuula'ande shook his head. "They speak of a war-torn world, but nothing of a dying one."

Darkness. Freezing darkness.

"You know that Yrmuunthal was destroyed?" Koruuksi ventured. "Darkside's World Tree?"

"We are aware of this tragedy. Even here, we felt the repercussions."

"They are greater than you might know, Your Highness," Koruuksi said. "Our spies within the Imaia have told us that the God King Ynuukwidas uses the entirety of his power to keep Efruumani in orbit. Apparently, he cannot do so indefinitely, and they plan to leave this world in three weeks and never return. They have already stripped most of the world of its resources and animals. My people are barely able to scrape by as it is even with supplies stolen from the Imaia. Without Ynuukwidas, this world will quickly become uninhabitable. We ask for your help in escaping Efruumani before that happens. Warriors to help us distract the Imaia's forces while we board everyone else into a stolen capital ship that will allow us to escape this world and find a new home among the stars."

Koruuksi looked between the king and the woman with the intense eyes once he finished speaking. Both appeared troubled.

"You bring grave news to me and my people," Kuula'ande said, "and a grave decision. I will need some time to investigate and think on this. No more than a week, likely less." He took a deep breath and his smile returned. "During that time, I extend to you the sanctuary and hospitality of my city, though I would request that you do not walk about with your weapons."

Koruuksi nodded. "Of course, Your Highness. Thank you."

He gestured to the woman with the intense eyes. "My daughter, Ymvesi'ia will help you find some quarters."

Koruuksi glanced at the princess, struggling to keep his expression neutral. He could see the physical resemblance, but difference in their respective demeanors nearly cancelled that out.

The princess bowed to her father, then stepped down off the dais toward Koruuksi and his companions.

"Follow me," she said in cold, barely accented Atongo.

Koruuksi hesitated for a moment, then bowed to Kuula'ande before turning to follow the princess and securing his helmet.

She led them out by what appeared to be the palace's main hall, passing through a few larger chambers sectioned off by galleries. Beautiful mosaics of stormy seas, large fleets of ships, and simple villages lined the walls, other than that, the palace seemed rather austere.

As they exited the palace, Koruuksi nearly caught up with Ymvesi'ia. He thought for a moment of asking her about the mosaics or even simply engaging in conversation, but a glance at her back and the tension her muscles held made him hold his tongue.

A few gasps and low whistles came from Koruuksi's team. He looked up and found his eyes wide as he took in the city. The hot, balmy air made sense now, as canals crisscrossed the city of E Kwekuue. Poled gondolas drifted down some at leisurely paces, while lily pads and other plants sat among the still, orange waters of others, bobbing with the ripples. Birds darted down to catch fish with their beaks. Blue stone rose from the waters as sheer platforms in some places and worn steps in others. Despite the canals, the city seemed constructed on hills, with stairs and even short waterfalls connecting different tiers and massive structures that rose high into the sky. Thin lines of silvery aluminum inlay seemed to dance about the buildings, lining them in intricate geometric patterns or simple, straight lines. Some even seemed to evoke the sea, or sea birds, for some reason. Plants grew everywhere, interrupting the orange and blue cityscape with large swathes of white and smaller blossoms of color within. Birds and small furry animals sat or scurried between branches as Koruuksi's escort passed beneath.

Next to all that, however, it was the oruu that made Koruuksi's chest grow tight. Wateroruu swam about in the channels, jumping and playing like tiny animated water droplets. Lightoruu flashed or spun around where bright surfaces caught the sun's rays just right.

Lifeoruu climbed trees and sat on leaves and branches. Heatoruu appeared among his team, making fanning motions at them. There were too many for him to count.

"I never believed it," Uuchantuu breathed from beside him. "The Silver City."

Koruuksi glanced at Uuchantuu and the rest of his team to find them just as awed as he felt. He had to nod in agreement. Though he now assumed his information was questionable, Koruuksi had heard that the name 'E Kwekuue' actually meant something like 'The City that Shines Like the Sun', though it was more colloquially known in stories as 'The City of Light' or 'The Silver City'. Most of the buildings were of a teal, blue, or white stone, but enough silver or aluminum covered them to give truth to the name.

Movement to their right caught his eye, and Koruuksi blinked at the sight of a woman heading for them at a brisk, if not exactly hurried pace.

That has got to be the most gorgeous woman I've ever seen.

She was topless, wearing only a colorful wrap like the princess and the other E Kwekuue women Koruuksi had seen so far. Her face was thinner than the princess's, and her features softer, with higher cheeks and large eyes and lips. Hoop earrings adorned her ears, and a thick collection of necklaces of beads and chains covered the entirety of her slender neck, the bottom few hanging down to her violet gemcrest. Matching anklets and bracelets adorning her arms and legs, and a similar headband encircled her brow, straight-cut bangs hanging down to obscure some of it. Her hair wasn't crimped like Kuula'ande's or Ymvesi'ia's, but not everyone in the throne room had shared that trait, either. She also wore the first genuine smile Koruuksi had seen since entering this place aside from Kuula'ande.

"That's just not fair."

Koruuksi barely held in a laugh at Uuchantuu's remark. The princess and some of the guards were attractive enough, but Koruuksi personally thought Uuchantuu, Ilona, and Muuzuuri were better-looking.

This woman, though... he had to agree with Uuchantuu.

The woman went immediately to Ymvesi'ia's side, exchanging a few hushed words in their own language. The princess seemed to soften a bit, the muscles in her back relaxing as she spoke to this woman. If only by a hair.

After a moment, the woman turned her dazzling smile on Koruuksi and Uuchantuu before settling on Koruuksi and falling back to walk beside them.

Keep your eyes on hers, or straight ahead. Don't be an idiot.

His helmet and mask would keep her from seeing where he looked, but experience had taught him that women always just seemed to know things like that.

"You all don't look nearly so run down as the groups we normally find."

Koruuksi blinked. This woman had less of an accent than the princess. It gave her voice a rhythmic, almost musical quality.

He shrugged, "We're not exactly refugees."

She smiled, spreading her arms, "Either way, I welcome you to E Kwekuue. I thought I might spare you some of Princess Ymvesi'ia's bad mood, as she does not much care for outsiders, especially armed ones."

Koruuksi glanced over at Ymvesi'ia just in time to see the princess tense before looking back to this beautiful woman and found himself gazing at her curves for a moment before he caught himself and returned his gaze to her face. His cheeks grew hot when he found her smirking at him.

"Uh, sorry," he said, making as though to run a hand through his hair before he remembered his helmet.

She laughed. "Don't be. I'll take it as a compliment as long as you actually pay attention to what I'm saying. Some of the refugees we've found have told me it takes some getting used to, but a few of them have even adopted our fashions."

Koruuksi blinked, an image flashing through his head of his team doing that, and he nearly laughed.

"Princess Ymvesi'ia tells me you just petitioned His Majesty, and he asked her to show you around and find housing for you while he thinks on his decision."

"That sounds about right."

"And you are the one who petitioned him? Koruuksi?"

Koruuksi grinned at her pronunciation. "Koruuksi."

"Koruuksi," she said again, getting it right, this time. "I am Vise, a friend and *mjakaazi* to the princess. I also manage the city's support staff and assist when we find refugees like yourselves, even though you are not exactly refugees."

Her tone implied that she was curious to know what he'd meant by that.

"It's nice to meet you, Vise," he said. "King Kuula'ande was very gracious in allowing us to stay here while he thinks on what we asked. Though I'm sure he has other reasons for keeping us here in the city."

Vise grinned. "We take our secrecy very seriously, as you can no doubt tell from Princess Ymvesi'ia and your escort."

Koruuksi thought he heard a low growl from the princess.

"While you remain here, however, you can go wherever you wish. Explore the markets, gardens, libraries, theaters—everything one of your cities probably has."

Koruuksi almost told her they didn't have cities anymore, but bit back the comment.

"Thank you. Is there any way one or two of my people could go back to our transport, though? We can do so under escort if we must. We have supplies there, but we did not bring money or much to trade. We weren't planning on an extended stay in an actual city."

Vise raised an eyebrow at that. "What were you expecting?"

Koruuksi looked to Uuchantuu, who shrugged. He caught the blush in her cheeks and the way it took a moment for her eyes to settle on Vise's face. "Hidden ruins? A homestead community, maybe? Refugees that wanted to fight like us but maybe didn't have the means? Definitely not..." She trailed off before gesturing around them. "This."

Vise laughed.

"I'm glad we were able to surprise you, then. I can arrange an escort of *Akjemasai* to bring you back to your transports if there is anything you really need, but you won't need to worry about money here."

Koruuksi looked to Uuchantuu, then back to Vise. "What do you mean?"

Vise rolled her eyes. "Being isolated has its perks. Our relationship with the Uumgwefili gave us access to hoards of information about the rest of the world, so we learned all about how your systems of trade and currency led to disparity and unrest in your society. Many of our scholars theorized that this was something brought on by your interconnectedness with other nations. Even if one of you had tried to eliminate currency with a sound system to replace it, the involvement of other nations would have derailed it. We don't have to worry about that here."

Koruuksi blinked. "So you're saying that we don't need to pay for food."

Vise nodded, smiling. "Food, clothing, anything, really. There are certain trade-offs, but I don't think they will be too much of a burden."

Koruuksi nodded, thinking about how the Remnant ran things. They had currency, but rarely used it. Instead making sure everyone did the work to make sure everyone was provided for. He wanted to ask for more details when the princess and the guards stopped.

"Ah, here we are!" Vise said, gesturing to a large building before them. Its geometric design and bright stonework adorned with lines of aluminum inlay matched the rest of the buildings in the city. A short flight of stairs led up to an arched, doorless entryway that reminded Koruuksi of the galleries in the palace throne room. It looked large enough to house an entire company.

Koruuksi looked at Uuchantuu, who looked to Vise. "Did you build extra housing once you started finding refugees more often?"

The woman's expression slipped for just a moment, and Koruuksi noticed Ymvesi'ia and a few of the warriors stiffen.

"After we sent warriors to help fight the Imaia," Vise said, her voice low, "many found themselves with most of their neighbors gone. They moved to other tenements where things felt more alive. This is one of the buildings left vacant after that."

Koruuksi nodded slowly. "I understand. I didn't have the pleasure of fighting alongside those you sent to fight, but I believe I know a few who did, and they had never seen a more impressive people."

Vise smiled at him. "I am glad to hear that. I hope they are to your liking. If you need anything, just ask."

"Thank you, Vise," Koruuksi said, returning the smile. He turned to Ymvesi'ia and tried not to react to the hardness in her eyes. "Thank you as well, Princess, for escorting us."

Ymvesi'ia held his gaze for a long moment before signaling to her guards. They started back toward the palace, but she and Vise did not.

Koruuksi looked between the two, confused.

Ymvesi'ia stepped close to him, her voice low and cold. "My father may have granted you sanctuary, Outsider, but I do not agree with him. I listen to the refugees that we take in, as do my guards. I know what the Remnant is, and I know you must be one of them. Praising our fallen will not change anything. I do not believe that you are here to save anyone, and I will not hesitate to protect my people and my city should you force my hand. Understood?"

Koruuksi should have just nodded, but despite the apologetic glance he caught from Vise, after the heat, humidity, and being led blindfolded for hours while stumbling over rocks, he couldn't help himself. He tried taking a deep breath. It still didn't work.

"I understand," he said, "that you're a princess living in a secret paradise who judges people she knows nothing about when they've done nothing to deserve it. My people are forced to hide in caves and steal what food we can just to survive, and yet we came to help *you*. Understand that, Princess."

Koruuksi snapped his mouth shut before he could say anymore. His fists were clenched, and if he didn't stop, he'd probably get far angrier than he should. Her turned away from Ymvesi'ia toward the building, gesturing to his team.

"Let's get some rest," he told them, leading the way inside. He didn't look back to see Ymvesi'ia's reaction.

"That probably wasn't one of your better ideas," Uuchantuu said once they entered the building.

Koruuksi raised an eyebrow at her, and Uuchantuu punched him in the arm.

"I'm not just saying that because she's gorgeous. You were an asshole."

Koruuksi shrugged. "I never said I wouldn't be."

"Anyone else find it incredibly unfair how gorgeous that Vise woman is?" Ilona asked.

Koruuksi couldn't help but agree with that.

"What do we do now?" Uuchantuu asked.

Koruuksi stopped halfway up the stairs and sighed. "For now, we rest. Once we've done that, I'll think of something."

9

The Silent Forest

Before we could make a decision, an Iron Fleet found us. Though our people had made these ships with their own hands and knew them well, we were too heavily laden to outrun the warships, and we had few weapons or warriors, while they had the Iron Marines. Then came the storm.

Exodus countdown: 17 days, 28 hours, 38 minutes

Estingai raised a hand to her forehead, trying to massage her temples through her helmet as the transport disappeared over the tree cover. With one last look off in that direction she sighed and started off into the forest to search for her quarry. Estingai pulled her cloak tight against the chill air as she hiked, dry leaves and twigs crunching beneath her heavy boots. Though she'd spent most of her formative years in Darkside, Estingai had become so accustomed to Lightside's heat that the once brisk, refreshing air of the twilight band now made her shiver even in her layered combat gear. At least the air was fresh—not stuffy and sweaty like Remnant Base.

As she searched the thick cover around her, Estingai tried to quiet her mind.

All I was trying to do was tell her to be careful.

Araana hadn't accepted that. Instead, she'd grown mad, convinced Estingai wanted to turn their one last chance at hope sour. Estingai hadn't meant it that way.

I want her to be telling the truth, but...

Estingai sighed, hoping like that was dangerous.

Estingai looked up to the sky again, a part of her wishing she hadn't let Araana drop her off. The original plan had been for Estingai to deliver everyone else to their coordinates, then keep the ship with her as she searched for Matsanga so that when she found him, she could take off and get the others quickly. The thinking was that if she could find Matsanga, he would be able to convince the others to come back and fight for them. Estingai knew, however, that she had made the right choice in letting Araana drop her off first and take the ship herself. She would have been too tempted to half-ass her search for Matsanga, get back in the ship and fly off with it.

Estingai didn't want to think she would do that, but she knew that she would have been tempted. Even now, looking up at the sky, she wished for some way to fly off to the stars and leave all of this behind.

Shaking out the stiffness in her limbs, Estingai blew out a groan and tried to clear her mind as she searched the forest for some sign of habitation. A mix of wood, dust, fresh soil, and some floral scents she couldn't place filled her head as she scanned her surroundings. Everything was brown or maroon here, a welcome change from Lightside's constant teal and black coverage with only the occasional shocks of white or maroon—not that she saw much of that anymore living in the desert. It did prove challenging for her current task, however. She blended in expertly in her brown and grey clothing, yet everything around her blended in with everything else. Perfect for an ambush.

Even after a few hours, she detected few signs of life: tracks, broken twigs and branches, even a few birds and rodents. But no spirits, no footprints, and nothing big enough to hunt if she somehow ran out of supplies.

That won't be a problem, she thought, *I won't be here long enough for that.*

As she walked, Estingai thought about her brother and her fight with him before they left.

Estingai wished she could be like him—still hopeful even after all they'd been through, instead of bitter and angry.

The argument with Araana had proven her brother's point.

But if I do find him?

The thoughts flooded through her head unbidden, and Estingai tried to snuff them out, but she couldn't. Instead, she decided to focus on what she would do if she found Matsanga. A part of her didn't even want to find him after he'd left them when they needed him most.

When I needed him.

Estingai took a deep breath, shoving those thoughts back down. She needed to convince Matsanga to fight Kojatere if things came to that. He was the only one with anything near the power to do anything about that. And he knew Kojatere's tricks far better than Estingai did.

He can also take the lead. Someone who can be the symbol the Remnant needs once I'm done.

Other thoughts—harder, more painful thoughts—would bring her to her knees if she thought about any other outcome.

She banished them, throat tightening, and had to resist rubbing at her eyes. She couldn't afford to think about anything other than the mission. That would bring too many feelings. Old feelings that didn't have a place in her life anymore.

As Estingai searched the forest, the thick cover and unsteady footing made her tense. The hair on the back of her neck, sweaty underneath her gear, stood up despite the weight, making her feel like she was being watched. Estingai tried to banish that feeling but watched her surroundings a bit more carefully. She nearly jumped when she slipped or tripped over the unsteady footing beneath.

As the minutes stretched into long hours, Estingai's paranoia turned to boredom and frustration. She looked up, checking the position of the moon, and blinked.

Five hours?

A sudden yawn confirmed that she had been searching the forest for far longer than she realized, and Estingai started searching for a place to camp instead of Matsanga.

At least I'll be able to get some good sketching done in this place.

Her sketchbook was filled with people, machines, old georaural schematics, and some words from her imagination, but as far as landscapes went, she had far too many rocky visages contained in her little book. A forest like this of tall, skinny birch trees poking out of the maroon blanket of fallen leaves would be a welcome change.

It took her a while, but Estingai finally found a place that looked good. A few thick trees had fallen into each other, forming a small thicket to shelter her from the winds or any searching eyes. She sat down her pack, reaching for her canteen, and heard something ahead of her.

Estingai looked up and her eyes grew wide at the massive, red-and-black icehound slinking out from behind a tree a few paces away, its golden eyes boring into her.

Something snapped behind Estingai, and she barely brightened her rednodes in time to bring up a sword of light to block an attack from the sword of a massive, hooded figure behind her. In that moment, she forgot about the wolf—this figure was very obviously the larger threat.

White hot rage burned through Estingai as she drew the weapons at her belt—a pistol in one hand, long knife in the other. She didn't want to give away her abilities unless she had to, though she brightened her greynodes just enough to give her a slight edge in speed.

I knew it!

That this assailant hadn't merely taken her out from afar, however, told her something very important.

He wants me alive.

That would make him sloppy.

Even as Estingai leapt into action, she realized she was outclassed.

A hardlight shield blocked her first shot, even as more of the golden substance enveloped the muzzle and crushed it. Nothing on her knife, however.

He wants a fight, then.

Estingai leapt forward, closing the distance between them faster than most would be able to react. This opponent caught her blade with one of his own, however, turning to the side and twisting his blade. If her blade had been a bit longer, the man might have trapped it.

Estingai extricated herself from the attempted hold, but that technique brought forth a memory.

Wait...

The thought fled as something pulled at the Auroralight within her gemcrest, as though it were draining. That didn't make sense. She wasn't using enough to deplete them that fast.

Her attacker's distraction nearly cost Estingai her arm, and even then, only her greynodes saved her, giving her the speed to dodge her attacker's blow. He'd tried to take her Auroralight—he was *still* attempting to do so—no point in hiding her abilities anymore. Her opponent was skilled if he could draw on her Auroralight this strongly without touching her.

Estingai's eyes widened as she desperately willed the Auroralight to stay, splitting her concentration between that and fending off her attacker's blows. She had her knife, but no sword other than what she could produce with her rednodes.

As she exchanged blows with the hooded figure, Estingai's rage faltered. Her opponent employed very basic, yet strong techniques. He did not stand in one place, unmoving, but neither did he leap around, seeking to confuse or flank her with complicated movements. Every step was purposeful, lending strength to his strikes.

It was almost...familiar to Estingai.

Can it—

Estingai gasped as she lost the battle for her Auroralight, nearly falling to her knees.

She'd trained for this, but nothing really ever prepared one for lightlessness.

With a roar to wake up her senses, Estingai threw herself at the hooded figure, a small, hateful part of her acknowledging the fact that she was doomed.

Her opponent had her Auroralight, and he moved with the speed of a greyarm, making him a full Auroraborn. Despite her training, Estingai's lightless movements were sluggish, as were her thoughts. A blow to her helmet knocked her to the ground, gasping for air.

"Now that that's over," the figure said in a grating voice like rocks sliding over one another, "you will tell me who you are and how you found me."

That voice.

It was like a jolt of energy to Estingai's lifeless state.

She leapt to her feet and flung herself at the figure, managing to throw back its hood even as he caught her with a massive hand and flung her back down to the ground, hard.

Estingai sucked in a ragged breath as she scrambled upright to see if she'd been right.

A familiar face with a strong jaw and thick, full lips stared back at her. He'd always been scarred, but a new, larger one marred his dark red complexion with a swathe of pink. She'd only seen the bandages of that wound. His dark brown eyes, however, were just as she remembered.

He peered at her through those ancient eyes, from under a heavy brow, then sighed, taking a step forward.

Estingai ripped off her helmet, tossing it aside. Her skin would burn if left uncovered too long, but not nearly as quickly as it would on Lightside.

"Matsanga, wait! It's me—it's me! Estingai!"

The massive man before her stopped, flinching as though from a well-placed blow. His eyes widened as he took her in.

"Estingai?" he breathed.

Silence stretched for a moment. Estingai glanced between Matsanga and the icehound, its tail still and its gaze seeming too piercing for a mere animal. Then Estingai gasped as light flooded into her, shocking her to her feet.

Just as training to be lightless could only prepare someone so much for the actual experience, the same went for becoming full of light.

Estingai's emotions and sense of the world around her went from zero to twelve. Her thoughts were clear again, but everything was so sudden that it swam. Her earlier rage exploded back to the forefront, nearly overwhelming her

"You left us!" she roared, pounding a fist against Matsanga's chest.

It was like hitting stone.

"You were all we had. The only thing keeping us together, and you abandoned us!"

Her screams turned more ragged. She tried hitting Matsanga again, but something closed around her wrist, restraining her. Estingai kept trying anyway. She needed to hit him, to hit *something*.

"We needed you*! I* needed you!" she screamed out.

Her wrists were restrained, then brought together. Estingai couldn't see anything. She'd shut her eyes to keep the tears from blurring her vision and stinging her eyes.

"Why did you leave us?"

Estingai's arms were brought before her, then something wrapped around her, holding her up even as her legs threatened to give out. Anger had made her face hot and her voice raw.

"Why did you leave me?"

10

Makala

At first, we thought it a sign of wrath and disapproval. Though the storm smashed the Iron ships and bore us far from them, it had also taken half our people with it—the blacksmith among them—and left us drifting for days.

Exodus countdown: 18 days, 9 hours, 29 minutes

"What would you think about placing a group of Redeemed aboard the capital ship to intercept the Remnant once they take control of the ship?"

Itese glanced to Othaashle, then over her shoulder at the dozen Redeemed following them through the tunnels a few paces behind, power-siphon georaurals in their hands as they flanked the same number of prisoners. These dimly lit tunnels connected the lower floors of Mjatafa Mwonga's military facilities and prisons like Makala—not that there were many of the latter—allowing for the transfer of Auroraborn prisoners between the various facilities while keeping them lightless and therefore much easier to manage.

The spies had already been lightless from being kept in the holding cells for so long, but Othaashle had been insistent.

Itese met the gaze of Aski, the closest of her brethren. They exchanged a nod and Aski straightened a bit.

"Itese?"

Itese returned her attention to Othaashle.

"Everything alright?" she asked.

Itese squared her shoulders and gave herself a shake. "Sorry. It's just the tunnels. Being down here makes us a bit... claustrophobic."

Shouldn't she feel it, too?

That wasn't the right word for it, but it was the best to describe how she and the other Redeemed felt. It was the darkness and underground location of the hexagonal tunnel that made her tense, not the enclosed space. The stark, metal walls reflected the Auroralight on their armor, at least.

Despite knowing the other Redeemed felt exactly as she did—though they all tried to hide it—Itese couldn't help but feel somewhat lesser because of it. She was supposed to be their leader's right hand. The tunnels didn't seem to affect Othaashle, so they shouldn't affect her, right?

Of course, she's the best of us. And now she has the power of the Throne of Darkness to aid her in situations like this.

Itese glanced back up at her commander, then tried to remember the question Othaashle had asked her.

"I think that would be a good idea," she said, "though I would suggest moving multiple ships to the location and using some of the Redeemed to funnel the Remnant into the right ship. If we have any fighters or equipment that is too outdated, we can task the Redeemed with ensuring they are destroyed during any fighting."

Othaashle nodded. "Yes, I believe that will work quite well. Thank you, Itese."

Itese couldn't help but smile at the praise. "Thank you, Mestari."

Othaashle walked in silence for a bit, then took a few quick steps, placing herself farther ahead, and gestured for Itese to join her. Itese did, signaling for the Redeemed following them to continue at their current pace.

"I want to apologize for keeping my visions from you, Itese," Othaashle said in a low voice.

Itese almost missed a step. She righted herself, but couldn't think of how to respond to that.

"Itese?"

She could hear the concern in her commander's voice.

"Thank you, Mestari," she said, "though I don't know if you need to. I'm not sure yet if doing so was the best call. I wish to be someone you would trust with information like this, especially so I can assist you if needed..." She sighed. "But it's a lot to take in."

Othaashle was silent for a while before nodding. "I understand."

Itese peered up at the woman as she continued forward in silence.

"What do you think of making some of the Remnant into Redeemed?" Othaashle asked, voice still low enough that the echoing footsteps of their party easily obscured it from the rest of the Redeemed. "I noticed quite a few good candidates among them," she continued. "Fighting and surviving the way they do has left only the strongest and most clever of their number."

"I would have no problem with it," Itese said carefully. She was one of the oldest Redeemed. She knew who most of the other Redeemed had been—or at least which side they'd fought for—but she honored their customs by not speaking about it and not treating them any differently, "the God King remakes us, after all. And I know that most of us with Iceborn abilities used to fight for the Union."

"Is that an assumption most Redeemed make?" Othaashle asked after a moment.

Itese shrugged. "It isn't spoken about much. The oldest of our number have figured it out, but as it is not our way to discuss such things and we have no way of confirming it... I don't believe the rest will have a problem so long as these candidates are handled in the usual way and no one makes a show of their origins."

Othaashle nodded, but otherwise did not respond.

Itese looked her commander up and down, recognizing the way she held herself.

What is she thinking about?

Though masks obscured the faces of new Redeemed, those masks came off when eating or bathing. Those Othaashle chose from the Remnant would likely stand out to any on the team they sent to trap the insurgents—especially if they were as skilled or powerful as Othaashle implied.

Can I use that?

Most of the Redeemed dutifully followed their strictures and avoided their taboos, yet Itese knew that such things would not be sustainable as their numbers grew. Not within their ranks, at least.

That line of thought was cut short as a door to a more well-lit area opened before Itese. Quickening her step, she followed Othaashle out of the tunnel and up a short flight of stairs to a much more open chamber.

Itese breathed in deep, feeling her body's tension slip away.

Alright, so maybe some of it was the enclosed space.

She glanced back at the other Redeemed. They seemed to stand a bit taller than they had a few moments ago, postures more relaxed. They were still indoors with no access to Boaathal's light, but the tunnels... the tunnels were just worse.

The building's front room matched the outer facade of a warehouse, with a wide mechanical door to the outside, high ceilings, and unadorned walls. This warehouse, however, had walls of reinforced aluminum, as well as a warden behind a desk and two pairs of guards flanking a heavy door behind him. The official purpose of this building was housing high-value weaponry, and it wasn't exactly a lie. Each prisoner transferred here awaited Redemption by Othaashle and the God King. They would be among the Imaia's deadliest weapons.

Itese signaled for Aski and the others to begin the prisoner transfer before walking over to join Othaashle near the center of the room.

"We need to find a way of capturing the Remnant if we do let them take the ship and try to escape," Othaashle said, half to herself as she looked toward the Redeemed and the prisoners.

"We could place a large enough team inside to detain them," Itese suggested. "They can hide in storage and ventilation compartments, then lock down the ship, holding most of their number in the main hangar and physically subduing anyone else until your arrival or until they can bring the ship back to Mjatafa Mwonga."

Othaashle nodded. "Figure out how large of a team we would need to do that while still making it small enough to effectively hide them on the ship. I want—stop! Don't send him through just yet."

Itese followed Othaashle's gaze to where the last prisoner, Phantom, stood among a group of guards and Redeemed.

Othaashle turned back to her. "Wait for me out here. I want to escort our friend inside personally and give him some last-minute encouragement. While I'm in there, think about what we would need for the more long-term plan of letting them get away. We would need plants among them, and Redeemed will be useless in that respect." She grinned. "If that turns out to be a viable solution, I might just need to orchestrate a heroic sacrifice to convince the Remnant they really will get away as planned."

SKADAATHA EYED Yndlova from across the geo-console, one of the Military Archive's prized jewels. It stood at the center of a collection of the building's digital access terminals off to one side of the main, high-ceilinged room of the Military Archive building. The woman wore a full, pristine dress uniform, as usual. She held her cap under one arm, and the beads at the end of her braids shone whenever they caught the light. Skadaatha kept expecting to see them glow with Auroralight, as had once been common, but she knew the people of this era—Yndlova especially—were too practical for such gaudy displays.

Except Makahaba and her people. But then, what else should I expect from the Whore Mother?

Beyond them, shelves stocked full of texts lined the walls with busts of influential scholars of Atonga and the Imaia standing on pedestals at the occasional gap between them.

Large windows above them let natural light into the spacious, high-ceilinged room where banners did not hang from the walls, though the geo-console's holographic displays required a dimmer section sheltered from the light. At the opposite room, past collections of desks and the shelves of standard texts, stood similar enclosures where scholars studied and maintained the older, more sensitive documents.

She and Adjunct Yndlova had each set up large datapads on the tables that pulled out from the sides of the console. These would allow for quick reference between the different points of interest.

"What is it about me that you find so interesting, Vizier?" Yndlova asked as she tucked a few braids behind her ear, keeping her attention on the blown-up holographic display of Mjatafa Mwonga. "Or have you already found the best place for the Remnant attack and you're just waiting to see how long it takes me?"

Skadaatha resisted grinding her teeth and turned her attention back to the display. Kojatere's adjunct wanted to find a place to execute her commander's plan that would be accessible enough to ensure the Remnant took the bait without the trap being too obvious.

"What materials does the Remnant have access to?" Skadaatha asked. "If we're going to set off explosions as a distraction, we should only consider materials that they would use. Nothing too advanced."

"I wouldn't know, Vizier. You're the one that has been to their bases, not me."

Swallowing her irritation, Skadaatha put forth as pleasant a front as she could manage without straining anything.

"From what I could tell, the Remnant has made use of a few old mining shafts and lava tubes in the Old Atonga region," she said, stepping around the console. She manipulated the map to show all of the Lightside hemisphere and circled the area with her finger. "They had a good deal of salvaged vehicles and technology, though much was in disrepair. Still, a few georaural devices wouldn't be out of place."

Yndlova nodded. "I'll work with some of our explosives experts to see if they can put something together that would leave nothing behind save residue that would point to the Remnant. Don't want to give any of our investigators a reason to be too curious after the fact."

"I'll take it to Aarnal," Skadaatha suggested, "he's the best we have, especially for unconventional matters like this."

Yndlova frowned, meeting Skadaatha's gaze. "Unfortunately, I must decline, Vizier. We want to keep the details of this operation known to as few as possible. While we appreciate your experience and expertise, you are technically not a part of the Imaia's military. Though I have no doubt you trust Aarnal, that question coming from you would raise too many questions, as would his involvement, given he is no longer in service."

Skadaatha could find no objection that didn't sound petty or pleading. "Of course, Adjunct."

Yndlova nodded. "Now, as far as moving the ship goes, I was thinking that rather than moving only a single capital ship, we move an entire flight group to one of the new hangars where the outer docks used to be. They will be easier to deploy and will make room in the shipyards for new projects."

Skadaatha held back a frown. "That is quite clever, Adjunct."

Kojatere's people would be easier to dislike if they weren't so competent.

She should be above that, however.

Just appreciate them for their competence despite their associations. Hopefully, that will make this a bit easier.

"Thank you, Vizier. That will also cover loading them with supplies, if that is the option we wish to go with."

Skadaatha raised an eyebrow at that. "What option, Adjunct? Surely we won't be stocking the ship with supplies if we're planning on capturing it or destroying it soon after the Remnant takes it."

The frown on Yndlova's full lips was slight, barely there for half-a-second. Yet Skadaatha caught it.

"One option Commander Othaashle discussed with us was that of allowing the Remnant to escape with the ship and some of our people among them," Yndlova explained. "They would allow the Remnant to find a new world to settle, establish a foothold there, then contact us when they looked ready for us to annex."

Skadaatha opened her mouth to object, but realized she couldn't argue the advantage in that. It would be best to focus all their efforts on finding and taming a single new world for the Imaia after Exodus, but if all it would cost them was a single ship to gain an entire colony...

Something about it still felt wrong to Skadaatha, however, even if it was simply Kojatere's involvement in such a plan.

Could she still truly serve the Imaia as she claims? Just with... divided loyalties, perhaps?

Skadaatha smiled at Yndlova. "That's the type of thinking I would expect from a general, Adjunct. I've often wondered why Othaashle keeps you running errands for her when you could serve the Imaia so much better from a position of higher authority."

The smirk Yndlova shot back was infuriating. "Commander Othaashle has recommended me for promotion quite a few times, actually. I turned her down because I believe I can serve the Imaia best in my current position. I can lend my perspective and skills to the Commander's authority rather than competing with it."

Skadaatha held back from frowning at that as Yndlova switched the geo-console back to a map of Mjatafa Mwonga, zooming in on one of the outer districts.

"I thought some of these empty warehouses might work for a distraction. We can make people believe that we were storing food and medical supplies there. Having their food and medicine destroyed is something people can rally behind."

Again, that competence.

"I appreciate the sentiment," Skadaatha said, "but that area won't work. Those warehouses disguise access points to Mjatafa Mwonga's cooling systems. These ones specifically connect to Reactor Three."

Yndlova blinked, raising an eyebrow. "Maintenance on that must be fun."

Skadaatha nodded. "Vysla is working on a way to alleviate that, thankfully. He wants to find the right balance between security and accessibility so that the city's infrastructure can be easily updated at need with minimal civilian impact."

"If anyone can do it, he can," Yndlova said, zooming back out and marking different areas of the city. "I'm always amazed whenever I get the chance to read about his latest projects."

Skadaatha narrowed her eyes at that.

Is she just saying that to throw me off guard?

"Here," Yndlova said, pointing at the various marks she'd made on the projected map. "Instead of those, we can target some monuments, some of the older buildings and tenements in need of renovation, and some known food and medical warehouses that we can quietly empty most of beforehand. Damaging some of the older hangars might work, too. It will make it seem more plausible when we don't send as many fighters as we should to intercept the Remnant."

Skadaatha peered at Yndlova's markings. Many indicated structures built before Mjatafa Mwonga had even been an idea, when the Imaia had terraformed islands just outside the Boaathal Sea in order to control access to the World Tree.

"This is good," she observed. "We can devote most of our resources to ensuring civilian safety and locking down the more populated areas, while we send smaller forces to deal with the outer attacks. They will take some time to get there, and people will be so preoccupied with ensuring Exodus' success that telling the fighters not to pursue beyond sight of the city won't seem out of place."

"Attacks on their symbols, food, and their homes will also rally people together," Yndlova said, "making it easier for us to work as one body after Exodus when we establish our new home."

Skadaatha agreed. She also saw what Yndlova was doing, however. An 'attack' like this would give the military and security forces—Othaashle's part of the government—much more leverage and power within the Imaia.

If I don't handle this right, it could bring things back by a few decades, at least.

Or work to her benefit if she managed to take control of that branch.

"The Imaia was made to fight a greater enemy than just the

Remnant or the Union," she said, meeting Yndlova's golden gaze. "We fight an enemy with the power to threaten gods."

The Adjunct nodded, expression grave. "Then we should work to make sure the Imaia has no weaknesses for them to exploit."

Skadaatha nodded, hiding a grin. Yndlova's loyalty to Kojatere would be a problem, but if the woman's loyalty to the Imaia proved to be greater, as Skadaatha suspected it was...

I might be able to use that.

11

To Fight Again

Then an unsettled coast came in sight, thick with forests at the foot of great mountains that climbed toward the clouds. Some believed we should settle the coast. Others wished to return to the seas and search for those lost in the storm. In the end, we decided to venture inland toward the mountains and hide from the Empire, should they come searching again. There, we found a pass through the mountains and the paradise within. Upon seeing it, all agreed that this would be our new home. Our Sanctuary.

Exodus countdown: 17 days, 21 hours, 20 minutes

Estingai breathed deep of the warm, spiced air of the room as she huddled next to the fire under a warm blanket, watching Matsanga prepare food. Between the pepper and *paprik* he'd thrown into the fire pit, and the savory aromas of venison, thyme, and rosemary mixing in the simmering stew, simply breathing made Estingai's mouth water.

How long has it been since I've had fresh food? Fresh meat? Anything that didn't come from a can or vacuum-sealed container?

Or anything without fungi in it?

She couldn't remember.

Estingai glanced at Matsanga, who seemed to have forgotten her as he presided over his stew, boiling in a large ceramic-titanium cauldron.

Where did he get that? Did he steal or salvage it? Or did he make it?

She hadn't asked. She was still embarrassed by her earlier behavior—both her breakdown and being so easily outclassed—even though she knew she shouldn't be. Matsanga had seen far worse from her, and she'd come to find him because his skill was so far above that of anyone else in the Remnant. He'd trained her, Kojatere, and most of the other Knights.

It still made her angry at herself that she'd been so easily defeated.

A rustling from the corner of the room made Estingai glance away from Matsanga. She immediately dropped her eyes.

Matsanga's icehound—she didn't know its name—kept looking at her with eyes that seemed far too inquisitive for a normal animal. The beast was unlike any other she'd seen. Its coat was black, but with strange red markings and shocks of gold that held her attention almost as easily as its ancient eyes. She shifted, pulling the blanket tighter despite herself.

Eventually, Matsanga rose from his seat beside the cauldron and took two earthenware bowls from a shelf. He ladled steaming stew into each, then walked around the cauldron to hand one to Estingai.

She forced a tight smile as she accepted it.

"Thank you," she said, voice smaller than she would have liked.

Matsanga just grunted as he took a seat between her and the icehound.

Estingai brought the soup up to her face and breathed in deep, shivering at how incredible it smelled, eyes fluttering closed.

She looked back to Matsanga just as he held a small wooden spoon out to her.

"Sorry for hitting you earlier," she said, taking the spoon and stirring the stew, blowing on it a few times before testing a sip. It was still a bit too hot.

Matsanga just grunted and blew on his own stew.

They ate without speaking for a while, but by the time Estingai had consumed half her bowl, the silence grew to be too much.

"What are you doing here, Matsanga?"

Her former mentor shrugged his massive shoulders but didn't answer.

She narrowed her eyes at him until he glanced up at her, then sighed, rolling his eyes.

"It's as good a place as any. Hunting is still good, and it's private and hidden," he paused, giving her a pointed look. "It was supposed to be, at least."

Estingai shrugged, looking around the room. She'd already noted the newer conditions of the metal hinges and banding on the main door, as well as the new wood, but a few more hinges, screws and signs of recent metalwork caught her eyes, as well as a few spots of plaster that didn't match the faded paint on the walls. She hoped that was a good sign. The large room within held a spit over a firepit in the middle, with low-burning coals that gave off a sweet scent akin to the unknown flowers she'd smelled but seen few of on her way here. A few cabinets and shelves of metal and wood stood against the walls, holding pottery and a few jars of various materials. Near an opening with no door on the opposite side of the room, a collection of large barrels clustered next to a pile of wood that reached almost to the ceiling. Estingai noted the newer metal banding around those, as well. Furs hung from a rack on the wall to one side near a pile of furs and blankets, and a cauldron rested in one corner. She could see a few supports that had been put up a few years prior at most. Matsanga had been here for a while and didn't seem to plan on leaving any time soon.

Mwyndobir, Matsanga's iconic blade, rested against the wall back with his pots and cabinets. It shone even in the cave—and Estingai thought he might have used it recently. She wondered why he hadn't been carrying it when he encountered her, but after taking a moment to think, she decided not to ask.

"Estingai?"

Estingai blinked, realizing he'd asked her something.

"What?"

"How did you find me?"

Estingai shrugged. "I'm still not entirely sure of that. I was given these coordinates to supposedly find you, but I thought it was a trap until I recognized some of your old tricks."

"Why would you come here if you thought it was a trap? Is that ship that dropped you off still flying around here somewhere?"

Estingai shook her head. "It's not. I came here because if it wasn't a trap, I'd have found you, and if it was, I'd have had my proof."

Matsanga gazed at her for a while in silence.

"Proof of what?"

Estingai bit her lip for a moment, then sighed. "That Kojatere will betray us."

Matsanga blinked, then frowned. He said nothing.

"She's back," Estingai elaborated. "Never really was gone to begin with, I guess."

"What do you mean?" he asked, slowly.

"She's Othaashle," Estingai said. "I've known—" She cut herself off, taking a deep breath. "I've known for seven years now, but no one believed me until two days ago when she approached our base with Koruuksi as her hostage."

Matsanga's eyes widened at that, "Is he—"

"He's alright. She used him to get to the Throne," Estingai continued, ignoring the concern he showed for her brother.

"Apparently it backfired and restored her to her former self. Now she is Kojatere again instead of Othaashle." She met his eyes, shaking her head. "I don't trust her. It seems too convenient. Now Kweshrima is gone and Kojatere holds the Throne's power. According to her it's still diminished, but..."

Estingai trailed off with a sigh, then smoothed the hair from her face and met Matsanga's gaze. "I don't know what to do or who to trust. Koruuksi wants to trust her, and I want what she says to be true, but even now, this—me finding you here as she said—could be some sort of ploy to gain my trust now so she can betray me later."

Matsanga frowned. "Being unable to trust one's family is a terrible thing. It pains me that you are now forced to suffer that."

Estingai's lips twitched in a slight smile.

"That still doesn't explain *why* you came here," Matsanga said as she ate some more of her stew. "Especially if your transport isn't waiting nearby to pick you up."

"I came because we need you back, Matsanga," she said. "I need you. I've missed you so much, and I'm not the only one."

Matsanga didn't respond, instead taking a few more sips of his stew. It irritated Estingai a bit, but she forced herself to swallow that emotion—this was how Matsanga had been for as long as she'd known him.

"How is your family?"

Estingai flinched at the question.

"You and Koruuksi are still alive. What about Uuchantuu? How is Sve—"

"Dead."

Estingai's voice was cold and tight as she cut off Matsanga.

"Koruuksi, Uuchantuu and I are all that's left."

"I'm sorry to hear that," Matsanga said eventually. "Does your brother still have a mouth on him?"

Estingai snorted. "No matter the rank of the person on the receiving end."

Matsanga barked a laugh, the genuine mirth surprising Estingai. For a moment, she found herself smiling as well. Then she met his eyes as his expression dropped a little and felt hers do the same. She knew exactly what he was thinking.

Just like Svemakuu.

"I worry about him. And Uuchantuu," Estingai said, looking back to her stew as she shoved the thought away. She tasted a bit, then brightened one of her violetnodes. A few seconds later, steam rose from the bowl once more.

Estingai took a sip. "I was all they had for so long, but I couldn't give him the attention they needed. They both turned out like their older siblings, thankfully, but I still worry that I scarred them in some ways."

"That was never your responsi—"

"Like hell it wasn't," Estingai snapped. "I was all they have left. No one else was going to do it. If I let everything that was 'never my responsibility' slip by, the Remnant wouldn't exist."

Matsanga sighed. "Why are you here, Estingai?"

"I told you: we need you. Everyone thought you were dead. Now that we know you're not, we need you to come back and lead. You can still fight better than anyone in the—"

"I can't."

Estingai frowned at the statement.

"Why?"

"What would I fight for? Even in my prime I couldn't take on the Imaia. Even fighting alongside Kojatere as Kweshrima's champion, endowed with her power, we lost. What makes you think things will be any different now with your forces diminished and the Imaia's bolstered?"

Estingai raised an eyebrow. "How do you know their forces have grown?"

Matsanga's face darkened. "I helped create the damned thing, remember?"

Estingai frowned but did not let her former mentor's demeanor intimidate her to silence.

"I need you to help me against Kojatere if she betrays us—not the Imaia."

Matsanga eyed her for a moment, then sighed. "And how exactly is it that you expect her to betray you?"

"She's going to procure a capital ship for us," Estingai said. "Or put one somewhere that will be easy for us to take and cause a distraction so that we can be quick about it and not only need to distract the Imaia's forces for a bit."

"And you think that sounds too good to be true."

Estingai nodded. "If she's telling the truth, we find a way off this dying world. If not, it's much easier to capture or kill all of us if we're all on one ship. I plan to see my people off this world and out of the Imaia's reach, whether or not she betrays us, but I'll need your help with that. You tamed a draakon once, Matsanga—"

The icebound grumbled, and Estingai frowned at it for a moment before continuing, "If anyone has even the slightest chance of standing against her, it's you."

Estingai's words hung in the air as Matsanga gazed at her in silence. After a few minutes, his eyes took on a distant look, and Estingai tried not to grin.

He's at least considering it.

By the time she'd finished her stew, he sighed and rose to his feet.

Hope swelled within Estingai as she followed, though she tried to reign it in.

Even if he does help, there's still a long way to go.

Still... the emotion was so unfamiliar to her it made it hard to keep her expression neutral.

Matsanga began ladling the stew into an assortment of metal, glass, and ceramic containers, emptying out the rest of the cauldron before taking them deeper into the structure, all without saying a word. When he came back into the room, he spent a few minutes pulling on his hooded cloak and belting on his quiver and knives before turning to her.

What little hope had risen within Estingai shriveled and crumbled as she met Matsanga's eyes.

"You're welcome to rest and eat, Estingai, but you should have your ship come back here and pick you up." He sighed. "I'm sorry that you wasted your time."

He turned toward the exit and made a gesture with his fingers, striding out before Estingai could think of anything to say. His icehound followed.

For a moment, Estingai considered running after him.

"Shit."

She sank to her knees.

"Shit, shit, shit."

Tears burned behind her eyes again, but she held them back.

I won't cry like a freezing child.
Estingai pulled out her comm, hand trembling as she gazed at it.
No.
She shoved it back into her pocket.
I found him. I'm not giving up that easy.
If she went home now, she would be consigning herself to death at the very least—maybe the whole of the Remnant.
Estingai looked toward the exit, then yawned and shook her head.
Tomorrow.
She needed some sleep. After that, she would find a way to convince Matsanga to fight again.
The sword pulled her gaze.
Even if it's not in the way I want.

12

What Now?

We burned a single ship as an offering to sea and storm for leading us to this place, and as a farewell to the lives we had once known, and those we had lost. The rest, we took apart and carried into the mountains to build our new homes. Though things were peaceful at first, as all groups do, we found grievances to bicker about and came to disagreements about how to live our new lives in secrecy without fear, and comfort without excess. The struggle nearly broke us, but what emerged were the Buuekwenani.

Exodus countdown: 15 days, 3 hours, 11 minutes

Koruuksi tried not to be embarrassed by his singing voice as he joined in with Kinjaga and the others. He could match pitch with no problem, but that didn't mean his instrument was any good. Still, he tried his best.

Kinjaga dropped out and Zadia joined in after a few syllables, harmonizing with him, wide mouth curled into a grin as she met his gaze and bobbed along with their singing.

Vise's friends spoke just enough Atongo to communicate perfectly half the time, and completely confuse him the rest. When they'd tried to explain *obwisa*—a singing game—to him, they'd ended up laughing and telling him just to follow along. So far as Koruuksi could tell, there wasn't really much of a way to win the game—it was just a way to have fun.

One person would start out singing, using the syllables of their name, and then others would join in, harmonizing with them. Each participant would come in and drop out in turn. The point of the game seemed to get as many voices as possible singing different lines —or at least octaves—at once while still producing something that sounded like music.

Koruuksi was glad for the distraction after his meeting with Kuula'ande earlier. He shook his head, trying not to think about that. It wasn't failure, but it made everything *much* harder. He took a deep breath in an attempt to stave off that feeling of being overwhelmed, then joined back in the game.

He'd found Vise on his first day, asking her to show him about the city, since he didn't have much else to do while waiting for Kuula'ande's decision. She'd given him a tour of the district nearest the housing his team had been given, showing him the markets, theaters and gardens, and explaining a bit more about how their society worked and the way they functioned without currency. Koruuksi still didn't entirely understand that last part despite the Remnant's similar situation.

After the tour, she'd introduced him to her friends. Kanelo was one of the Akjemasai —the city's guard that had escorted them in from the forest—and Majele, Zadia, and Kinjaga just seemed like regular people. They all had the height, strong features, and dark red, striped skin Koruuksi had come to associate with the people of E Kwekuue. Matondo, on the other hand, was a refugee with spots instead of stripes, and a bit more orange to his complexion. He was also much closer to Koruuksi's height. Koruuksi enjoyed speaking with the man, as he spoke Atongo even better than Vise, and had been here long enough that he could translate for Koruuksi and the others when needed.

Koruuksi had pried about Matondo's past a few times and

suggested he help them but had decided against both after the man deflected a few times. Koruuksi found it hard to blame him for that.

Instead, he'd settled for enjoying himself for once. He'd decided to get to know Vise's friends, even if it meant sitting in sweaty clothing at the edge of a sunlit plaza.

"Koruuksi?"

Koruuksi froze at Uuchantuu's voice, a lump forming in his throat. The singing stopped and the others looked past him, back toward the plaza. Swallowing the lump, he turned toward his friend and grinned. "Hey, Uuchantuu, want to join in?"

She didn't respond as she approached. She just glared at him.

Fuck.

Uuchantuu had shed her kit and uniform since they'd been given housing, opting for a lighter, sleeveless white shirt and light brown pants that she'd rolled up around her ankles. She still wore her boots, however, which made the outfit look a bit ridiculous.

Maybe we should find somewhere to get sandals like everyone here wears.

"I need to talk to you," she said once in earshot, voice harsh.

Koruuksi forced himself to hold his grin and moved over a bit, patting the spot next to him. "Come sit. We can talk and—"

Koruuksi grunted as Uuchantuu grabbed his arm and yanked him to his feet, pulling him away from the circle of concerned-looking people.

Koruuksi waved and smiled at them as Uuchantuu pulled him a bit further away. "I'll be right back."

Once Uuchantuu stopped a short distance away—there wasn't really anywhere that private in the square, but they were out of earshot, at least—Koruuksi yanked his arm back and rubbed his wrist. "Ow. What the shit, Uuchantuu?"

"What do you think you're doing?"

"Singing. I think that was pretty obvious."

Uuchantuu glared at him. "We've been here three days and we've done nothing. That's half-a-week gone. Rather than working to complete our mission, you're just going out every day and acting like you've forgotten about the world outside this place. The *dying* one."

Koruuksi sighed, frowning, "I haven't—"

"We can't stay here, Koruuksi, as much as we'd like to, and neither can these people."

She paused, taking a deep breath. Her expression had sobered when she met his gaze again. "Me and the others... we need this win. I know you do, too. Right now, it doesn't feel like we're winning anything. Maybe we should ask the king—"

"That won't do any good."

Uuchantuu frowned at him, raising an eyebrow. "You already tried?"

Koruuksi sighed. "That idiot king gave me his answer this morning. He said he appreciates our intentions, but that this Vale will keep them safe even from something that ravages the rest of the world, and he does not wish to panic or disrupt the lives of his people. He extended his hospitality to us indefinitely if we wish to stay here and said that depending on the number of people we have, if we prove to be good guests, we might be able to bring the rest of the Remnant here to live in peace and safety."

Uuchantuu's face dropped, then hardened. "Then we just need to find some way of going around him. Kuula'ande can't be the sole authority here—they have to have some sort of legislative or bureaucratic body."

"They have a council that rules along with Kuula'ande," Koruuksi said. "Each of them apparently governs some specific area of life here, and they serve as both advisors and a check to the king's power."

"Then why aren't we trying to convince them to help us right now?" Uuchantuu hissed, throwing her hands up. She sighed, and when she looked at Koruuksi again, her eyes held pain.

"Why didn't you tell the team about Kuula'ande's answer?" she asked, voice much smaller and less heated than before. "Why didn't you tell me?"

Koruuksi dropped his gaze, unable to meet her eyes. "I never signed up for this."

"You practically sprinted to Kojatere to volunteer for this."

"I volunteered because I wanted to do something good," Koruuksi snapped, "not because I wanted to lead. You're the team leader, not me. And neither of us have done anything like this, before. I thought we would just be recruiting a group of people as desperate and as eager to escape as we are, not trying to convince an entire population to leave their fucking paradise of a home. Even then, I thought they would listen to science and reason, not say no."

He paused, gritting his teeth, then sighed. "When Kuula'ande told me his answer, everything just caved in on me at once. We won't be able to do this the easy way just ferrying people out of here, and I don't know what we're going to do now, if we just try to find whatever secret it is Kojatere wanted us to find, or if we just try to save them or both. Even once we decide, I have no clue *how* to do any of it." He put a hand to his head. "I just—"

He glanced over his shoulder at the circle of Vise's friends, then returned his gaze to Uuchantuu. "I needed to blow off some steam for a bit. I didn't want to share the news with the team without a plan to move forward, but I haven't been able to think of one."

Uuchantuu stared at him for a while, expression neutral. Finally, it softened. "I'm sorry for yelling at you," she said. "I was so worried about the team and my own issues that I forgot about all the pressure that's on you."

Koruuksi shook his head, giving her a bit of a smile. "Don't be. I need you to yell at me every now and then to keep my head on straight."

"And to keep your ego from over-inflating."

Koruuksi snorted, and Uuchantuu grinned.

She reached up and put a hand on his shoulder, meeting his gaze. "The team does need a leader—not me. Like you said, this isn't my thing. I can do tactics, but you're better with people. They're growing lax and a bit grumpy and combative. Tshala and Luuhuuta have started alternating between pestering and enjoying each other, and Lysanda and Andor have apparently gotten bored of... uh, you know..."

Koruuksi snorted at the color in Uuchantuu's cheeks, then sighed, sobering a bit. "I know."

"Do you know you don't need to bear that alone?"

Koruuksi met her gaze again, and smiled. "I don't think I deserve that."

Uuchantuu raised an eyebrow. "Of course you don't. You're just stuck with me. If something's hard on you it usually ends up biting me in the ass as well. I had enough of that with those bugs in the jungle."

Koruuksi laughed.

"Plus, I'm under strict orders from Estingai to make sure you're okay, and I'm pretty sure that includes not cracking under the stress of leadership." Koruuksi groaned, giving her a pointed look.

"What? You know I'd do it anyway. Estingai just made it clear she'd probably kill me if I didn't."

Koruuksi rolled his eyes. "Why does she always have to do that? She treats me like a fucking child. Ow!"

Koruuksi glared at Uuchantuu, rubbing where she'd punched his arm.

"She treats both of us that way. You're just trying not to feel bad about fighting with her just before we left."

Koruuksi folded his arms over his chest, looking away. "She started it."

"I guessed as much when she came to speak to me right after," Uuchantuu said. "You shouldn't be so hard on her. You know she's just looking out for you. She just—"

Koruuksi looked back to Uuchantuu as she sighed. "You two broke in different ways when you lost Svemakuu. You cracked a little bit and threw some patches over it. She shattered and somehow put the pieces back together. Sometimes it seems like she did that through sheer rage. You can give as good as you get, but she's basically a glass cannon emotionally. It's not her fault."

Koruuksi sighed. He knew she was right.

She usually is.

Then he thought of something.

"What?"

"The princess," Koruuksi said, "she reminded me of Estingai."

"Confident and strong-willed?"

Koruuksi snorted. "More like fucking infuriating."

Then he sobered a bit. "Do you think she's lost someone, too? I haven't heard anything about a queen in the past few days." Uuchantuu frowned at that. "Or were you too busy staring at her to notice that?"

Koruuksi barked a laugh as Uuchantuu's cheeks darkened.

"What about you? You stared at that woman Vise almost constantly once she appeared."

"At her face. And that was only because I was making sure I didn't stare at her chest."

Uuchantuu's face grew even darker. She ran a hand through her hair, "Yeah, still haven't gotten used to that."

Koruuksi shrugged. "I'm starting to. It makes sense—they live in perpetual heat and isolation probably kept them from adopting any of the oppressive modesty-customs some religions pushed. I'd walk around with my shirt off if the sun wouldn't give me severe burns."

"Have you seen her since then?"

"Who, the princess?"

"No, Vise?"

Koruuksi nodded. "A few times. I had her show me around the city, and those are some of her friends back there that she introduced me to."

"You try to sleep with her yet?"

Koruuksi cleared his throat. His own cheeks grew hot. "That's— No. That's not why we're here."

Uuchantuu raised an eyebrow. "I don't think that's ever stopped you before. And she's insanely gorgeous."

Koruuksi eyed Uuchantuu. "Then why haven't you tried talking to her? Not your type?"

Uuchantuu snorted, folding her arms beneath her chest. "I'm pretty sure she's *everyone's* type. It's not even fair. But, no. One, I *am* focused on our mission," she said. "And two, Natari women usually don't prefer other women. That's what makes me special. She also flirted with you quite a lot."

"I think that's just because I was the one that spoke with her the most. Her friends said that's just how she is."

"She also snuck quite a few looks at you."

Koruuksi smirked. "Did she actually sneak them, or was it like how you practically drooled over the princess? In front of her father, I might add."

Uuchantuu's cheeks grew darker than Koruuksi thought possible. He laughed, fending off a few half-hearted punches from her. Once he was done laughing, he smiled at her.

"Thank you, for getting me out of my head."

She smiled, most of the darkness still in her cheeks. "You're welcome."

"I need to go think about how best to approach this," Koruuksi said, "but you're having some fun while I do that."

Uuchantuu raised an eyebrow. "What do you—Ah! Koruuksi!"

Koruuksi pulled Uuchantuu back over to Vise's group of friends.

"Everyone, this is Uuchantuu. Uuchantuu—Kanelo, Kinjaga, Matondo, Zadia, and Majele."

They all smiled and waved at her as Koruuksi pushed on her shoulders, forcing her to sit down.

"Stupid tall people," she grumbled, taking a seat next to Matondo, who laughed.

"Tell me about it."

"I have some things I need to go take care of," Koruuksi told them, "I would appreciate it if you could teach her *obwisa* or *ago'ame* and make sure she has some fun—she doesn't do that enough."

"We'll take good care of her, Koruuksi," Kinjaga assured him in thickly accented Atongo.

Koruuksi grinned, then started off at a quick pace in the other direction before Uuchantuu could stop him. He needed to find somewhere quiet to think.

How the fuck am I going to pull this off?

13

The Right Course

As we settled into our new home, we found a strange, silvery metal that those of us familiar with metalwork could not identify. Some had heard myths of a silvery metal that came from the sky, yet in our valley it was as plentiful as fish on a reef. We discovered its strength and its ability to disrupt Auroramancy, and used it in many things from construction, to jewelry, to armoring our warriors. Though even our own people had trouble finding the pass if they ventured outside our borders, we had learned to be prepared. After a generation spent in this new home, we learned of another gift of this new sanctuary: every child born within the Vale became an Auroramancer.

Exodus countdown: 16 days, 20 hours, 32 minutes

For the first time in months, Skadaatha found herself truly at peace without the aid of her husband. She sat in one of Mjatafa Mwonga's concert halls, eyes closed and clearnodes brightened as Dymbajat's ensemble filled the space with music. They rehearsed rather than performed, and she was the only person in the audience, able to focus only on the music. No distractions.

She'd even managed to reduce that voice in her mind—the one that told her she should be gaining something from the music—to a faint whisper.

Dymbajat had run the ensemble—a full orchestra of seventy-two master musicians—through a number of older pieces by composers long dead, before getting to his own music. Skadaatha had suggested establishing a canon of the works of Efruumani's musical greats—pieces that people could learn and grow familiar with that would keep them coming back to the concert halls to hear their favorite works. Programs could then combine those with the works of more modern composers like Dymbajat to give them the chance to enter the ranks of the greats like Jansi Balys, Arva Pir, Muusadi Awaara, and Babasi Oko.

Though in Skadaatha's opinion, Dymbajat had the potential to become greater than any of the old masters in the canon.

Skadaatha opened her eyes. Brightening her clearnodes just a bit further, she breathed in deep, taking in the grand, yet somehow still intimate atmosphere of the concert hall. The only scent was that of the instruments and the various oils and rosins the musicians used to maintain them. Otherwise, the room smelled clean. The smell of the hardwoods that made up the chairs had long faded, as had that of the leather cushions. Thick, ornate pillars rose at the edges of the massive chamber, extending to form magnificent archways. Tiered, arched galleries and balconies lined the walls four levels high. Windows of stained glass illuminated them with natural light. Bright electric lights and sconces holding large gemstones infused with Auroralight lit the rest of the massive chamber, making the myriad mosaics of red, gold, and white sparkle. As she turned her gaze again to the musicians, Skadaatha's enhanced vision allowed her to pick out the concentration of the performers' faces, the shifts in their embouchures, and the way their eyes darted across the sheets of music before them. Most incredible was the music itself, however.

Not for the first time, Skadaatha wondered how she'd ever listened to music without enhancing her senses. The minor variations in tone, pitch, and color that her ears picked up gave the music another magnitude of depth. With a skilled ensemble, at least.

However, Skadaatha's enhanced hearing risked inviting distraction. She sighed when she heard footsteps and a door opening at the back of the hall, signaling the arrival of her elites. She could tell simply by the way they walked that they were still upset about how she'd left them after the confrontation with Kojatere.

Once all seven had taken seats around her, Skadaatha dimmed her clearnodes and turned to face them, meeting each of their gazes in turn. Most wore neutral expressions. Mnene didn't bother. Skadaatha still hadn't entirely gotten used to his lack of a mask. He wore one outside, but ever since his defection to the Imaia, he'd forgone a mask whenever he could.

For a moment, Skadaatha considered putting forth the iron front that had originally won their loyalty and respect.

"I called you here because while taking the Throne's power is no longer an option," she said, keeping her voice low, "Kojatere is still a threat. I also wanted to apologize. I should not have left you like that, but I needed to think."

As she looked around, their expressions relaxed. A few nodded.

Satisfied, Skadaatha continued, allowing herself a small smile. "She seems to be following through with the plan she told us of back on Atonga, but I do not have all the details. They will be using explosives to cause a distraction to blame on the Remnant while allowing them to commandeer a capital ship from one of the outer hangars. Adjunct Yndlova let slip that they have toyed with the idea of letting the Remnant slip away with spies in their midst to later reclaim whatever settlement they found rather than simply capturing or destroying them once all of their number are on the ship."

Her companions showed some surprise at that.

"I believe that option could work out well for the Imaia, but I do not trust Kojatere to ensure it does. The way they have laid out this plan so far will also give the military and Kojatere a great deal of leverage following its success. That could end poorly unless—"

Skadaatha cut off as something in Dymbajat's piece caught her attention. It tugged at her memory, though at first, she couldn't place it. When she realized where she'd heard it, she stiffened, and brightened her clearnodes again, trying to catch it again. The fragment of music did not repeat, however.

"Skadaatha?"

Skadaatha held up a hand and looked to the stage. For a moment, she considered interrupting the rehearsal, but dismissed the thought.

What would I say? That a part of his piece reminded me of a strange melody I heard on Darkside atop Mount Saanad eight days ago?

Skadaatha sighed, turning back to her companions. She had more important business to attend to than idle curiosities.

"Skadaatha?" Mnene asked again. "Unless...?"

"Kojatere gaining such leverage could end poorly unless we manage to come out on top," Skadaatha said. "We need to find a way to out-maneuver her. Catch her in the act if she plans betrayal, or manipulate the public perception to make it appear that her plan would have failed catastrophically if we did not step in."

The last sentence came out almost as a whisper. Skadaatha's companions stiffened. Mnene in particular wore a troubled expression. Despite his Samjati roots, he'd always worn his emotions plainly for all to see. Perhaps that came from having a mask to hide behind for so much of his life.

"What you propose," Symen said finally, "would it be sanctioned?"

Skadaatha considered for a moment, then shook her head.

They deserve to know what they are getting into.

"You know that, normally, my word alone would sanction any actions we take, but when Kojatere can do the same, I would need to go through official channels. That would give us away."

A few of them gave grave nods.

"What chance do we have, Skadaatha?" Synova asked, "with the Mestari wielding the power of a Throne...if we couldn't stop her in Old Atonga, how do we have any hope of doing so now? What has changed? Did Vysla come up with something? I won't risk my career for nothing. Even with your help, I doubt I would be allowed to keep my clearance and position in the Ministry if we moved against Othaashle and failed.

"He has a few ideas," Skadaatha said, "but that is not something we will need to rely on. Even if Othaashle held the power of the Throne of Darkness in its entirety, which she does not, Ynuukwidas is..."

She paused to take a deep breath, trying not to grate as she forced out the words. "The God King is still more powerful. Our only chance is to appeal to him. We must either uncover her plot at the last minute to show the God King that she is a traitor, or make her plan fail in a very public manner and swoop in to save it, as I suggested."

They remained silent for a while after that, Dymbajat's music the only sound in the hall. The tense, anticipatory mood set by the extended chords in the strings that seemed to just hang in the air felt almost physical, a manifestation of the decision she had laid before her companions.

Mnene nodded first. The rest followed slowly, one by one.

"Thank you," Skadaatha said, meeting the eyes of each. "For now, I need you to keep an eye on Kojatere and her people. We want information on their movements and the details of their plan, anything we can examine for discrepancies. Aarnal, I want you to look into the conditions of and protections afforded to Samjati refugees. Othaashle may simply be concerned for them, but let me know if there are any individuals or activity that stand out. Synovi, I will speak to my husband and see if there is any way in which you can assist him. Mnene, look into Makala, specifically the spies we just placed there —Phantom is one of them."

Mnene blinked at that, nostrils flaring. He'd served on Symuuna Team with Kojatere under Phantom, and had been there when Kojatere had taken the man's eye in an act of rage. Mnene had called Kojatere an enemy once coming to the Imaia, but when he'd relayed that story to Skadaatha, he'd seemed to respect Kojatere's actions.

The man must be even more of a raging bitch than most people think I am.

"I'll give you the clearance," she said before looking around. "The rest of you will receive more specific orders as we gather more intelligence. Any questions?"

"You're sure this is the right course?" Ljamyla asked.

Skadaatha nodded.

"Then I am satisfied."

The rest nodded, then rose, starting out the hall. Skadaatha looked after them for a moment, then settled back into her seat, enjoying Dymbajat's music once more, enjoying the manner in which he drilled the ensemble, coaxing perfection from them. She listened for that strange melody, clearnodes shining bright with Auroralight, yet it never returned even in variation or transformation.

When the rehearsal finally ended, the musicians gathering up their music and cleaning their instruments as Dymbajat gave them some concluding notes, Skadaatha rose and turned toward the back.

She blinked upon seeing Mnene.

He stood at the back of the hall, leaning against the ornate stone doorframe of one of the six entrances on this level, arms folded, expression contemplative.

"I didn't realize you enjoyed concert music," Skadaatha said upon approaching him.

"I don't always," he said. "Dymbajat's music holds such emotion that it is hard not to be enthralled by it."

Skadaatha nodded.

"I know what you said to Ljamyla, but..." He sighed, then took a long pause, meeting her gaze. "I did a lot of things for the Union—for Kweshrima and the Knights—that I am not proud of. Things I believed were right at the time because they worked toward some higher purpose. I need to make sure I do not repeat those mistakes. And that I atone for the ones I've made."

Skadaatha studied the man for a moment, then reached out and placed a hand on his shoulder. "I am sure, Mnene. And you have already redeemed yourself many times over."

The corner of his mouth twitched in a brief smile. "Thank you, Skadaatha. But no, I have not. Not yet."

14

The Workings of the Stars

Despite this, as our people grew, some wished to expand our borders. Longing for the sea, we built settlements on the coast where our people could live as we once did and bring back fish to feast upon. When they did, we realized that many of our children had never tasted the sea's bounty before that, and our conviction to keep a strand of the coast for ourselves grew.

Exodus countdown: 15 days, 1 hours, 34 minutes

Koruuksi drew himself up as he entered the room, taking in a deep breath to steady himself. They'd all quickly learned that buildings in E Kwekuue—or this building, at least—didn't divide into rooms as completely those in Remnant One or the other bases. The walls instead were carefully arranged to form semi-private alcoves with narrow entrances, sometimes blocked with curtains or strings of colored beads. That had led them to spread out somewhat within the building itself, but they'd met in one of the larger rooms rather than the building's central atrium so that they could pull the curtains and shutters closed to keep out the light.

"Finally," Kakengo said, tossing Koruuksi a salted sardine ration. "What did you call us all together here for, Koruuksi?"

Koruuksi caught it and took a bite. He had to hold back a frown as he looked around at his team. Uuchantuu was right. All of them had frizzy hair from the humidity, but none of those with Natari blood and crimped hair had tied their hair down into tight, thin braids as they usually did. They'd all abandoned their gear and uniforms for looser, more comfortable clothing that looked worn, and Luuhuuta and Lysanda had foregone even their minimal make-up for the first time he could remember since meeting them. Though that could have been due to the humidity for all he knew.

"We need to figure out how to proceed," Koruuksi said, taking a seat next to Uuchantuu. He had to force the next part out. "We don't have their king's support for evacuating this place. He declined."

Lysanda jerked upright. "What? But—"

Koruuksi raised a hand, halting the objection.

"At this point, his reasoning doesn't matter, and we're not here to discuss that. We've lost three days already as it is, and there are only eleven hours left in this one." He paused, sighing. "Since Kuula'ande has chosen to be dense on this matter, we need to go around him. We need to convince someone that he will listen to that his people are in danger and that this paradise will soon be just a lie."

The team went silent. A few tensed, others looked down at the floor or busied themselves fiddling with something.

"You mean insurgency," Tshala finally said, voice tight. "You want us to usurp the king's rule."

Koruuksi shook his head. "No. There will be no violence in this under any circumstances."

A collective sigh resounded throughout the room, the tension leaving his teammates.

"These people have a council that rules along with Kuula'ande and serves as a check to his power," Koruuksi continued. "Tomorrow, Uuchantuu and I are going to meet with Vise—"

He cut off, rolling his eyes at the grins and snickers.

"Of course, you're meeting a gorgeous woman for information," Ilona said, voice dripping with sarcasm.

"Any chance I can come instead of Uuchantuu?" Akseli volunteered.

Koruuksi gave them a flat look. "Vise is that bratty princess's bodyservant or something like that, so I figure she will be a good source of information about the council. If the princess is smarter than her father, maybe Vise can get her to help us."

Wemba snorted. "After that shit you pulled with her the first day? Not likely."

"Yeah, pretty sure she wants nothing to do with us."

Koruuksi waved them quiet.

"I still need to try though. While we do that, I want the rest of you exploring the city and engaging the people in conversation. I want info about the council, their supplies, their numbers. Do we need to file people out to the edge of the forest, or can we land several transports in here without the tech being affected? Whatever you can find."

"And what about their secret?" Muuzuuri asked. "The thing Kojatere sent us after that supposedly protects this place?"

Koruuksi thought for a moment. "That needs to be handled carefully. Let Uuchantuu and I worry about that for now. I want you to ask about the spirits and how long they've just been here, get them to ask you about yourselves and the outside world. It will be easier to get these people to move if they're already considering their home might not be safe once their council orders it. Ask about how many of them are Auroramancers, too. Almost everyone I've met seems to be one. That might have something to do with their secret."

They nodded. Most were his and Uuchantuu's age, raised during a time of conflict where people were a bit more motivated to make progress, but they'd all read the histories. Aliz and Andor were old enough to remember exactly how much people would resist change, simple or large, even if doing so put their lives in danger.

Satisfied, Koruuksi allowed himself a smile, "Now what about you all, any ideas?"

Luuhuuta raised a hand.

VISE GRINNED. "OKAY, SO THE ANTLERS..."

Koruuksi cocked his head, raising a hand to the base of them. "What about them?"

He and Uuchantuu had managed to find Assyn near the palace, who had sent someone to find Vise. The gorgeous Buuekwenani woman had led them away from the palace through some residential areas, though what looked like shops had begun popping up as they continued on through the city's colorful, vibrant streets. All that distinguished those buildings from the homes, apartments and other buildings they'd passed were the symbols inlaid in aluminum over the storefronts and the crowds of people outside of a few.

"How do they work?"

"They don't really do anything special," Uuchantuu said. "They're just there."

Vise shook her head. "No—I meant do they grow at a certain point or stop growing ever? Is this the biggest they will get? Can you feel things through them?"

She reached up and ran a finger along one of the branches. "Like that?"

Koruuksi was glad his mask hid the heat in his face.

"Yes and no. I can feel the pressure of you touching it at the root of the antler, but it's similar to the sensations with your hair." He hesitated a moment, then took a strand of Vise's hair between his fingers. "You can't feel that, but if I were to tug on it—"

"I get it," Vise said, taking her hair back. Her fingers brushed against his, and Koruuksi thought her cheeks grew a shade darker. "How often do you bump them on things?"

Koruuksi sighed as Uuchantuu snickered. "More than I would like. Not everything is built for their width. Your people seem to like high ceilings and doorways, at least, which helps. It's getting to the point where I just want to shed them, though."

Vise's eyes went wide, "Shed them?"

Koruuksi nodded, touching the base. "They start growing at around six cycles, and don't shed for the first time until usually around nine cycles, because they grow slowly the first time. After that, it takes about two cycles, then one, then it's every year that they shed. There seems to be some arbitrary limit on how large each person's can get, but they usually grow until you shed them."

"They just fall off?"

Koruuksi shrugged. "They usually get a little loose first and you can pull them off or let them fall."

"What do you do with them after that?"

"People used to make weapons, tools and art out of them. For a while, they were either discarded or used for ceremonial purposes, but now, we need everything we can get, so we usually break them up and make sewing needles or handles or anything else we can use them for. Skolan, one of our furniture makers, got creative enough a few times to make chairs out of them."

Vise blinked, then glanced up at his antlers skeptically.

"They're not the most comfortable," Uuchantuu said. "But they're functional, which is all we really care about."

Vise nodded at that, frowning as she looked down for a moment. Koruuksi took the opportunity to steal a glance at her. She was just as insanely beautiful as the first time he'd seen her. The faint smell of citrus that emanated from her hair enhanced the effect. Koruuksi thought he'd gotten used to the sight of topless, barely clothed women over the past few days of hanging out in the city with Vise's friends. Now that he was with Vise again, he found it almost more difficult than he had upon first arriving in the city.

"What about your mask and the clothing?" Vise asked, nearly catching him. She gestured to Uuchantuu. "She changed, so I imagine that must get hot."

Uuchantuu seemed a deliberate contrast to Vise. Both were petite in build with full lips and prominent cheekbones, but Uuchantuu's strong jaw and nose fit with her longer, more muscular limbs, while Vise's soft features complemented her warm, inviting demeanor.

Uuchantuu wore loose grey trousers and a loose white vest that obscured her figure with its neckline barely below her gemcrest, while Vise wore only a few items of jewelry, and her bright blue and violet *maopa* wrap that barely covered her hips and revealed nearly all of her legs with every swishing step. She wore the same sort of sandals that everyone in the city seemed to have a pair of, with the laces travelling halfway up her calf, though hers were white, while most of the others he'd seen were of uncolored leather.

Koruuksi shrugged. "I've gotten used to it. Don't you have any other Samjati refugees that have come here?"

Vise shook her head. "Just you and your team so far. I've heard stories and read accounts that say you wear it for protection from the sun. Is that true?"

Koruuksi nodded. "Somewhat."

He tapped his mask. "These were ceremonial for the Jusanariti'i and Nimikadeka peoples for a long time—two of the major ethnic—"

"I know," Vise said. "Go on."

"They were originally adopted by the Jusanariti'I to protect their faces from the sun, as was the clothing and the eye shades of the mask," he continued. "Since they were the first to travel beyond the twilight band and into Lightside. Since most Samjati peoples live on Darkside, our skin is used to absorbing very faint light—just that which reflects off Myrskaan."

Vise frowned at that. "How do you refill your gemcrests on Lightside, then?"

Koruuksi raised two fingers to the lenses at his mask.

"It takes a bit longer," he explained, "but it works just like glass windows do for Natari. We just have to look directly at the auroras on Auroraday."

"It took decades for glassmakers to get the tint and thickness right, though," Uuchantuu added.

Vise thought about that for a moment. "What happens if you're exposed to Lightside's sun?"

"Burns," Koruuksi said, "very quick and very bad. It's not too bad in the twilight band, but...if you were to leave me out in the sun with even just my shirt off for twelve to eighteen minutes, I'd be burnt past recovery."

Vise's eyes bulged. "Why would you ever venture outside?" She stopped, looking around frantically for a moment before grabbing Koruuksi's wrist. "Here, this way."

Koruuksi looked to Uuchantuu as Vise pulled him along. She just shrugged and followed after.

Vise stopped once they were under one of the many shaded areas along the side of the plaza. Natari didn't have to worry about constant sun-exposure, but certain wares were best kept in the shade and out of direct light or heat. This particular overhang happened to be near the river, not in front of any particular shop or vendor.

"There, is that better?" Vise asked, looking to him.

Koruuksi grinned. "I wasn't in any danger out there, but this is certainly cooler."

Taking a seat on the paved edge of the street that overlooked one of the many canals, Koruuksi checked to make sure he wouldn't accidentally lean into direct sunlight, then took off his mask and hood. He had to squint at first as he ran his fingers through his hair—even in the shade, it was still bright without his mask's lenses—but adjusted after a few moments. He let his mask hang from the strap that connected it to the back of his shirt and turned to Vise to find her gazing at him, expression unreadable.

"What?"

Vise blinked. "Nothing, it's just nice to finally know what you look like."

Koruuksi grinned, untying his sweat-soaked headband. "Not too disappointing, I hope."

Vise shot him a flat look as he folded the cloth into a small square and stuffed it into one of his pockets before fishing out a fresh one. He reached down to dunk it into the water, then wrung it out and tied it around his temples. He closed his eyes and took in a deep breath, enjoying the cool damp on his skin, then looked to Uuchantuu. She was giving him a look similar to Vise's.

"You have no idea how hard it was not to just push you into the water right then."

Koruuksi narrowed his eyes, scooting back from the edge a bit before he turned to Vise.

"So, what exactly is it that you do for the princess?" Koruuksi asked. "I heard you're some sort of body servant or handmaid to her?"

Vise shrugged. "Partially. That doesn't entirely describe the duties of a *mjakaazi*, though. I also manage the palace staff and carry out certain administrative duties between King Kuula'ande and the Diwani."

"Really?" Uuchantuu asked. "But you're so..."

"Laid-back?" Koruuksi supplied, looking between the two women.

Uuchantuu nodded. "Most of the aides we know are always running about everywhere, always pressed for time, never with a free moment."

Vise frowned. "That sounds awful. Don't they know how to delegate?"

Koruuksi snorted at that, thinking of Marjatla—the commander still acted like an assistant sometimes. "They're usually of the mindset that if they don't attend to something personally, it won't get done right or in a timely manner."

Vise grinned. "That sounds like the men and women I usually choose to delegate to." She paused, peering at Koruuksi. "You didn't exactly endear yourself to Ymvesi'ia, by the way."

"Oh, don't worry, he knows," Uuchantuu said. "We made it very clear to him how much of an asshole he was."

Koruuksi narrowed his eyes at Uuchantuu.

"She deserved it," he muttered, looking down.

Uuchantuu hit him in the arm and glanced pointedly at Vise. The woman just grinned and shook her head.

"I'm not arguing. Ymvesi'ia's not always so bad, though. She just takes protecting her people very seriously. She had to bully her father into allowing her to train and patrol with the *Akjemasai*. That work has warmed her up to the idea of taking in refugees, but they usually don't come into the forest fully armed, marking their way through."

Koruuksi's eyes widened. "She knows we did that?"

Vise nodded, grinning. "They followed you for a while before revealing themselves to you. She and most of the guard speak Atongo, so they like to have an opportunity to listen and see what people are like before revealing themselves."

Koruuksi nodded. "That's pretty clever."

Vise grinned.

"Have they had to deal with much other than refugees?" Uuchantuu asked. "Any groups that they didn't let into the city?"

Koruuksi thought back to the bones and equipment he'd found and looked to Vise.

Her expression fell a bit, and she nodded. "A few times. From what Ymvesi'ia has told me, usually, if they find someone or a group that appears unfriendly, they don't reveal themselves unless it seems like their quarry might actually find the way into E Kwekuue. That doesn't happen often."

"But it has happened," Uuchantuu said.

Vise nodded. "Not so frequently in my life or Ymvesi'ia's, but yes. Ymvesi'ia was very shaken the first...they first time her squad had to kill someone. None of her warriors died, but she killed one of the intruders, and a few of them were injured."

Koruuksi blinked at that. The hard intensity of Ymvesi'ia's gaze took on a whole new light with that.

"You call her by her name," Uuchantuu said. "Rather than 'Her Highness' or 'Princess' or something like that. Is that just something people do in stories or something they used to do?"

Vise grinned, shaking her head. "I always refer to Kuula'ande and Ymvesi'ia and the Diwani by their titles or honorifics in formal situations, but I know Ymvesi'ia far too well for her to require that from me in any other circumstance. Part of the reason I'm her mjakaazi is because we grew up together and we just work well together. I've been around her and the court in some way or another for most of my life, so there wasn't really that much for me to learn once I took on that position or my other responsibilities."

A few lightoruu—long, ribbons of faintly red light—zipped

through the air overhead, looking as though they were chasing each other.

"Still haven't gotten used to that," Koruuksi said, looking after the spirits as they flitted away, but did not vanish. "Do they always just... float around like that?"

When he looked back to Vise, she wore a frown. "Not always."

Koruuksi waited for her to elaborate, but she did not.

"Why are you here?" she asked instead, looking between the two of them.

"The princess didn't tell you?"

"I want to hear it from you," Vise said. "Not something with Ymvesi'ia's annoyance or Kuula'ande's ruling perspective as a bias."

Koruuksi looked to Uuchantuu, then back to Vise, holding back a grin. This was exactly what they'd wanted. "Alright. What is your understanding of planetary physics?"

"We know how the planets in our star system work," Vise said, "And have theories about other star systems and celestial bodies in the aioavere. Our observatory up near the edge of the Vale provides us with a great deal of information on things beyond our world."

Koruuksi blinked at that. The idea that this isolated civilization had an observatory with equipment powerful enough to observe distant stars gave him an idea. He tucked it away for later.

"Do you know about LaGrange points?" he asked. "How they work and how unstable they are?"

Vise frowned. "I know the term—our scientists have had a fascination with the stars ever since we built our observatory after making our arrangement with Uumgwefilo—but don't remember much about it."

Koruuksi nodded. "Well, you know that our world is a habitable moon, not a planet, correct?"

Vise nodded, smiling. "That, I do know."

Koruuksi grinned, glad to have a baseline. "Good. So, rather than orbiting Myrskaan as Atjakuu orbits our world, Efruumani appears to orbit the sun at nearly the same rate as Myrskaan. Rather than rotating on an axis perpendicular to our sun like Myrskaan, our world is tidally locked."

Vise nodded. "Which makes its axis point toward the larger celestial body—Myrskaan, in this case—resulting in Lightside and Darkside."

"Exactly."

Vise nodded. "And where do LaGrange points come in?"

"Every celestial body has LaGrange points," Uuchantuu said, picking up the explanation. "They're sort of resonant points in space that stay constant with their parent celestial body."

Koruuksi rolled his eyes. "Or, more plainly, something in a LaGrange point will orbit at the same rate as its parent."

"Isn't that what I said?"

Koruuksi rolled his eyes, then looked back toward Vise. "If Atjakuu had something in one of its LaGrange points, that object would orbit Efruumani at the exact same rate as Atjakuu, regardless of whether it was beyond the moon or between it and our world. Efruumani is in one of Myrskaan's LaGrange points, tidally locked between the gas giant and the sun. However, normally, LaGrange points are incredibly unstable. The Imaia tried creating satellites that would orbit Efruumani at these points, but found that unless the satellite had thrusters that would allow it to constantly adjust its position, the orbit would rapidly decay."

Vise narrowed her eyes. "But that makes no sense. If our world orbits at a LaGrange point, and they are as unstable as you say, our world shouldn't have lasted nearly as long as it has, correct? It should have been pulled into either Myrskaan or the sun?"

Koruuksi nodded grimly. "Even beyond that, while Efruumani is in our star's habitable zone, its tidally locked position should have rendered most of Lightside as desert, rather than the mix of rainforests, plains, deserts and other ecosystems it holds. Darkside should be a frozen wasteland too dark and cold for any life to survive much less evolve, and the auroras are the result of massive solar flares that hit our planet regularly with enough energy to somehow span across the entire sky rather than simply the poles."

Vise frowned. "Alright, I understand up to that point. If that's what should happen, why doesn't it?"

"That's where the Aathal come in," Uuchantuu said. "From what scientists—mostly the Imaia's—can tell, the Aathal perform some sort of geoengineering for Efruumani. They've made both Lightside and Darkside more habitable, turn the auroras into something with substance rather than just colorful lights, and they keep Efruumani from falling out of its orbit."

"When Yrmuunthal was destroyed," Koruuksi said, "the world shifted a bit. Darkside is even colder than it once was. Our reports from inside the Imaia say that the God King has retreated from most daily life, using every last scrap of his power and will to keep Efruumani stable and keep the auroras coming."

Uuchantuu looked to Koruuksi, then looked to Vise when he nodded.

"You know about the city the Imaia has built around Boaathal?"

Vise nodded. "We've heard stories from the refugees."

"Our intelligence tells us that it's more than just a city. It's some sort of vehicle they plan to use when leaving Efruumani. Our reports also say that they plan to take Boaathal with them to power their city and transplant on whatever new world they find to call home. Once they leave, it won't be long till the solar flares batter Efruumani's atmosphere away or the planet falls out of orbit and into Myrskaan or our sun. If it takes longer than nine days, we'll all be lightless by then."

Vise peered at them, and Koruuksi frowned at the skepticism in her gaze.

"Everything you said makes sense," she said, "up until the part about the Imaia taking the Aathal with them. The World Trees are bound to Efruumani—there is no way the Imaia could separate one from this world, no matter the technology they have."

Koruuksi sighed. "That's what a lot of us thought at first. It sounded so absurd that we didn't take it seriously."

"The Imaia takes it very seriously, though," Uuchantuu said. "They seem intent on leaving this world and taking everything they can with them, including Boaathal. Part of the reason we came here so heavily armed is because we were convinced this would be a trap set by the Imaia. They've stripped the rest of the world of every resource they can, so we thought there was no way they would have missed this place."

"That doesn't explain how they would be able to separate a World Tree from its world," Vise objected.

"We don't know exactly how they plan to do it," Koruuksi admitted, "but we also don't know much about the Aathal in general. And the Imaia has the God King on their side. He is more powerful than Kweshrima was, and Kweshrima found a way to destroy an Aathal—something no one thought was possible. Surely you can't deny the effects of that. Kuula'ande said you felt something from that, even here."

Vise shook her head, "We did, but..." She trailed off, then looked between them with a slight hardness to her gaze. "You knew she did that, and exactly how detrimental that was to the world, yet you continued to follow her?"

Koruuksi sighed, "That's complicated."

It was a distraction from the real topic at hand, but he'd expected it to come up at some point. Though he'd thought the questions would come from Ymvesi'ia before Vise.

"We did," he said, meeting Vise's gaze. "She was all we had left to cling to while everything else crumbled around us. It wasn't right. What she did or continuing to follow her. Most of what we've done since hasn't been good or right, just necessary. We're trying to do something good now, though. Here. We've been unable to prevent a lot of terrible things. All we want to do is save your people from a threat it seems you are all unaware of." He looked around. "This place is beautiful, but wouldn't you like to be able to see an entire world instead of just one little plot of it?"

Vise frowned.

"We've learned some of the rules you have in place to maintain your way of life here," Uuchantuu said. "The way your society operates is fascinating, but it has to get frustrating at some point. The limits on occupation and areas of study, tiered job rotations, restrictions on space...I know that sort of thing wears on our own people. We just want to be free of restrictions like that, and I imagine you would, too."

"This place truly is a paradise," Koruuksi said, "but it won't last once the Imaia leaves and takes Boaathal with them. Even if Efruumani doesn't fall out of orbit and whatever has kept you safe and hidden here for so long manages to keep the Vale safe and habitable, you won't be able to leave it. Likely even the forest will turn to desert."

Vise rose to her feet, a strange look passing over her face.

"I'm sorry," she said, voice tight, "I need to go."

Koruuksi jumped to his feet as she trotted off; he barely remembered that he had his mask off in time to stop himself from pursuing her. He fixed it in place and took a step forward, but Uuchantuu put a hand on his shoulder.

He looked to her, cocking his head.

"Just let her go," she said.

Koruuksi sighed, shoulders sagging. "Did I screw that up, too?"

Uuchantuu shook her head. "I don't think so. We dumped a lot on her. She just needs some time to process it."

Koruuksi looked after Vise's curvaceous, shrinking form and took a deep breath.

"You're right. Come on, let's go meet with the team and see what they've learned. Hopefully they might have discovered a few other options if it ends up taking Vise a while to speak with us again."

15

Mshauuri

As we had feared, outsiders soon found that settlement, and attacked. The ships that came did not bear the Iron Hammer, yet we could not risk word of our people's location spreading. Our warriors fought off the attackers, yet we knew more would come searching. A brave group of volunteers feigned flight when the invaders came again, vowing to never return to our sanctuary. They protected not only our safety, but that which we hid from the world: the gift we had discovered at the Heart of the Vale of E Kwekuue.

Exodus countdown: 16 days, 3 hours, 54 minutes

Estingai awoke to find Matsanga still gone. Or he'd come back and left again, enough time had passed for either. Rather than search for him, Estingai fished her sketchbook and a pencil out of her bag and decided to pass the time productively. He'd left his sword here. He would be back.

Drawing in a deep, shaky breath, Estingai tried to clear the tightness in her chest. She tried to relax for a few minutes, but she'd never been very good at that, even before training to become a soldier. She either needed to sleep or do something. Svemakuu had been the only one that could get her to truly just relax.

She warmed up with a few simple sketches of the cauldron and the various bowls and containers Matsanga possessed, writing little notes about where he might have acquired them, and looking around the room. Estingai had seen homes like this before they were taken by the ravages of time and war—places with far more space and luxury than anyone could need while children like her had gone without knowing where their next meal or bed would be. She'd fought in these same homes when noble families had transformed them into fortresses to protect their own wealth and power rather than those who depended on them.

After her warm-ups, Estingai moved on to more complex subjects like her former mentor and his new canine companion. Sketching often helped Estingai think more clearly, and sketching a specific person helped her think about them.

Sketching the icebound made Estingai frown as she replicated its likeness. It didn't have biomes in the usual spots.

It's fur is pretty shaggy. Is that hiding it?

Estingai drew the creature as though that were the case, then moved onto Matsanga.

As she worked through the sketch, orangenodes bright to keep the image of Matsanga crisp in her mind, Estingai gave the man's eyes and scars a bit of extra attention. She knew that Othaashle had given him the burn, but he'd been closed-mouthed about most of the others.

Her former mentor was a stubborn, implacable man who had lived long enough to see through any tricks she might employ.

How do I convince someone like that to help?

By the time he returned, Estingai had her answer.

Matsanga seemed surprised to find her there.

"I figured you'd be gone," he said when she met his gaze, the red-and-black wolf walking past him to curl up in the corner and glance between the two of them. "Or waiting for your ship, at least."

Estingai shrugged. "I never said I was leaving. My ride won't be here for another week. Communication is too risky."

Matsanga sighed, looking between her face and her sketchpad. She made no effort to hide the sketch of him. Koruuksi had annoyed any sense of embarrassment about her sketches—immaculate, incomplete or personal—out of her long ago.

"At least you'll have something to keep yourself busy."

"I've thought of something that will keep both of us busy, actually," she said.

Matsanga looked over his shoulder and raised an eyebrow as he walked over to the shelves and started taking bundles of herbs from his bag and setting them out.

"You going to ask me to pose for your sketches like when you were learning?"

"No—I have enough sketches of grumpy old men to fill a museum if I could find the remains of one."

Matsanga grunted with something that sounded almost like amusement.

"Since you won't come back with me," she continued, "you're going to teach me enough to give me a chance against Kojatere if it comes to that."

"Why bother?"

The wolf let out a soft, rumbling growl.

Estingai looked at the animal, jaw clenched, then took a deep breath, looking back to Matsanga. "I didn't stand a chance against her when she was just one of the Redeemed. Now that she has the power of the Throne, I have absolutely no chance against her. Not as I am, at least. I'm not some legendary hero like you."

Matsanga sighed, shoulders slumping. "Othaashle was never 'just one of the Redeemed,' and I'm no hero, Estingai. You know that. What makes you think there's anything I could teach you that would allow you to go toe-to-toe with a god, if a fledgling one? Like you said—I'm a grumpy old man. You were always the one coming up with new ways to use georaurals. Did you think of making one to deal with her?"

"You're no grumpier now then you were when you trained me," Estingai said, "and barely any older by your standards. Kojatere respected you before she died, even with the power of a god at her disposal. Kweshrima held you in equally high regard, as did everyone else. As for the georaurals, I gave that up a long time ago. Even if I had the right materials to work with, I don't know how to make something that could challenge her."

Matsanga said nothing.

Estingai waited, but he didn't even turn around.

"Please," she finally begged. The unsteadiness of her voice surprised her.

Why should it? This is the last chance I have left to be anything more than a sacrifice.

"Please, Mshauuri."

Matsanga turned his head, and Estingai followed his gaze to the wolf, who looked up and met his gaze.

After a moment, Matsanga sighed and turned to face her.

"I'll teach you."

Estingai beamed—she nearly laughed.

Before she could say anything, though, Matsanga held up a hand. "Tomorrow. I will give you three lessons, but they start tomorrow. I need some time to think about what to teach you, and some more time to sleep on it. While I think...give your body a little exercise. You still keep up with the acrobatics I taught you?"

The smile didn't leave Estingai's lips. The expression was so unfamiliar, it felt odd on her.

"Thank you, Mshauuri," she breathed. "I do. I will."

Matsanga nodded noncommittally, putting the bag away.

"I'll be back," he said, then strode out of the room.

Relieved, Estingai tilted her head back against the wall, closing her eyes.

When she straightened, opening her eyes, she found the wolf staring at her again.

Rather than look away, Estingai narrowed her eyes and held its gaze. She soon found herself wishing she'd brought some paints or colored pencils—she still had some, though a few were almost too small to hold—so she could try and capture the incredible mix of blues in its eyes.

Instead, she flipped to a new page of her sketchbook—she could finish the other one later—and began a new sketch of the wolf.

Light, I never asked Matsanga its name.

"For right now," she said to it, "your name is just 'Wolf,' alright?"

Estingai could have sworn the animal smirked at that.

16

Protected No Longer

We never learned what became of them, but after that we withdrew into the mountains. Only our Akjemasai warriors ever ventured out into the forests beyond, keeping watch for any who grew too curious, and ensuring none ever found the pass. For a time, our people lived in peace and isolation, and likely would have forgotten about the world beyond our mountain walls if not for our time of remembrance every Auroraday.

Exodus countdown: 14 days, 34 hours, 5 minutes

Ymvesi'ia tried not to stomp like a striped mountain horse as she finally returned to her quarters. She enjoyed training and patrolling with the rest of the Akjemasai, but even after eleven years patrolling with them, she hadn't gotten used to the thick, clammy air of the jungle that surrounded the Vale. The city itself was usually just as humid, if not more, but it was more open. Sneaking through the jungle sometimes felt like being in a tight, sealed box that had been left out in the sun next to the river.

It didn't help that she'd been distracted all day.

Closing her door behind her, Ymvesi'ia set her spear in its usual place hanging on the wall at a slant. She stripped off her mask and hood, then grinned when the sweet, citrusy aromas of a bath reached her nose. Ymvesi'ia hurriedly stripped off the rest of the unadorned white uniform that hid all but her eyes, granting her near-perfect camouflage in the white forest.

"You're late."

Ymvesi'ia turned as her tunic fell from her torso to see Vise standing in the doorway to her bathing chamber, wearing her characteristic smirk as she looked at Ymvesi'ia.

A pristine white *maopa* with aluminum thread embroidery hung from Vise's ample hips, matching the woven anklets and bracelets she'd chosen today. Ymvesi'ia held in a sigh at how incredible her friend looked, as usual. She was everything Ymvesi'ia was not: curvaceous where Ymvesi'ia was thin, soft where she was muscular, petit where Ymvesi'ia was tall. Ymvesi'ia had mostly gotten over her jealousy at that some time ago, along with other things, but on days like today, old emotions flared up.

"Rough day?" Vise asked when she didn't respond.

Ymvesi'ia drew in a deep breath in an attempt to clear her head, then nodded. "We did not find any more refugees or soldiers, but we did find their transports."

Those had been strange. The city's libraries held diagrams and sketches of the various vehicles other civilizations had used in the past to travel over land, water, and even the skies more recently. Those transports had borne only the slightest resemblance to the airborne vehicles.

Vise's eyes lit up, as Ymvesi'ia had guessed they would. "Their transports?"

Ymvesi'ia couldn't help but smile at her friend's excitement. Some of her earlier frustrations melted away at the expression.

"Help me get out of these and into the bath," Ymvesi'ia said, gesturing at her remaining clothing, "then I will tell you all about them."

Grinning, Vise darted forward to help Ymvesi'ia with her gloves, boots, pants and breastwraps.

"I still don't know how you and the others stand these things," Vise said, making a face as she loosened the wraps around Ymvesi'ia's chest.

"Not all of us are as blessed as you. We do not have as much to squish down and hold in place. It iss not really that bad."

Vise grinned. "They're only a blessing because I have a strong back and make a point of never running anywhere."

Not for the first time, Ymvesi'ia grinned at the thought of what her friend would look like, sprinting through the city with nothing holding her generous chest in place.

Vise gave her a light swat on the arm. "I know what you're thinking, and it's much more painful than it is amusing. Come on, let's get you in the bath. You smell terrible."

Ymvesi'ia gaped, but Vise had already moved clear of her before she could think to do anything. Vise didn't run, but she found ways to move very quickly when she wanted to.

Ymvesi'ia followed Vise into the bathing area and took a deep breath, closing her eyes and letting the wonderful scents wash over her.

When she opened her eyes, Ymvesi'ia grinned at the steaming bath before her. The aluminum edges shone, reflecting both the natural light from outside and the Auroralight from the georaurals set into one section that controlled the temperature and flow of the water. She stepped up to the rim of the tub and let out a relieved moan when she dipped her toe into the wonderfully hot water.

Vise giggled behind her.

Ymvesi'ia turned around and eyed her friend as she stepped deeper into the large pool, "What?"

Vise grinned, removing her own clothing before joining Ymvesi'ia in the bath. "That's a noise most women only make in the bedroom."

Ymvesi'ia rolled her eyes despite the heat in her cheeks. "Let us just say that after being in that forest today, I am as happy to see my bath as Arafaa and Nia are to return to their husbands."

Vise laughed before dunking herself beneath the water. Ymvesi'ia followed suit, remaining submerged just long enough to soak her face and hair before standing straight again. The water up to her navel.

Ymvesi'ia looked back to Vise to find the woman with hers eye closed, hair plastered to her face and neck, feeling toward the edge of the tub. Ymvesi'ia shook her head and grabbed one of the smaller towels Vise had set near the edge of the water.

"Here," she said, handing it to Vise. "You always forget."

Vise dabbed at her eyes and face, wiping away her make up, then smiled. "Thank you. You are not the only one that gets excited for a bath."

Once she was done with the towel, Vise set it down, then reached over the side and grabbed the bottles of shampoo and conditioner, bringing them closer to Ymvesi'ia. She took a seat on the edge of the tub and gestured for Ymvesi'ia to sit down on the step before her, as usual.

"So, what's bothering you?" Vise asked as soon as she had her sudsy hands in Ymvesi'ia's hair.

"Did you specifically wait to ask that until you could literally hold me captive?" Ymvesi'ia asked.

"Wouldn't you?"

Ymvesi'ia sighed, rolling her eyes behind her lids.

"That...Koruuksi and his people."

"The transports? You are going to tell me about them, right?"

"It is not just those—he was frustrating me before we came across them. His team hid them well. We did not get too much of a look inside, though. I did not want to accidentally set anything off or break something. I do not want them to have any trouble leaving."

Vise sighed, and Ymvesi'ia could imagine the overly dramatic expression of despair on her friend's face. "You're no fun. Can you at least tell me what they look like?"

Ymvesi'ia snorted. "Like big, unwieldy boxes." Vise groaned, rolling her eyes.

"I am serious! I do not know how these things get people anywhere. They have things that *look* like wings on them, but they do not resemble ships or birds or any of the vehicles the Uumgwefili used. I cannot even think of anything close to them that our warriors described seeing when they fought. Though I suppose that makes them more impressive. They looked well-taken care of, at least, if with a few parts that appeared patched on. And they were all orange—something between the sky and the sea."

Vise eyed her for a moment, then smiled. "Thank you. You're certain you didn't get a look inside?"

"No way to do so without possibly damaging them. I do not want them to have any reason to stay here when they finally leave."

Vise sighed again. "I guess that makes sense."

Ymvesi'ia snorted, smiling.

"What was bothering you before that?"

"Something he said when he petitioned my father, and on the way to their quarters," Ymvesi'ia said, eyeing the few reddish mistoruu and heatoruu that hung about this part of her room, imitating small clouds of steam. They'd become so commonplace she barely noticed them anymore.

"About the spirits and the outside world. I tried to attract some while patrolling, but nothing worked, even though I had no problem doing it on this side of the mountains both before and after. It was also..."

Ymvesi'ia trailed off for a moment, thinking back to what she'd felt in the forest. "Eerie. There is no life in the forest outside the Vale. Even right up next to the mountains. No birds, no firefoxes or panthers or monkeys, just insects, and few of those."

Vise was silent. For a while, Ymvesi'ia was able to dispel her frustration and focus on Vise's soothing fingers.

"Have you heard what he and his people are doing?" Vise asked.

Ymvesi'ia frowned. "Who, Koruuksi?"

"A few of the friends I've introduced him to are a bit worried by the things he's said when they asked about the outside world."

Ymvesi'ia nodded. Assyn, one of the Akjemasai that was friends with Vise, had spent some time with him at Ymvesi'ia's suggestion.

"He was clever," Ymvesi'ia said. "Appearing to just enjoy himself for a few days, getting to know people, and then manipulating them into asking about why he is here and the outside world."

Ymvesi'ia paused at a twitch from Vise's fingers. She turned, meeting her friend's gaze, "Everything alright?"

Vise nodded. "Dunk your head."

Ymvesi'ia held her breath as she did so, then smoothed out her hair behind her and out of her face as she sat between Vise's legs again to let her put on the conditioner.

"I still cannot believe my father even considered his ridiculous petition, much less granted him and his team sanctuary if they desire it."

The words came out with a bit more bite than she'd thought.

It has to just be some ridiculous scheme. It can't be real, no matter the spirits and the forest.

Ymvesi'ia shivered, then shook her head. She couldn't let these baseless rumors get to her.

"Watch it!" Vise said.

Ymvesi'ia's cheeks grew hot. "Sorry."

"Mhm."

Silence stretched again. Once Vise was done with Ymvesi'ia's hair, she did her own as usual, despite Ymvesi'ia's insistence that she return the favor. Ymvesi'ia counted each of the seven time's she'd convinced Vise to allow her to wash her hair as a personal victory.

Ymvesi'ia tried to lose herself in the routine as they continued bathing, to keep from her thoughts her troubling experience in the forest earlier, as well as the research she'd done earlier this week.

About halfway through scrubbing each other down with coarse cloths, Vise paused and looked up at Ymvesi'ia.

"What?"

"Would you really want them thrown out?" Vise asked. "Even Uuchantuu?"

Ymvesi'ia's cheeks lit up. "I do not know which one—"

"Don't lie to me. I wasn't able to learn too much about her, but she seems like a good friend to Koruuksi. And she's intelligent. Both of them are."

Ymvesi'ia cleared her throat and went back to scrubbing Vise. "I do not know what you're talking about. She was probably just staring because my breasts were out. You know how other peoples are."

"She didn't stare at mine, that way," Vise shot back. "Well, only a few times."

She grinned.

"What?"

"Uuchantuu seemed annoyed at Koruuksi for how he spoke to you the other day," she said, "even if you deserved it a bit."

Ymvesi'ia groaned. "Yes, I know—you've made it very clear that I should not have threatened our guests on their first day here."

Vise grinned. "Just making sure."

Ymvesi'ia frowned, then locked her eyes on Vise's. "When did you speak with her?"

Vise chuckled and continued scrubbing her down. "You're a bit too excited for someone who didn't know who I was talking about a few moments ago."

Ymvesi'ia glared at her.

Vise grinned.

"Koruuksi asked to speak with me today under the pretense of a tour around the city, and Uuchantuu came with him."

Ymvesi'ia frowned at that. "Are they together?"

Vise snorted. "You wouldn't ask that if you'd spend even twelve minutes with them. The way they treat each other is somewhere between extremely close friends and bickering siblings."

Ymvesi'ia found herself smiling at that. "You said 'pretense.' What did they actually want?"

Vise frowned and set the cloth down on the side of the pool. She dabbed a bit of oil into her hands and rubbed them together before starting to massage Ymvesi'ia's shoulders.

"Well, they did seem interested in the city," Vise said, her fingers working magic, melting away the tension and fatigue of Ymvesi'ia's day, "but I feel like they manipulated me into asking them about why they were here. I don't know how they did it, but I'm certain they did."

Ymvesi'ia frowned. "I—"

"I think I believe them," Vise said, cutting her off.

All the tension Vise had managed to dispel returned as Ymvesi'ia turned toward her friend.

"You believe them?" she said, chest tight.

Vise nodded. "And I think you know they might be onto something. You wouldn't have spent so much time researching what they said if you thought their claims were entirely baseless."

Ymvesi'ia's mouth drew to a thin line. "I researched the issue to make sure I could disprove it and refute any of their claims that did not check out."

"And could you?" Vise asked, folding her arms.

Ymvesi'ia's jaw bunched. She wanted to yell and scream. Anything to keep from talking about this—from giving it any hint of legitimacy.

The fear in Vise's eyes shut all of that down in an instant.

"Auroras, you really do believe them, don't you?"

Vise nodded, and Ymvesi'ia took her friend into her arms. She held onto Vise just as tightly as the other woman held onto her.

Light. Light, burn it!

Ymvesi'ia prided herself on her intelligence, but Vise stood above her in that.

If she believes them...

With a sigh, Ymvesi'ia pulled back just enough to meet Vise's gaze. "I am sorry."

Vise raised an eyebrow. "You thought you were looking out for your people."

"Instead, I may have wasted valuable time. And now that my father has rejected their petition..."

Ymvesi'ia let out a breath of frustration, closing her eyes as she rubbed at her forehead.

"Don't worry about that right now," Vise said, taking her hand. "Just come with me to meet them tomorrow and speak to Koruuksi with an open mind. Let him explain everything to you."

Ymvesi'ia nodded, "Okay."

She looked down at herself and became aware of the now-tepid water. Reheating it wouldn't be a problem, but...

Holding her breath, Ymvesi'ia bent her knees and dunked her head between the water. She scrubbed, then raked her fingers through her hair and over her scalp, getting all the conditioner out, then popped back above the surface.

Vise raised an eyebrow. "Done with your bath, I take it?"

Ymvesi'ia nodded, and Vise disappeared under the water for a few moments.

"You're still giving me a massage later," Vise said once she popped back out of the water, smoothing her hair back out of her face. "You're not the only one who has long days."

Ymvesi'ia grinned as they stepped out of the water. "Fine."

Vise crossed the room to where two fluffy towels laid out on the balcony in the sun and tossed one to Ymvesi'ia.

The warm fabric soaked up all the moisture on her body as she dragged it back and forth across her skin before tying her hair up within it.

Vise set a pot of tea over the fire, then came over with a bottle of moisturizing lotion that would keep her skin from drying out in the constant heat and sun. She poured some over Ymvesi'ia's shoulders, then smoothed it into her skin as it dripped down her back.

"You were right on one thing," Vise said. "If they're right, we need to move quickly to get everyone out in time."

Ymvesi'ia sighed. She'd trusted Vise's intuition and had promised she would listen to Koruuksi with an open mind, but a part of her did not want to face that reality.

"What about the Heart of the Vale?" she asked, "It has protected us from everything else that has tried to bring us harm."

Vise's hands stopped massaging the lotion into Ymvesi'ia's skin. She sighed. "I don't think it can protect us from this." She resumed her massage. "Try not to focus on that part, though."

Ymvesi'ia cocked her head. "What should I focus on, then?"

"The thought of seeing somewhere new," Vise said, a hint of longing in her voice. "Of being able to explore and go wherever you wish. Of not needing to live under such strict conditions to sustain our existence."

Ymvesi'ia glanced over at the pot of tea Vise had set over the fire. She felt Vise's gaze follow hers, even though she couldn't see it.

"You don't plan on ever bedding a man," Vise said, "yet you drink it every day like the rest of us because we need to plan even for possibilities we hope never happen. It's not the worst way to live, but those little things add up."

Ymvesi'ia reached over her shoulder to squeeze Vise's slippery hand. "I will meet with him tomorrow. I promise. But *only* because you think I should."

Vise squeezed her hand in return, then resumed the massage. Ymvesi'ia closed her eyes and tried to relax and focus on the positives of a new home. For the most part, she succeeded. By the time she and Vise switched places, almost all the tension of her day had disappeared.

The fear remained, however, stuffed back into the recess of her mind. The dread of what would happen if Koruuksi was right, and they acted too late.

E Kwekuue, her people's home and paradise for so long, would be a sanctuary no more.

17

Tower Six

Until one day when our Akjemasai encountered a party from a neighboring peoples, and instead of frightening them away or killing them all, they let one live: a young woman one of the Akjemasai judged deserving of mercy, and brought back into the city. The young woman and the Akjemasai who brought her to E Kwekuue survived only because the latter was the daughter of our king, and loved by many.

Exodus countdown: 15 days, 31 hours, 26 minutes

"Pardon, Mestari, you are asking permission to destroy my hangars and aircraft?"

Itese held in a snort at the Air Marshal's tone.

When he puts it that way...

"I'm doing you a courtesy by informing you of my plans, Marshal, not asking for permission. And I will only be destroying those you believe are obsolete or in need of renovation," Othaashle replied, voice holding a bit of the same amusement Itese felt.

The chill of the metal floor seemed to penetrate through the soles of her boots as she accompanied Othaashle and Marshal Jynos through Tower Six's hangar. Oil mixed with fumes from fuel and industrial cleaner, penetrating even through her helmet's ventilation as they passed by Tridents, 4-Tails, transports, and some newer, experimental aircraft. Each sat in its respective bay, most with mechanics performing routine maintenance on them.

Itese still found it hard to believe that these floating fortresses had once been made entirely out of ice, with people living in them for years at a time. The Imaia had gutted them, leaving only the ice and georaurals that maintained the overall structure. If deployed outside the city they would be incredibly energy inefficient—only able to operate for a short time without melting—but Boaathal's light kept the georaurals full, which ensured the ice remained as cold as though the fortress was still in Darkside waters.

"We need to create a diversion for the Remnant to get to their promised ship without too much trouble or attention," Othaashle elaborated, voice low enough so that only Itese and Jynos could hear. "The simplest way to do that is by setting off controlled explosions for our forces to respond to. However, we also want to do as little real damage to the city as possible."

The Air Marshal nodded. "And damage to a hangar could limit the number of fighters we send to intercept the Remnant and create a need for repairs or replacement ships. I see the reasoning, but—"

"If older ships or hangars happened to be damaged in the attack, Marshal," Itese interjected with a shrug, "then you could request newer, more up-to-date equipment for your airmen."

They walked in silence for a time as the Air Marshal considered, a hand to his chin, eyes downcast. Itese glanced at Othaashle. Her commander seemed to be scanning the hangar, so she did the same. Most of the airmen here tended to their ships in their standard-issue utilitarian jumpsuits, inspecting the aircraft and various points on the hangars, and walking this way and that on various assignments. Itese glanced at Othaashle again, knowing what she must be thinking. They didn't want to damage any of the ships if that meant casualties on their end. The massive doors that sealed off the hangar, however, were a prime target for their plan, and this hangar contained more functional fighters than transports or anything else. It would be a perfect distraction.

"I assume the Senti and Mkuutana are unaware of this... operation?" he asked eventually.

"The legislature knows nothing about this, and neither does the Council of Six," Othaashle confirmed. "Even the other members of High Command won't know, save for my adjuncts and yourself. Though I might need to read in Takina somewhat since we will need to use the outer hybrid hangars. However, Marshal, I believe that this will gain you greatest leverage to scrap obsolete equipment and gain the sympathy needed for the legislature itself to grant funding for new production."

The Air Marshal halted, raising an eyebrow at that. "That sounds like something I could agree to. I've also been meaning to discuss the conflicting responsibilities of the air force and the navy once we embark on Exodus. I know Kanysile believes she should assume command, as our spacecraft will technically still comprise a fleet, but my men have the experience operating the craft. I was thinking—"

Jynos cut off as Othaashle raised a hand. Itese smirked. Othaashle —and even Skadaatha before her—had done a remarkable job of cutting any undeserved legacies or bureaucrats from the ranks of the Imaia's armed forces, especially in the command structure. Neither of them could blame Jynos for trying to leverage his position in this case, however.

"I've thought up a few different ways to divide responsibilities and command, Marshal. They involve you and Kanysile proving who can adapt best to the new circumstances once we leave Efruumani behind. Do I have your permission to 'destroy your hangars and aircraft,' as you put it?"

The Marshal nodded. "Of course, Mestari. I'd like to discuss the details of that, though, if you wouldn't mind."

"Not at all. Let's talk while you show me a few of the prototypes your pilots have been testing."

Itese grinned. She'd never tried flying, but Othaashle loved it. She kept her tone reserved for Jynos, but she'd let that slip in front of

Itese a few times. For some reason, that had made Itese even more eager to serve the Imaia's Champion. She might be a living legend, but she still grew excited at things like Itese and everyone else.

The Air Marshal gestured toward that area of the hangar. Othaashle turned to Itese and handed her a small data drive. "Go to the control office and ask for the blueprints and maintenance assessments for all hangars within the city."

Itese took the drive, then saluted both Othaashle and Marshal Jynos before heading off in that direction. She tried not to make her pace seem too eager.

Downloading that information would mean accessing a terminal without the access restrictions in place on those within the archives on the Isle of the Redeemed. If she could gain access to one, she could search for files about the Redeemed without giving herself away.

About halfway to the control office, Itese thought she spotted someone familiar, a Natari man in a uniform that didn't quite fit as well as it should have. She stopped for a moment, looking again, but decided there were too many mechanics, engineers and airmen walking around for her to not have recognized at least one of them by site, and continued on toward the office.

The control room was like most in Mjatafa Mwonga, with six large displays for tactical information at one end of the room, and windows looking down on the hangar at the other. This was one of the few rooms that did not conform to the hexagonal architecture most followed, as a simple square was deemed more functional. Still, six hexagonal clusters of desks dotted the floor, uniformed officers with headsets working at their station computers. Balconies lined either side of the room, doors in the middle of them leading to the offices of the ranking personnel for the hangars. Imaia banners and symbols of the air force hung from them, with weapon racks beneath, just in case. From the entrance, the faint citrus of industrial cleaner tinged the air, but as Itese ventured toward the middle of the floor, that was quickly replaced by colognes, perfumes, and the natural odors of the sixty men and women that kept this hangar running.

Everyone stood at attention, snapping salutes within seconds of Itese entering the space. The rapid attention, as well as the mix of awe and nervousness on almost every face in the room almost made her sick. Itese had earned a formidable reputation on the battlefield, but she doubted any of these people knew who she was by sight. Even if they had, she knew it wasn't that. They looked at her this way because she was one of the Redeemed, and and it seemed even military personnel didn't how to act around Itese's or her people.

She snuffed out the impulse to snap at them. That would only add to their nervousness, which was the part that annoyed her. Itese knew her mask and mane didn't help, but it had been important for the first few Redeemed to cultivate as much mystery around them as they could to make them more intimidating to their enemies, and more heroic to those they protected. That would be especially important in the days to come when they searched for a new home among the stars.

Our role as symbols is more important than how I feel about the way they regard me.

It helped that Othaashle had plans to better integrate the Redeemed into daily Imaia society.

Itese rolled her eyes at the display but nodded to them as she made her way toward the nearest terminal. It was occupied, as they all were. The young man sitting at this one, however, had eyes as wide as saucers by the time Itese stopped next to his workstation.

"Airman Davara?" she asked, reading the man's name tag.

"Yes?" the airman asked. His freckled cheeks darkened a moment later. "Sorry, sir. Yes, that's me. Shaan Davara, I'm—uh..."

He trailed off for a moment, then took a deep breath and drew himself up. "What can I help you with, Redeemed?"

Itese took a moment to assess Shaan. He looked to be on the younger side, which matched up with his lower rank of airman. His particular brand of nervousness wasn't what Itese was used to. He seemed almost excited.

That would be a first.

Despite the man's scattered, unsure demeanor, his gold and black hair was held back in a tight, orderly bun, his uniform was pressed and clean, fitting him well with an orange bar on the left breast to mark his gemcrest and his workstation...

Itese cocked her head, leaning in as she moved around for a better view of the sketch pad on Airman Davara's desk.

"Is that a technical sketch?" Itese asked.

Airman Davara's cheeks grew dark again, and his hand darted halfway to the pad before he stopped it.

"Just a sketch, Redeemed."

"Itese."

"Sorry, Redeemed?"

"My name, Airman Davara," Itese said, "You may also refer to me as Adjunct Itese. What type of fighter is this? It looks a bit like a Trident-class, but not exactly."

"It isn't," Davara said. "Not a fighter, I mean. Well, not one that currently exists. I just like to sketch. Drawing things by sight or from memory is easy, so I thought I would try something new."

Itese gave the young man another look. "That is quite impressive, Airman."

"Thank you, Redeemed," he said, cheeks growing dark again. "Redeemed Itese. Sorry, sir."

"Relax, Airman. We don't bite. That's what the masks are for."

Davara's eyes widened again.

Itese held in a sigh. "That was a joke, Airman."

Somehow, the man's cheeks grew even darker. "Oh, right."

He relaxed. Barely.

"Redeemed, Itese? Not that I don't enjoy compliments about my sketches, but is there something you wished of me?"

Right.

Itese nodded, holding out the drive. "I need you to copy files onto this that contain blueprints and maintenance assessments for all hangars in the city, active and inactive."

The man nodded, taking the drive, suddenly all business. "Yes, Redeemed Itese."

As Shaan inserted the drive and pulled up an instance of the digitized military archives, Itese reached for the man's sketchpad.

She noticed the airman tense.

"Do you mind if I look?"

Davara gave her a nervous smile. "Not at all."

Nervous because of me? Or what I'll think of his art?

Itese quickly decided it was the former as she flipped through the sketchpad. There were a few pages with various sketches, notes and diagrams of different aircraft and trans atmospheric vehicles, all skillfully done, if not always realistic or practical. When she reached the section with sketches of people, however, Itese felt her jaw drop.

"These are incredible," she breathed.

Looking around, Itese found that Davara had sketched a few of his fellow soldiers. There was something about the drawings that made them seem more, though. More passionate or heroic.

"Thank you," the airman said.

Itese smirked at the hint of embarrassment in his voice and set down the sketchpad, finished looking through it.

A few minutes later, Davara handed the drive back to Itese. "That should be everything you need, Redeemed Itese."

"Thank you," Itese said, taking the drive. She did not pocket it yet, however, instead looking around the room. Still no open terminals.

"Would you like to deliver this back to Commander Othaashle, personally?" Itese asked, brightening her yellownodes for a little luck as she returned her attention to the young man.

Davara's eyes bulged. "The Mestari? She requested this?"

Itese nodded, holding out the drive. "I'll watch your station."

The man took the drive, then stood, shooting a wide grin at Itese before rushing off into the hangar.

His excitement was almost enough to make Itese feel bad about deceiving the airman.

Just to be safe, she remained standing for a bit. Once she was sure no one was actively paying attention to her, she sat down, facing the terminal. In his haste, Airman Davara had left an instance of the archives open. Exactly as Itese had hoped.

Itese pulled out her own drive and connected with the terminal, then began searching, keeping her yellownodes at a low burn. After a moment, she brightened her ambernodes as well to process the information faster.

She looked for information on Phantom and Symuuna Team first, then the battles following Kojatere's defeat and Othaashle's appearance. At first glance, nothing looked particularly helpful, but Itese downloaded all of them. She would likely need to study these and let the information within direct her to other files that would hopefully have what she needed. That way she wouldn't need to spend too much time looking here or at the central archives.

Retrieving the drive, Itese stood and slipped it into her pocket. She picked up Davara's sketches again to occupy herself

Itese's decision to skim and download the files rather than trying to look through them proved the right one a few minutes later when Airman Davara returned to the room, beaming. He strode over to Itese and saluted before extending a hand.

"Thank you, Redeemed Itese," Shaan Davara said, still beaming, "for that and for all you and your people do for the Imaia."

Not for the first time, Itese wished for the ability to smile through her mask. She set the sketchpad back down and shook the airman's hand.

"It was my pleasure, Airman Davara."

18

A Different World

Though both were almost executed anyway, Princess Ymbandi used her influence with her father and the Buuekwenani to sway opinion and judgement in her favor. Princess Ymbandi worked with the foreigner, Taatuube Rabesala, an influential woman among her own people, the Uumgwefili, to reach an accord between our two people. The Uumgwefili would keep our secret and help protect our interests in addition to supplying us with information of the outside world. All in exchange for aluminum and sanctuary, should they ever need it.

Exodus countdown: 14 days, 14 hours, 17 minutes

Koruuksi tried not to fidget as Vise approached him and Uuchantuu from across the plaza. It was shaded for once, as pink, puffy clouds hung in the sky above them. He couldn't remember the last time he'd seen clouds that large.

Vise wore an assortment of jewelry about her wrists, neck and ankles, a maopa wrap of various shades of violet and sandals of a darker leather along with her customary amused smile. Koruuksi hoped that was a good sign after the way she'd left the day before, but flirting and smiling seemed to be something she did just as easily as Koruuksi could spew out words.

"Thank you both for meeting me," Vise said as she came within earshot.

Koruuksi opened his mouth, ready to apologize, but Vise gestured for them to follow her, not breaking stride. "I wanted to show you the markets today. I know you've had some of our food, but you need to try something fresh. Some don keb, perhaps? Or kebab?"

Koruuksi's mouth started to water. He remembered having those with her friends.

She eyed Koruuksi and then Uuchantuu. "I'm assuming you don't have things like that where you come from."

Uuchantuu shook her head and Koruuksi fished a ration packet out of one of the pouches at his belt.

"These are about as good as it gets," he said. "Nutritious, high calorie, high energy, long lasting, and a *very* acquired taste."

Vise laughed at that. "That sounds terrible."

She grabbed both him and Uuchantuu by the wrist. "Come, let's get you something real to eat."

Koruuksi exchanged a look with Uuchantuu, both their eyes darting back and forth between each other and Vise's hands, but they shrugged and let the woman tug them along.

When they rounded a corner, color overwhelmed Koruuksi. It filled the market, different shades and hues running together with no sense of reason, and it was wonderful. A few shops along the edges had permanent, stone structures, but most were stands made of wood and colorful canvas. As he and Uuchantuu followed Vise through the conflicting currents of people, a few stopping to greet her or offer her something, Koruuksi got a better look at the design of a few of the stands, noting fine metalwork and hinges near the joints.

They're collapsible.

He'd heard that these markets set up quite frequently, but something about this one seemed different—those that Vise's friends had taken him to for some street food hadn't been this extensive or overwhelming. Spices and the sizzling scent of cooking meats cut through the odor of so many bodies so close together as they passed stall after stall of smiling people and finely crafted goods. When he asked about it, Vise explained that the market was permanent, but most of the vendors circulated daily. The more permanent structures were those shared by a few different families and vendors, or those that required larger or more specialized equipment to run, while the collapsible stalls were those that changed out daily.

They stopped at one of the stands with no line or crowd, where an older, squat man—for a Natari, at least—tended to a pile of sizzling meat and vegetables on a smooth metal plate, with a few long skewers of larger pieces of food grilling off to one side. Vise greeted the man with a warm smile and ordered them some food. The man handed her five of the skewers, calling them kebab, and scooped some of the sizzling pile of food onto three circles of flatbread, drizzling some sort of sauce over them before wrapping them up and handing them to Vise. She thanked him, then distributed them to Koruuksi and Uuchantuu as they walked away, deeper into the market. Koruuksi glanced back at the man and his stand a few times, still unable to fully grasp the lack of any exchange of goods. The Remnant didn't use currency, but that was due to everything being rationed. He was about to ask Vise about it again when she interrupted his thoughts.

"How do you eat with that thing?" Vise asked, gesturing to his mask.

"Carefully," Koruuksi said, tugging his hood forward a bit and taking a small piece of the kebab in his fingers. He used the backs of his fingers to push the mask out just a bit and slipped the bite between his lips.

Vise gazed at him with wide-eyes. "That looks terrible. Come on —the clothing market is more shaded."

Koruuksi looked to Uuchantuu, a few spots of shade nearby, then to Vise. "Why the clothing market?"

Vise rolled her eyes and gestured at Uuchantuu. "Because she needs something nicer to wear. I haven't figured out what to do about you yet, but we're getting her something lighter and more comfortable to wear."

Koruuksi looked to Uuchantuu, who seemed to be hiding a grin. He shrugged and gestured toward the way Vise had pointed. "Lead the way."

Vise grinned and darted off at a trot. They followed her past various shops and stalls—and more mouth-watering scents—until she stopped for just a moment before an actual storefront rather than a stand. Vise barely gave Koruuksi any time to take in the shop's outer façade, pulling him and Uuchantuu in after her. As soon as he was inside, however, he found it hard to care. The cool air was immediately apparent, and even the humidity seemed to have dropped somehow. Koruuksi noted a few georaurals at intervals along the wall.

And the lights. The room was far dimmer than any he'd entered since coming to this city, illuminated only by the light in the cracks around the window shutters and Auroralight lamps. He checked first, of course, just in case, then removed his mask and grinned, taking in a deep breath as he threw back his hood and loosened the laces at his chest. He caught Uuchantuu's grin out of the corner of his eye as Vise disappeared into a collection of mannequins dressed in different wraps, calling out something in Buuekwenani. Koruuksi was surprised to find a few with torsos, displaying what could only be ornamental mantels and drapes that would barely cover the chest and shoulders. Bolts of cloth in myriad colors and tones hung from bars bolted to the bare stone walls, almost like decorations.

Another voice called back from deeper within the shop. A few moments later, an older woman stepped out from the mannequins and racks of cloth. She wore a dark green high-waisted wrap that covered a bit more of her thighs than Vise's, with a matching headband, and had the height, dark eyes, strong features, and deep red skin with black stripes that Koruuksi had learned were common among the Buuekwenani.

She and Vise went to the windows, closing them tight before Vise brought the woman over to Koruuksi and Uuchantuu and introduced them.

"This is Afria," Vise said. "Her Atongo is a bit rusty."

Koruuksi took off his mask and hood and gave the woman a smile. "Pleased to meet you."

Uuchantuu echoed him.

The woman smiled, then eyed him and Uuchantuu up and down. Koruuksi blinked. The woman's gaze made him feel like she'd catalogued everything about him. Including things he didn't even know. She turned to Vise and they began exchanging words in the Buuekwenani tongue.

Koruuksi nodded.

"I haven't figured out what to do with him yet," Vise said. "He needs to be fully covered at all times, but I have some ideas for her."

Uuchantuu shot Koruuksi a wary glance at that. "I'm about to be a dress-up doll, aren't I?"

Koruuksi rolled his eyes, grinning. "Don't act like you won't like the new clothes."

"It's the poking and prodding part that I'm not a fan of. And the clothing around here is a bit more... revealing than I'm used to."

Koruuksi barked a laugh, catching Vise and Afria's attention.

"Something funny?" Vise asked.

Koruuksi grinned, pushing Uuchantuu toward them. "You'll see."

As Afria shuffled Uuchantuu toward a raised platform near the middle of the room, Koruuksi popped the last of his kebab into his mouth. It *was* quite good. He had no clue what was in it, but found it hard to care.

"You live in a pretty amazing world," Koruuksi said as Vise approached. He held up the empty skewer. "And this is fantastic. I'm tempted to try and suck the juice out of the wood."

Vise giggled. "I thought you would like it. Assyn and Babanir said you didn't really eat much when you spent time with them."

"Spying on me?"

Vise just grinned.

Koruuksi had figured that was the purpose of her introducing him to her friends—one of whom was a guard and therefore friends or at least colleagues with Ymvesi'ia. He didn't mind, though, as it wasn't incredibly devious.

"About yesterday—" he began.

Vise waved him off, smiling at him as she patted him on the arm. "Don't worry about it, alright?"

The smile was genuine, but just a bit off.

Koruuksi searched for something to say—anything that might get her to open up a bit more without being too direct—but Uuchantuu and Afria came back out into the shop's main room, the latter carrying a few bundles of fine fabrics while Uuchantuu wore a plan white garment of the same cut as Afria's wrap. Other than that, she wore only a frown, arms crossed tight over her chest.

"It's a fitting cloth," Vise explained. "Afria will use a few of those to get the cut and measurements right, and the other cloth will be to see how well the colors match her skin, eyes and hair."

Koruuksi nodded, grinning. Uuchantuu glared at him.

Vise looked between them, raising an eyebrow. "Am I missing something?"

"Uuchantuu likes to keep covered up."

"Even in this heat?"

Koruuksi nodded.

Vise frowned, looking to Uuchantuu, then down at her own breasts as Afria made a few measurements. Koruuksi nearly lost it, looking away when she hefted one in each hand while frowning at Uuchantuu. "They're just breasts."

Koruuksi didn't think he'd ever seen Uuchantuu's face turn that particular shade of purple. He still couldn't resist.

"And nothing I and the rest of the team haven't seen before."

Uuchantuu balled her hands into fists at her sides as she stomped on the platform, letting out a huff. "That's not the same, and you know it."

Koruuksi just smirked at her.

It took her a moment, but Uuchantuu went even darker purple, the flush spreading to her exposed chest when she realized what she'd done, quickly folding her arms again.

Vise laughed. "Don't worry, Uuchantuu, I think we can work something out."

She said something to Afria that caused the woman to straighten with a confused expression on her face, and it took a bit of back and forth before Afria sighed and turned back to Uuchantuu and ushered her toward the back of the store.

"What did you tell her?"

Vise shrugged. "To come up with something that covers her chest so she will be comfortable, but still works with her figure.

Koruuksi nodded, grinning as Afria began the poking and prodding.

"Koruuksi?" Vise said in a lower voice.

He glanced over at her. "Yes?"

"Don't try to manipulate me into anything like that again."

Koruuksi grimaced. "You saw through that, did you?"

Vise nodded.

Koruuksi sighed. "It won't happen again. Not on purpose, at least. I'll try to make sure it doesn't happen by accident either. Sometimes it's the only way we can get things done. My sister is a bit bull-headed. Like Ymvesi'ia, but angrier. Sometimes—most of the time, actually—the only way to get her to engage about something she doesn't want to is to manipulate her into bringing it up. It won't happen again, though."

Vise smiled at him. "Good."

They stood in silence for a short time after that, watching as Afria led Vise back out and onto the pedestal, this time wearing a deep blue wrap that fit her far better than the white one. Afria took a few other pieces of similarly colored cloth, draping them over Koruuksi's friend as Uuchantuu's frown turned to a pout. Eventually, Afria turned toward them and said something to Vise.

"She's done," Vise translated.

Koruuksi looked Uuchantuu up and down and grinned. Afria hadn't altered much of the wrap Uuchantuu had originally come out in, though she'd added a mantle that came down just far enough to cover her chest. The blue looked good on her. Glancing down at his hands, Koruuksi noted it was very close to his own skin tone.

"Isn't this showing a bit too much skin?" Uuchantuu asked.

Koruuksi snorted, earning a glare from her while Vise circled the pedestal, inspecting Uuchantuu.

"You need to relax," Vise said. "This clothing is light enough to let you move and keep you cool in the heat and humidity, and it looks fantastic on you."

Uuchantuu looked between Vise and Afria, a hint of a smile tugging at her cheek. "You really think so?"

Vise nodded.

Africa rolled her eyes and said something to Vise. Uuchantuu looked at her expectantly.

"Of course, it does," Vise said. "Even with that silly part covering your chest. Afria wouldn't let you leave this shop if you wore something that didn't enhance your natural beauty."

Koruuksi kept himself from laughing at how dark his friend's face grew. It was nice to see her get pampered for once.

"You."

Koruuksi turned to find Afria standing next to him, analyzing him with that discerning gaze. She plucked his mask out of his hands, then fingered his hood and mantle before saying something to Vise.

"You need to have these on at all times when in the sun?"

Koruuksi nodded. "I need all of my skin covered."

"Hmm, so it is true, then. How thick does the cloth need to be?"

Koruuksi shrugged. "As long as you can't see through it, I will be fine." He gestured to Uuchantuu. "That fabric is probably as thin as I can go, though it might be pushing it."

Vise blinked.

"Wait, can you see through this?"

Koruuksi grinned. It grew even wider when he noticed Vise's laughter. Afria waved her off, then eyed his antlers. She pointed to them, asking Vise something. The woman laughed as she answered, nodding.

"She asked if they were permanent," Vise explained when Koruuksi caught her eye.

Afria said something else, and Vise translated again.

"She has a few ideas she can try out, but it will take a bit longer than she did."

"I'll make sure he returns so you can try them out," Vise said. "Right now, these two have somewhere to be."

She turned to Uuchantuu and gestured for her to follow.

"Wait, what about my clothes?" Uuchantuu asked.

Vise translated for Afria, then laughed at Uuchantuu as the seamstress rolled her eyes.

"Those *are* your clothes, Uuchantuu."

Afria started up again.

"Your figure will hold up that wrap without any modifications so long as you don't try to run or do anything too athletic in it."

"What about my other clothes?" Uuchantuu asked.

Vise translated, and Afria sighed, rolling her eyes. After a moment, she walked to the back of the building and came out a few minutes later with a bundle of clothing.

Koruuksi took them and folded them up before Uuchantuu could take them.

She glared at him, face dark.

"You should wear that the rest of the day," he said, grinning. "What's the use in getting new clothes if you don't let everyone see them?"

Her face grew even darker.

Koruuksi had to raise a hand to his face to keep himself from laughing.

Vise thanked the woman and led them out of the shop. Koruuksi frowned at that, though Uuchantuu's nervousness soon distracted him.

"Uuchantuu," Vise said, slinging her arm around Uuchantuu's shoulder's and drawing her close. "Relax. You're far more covered up than anyone in the Vale save for any on-duty *Akjemasai*. If anyone looks at you, they'll be looking at your clothing, not the skin you think it should be covering."

Uuchantuu swallowed, but nodded and drew her shoulders back, standing a little straighter.

Vise raised an eyebrow at her and Uuchantuu shrugged.

"I guess it's a start," Vise said "We'll just need to have some thibara with our meal."

Uuchantuu raised an eyebrow, looking between Koruuksi and Vise.

"Alcohol," he explained before turning to Vise. "Is that where we're going? To get some food?"

Vise nodded, smiling. "I could use some food, and I'm guessing the kebab and don keb didn't really fill you up."

Uuchantuu shrugged. "I could eat."

Vise grinned and walked between them, putting a hand on the small of Koruuksi's back and pushing him forward, along with Uuchantuu.

Koruuksi breathed in deep as they entered the restaurant and found his mouth watering. Vise led them past tables of people, some laughing and speaking for any to overhear while others engaged in quiet conversation. He noted how many smiled and waved when they noticed her, especially the men. Earthen, nutty spices made his nose flare in anticipation, and he thought he caught the scent of a few different meats cooking, and—his eyes bulged as he looked to the surrounding tables, then touched Vise's arm. She turned to him with an expectant look. "Is that fresh bread baking?" he asked.

Vise grinned, nodding, and led them deeper into the restaurant to help them order their food.

"You really don't pay for anything here, do you?" Koruuksi asked as they sat down with two cups of fine metal-and-glasswork each. One filled with sweet thibara, the other with water. After looking around to make sure they were far enough under the building to avoid direct light, Koruuksi took off his hood and mask and hung the latter from his shirt before undoing a few of the ties on the front.

Vise raised an eyebrow. "We don't need to. Is money really so important where you come from?"

Koruuksi shook his head. "The Remnant is a military body, and since we don't really have the ability to set up much infrastructure or means of production, everything is rationed. But money used to drive everything in the world. I've read enough to know that it played a large factor in how the Imaia turned certain corporations or even entire nations to their side against the Union. Surely you experienced some of that mentality when you traded with Uumgwefilo."

Vise nodded. "That all stopped a long time ago, but yes, we did. It's just hard to wrap my head around. I do remember reading about how confused the Uumgwefili first were when we told them their coin was no good to us."

Uuchantuu snorted. "I would have liked to see that."

Koruuksi looked to Vise to find her eyes on him. He followed her gaze down to the sliver of exposed blue skin at his chest, a line of lighter skin running through it. He looked back to Vise and raised an eyebrow. When she looked up and realized he was looking at her, rather than blushing as Uuchantuu would have, she raised an eyebrow and grinned in return.

Koruuksi's cheeks grew hot.

Was that a challenge?

"Uh... you two need a minute?" Uuchantuu asked.

Vise turned her grin on Uuchantuu. "Just seeing if I could make him blush—he's a bit more difficult than you."

Koruuksi eyed Vise, not entirely sure about that.

As one of the restaurant staff brought them their food—some sort of chicken dish with vegetables and a sauce similar to whatever the vendor had drizzled on their snacks earlier—Koruuksi thought about how Vise had been acting since she met up with them.

She flirts to deflect when she's nervous or doesn't want to talk about something.

Just like how he usually started running his mouth.

"You mentioned your sister earlier," Vise said once they had their food and the staff member was out of earshot. "Older or younger?"

"Older," Koruuksi said, taking a drink in each hand and brightening his violetnodes to chill them.

"And perpetually angry?"

Koruuksi barely stopped himself from launching into some tangent to get away from the topic.

She deserves some honesty after I manipulated her.

He nodded, taking Uuchantuu's drinks, then Vise's to cool them as well. "Not entirely undeserved. She's not my sister by blood—my brother's widow—but she's treated me like something between a kid brother and a son for most of my life, so I just think of her as my sister."

Vise's face fell. "I'm sorry for your loss."

Koruuksi shrugged. "You don't need to be, I'm used to dealing with it."

They ate in silence for a while before Vise spoke again.

"How do you deal with it?"

Koruuksi looked up from his food, raising an eyebrow. He swallowed his current mouthful of food and washed it down with some of the thibara.

Light, that's good.

"With Svemakuu's—my brother's—death?"

Vise started to shake her head, then stopped "No, but... well, I guess that might be part of it. How do you deal with...?" She paused, looking around, then leaned in. "If the world really is ending, and you've known about it for some time now..."

She trailed off, leaning back and looking down into her food.

Koruuksi looked to Uuchantuu. The despair in Vise's voice made his chest tight. He knew that tone all too well.

Koruuksi nudged Vise's chilled thibara a bit closer to her and grinned when she looked up at him.

"That helps a bit," he said. "Just to take the edge off sometimes. The soul-crushing weight of existential threats requires a mix of a few different tactics to bear correctly, however."

Vise took a sip of her drink, then blinked, holding it up a bit to study it, then looking at Koruuksi. "That must come in handy."

He grinned, then looked to Uuchantuu and held up one finger. "There's dark humor. That's the easiest one and the common go-to for most of us."

Uuchantuu grinned. "Old age, for instance—if we manage to escape the world's end, we'll have that terrifying future to live through."

Koruuksi shuddered, looking to Vise. "I know I'm charming, but there's only so far that can go once I get all pale and wrinkly."

"Don't forget about your hair falling out," Uuchantuu reminded him.

Koruuksi narrowed his eyes. "Or yours."

That made Vise crack a smile, if a small one.

He held up a second finger. "Then there's just not thinking about it and finding distractions. Watching Uuchantuu turn sixty different shades of red while trying on clothing was working very well, as was this food and your company until you decided to get all depressing."

Vise frowned. "I—"

Koruuksi cut her off with a third finger. "Then there's just rolling with it. Knowing it is going to happen and, in some ways, there isn't much you can do about it, so you just don't worry about it. I would suggest that method or the dark humor for you right now."

A bit of the light returned to Vise's eyes.

Koruuksi lifted a fourth finger, but Uuchantuu cut him off.

"Then there's looking at the positive end of things. Koruuksi isn't the best at it, but it's doable. Instead of thinking about how the world is going to end, I can focus on how great this food is. Just like I can focus on how pretty these clothes are and not on how much of my skin they show."

Koruuksi grinned and took another bite of his food as Vise laughed at that.

"You do look very good in them," Vise said, "Though it would look better without the top part."

Koruuksi almost choked on his food at how purple Uuchantuu's face turned. She slapped him on the back a few times, a few of them a bit more forceful than absolutely necessary.

Vise handed him his glass of water while grinning at Uuchantuu. "You make it too easy, Uuchantuu."

Koruuksi washed down the rest of his food, coughing a few times as Uuchantuu continued. "The last tactic is working toward a goal. It's easier to not feel crushed under the world's end all the time if you're trying to do something about it."

Vise gave both of them a tight smile. "Thank you. I think I'll give that last one a try for right now."

She looked past them and nodded.

Koruuksi turned and looked over his shoulder to see a Buuekwenani woman walking toward their table. He almost didn't recognize her until he met her eyes.

Ymvesi'ia.

Koruuksi frowned, fingers tightening around his cup.

Instead of the white clothing she'd worn when ambushing them in the forest or the finery she'd worn in the palace, Ymvesi'ia wore a simple maopa of rich, golden brown with no anklets or bracelets, just two small aluminum earrings in each ear. One pair held small ovals of jasper, the other some sort of lapis. She didn't wear any necklaces, but with a full gemcrest that sparkled with aurora light, she hardly needed to. Somehow, the simple change in clothes made her seem less standoffish.

Koruuksi glanced at Uuchantuu and rolled his eyes at the heat in her cheeks and how intensely focused she suddenly decided to become on her food. When he met Vise's eyes, she glanced to Ymvesi'ia and back to him, then smirked.

Koruuksi frowned.

"What was that you said about manipulating people?"

Vise raised an eyebrow. "That *you* shouldn't do it. I said nothing about me. Play nice. I asked her to hear you out."

Koruuksi rolled his eyes, then turned to Ymvesi'ia as she came around the table.

You need her on your side. No matter how much of an asshole she was.

He started to rise, meeting Ymvesi'ia's gaze, but she held up a hand and shook her head.

"Please," she said, taking a seat next to Vise. "I do not need all the attention that will attract. I came here to speak with the two of you, not everyone else."

Koruuksi eyed her, then looked around, trying to pick out anyone new in the restaurant.

"What?" she asked.

"Trying to find your guards," he said, glancing back at her. "Your Akjemasai."

Ymvesi'ia frowned, "Akjemasai? Why would I need guards to accompany me to a restaurant?"

Koruuksi peered at her for a moment before shaking his head and taking a deep breath, "Right, I forgot. Different world here."

Ymvesi'ia and Vise exchanged a glance and Vise shrugged. "You remember how the Uumgwefili used to do that, right?"

Ymvesi'ia frowned but nodded.

"I wanted to apologize for how I first acted," Ymvesi'ia said, turning her attention to Koruuksi and Uuchantuu—mostly Uuchantuu. "When I saw your weapons and heard your claims about why you were here, I assumed your intentions were malicious, and believed I was acting in the best interest of my people by not welcoming you to my home. The outside world has not been kind to us for the majority of my life. I say this not to excuse my actions but explain."

Koruuksi had to hold in a grin as Ymvesi'ia spoke almost entirely to Uuchantuu. He wanted to be annoyed with the woman, but he'd be a hypocrite if he blamed her for the sins of her parents.

"I want to apologize, too," he forced out. "I wasn't as gracious for your hospitality as I should have been."

Ymvesi'ia looked to him, blinking as though she'd forgotten he was there, then looked between him and Uuchantuu and nodded, a slight smile on her lips. "Thank you."

"We are here to help," he assured her.

Uuchantuu nodded. "We've had our fill of fighting and conflict and intrigue. We just want to do something good for a change."

Ymvesi'ia glanced back at Uuchantuu and a hint of sadness

entered her eyes. Not pity, but an understanding of that weight and desire. She looked to Vise then, who nodded, and back to Koruuksi and Uuchantuu.

"I want you to explain to me what you told Vise," she said. "I want all the technical, esoteric details of what you believe will happen."

She put a hand on Vise's. "She has a better knowledge of physics and the sciences than myself, but I spent the morning refreshing my memory."

Koruuksi stuffed the last bite of food into his mouth, then nodded as he washed it down with his water.

"We'd be happy to," he said, then glanced around at the restaurant. "Do you want us to do so here, or...?"

Ymvesi'ia looked around, then shook her head, "No, you are right. We should go somewhere a bit more private."

Koruuksi downed the last of his thibara—with the food and water, it was barely enough to give him a faint buzz—and waited for a moment as Vise and Uuchantuu finished the last bits of their own food. Once they were done, he put on his mask, earning a curious look from Ymvesi'ia.

"It is true then?" she asked. "People with your skin tone must cover up in the sun?"

Koruuksi nodded, closing back up his shirt. "Unfortunately."

The woman eyed him for a moment, her eyes darting to his antlers a few times, then nodded. "I will make sure we talk somewhere with plenty of shade, then."

"Thank you."

When Vise stood up, she picked up her plate and gestured for Koruuksi and Uuchantuu to follow. He took a few quick steps to get close to her before Uuchantuu could catch up.

He leaned in close to Vise. "You got her all dressed up on purpose, didn't you?"

Vise smirked. "What, I can't have my fun? You saw the way she looked at her back at the palace."

Koruuksi snorted.

"What are you two talking about?"

Vise turned to Uuchantuu as she caught up. "Just explaining to Koruuksi how things work here. We're going to return the dishes and let Fafa, the chef, know just how much you enjoyed his food."

"And there's no payment?" Koruuksi asked.

Vise rolled her eyes. "That *is* the payment."

"What about the staff?" Uuchantuu asked.

"Volunteers," Vise said "He makes them some special treats in thanks for helping him out. Now come on, let's not leave Ymvesi'ia waiting too long."

Koruuksi glanced over his shoulder at the princess.

I hope she takes it as well as Vise did.

YMVESI'IA SAT at the edge of one of the canals, toes dangling just above the surface, trying not to shake. The clouds had opened up in a light drizzle, the tiny droplets creating patterns of ripples on the water.

A soft hand squeezed her shoulder. Ymvesi'ia looked up to find sympathy on Vise's face as her friend peered down at her.

"I know it's a lot," she said.

Ymvesi'ia nodded, looking at Koruuksi and Uuchantuu.

Koruuksi seemed so out of place with his emotionless mask and all of his skin hidden, though not nearly as intimidating as when she'd first seen him in the forest, or in the palace even after the Akjemasai had disarmed him. He no longer matched Uuchantuu now that she'd adopted Buuekwenani clothing.

Ymvesi'ia's face warmed as she glanced at the petite, red-skinned woman, trying not to be too obvious. The way Uuchantuu had stared at her in the palace had made Ymvesi'ia uncomfortable, but mostly because of how warm it made her feel all over. The woman's prominent nose and full lips drew Ymvesi'ia's gaze like a lodestone. Now that she wore clothing that didn't conceal her sleek, muscular figure, Ymvesi'ia had an even harder time not staring at the woman. That Uuchantuu was so concerned about making sure her clothing covered as much of her as possible—especially the mantle—made it even worse. Ymvesi'ia found it adorable.

You're supposed to be thinking about more important things than a beautiful woman.

Ymvesi'ia sighed. Thinking about Uuchantuu was so much easier.

What they'd told her about Efruumani's place in their planetary system and their scientists' projections once the Imaia left terrified her.

Efruumani is not a planet, but a habitable moon of Myrskaan, tidally locked between Myrskaan and their system's star at one of the gas giant's LaGrange points, allowing it to keep a steady orbit and stay within the habitable zone despite the fact that those are incredibly unstable. The World Trees must be what stabilized Efruumani, and if both of them were no longer on the planet...

Ymvesi'ia shivered. It seemed too fantastical to be true, yet with her recent research on the topic, she knew it was true. That made it all the more horrific. She tried to find holes in their science or their logic but found she couldn't. They'd answered all the clarifications and questions with a confident, yet almost resigned manner.

She sighed, and looked to her companions. "So the world really is ending, then?"

All three nodded.

"And you have known this since Kweshrima destroyed Yrmuunthal?" she asked, looking to Koruuksi. "Why did you still follow her? Why did you not just join the Imaia after her betrayal?"

Uuchantuu's face fell a bit, and Koruuksi's shoulders sagged.

"We knew something was wrong with the world very soon after Yrmuunthal was... after she destroyed it," Koruuksi said. "It was at least a year or two before we found out that Kweshrima was responsible."

Koruuksi paused head cocking as a group of violet timeoruu lazily floated past, spelling out the exact amount of time it had been. Ymvesi'ia thought she could see Koruuksi tracking the spirits. When she glanced at Uuchantuu, Ymvesi'ia found the petite woman doing the same, a tight expression on her features.

"By that point, there was no going to the Imaia unless we wanted to end up dead, imprisoned, or worse," Koruuksi continued, "and not many would have wanted to. The fighting had grown even more bitter by then."

Ymvesi'ia nodded. She could understand that.

"Kweshrima was all we had by that point," Uuchantuu said. "No home, no nation, no World Tree, barely any leadership... it doesn't excuse our actions, though."

"We hope that helping your people escape Efruumani's fate will at least start us on the path toward redemption," Koruuksi said. "It's the closest we've come to doing something good without needing to justify the means we take or make some argument about how it is just something necessary."

Ymvesi'ia looked between him and Uuchantuu. Their explanation was sound, but the haunted pain in their eyes was what sold her. "I believe you."

She glanced to Vise. "Auroras, you were right. I believe them."

Vise gaze her a reassuring smile and squeezed her hand.

"So you will help us?" Koruuksi asked.

Ymvesi'ia didn't respond immediately. She'd initially challenged Koruuksi out of her duty to her people. Would she be a hypocrite for turning that decision around and aiding him?

He's trying to help, and the threat is real. I need to do something about that, and he is the best avenue.

Ymvesi'ia met Koruuksi's gaze and nodded. "I can find some volunteers to help with your attack on the Imaia's city. Getting my people to leave, however..."

"That is our main goal," Uuchantuu said. "We welcome the help with our distraction, but our main concern is getting your people to safety."

She sighed but smiled at Uuchantuu. The other woman's cheeks darkened as she returned the expression. "That will take some delicate work. You must advise your people to be a bit more subtle in their conversations about why they are here. Now that he has made his decision, my father will be quite angry if he discovers that you are still working toward your goal after he made his mind known to you. He would likely rescind the hospitality he has offered you."

Koruuksi nodded. "We can do that." He paused, looking between her and Vise. "Do you think we have a chance?"

Ymvesi'ia nodded. "I can take you to the Diwani—the council members. We will need to be quiet about it, but if we can convince each of them, they can overrule my father."

"That is the better option, anyway," Vise said. "The people respect your father, but if he asked them all to pack up and leave without the support of the council, not everyone would do so willingly. If he and the Diwani are united in this..." She shrugged. "Some will likely still drag their feet, but most will pick up on the urgency of the situation."

Ymvesi'ia eyed Koruuksi as Vise spoke.

That way he looks at her.

Even though the mask obscured his face, Ymvesi'ia found she could tell through the man's posture. It didn't seem like the usual appreciation Vise received from most people, but something more interested, more intense.

Koruuksi's masked face turned to Ymvesi'ia, catching her. She didn't let her embarrassment show on her face.

"There is one other thing," he said slowly. "Kweshrima told us to see if we could find...whatever it was that keeps this place safe and makes it what it is. She said it would make finding a suitable world to call our new home much easier once we leave Efruumani."

Ymvesi'ia swallowed and exchanged a look with Vise. Her friend looked as troubled as she felt by his question.

He means the Heart of the Vale... but how could that make finding a new home easier? It did not call to us—we found it by accident. Something to do with the spirits, maybe?

"That," she began, choosing her words carefully, "is something you will need both Kuula'ande's and the Diwani's united support on as well. And I would caution you not to bring it up until they have decided that we do, in fact need to leave. I would help you with that if I could, but it is beyond me. For now, let us focus on the Diwani. Vise and I will need to do some research on how best to plead our case, and I will schedule the meetings immediately."

Koruuksi's masked face stared at her for a moment. Then he nodded, head wobbling, "Thank you."

As Ymvesi'ia looked between the two of them, she saw some of the pain in Uuchantuu's eyes fade, replaced by hope. Koruuksi's shoulders seemed less bowed than before. When Ymvesi'ia met Uuchantuu's gaze, a warm smile spread across the woman's face, and Ymvesi'ia thought she caught a hint of something new in the woman's golden-brown eyes. Something that made her blood run hot, and her heart beat a bit faster.

"How can we help in the mean time?" Uuchantuu asked.

19

Fundamentals

Despite some initial back and forth, the arrangement resulted in prosperity for both peoples. The Uumgwefili helped create the illusion that the mountains and forest surrounding E Kwekuue were undesirable land and hid the caravans that flowed between the two people, running everything out of their nearby city, Uumgwefilo. Taatuube's family ensured that the rulers of that city saw guarding E Kwekuue's secret as a near-holy cause, and made sure everyone privileged to such information understood that the relationship with E Kwekuue was Uumgwefilo's lifeblood.

Exodus countdown: 15 days, 33 hours, 28 minutes

Estingai woke to the soft rustling of cloth and clinking of metal buckles. She carefully reached for the dagger under her pillow before remembering where she was, and that she'd set her equipment leaning against the wall next to her.

She had to take a deep breath to help swallow her frustration. Matsanga or his pet would likely be alerted to any intruders long before her, but she still didn't like the thought of growing lax.

Cracking one eye open, Estingai found Matsanga shrugging on a cloak and shouldering the massive bow he carried. She realized he was singing to himself. Voice so soft she could barely make out the lyrics.

Estingai pushed herself into a seated position, stifling a yawn.

"Trying to sneak out before I woke up?"

Matsanga paused in readying himself, though only for a moment "You're a light sleeper."

"My life doesn't leave me much choice in that. Aquanodes help, too."

Matsanga grunted.

Estingai frowned, though Matsanga still had his back to her. Movement pulled her gaze to his large wolf, and she found the creature studying her again. Estingai turned her frown on it for a moment, narrowing her eyes, then looked back to Matsanga.

"What was that you were singing?"

Matsanga blinked at her, cocking his head, "You didn't recognize the lyrics?"

"I just heard the melody, and barely that."

Matsanga studied her for a moment, then drew in a deep breath that kept his shoulders still while his midsection swelled. His voice was deep and rich, making the melody even more haunting.

> "Under the light of Myrskaan and star and moon
> When the fiddler's songs fill the night
> The dancing lights travel o'er icy dune
> Grant us life, and let us shine bright.
>
> She plays for her friends, for family and love,
> For the ancient days of her youth
> For those gone so long that without the dancing lights
> Their names would have vanished, too
>
> But in song, their memories live on.
> In her songs, their souls dance again,

When the Fiddler plays to the night,
Their souls shine bright again.

She plays when the moon shines high in the sky,
And when stormclouds gather like a shroud
From the frozen coasts, to the top of the world,
Her songs raise spirits and warmth.

And in song, their memories live on.
In her songs, their souls dance again,
When the Fiddler plays to the night,
Their souls shine bright again.

And in song, their memories live on.
In her songs, their souls dance again,
When the Fiddler plays to the night,
Their souls shine bright again.

Under the light of Myrskaan and star and moon
When the fiddler's songs fill the night
The dancing lights travel o'er icy dune
Grant us life, and let us shine bright."

Estingai blinked. The hairs on her arms stood on end, and her chest felt tight. She recognized "The Fiddler in the Night," but the first and last verses were different that what she knew.

Taking a deep breath, she shook herself a bit before looking back to Matsanga. She hadn't expected such an emotional response to his singing.

"Are those older lyrics?"

Matsanga shrugged, "Probably. How do you know it?"

Estingai recited the verse.

"High in halls of ice that hang among the stars,

*Kept aloft by dancing lights.
Memories arise of ages long past
When the Fiddler plays to the night."*

Matsanga raised an eyebrow, "No singing."

She frowned, "I haven't in a long time."

Matsanga stared at her for a moment, then nodded, "You know who that's about, right?"

"A fiddler people thought brought the auroras before they knew it was caused by the flares?"

Matsanga rolled his eyes, "That's *what* it's about. I asked you if you know *who*."

Estingai shook her head, then stopped as she remembered the first time she'd heard the song played rather than sung. Played on a fiddle, "Really?"

Matsanga nodded, "She told you she was older than Kweshrima."

"I thought that was just part of her mystique. Or that she was trying to mess with me because I annoyed her."

Matsanga grinned, "You did, but Nevisi rarely lied."

"Yeah. Just deflected a lot."

Estingai took a deep breath. She didn't want to talk about Nevisi. It would only make her angry.

"You sing to yourself often?"

He snorted, "When I was your age, we either had to sing to ourselves or find someone to sing for us. I didn't do it much at Bastion because we had the audio players, but out here…"

Matsanga trailed off with a shrug. He nodded to the wolf.

"Ajida likes it."

Estingai looked to the wolf—Ajida—blinked when the animal moved it's head in what seemed like a nod, then looked back to her former mentor, frowning.

He named it after his friend?

That seemed a bit strange to Matsanga, but he'd lost a lot. She'd remembered the reserved, stately Natari woman with black hair that had often accompanied Matsanga in Bastion and on assignments.

Estingai had rarely approached when the two were together, sensing a bond she didn't want to disturb. She didn't think they'd been romantic, but...

I can understand missing someone that much.

"You need to teach me before you go..." She trailed off, frown deepening. "What exactly is it that you do out there? Hunt all day?"

Matsanga was silent as he took his bow and leaned it against the wall before turning to her and taking off his quiver as well.

"Very well. It will give you some time to practice."

Estingai smiled, then frowned, feeling as though she'd been played.

With a heavy sigh, Matsanga sat down with legs crossed, facing her. The black and red wolf, Ajida, padded over to sit beside him, and he scratched her behind the ears.

Estingai looked between the two of them expectantly. "Well?"

"You sure you're awake enough?"

Estingai nodded, taking her canteen from where she'd set it against the wall and bringing it to her lips for a long draft of water. She gave her clearnodes a quick flare as well. The sudden flood of sensory input shocked her awake.

"Now I am," she said, wiping her mouth as she blinked a few times and dimmed her clearnodes again.

Matsanga grunted. "What do you remember about Aioa? Cosmic Theory, specifically?"

Estingai frowned again, "What does that—"

"Just answer the question."

Estingai's frown deepened. "There are two realms—ours and that of the spirits. Ours effects the other realm to a certain extent, the Thrones are manifestations of the world's power, and there are about twelve different theories about the nature of the oruu."

Matsanga nodded. "As I expected. What about the Aathal and their effect on this world?"

Estingai shrugged. "No one knows much about them. Even Kweshrima couldn't—or wouldn't—tell us too much about them. There are theories, but none of them have been conclusively proven.

The most we really know is that they seemed to be the mechanisms that held our world's orbit stable when it never should have been, and what cause the auroras."

"They do much more than that," Matsanga said.

Estingai narrowed her eyes. "They why are you having me tell you all of this instead of just teaching me whatever it is you have in mind?"

Matsanga grunted. "Remember when you first started training with me and you wanted to learn the more advanced techniques of fighting and Auroramancy?"

Estingai sighed. "You demonstrated all the different ways you could knock me on my ass using just the fundamentals."

Matsanga nodded. "Do I need to do that again?"

Estingai flexed her fingers. A part of her wanted to challenge him just for the fight. She shook her head. "Go on."

"I learned about the realms and the Thrones long before they became common knowledge," Matsanga said. "First from Skadaatha, then Nevisi. Their own learning experiences were very different, as I'm not sure Skadaatha ever really 'learned' of that as we do, but what each taught me complemented the other. The Thrones, however, are only one part of Efruumani's power, and by extension, the secrets of Auroramancy and georaurals."

"The other part is the Aathal?" Estingai asked.

Matsanga nodded.

"Skadaatha and Nevisi both believe that some of our Auroramantic abilities, as well as the latent abilities granted to all by gemcrests, come from the Aathal," he elaborated. "Unfortunately, there is not much of a way to directly study the Aathal, so both had to use alternate methods."

Matsanga rose from his seat and walked over to where Mwyndobir leaned against the wall and a tall chest of drawers. He opened one of them, then took out what looked like a false-bottom and fished out a small pouch.

He tossed it to Estingai as he sat back down.

She caught it and looked at him expectantly. The pouch didn't jingle or clink, and the lumps inside just felt like rocks.

"Open it," he said. "Take one out and hold it."

Estingai pulled the tiny wash-leather pouch open and dumped the contents into her palm: a few nuggets of some silvery metal with a reddish tint.

As Estingai peered at the largest one, she realized that she could make out incredibly fine details on the surface.

Is that just how this metal forms? Or...

Estingai sat up straight, studying the room around her. What little heat the firepit's smoldering embers gave off seemed more intense. The room's odors made her wrinkle her nose as she tried to pick through them and identify the individual scents.

She furrowed her brow, looking to the nuggets, then at Matsanga. "What are these?"

"Honestly?" he shrugged. "No idea. Nevisi and I have just called them 'powermetal'."

Estingai nodded slowly. "That seems to fit. Do they hold their own power, or enhance that of whoever holds it?"

"The latter, as far as I can tell," Matsanga said. "You can feel it enhancing your latent abilities, can't you?"

Estingai nodded slowly. As a full Auroraborn, she bore a gemcrest with all twelve colors, and so received the latent abilities of all twelve gems, as well as the use of their Auroramantic abilities. As her gemcrest was divided, however, she did not receive as great a latent benefit as others would and found it hard to notice the difference when she was low on Auroralight.

"Here," he said, rising and taking an earthenware pitcher in one hand and silver cup in the other. He poured some water, then returned the pitcher before walking over to hand her the cup.

Estingai accepted it with a questioning look.

"Set the powermetal down and brighten your violetnodes," he said, "just enough to boil the water. Be conscious of exactly how much Auroralight it takes."

Nodding, Estingai set down the chunks of powermetal before her and blinked at the sudden dullness of her surroundings. She shook herself, then looked down at the cup.

She brightened her violetnodes just barely, holding that miniscule level of intensity until the water bubbled.

"Now let it cool."

Estingai did so, waiting patiently until the cup stopped bubbling, then steaming.

"Now do the same with the powermetal?" Estingai asked.

Matsanga nodded.

Estingai took the powermetal and the cup each in one hand, then gazed at the cup as she brightened her violetnodes.

She flinched, dropping the cup as the water steamed, then boiled almost instantly, the silver too hot for her to hold.

Matsanga snorted.

Estingai gazed wide-eyed at the cup, then Matsanga. "That's incredible. Is it always the same amount, or does it have a limit?"

Matsanga shrugged. "I haven't been able to do many conclusive tests, though from what I can tell in the difference between those nuggets and the bits of that metal contained in Mwyndobir, I believe the more you have, the more potent its effect. Though it seems that it needs to be touching your skin. Those should give you some edge against the Imaia. And Kojatere, should it come to that."

Estingai blinked. "You're giving them to me?"

Matsanga raised an eyebrow. "What need of them do I have other than to postulate? Especially at the end of the world."

Estingai frowned at that and looked back down at the stones. "Thank you, but...Why do I feel like this won't be enough?"

"Because it won't," Matsanga said. "Maybe if you were just facing Othaashle wielding Ilkwalerva, but not now that Kojatere has the power of the Throne."

Estingai made a fist around the nuggets. "Then why even give these to me?"

Matsanga frowned. "Because I can't teach you what I had in mind unless I first gave you those to use as a handicap." He rose, the icehound rising with him. "Come. You have some practicing to do, and it will give Ajida some exercise."

The icehound grunted, then padded out ahead of them.

Frustrated and disbelieving, yet eager, Estingai followed, beating Matsanga out of the dwelling.

20

Diwani

Eventually, however, problems arose. There were initial border disputes between nearby farmers and wanderers with the Akjemasai, but those were the least of our worries. With finite space and resources, the Buuekwenani had adapted to a very specific way of life. The influx of new ideas, luxuries, and materials not just from Uumgwefilo, but every people our allies came in contact with, challenged that way of life.

Exodus countdown: 12 days, 33 hours, 29 minutes

"If you do not mind me asking, what is your... relationship with Uuchantuu?"

Koruuksi looked to the princess and cocked his head, grinning beneath his mask as they walked through E Kwekuue's sunlit streets toward the edge of the market district.

Ymvesi'ia waited a moment for him to answer, then rolled her eyes. "I thought you were lovers at first form the way you seem glued to one another, but other than that, you don't behave that way."

Koruuksi laughed. "No, we aren't together. I've never thought about her that way even before she told me she's only interested in women."

Koruuksi caught the way Ymvesi'ia's cheeks grew dark at that, but didn't acknowledge it.

"I would say that she's been like a sister to me, but our relationship is nothing like what my sister and I have, or what I had with my brother," he continued. "We're just very close friends. Like it seems you and Vise are."

Koruuksi thought Ymvesi'ia's cheeks darkened just a shade more at that comment. He held in a laugh. *If she's attracted to women, she probably occasionally finds herself wishing Vise was as well.*

He'd never had that problem with Uuchantuu, though he knew she was attractive. Vise, though...

Koruuksi shook himself, realizing Ymvesi'ia had said something. "Sorry, what was that?"

"I said that you are probably correct," Ymvesi'ia told him. "Vise and I have been friends since childhood. She was the daughter of my mother's body servant, so we spent a lot of time together even before Vise began to take on that role."

"Is that a hereditary position?"

Ymvesi'ia shrugged. "Technically, no. I cannot imagine anyone else in Vise's place, however. She and I are so close that having someone else in the mix who took the position out of some sense of duty or honor just seems strange."

Koruuksi nodded. "It's nice to see someone in a service role treated with such respect."

Ymvesi'ia frowned at that, then sighed. "Right, I forgot. The way the Uumgwefili acted is probably more like what you are used to—though they were better than most, from what I heard. Vise is my *mjakaazi*, my body servant, but the translation is misleading—it evolved from the old role long ago when we still had such things as true servants who had to be paid and such. Vise commands more respect than anyone else in the palace besides my father."

Koruuksi cocked his head. "Even more than you?"

Ymvesi'ia snorted, nodding. "She does far more work than I do, and she is the one who has to deal with me most often."

Her cheeks darkened a bit, and she tucked a loose strand of hair behind her ear, "I am not always the easiest person to deal with."

Koruuksi barked a laugh, "I hadn't noticed."

Ymvesi'ia glared at him.

"What? I didn't say I was easy to deal with, either."

Ymvesi'ia rolled her eyes.

"You remind me a bit of my sister, Estingai."

"Oh?"

"She can be very harsh when she feels it's necessary, but she's always working in the interests of those she protects. She would do something like spend a few days researching planetary physics if she thought it would be of help to those who depend on her."

Ymvesi'ia smiled. "I will consider that a compliment, then."

Koruuksi returned the smile, though he knew she couldn't see it.

Ymvesi'ia pursed her lips, then looked away.

"What?"

She looked back at him, hesitating a moment before she spoke. "Your mask. Does its design have any meaning? Or is it just to protect you from the sun?"

"Let's walk in the shade?"

Ymvesi'ia nodded and led him over to a smaller street between some buildings. Koruuksi had discovered that thanks to the sun's fixed position in the sky, certain parts of the city were always in the shade. Once out of the sun's harmful direct light, Koruuksi took off his mask and smoothed back his hair. He held it up to her, adjusting the headband to wipe off a bit of sweat before changing it out for one of his spares.

"Do you carry a lot of those?" she asked.

He nodded, then pointed to the mask.

"The masks started out as a cultural thing very early in Samjati history. There was a notion of not displaying your emotions to just anyone—only those you were most intimate with, or something like that. It varied from culture to culture, as did the masks. Some just covered the eyes at first, then others covered half the face, others covered everything except the mouth, and so on. Only the most conservative cultures used those that covered the entire face for a while, and the masks took on different meanings in different areas. When Samjati—particularly the Juusanariti'i, one of the major ethnic groups—began exploring and settling on Lightside, they adopted the full-coverage masks as well as the clothing. They could get away with just masks and limited time outdoors in the twilight band, but once they were fully on Lightside, the sun would burn them, even those with dark blue or violet-hued skin."

"I imagine that gets old at times," Ymvesi'ia said.

Koruuksi shrugged.

"And what do the markings mean?"

"Adornment was a big thing in the past," he explained, "but we don't really have the time or resources for that anymore. Plus, I have quite a few of these just in case one gets damaged. The twin symbols on the cheeks are my name in the old snowscript. Supposedly created by the goddess herself to make every word look like a snowflake."

Ymvesi'ia frowned ."A snowflake? Is that not just a frozen raindrop?"

Koruuksi laughed. "Yes, but when the water freezes, it forms tiny ice crystals. If you look close enough before they melt or break, you can see the intricate design. Supposedly no two are alike."

Ymvesi'ia blinked. "Darkside sounds strange."

Koruuksi grinned. "I imagine it would."

"And what about the marks on the edges? More names?"

Koruuksi nodded. "My family. Kojatere and Aiteperit—my parents—my uncle Suulehep, my brother Svemakuu, Estingai, and Uuchantuu."

Ymvesi'ia smiled at that as Koruuksi put his mask back on for the sunlit section up ahead.

Koruuksi looked at her, wondering if she would pry. He didn't want to need to deflect if she did. "If you don't mind me asking, how do the other refugees adjust to the clothing here?"

"What do you mean?"

Koruuksi cocked his head and gestured to his chest, then hers.

"Ah," she said, cheeks darkening a bit. She made no move to cover up, however. "Yes, I forgot about how other cultures sexualize breasts. Though just the female ones."

Koruuksi shrugged. "I didn't make the rules."

Ymvesi'ia grinned. "From what I can tell, they simply adjust. Is that why Uuchantuu seemed uncomfortable yesterday? Was she raised in that kind of background?"

Koruuksi shrugged. "Yes and no. Despite her skin and lack of antlers, she's basically Kysuuri. Her people used to live in Darkside's Ice Wastes—a cold, brutal environment. They have... complicated views on nudity. Because it was so cold, they wouldn't exactly have a chance to wear clothing that revealed much unless they were inside their homes or bathhouses, so their culture eventually developed the mindset that it's inappropriate to reveal much skin unless you're being intimate or in private."

Ymvesi'ia raised an eyebrow. "Or in a public bath?"

Koruuksi shrugged. "See what I mean? She's completely fine with that, partially because our lifestyle involves a lot of communal spaces, so most of us are desensitized to nudity in communal bathing. Outside of those situations, however..."

"She will grow uncomfortable just wearing clothing that shows any skin, much less any that gets transparent when wet?"

"Exactly."

"And that's why she seemed so reserved most of the time yesterday?"

Koruuksi laughed. "Part of it."

"The other part?"

Koruuksi stopped and met Ymvesi'ia's gaze, even though his shades hid his own eyes from her. "I think you know."

Ymvesi'ia's cheeks darkened, and Koruuksi had to hold in a laugh.

"Are we almost there?" he asked, taking pity on her.

Ymvesi'ia shot him a grateful smile. "Yes."

"What do I need to know about this Diwani?" Koruuksi asked as they neared some larger, more impressive buildings than most of those Koruuksi had seen in the district this far. "The history that Vise read to me just mentioned their origin and general functions, not how they've developed since."

"Diwana Duubaan is in charge of our economy and distribution of resources," Ymvesi'ia said. "We are approaching him first because I believe he will be the most difficult to convince."

"Because leaving would probably upset the system he and your people have worked so carefully to maintain?"

"Exactly. If he refuses to help, we can approach other Diwana, and hopefully their support will convince him to change his mind."

"Got it."

"I need to let you speak, since you know the science better than I do, but make sure to pause every now and then so I can interject, if needed."

They stopped before a building the size of the tenement Koruuksi was staying in. It rose six stories into the air, the levels tiered so that they grew narrower with each one. As with most of the buildings, lush vines, leaves, and flowers spilled over the sides almost like a waterfall. Twin columns with intricate aluminum inlay rose on either side of a wide, open entryway with a steady stream of clerks flowing in and out. Koruuksi frowned as he saw more of them, however, noticing that none of them carried papers or files, and that a few carried what appeared to be chalkboards.

Maybe they're as short on paper as we are.

"Any advice for my approach?" Koruuksi asked, bringing his focus back to the matter at hand.

"Be direct. Present only the facts. Duubaan tends to see things from a removed position, considering the numbers rather than the individual."

Koruuksi took a deep breath. "Let's go."

Ymvesi'ia led him into the building and up through the various floors. Officials and clerks all bowed to Ymvesi'ia if they saw her, but no one went out of their way to do so. Koruuksi received about as many curious looks as he'd expected. When they reached the Diwani's offices on the top floor, Koruuksi was surprised when the

Diwani's assistant, a young man with a slim build named Bewa, told him and Ymvesi'ia to wait. He was even more surprised when Ymvesi'ia didn't object. It made sense, as they wouldn't want to appear rude before asking for the Diwana's help. It also gave him hope that their plan would work, as he couldn't think of any stories or histories he'd heard of where a functionary—even a high ranking one—had the authority to make royalty wait.

It only lasted a few minutes, however, and the three clerks that exited the offices all bowed and moved aside when they noticed Ymvesi'ia. They gave Koruuksi similar looks to those he'd received on the way up.

"Diwana Duubaan will see you, now, Highness," Bewa said, smiling as he gestured toward the door.

Ymvesi'ia smiled and gestured for Koruuksi to follow.

Once the doors closed behind them, Koruuksi sighed. Duubaan's office opened up to a wide balcony in the back with no curtains to pull shut. The office itself was simple. A sturdy wooden desk faced three chairs atop a colorful rug, and shelves filled with thick books lined the walls from floor to ceiling. Duubaan himself was a sturdy man of average height. For a Buuekwenani, at least—he was still taller than Koruuksi. He wore spectacles and a thin, trim beard that outlined his angular jaw and matched his close-cropped hair. Open robes revealed a rainbow gemcrest at his clavicle.

Light... how many Auroraborn do these people have? I'll have to ask Ymvesi'ia if that has any bearing on their positions in society.

Duubaan rose and bowed to Ymvesi'ia—and she in return—before studying Koruuksi through a pair of spectacles.

Koruuksi realized that if Ymvesi'ia had bowed to this man, he should follow her lead, and bowed a bit lower than she had. It seemed to appease the man.

He greeted Ymvesi'ia in their language as she and Koruuksi sat in the empty chairs.

"Thank you for seeing us, Diwana," Ymvesi'ia said in Atongo, "This is my friend, Koruuksi. He and a group of his companions arrived to petition my father and inform him of a matter of great importance."

Duubaan glanced to Koruuksi again, then back to Ymvesi'ia raising an eyebrow. "His Majesty has not asked my counsel on anything so far." He looked to Koruuksi. "You arrived here a week ago?"

Koruuksi nodded. "Yes, Diwana."

"That is why we came to you," Ymvesi'ia said. "My father denied Koruuksi's petition, but I do not believe he considered it with the gravity he should have."

The Diwana nodded slowly, "Very well."

Ymvesi'ia smiled, "Thank you, Diwana. Koruuksi will be able to explain it best."

Duubaan turned his gaze upon Koruuksi.

Koruuksi cleared his throat.

"My petition to His Majesty was for aid from the Akjemasai against the Imaia, and that he begin the evacuation of the city so that my companions and I will be able to get everyone off-world before Efruumani is no longer inhabitable."

Duubaan's eyebrows rose, but he said nothing, so Koruuksi continued.

"I did not have much time to explain the reasoning behind my request when I first met the king," he continued, "which I believe is part of why he denied my petition. Princess Ymvesi'ia came to me yesterday asking for more detail on the science and reasoning behind what I am sure sounded like an outlandish claim, as she thought the same."

Duubaan looked to her as if for confirmation, and she nodded.

"The first part of your petition," the Diwana said, looking back to Koruuksi, "I assume Princess Ymvesi'ia has informed you that we already sent warriors against the Imaia and have very few left?"

Koruuksi nodded. "We ask for aid not to fight against the Imaia in hopes of defeating them. We just need to distract them long enough to be able evacuate our people—and yours, now—unmolested by the Imaia's forces."

Duubaan nodded. "And your second claim? You believe Efruumani will soon become uninhabitable?"

Koruuksi nodded. "The Imaia plans to leave Efruumani in two weeks' time on a massive spacecraft the size of a large island, and they plan to take the World Tree Boaathal with them when they go."

Duubaan narrowed his eyes. "Impossible."

Koruuksi nodded. "My people once thought so as well. The Imaia seems to believe they can do so, however. They have Ynuukwidas on their side, and after Kweshrima destroyed Yrmuunthal, the claim is unfortunately not as outlandish as it once would have been."

Duubaan's full lips drew to a thin line. "The loss of both World Trees would be devastating, but the belief that it would render Efruumani uninhabitable seems…a stretch to put it mildly. Especially in such a short amount of time."

"That is the best-case scenario, unfortunately," Koruuksi said. "Our spies within the Imaia report that their scientists have concluded it is very likely that Efruumani will fall into our sun and burn up once the World Tree is separated from it. We are currently locked between Myrskaan and the sun at their LaGrange point, an orbital position which should be far too unstable to hold a satellite like Efruumani in the same place for more than a single orbit, much less the thousands for which life has existed here. The only explanation for our stable orbit that the Imaia's scientists could find was that the Aathal have somehow stabilized our world. They all but confirmed this when Efruumani lurched just enough after Yrmuunthal's destruction to alter the orbit. According to them, Ynuukwidas, their God King, puts all of his strength into keeping Efruumani in orbit long enough for the Imaia to find a way to escape."

Koruuksi stopped there. The three of them sat in silence for a time before the Diwana spoke.

"That is… a great deal to take in."

Ymvesi'ia nodded. "I agree, Diwana. We merely wish for the Diwani to give the issue the consideration it deserves."

Duubaan turned his gaze on her. "Meaning you want me to agree to compel your father to attend a session should the other Diwana agree that it is necessary."

"Yes."

"Have you been able to verify this man's claims?"

Koruuksi clenched his fists at the Diwana's tone but kept silent as Ymvesi'ia answered.

"As much as is possible, Diwana. There are, of course, gaps in our understanding of planetary physics, and we must assume that Koruuksi's information from the Imaia is correct. Especially if they are—"

"Forgive me, Princess, but we must assume no such thing. Nothing can be taken for granted when dealing with the Imaia. Their greatest leaps in power were not due to warfare but superior technology and masterful political and economic maneuvering. Many nations fell to them without a single spear raised by either side."

He looked at Koruuksi. "Can you be absolutely sure that your spies are not being fed misinformation on purpose?"

Koruuksi gritted his teeth. He wanted to believe his mother, but years of living a life in hiding could not prevent him from considering the opposite. It made his stomach turn.

"If we could, then we wouldn't need spies, would we?"

Duubaan nodded as though that was exactly the answer he'd expected.

"I must decline your request, Princess. There is not enough compelling evidence to prove your companion's claims. Even if there were..." he shrugged, "well, the Imaia has never had the chance to study the Vale has it? And remaining within our borders has protected us from all the other disruptions in the world. I believe your father made the right decision."

Koruuksi growled, rising from his seat.

"My people—my *friends*—did not die to get false information. We did not come all the way here and let your Akjemasai disarm us because we thought it would be fun. We came here to save you and your people. Maybe if you got off your ass and went outside—"

"Koruuksi!" Ymvesi'ia hissed, her hand closing tight around his wrist.

Koruuksi glared at the Diwana for a moment, then clamped his mouth shut.

Duubaan raised an eyebrow at him, then said something to Ymvesi'ia in their tongue that he didn't catch. Ymvesi'ia's face darkened. She rose from her seat and snapped something back at the councilor before dragging Koruuksi toward the exit.

"What was that?" he hissed, nearly stumbling as he adjusted to her pace, heart pounding, "What did he say?"

"Nothing that bears repeating," Ymvesi'ia said as they entered the stairwell. She paused for a moment after the first flight, the muscles of her face tight. Her eyes burned with the same emotions that roared through him.

"I need a drink," she said, "and I really hate drinking alone."

Koruuksi peered at Ymvesi'ia over his food as she drained a large glass of thibara and gestured for one of the staff to bring her another one without missing a beat. The restaurant was like the few others he'd visited so far, with minimal staff and filled with wonderful smells. This one served fish, from what he could tell, and Koruuksi found his mouth watering. He hadn't eaten fish in years.

"You're... not at all what I expected," Koruuksi said, running his fingers through his hair before taking another bite of his food. His mask rested on the table next to his plate, and he'd thrown back his hood. Ymvesi'ia had been nice enough to choose somewhere shaded.

"Likewise," Ymvesi'ia said, smiling at the staff member who brought her more thibara.

Koruuksi raised an eyebrow.

"From what I have read, Samjati are supposed to be more mild-mannered and reserved than you were with Duubaan. Your do not have a particularly long fuse, to use one of the Uumgwefili's idioms."

Koruuksi snorted. "On that part I probably take after my sister.

She probably would have just throttled Duubaan or beat him into submission."

Ymvesi'ia's eyes widened. "I imagine she would hate politics."

Koruuksi nodded. "She's a good leader, but not a good negotiator. She will take advice and listen to people's opinions, but if she thinks someone is being an idiot, she will make it clear to them that stupidity is not an option. What was Duubaan's problem, anyway?"

"You mean before you yelled at him and told him to get off his ass?"

Koruuksi cleared his throat, wishing for his mask to hide the color in his cheeks.

Ymvesi'ia smirked, then sighed. "He would not say it outright, but I think you were right with what you said before we met with him. Duubaan played a major role in revising our economic systems and way of life after Uumgwefilo fell. When that happened, we could no longer trade aluminum and medicinal plants for luxuries the Vale does not produce or goods it would not be sustainable for us to produce for ourselves. I think he sees anything that would disrupt that—even an offer of salvation—as a threat to his system."

"Especially since he can't actually see the threat he needs saving from."

"Exactly."

Koruuksi snorted. "So this place isn't entirely a paradise, after all. Your officials and bureaucrats can be just as infuriating as ours were."

Ymvesi'ia grinned. "I think it is something they are born with. There are no infuriationoruu, so politicians and government officials exist to fill the void."

Koruuksi laughed, and after a moment, Ymvesi'ia joined in.

"To get back to your initial question," Koruuksi said, "Samjati are more reserved and less emotive, but not mild-mannered. They have a long fuse, but when it goes off, it's frightening."

"They?"

"My father was Natari. Things like that get much more muddied when you're of mixed parentage. Some people seem to think that your emotional demeanor 'shows the strength of one's blood' or some shit like that, but they say the same thing about Auroramancy. And while I definitely have more of a Natari temper..."

He held up his glass and brightened his violetnodes just a bit, sapping the heat from the glass until the surface of the drink and the condensation on the outside turned to frost.

Ymvesi'ia blinked, eyeing the glass, then grinned. "That must be nice to be able to cool things down at will in Lightside's heat."

Koruuksi grinned. "Yes, it is. Though we're taught to treat our powers with more respect and discipline."

He took a sip of the freshly chilled drink. "I'd still much rather be able to walk around without my shirt on in this heat."

Ymvesi'ia chucked. "I will not argue with that."

She peered down her broad nose at him, then looked down at her food and shoveled a few quick bites into her mouth.

"Is there anything special about the fabric you make your clothes out of?" she asked.

Koruuksi shook his head. "What I'm wearing now was made to keep me cool in the direct sun, but the cloth just needs to be made out of a fine weave—something that lets as little light through as possible. Other than that, there just needs to be enough to cover all of me."

Ymvesi'ia nodded, then quickly finished her food and drink. Koruuksi did the same, sensing something was on her mind.

"Come with me," she said, touching his shoulder and nudging him toward the market district.

Koruuksi almost asked where they were going as she led him through the streets but decided not to and just followed her. He soon began to recognize their surroundings. He couldn't place them, however, until they paused before a familiar shop. Ymvesi'ia didn't even give him a moment to ask what they were doing here before pulling him into the store.

Ymvesi'ia called out something in her language as she entered the shop.

Koruuksi cocked his head at Ymvesi'ia. "We hurried here so you could get some new clothes?"

Ymvesi'ia turned and shot him an amused look but said nothing. She turned her attention back to Afria as the shop owner emerged into the store's main room.

The older Buuekwenani woman smiled, bowing to Ymvesi'ia when she saw her, then closed the distance between them and started speaking excitedly. After a few exchanges, Ymvesi'ia gestured toward Koruuksi, and Afria looked him up and down.

"Ah, Koruuksi."

She grinned, then said something to Ymvesi'ia before heading over to one of the windows.

Koruuksi looked after the woman for a moment as she started drawing the curtains closed, then turned to Ymvesi'ia. "Wait, me?"

She grinned before trotting over to the shop's windows and drawing the shades over them, shooing Afria away and gesturing toward Koruuksi.

"Come," Afria said, beckoning him toward the same pedestal she'd put Uuchantuu on.

When he stood atop it, she tugged at his clothing. "This, off. Measurements."

"Wait—" Koruuksi said again, looking between her and Ymvesi'ia, face growing hot.

Afria put her hands on her hips, looking at him expectantly. Ymvesi'ia grinned. "I thought you said Uuchantuu was the shy one."

Koruuksi swallowed. He was not as shy as Uuchantuu, but still didn't feel like stripping down in the middle of the room in front of Ymvesi'ia.

He sighed and took off his mask, handing it to Ymvesi'ia. "Hold on to this, please."

She grinned and nodded as Afria dragged him off.

After a few minutes of poking and prodding, Koruuksi walked back out onto the pedestal wearing a plain white wrap around his waist that fell to his ankles.

Ymvesi'ia grinned at first, full lips seeming even larger than usual. Then her expression sobered when her eyes fell to his bare torso.

"So many scars..." she said, putting a hand to her mouth as she took a few steps closer.

Koruuksi nodded. "Field medicine is more concerned with keeping you fighting or getting you out alive than making sure everything looks pretty when you're done."

Ymvesi'ia's lips drew together, one hand moving down to her hip.

Does she have a scar of her own there?

When Afria followed Koruuksi out a few moments later, Ymvesi'ia put a smile back on and exchanged a few words with her before looking to Koruuksi.

"It needs to cover all of you, right?"

Koruuksi nodded. "If we're fighting, we usually wear a balaklava that clings to the face and reveals only the eyes under our mask or helmet. Just to be safe."

Ymvesi'ia relayed that and a bit more to Afria before the woman pointed to his mask.

"Can she examine it?" Ymvesi'ia asked.

Koruuksi nodded and she handed the seamstress Koruuksi's mask.

"Is this a thing with the two of you?" Koruuksi asked Ymvesi'ia as Afria turned his mask over in her hands, inspecting it.

Ymvesi'ia raised an eyebrow.

"You and Vise. She brought Uuchantuu here for those new clothes."

Ymvesi'ia blinked, then blushed, putting a hand to her forehead. "I thought I recognized the work. Was that just before I met with you three?"

Koruuksi nodded, and Ymvesi'ia's face colored even deeper. "Oh, Vise."

"I have to say I'm surprised at how quickly your mood changed regarding Uuchantuu and me," he said as Afria handed his mask back to Ymvesi'ia before walking over to some of the cloth racks. "And your perspective on the science."

Ymvesi'ia snorted. "I do not really have a choice about the science

—only an idiot would argue with that. Science does not care if you believe in it, it just is."

Koruuksi nodded as Afria started draping different pieces of cloth around him. "And Uuchantuu and me?"

Ymvesi'ia's face colored again, though not as much as before. Koruuksi thought he saw the woman look away and wet her lips before she spoke. "Now that I know your claims of danger are real, it is my duty to protect my people from that danger, rather than be angry at you for sounding a false alarm."

Koruuksi grinned, and Ymvesi'ia smiled back.

"You realize that even if we have my father and the council on our side, we might still encounter some trouble," Ymvesi'ia said. "People are slow and unwilling to change their routines or beliefs if they still have some comfort or sense of normalcy in their current circumstances."

Koruuksi nodded. "I know. Many didn't move fast enough in the aftermath of Yrmuunthal's destruction and lost everything."

Ymvesi'ia sighed. "Sometimes I feel as though things could have been different if we had sent more warriors to fight alongside the Uumgwefili against the Imaia. Most didn't believe we needed to. My father did, but he was only able to convince the council and our people to allow the recruitment of warriors by framing it as something we needed to do to honor our history with Uumgwefilo rather than as a response to the threat of the Imaia. The force my mother led against them was the largest most of our people had ever seen assembled, yet it was not enough."

Ymvesi'ia's expression dropped at that last part.

"That's why you joined the Akjemasai, isn't it?" Koruuksi asked. "To honor her in how you protect your people?"

Ymvesi'ia frowned at him, but only for a moment. Her expression softened, and she nodded. "I heard stories of how incredible she was from those who returned." She smiled. "I heard stories about your mother, and the Knights, too."

Koruuksi smiled at that.

Afria said something then, gesturing to Koruuksi.

Ymvesi'ia smiled at the woman and took a step back, eyeing Koruuksi. He looked down at himself and nodded in appreciation. The clothing reminded him of what the seamstress had made for Uuchantuu, though with a lot more coverage. She'd given him long, baggy sleeves that crossed over his chest to sit just above the wrap that covered two thirds of his torso, with a long, high-collared mantle that covered the rest of him. It wasn't complete, but Koruuksi could see what Afria was thinking. A hood, leg wraps and a pair of gloves, and this would cover him perfectly.

Ymvesi'ia and Afria chatted, circling him as the seamstress pointed to different parts of the outfit.

"Do I get an opinion on this?" Koruuksi asked.

Both women shook their heads. "No."

They resumed talking, growing more excited until Ymvesi'ia clasped Afria's hands, prompting the woman to bow.

She turned to Koruuksi. "She said she can have a complete outfit ready for you in a few hours."

Koruuksi frowned. "Aren't we meeting with Diwana Nkruuma later?"

Ymvesi'ia nodded. "Exactly. We'll stop by here just early enough for Afria to make any last-minute adjustments. This should help make a bit better impression with Diwana Nkruuma. After Duubaan, I'll take any help we can get. She also agreed to make a few sets of clothing for the rest of your team, so you should send them over to get measured soon."

"Thank you," Koruuksi said, both to Ymvesi'ia and Afria. "Please let me know how I can repay—"

Ymvesi'ia grinned, and relayed what he said to Afria, prompting them both to laugh.

"Right," Koruuksi sighed, "I forgot, no money."

Ymvesi'ia followed this time when Afria led him over to a sheltered area where he could put back on his clothes. "How exactly does that work again? I'm assuming she's one of the best tailors in the city if you're coming to her, but the shop is empty, and it was the same when I came here with Vise. Where I come from, that would be a sign of a struggling business."

"That is the problem," Ymvesi'ia said, "you're thinking about this as a business, when it is not."

"You lost me."

"Vise explained to you how we sustain ourselves in isolation, right?"

"Somewhat. It's still hard to wrap my head around."

Ymvesi'ia was silent for a moment.

"The Vale is incredibly fertile, and with our population control measures, we have enough room to produce enough food for everyone with little effort. Everyone works a shift one day a week in some sort of essential function to keep the city and the Vale running."

"Even you?"

"Of course. Why do you think I waited until today for us to meet with the Diwani instead of yesterday, and why do you think Vise isn't here?"

Koruuksi shrugged. "I thought you just had work to do. I guess it just wasn't the type I was thinking of."

"Exactly," Ymvesi'ia said. "Tending to crops and animals, cleaning the city, distributing food, weaving, and checking for areas in need of maintenance are just some of the unskilled, essential labors that keep the city running. Vise has cleaning duty today, and I had harvesting yesterday. We have specialized professionals like engineers, smiths, masons, doctors, educators, researchers, bureaucrats and the Akjemasai, but for other professions like cooking or tailoring, people just do those because they enjoy it, not because they must. They're able to pursue whatever they want in the four days each week they have free after spending the other two working essential shifts."

"I gathered that," Koruuksi said, tugging on the last of his clothing, "but how does that work? How does Afria get the space and materials to make such clothing?"

"Some of it is allotted to her, but sometimes people will bring her cloth they want her to work with. Dyers, for instance, will try out new colors or patterns on a piece of cloth, then bring it to Afria or another seamstress to make it into some sort of clothing. She sees it as an art. She doesn't need to worry about food or a home, so she tells people to repay her by wearing her clothing about the city so more people will come to her asking to create more art."

Ymvesi'ia exchanged a few words with Afria before looking back to him. "Of course," Koruuksi said, smiling, "and thank you again."

Once they left the shop, Ymvesi'ia turned to Koruuksi. "I have some duties to attend to before we meet with Diwana Nkruuma. Go get some rest and let your team know to come by here and Afria will make them some new clothes—Samjati and non-Samjati."

Koruuksi shook his head. "That's too much. We can't—"

Ymvesi'ia raised an eyebrow. "You are working to save my people, Koruuksi. The least I can do is make sure that you and your friends look good while doing it. Afria said that's how you can repay her. That, and wearing the clothing she makes you around the city."

"Wouldn't that require more material than she is allotted?"

Ymvesi'ia shrugged. "I can cover that." She grinned. "Being royalty does still have some privileges here."

Koruuksi shook his head. "Honestly, it seems too good to be true."

"That's because you have only been told about it. We work hard to maintain a society that benefits us all. I do not excuse Duubaan, but I can understand why he is reluctant to agree to something that can disrupt that, even if it is for a very good reason. I will see you later?"

Koruuksi nodded.

Ymvesi'ia half-turned in the direction of the palace, then stopped, "And... if she's interested, tell Uuchantuu her presence would be welcome when meeting with Diwana Nkruuma."

Ymvesi'ia blushed again as Koruuksi gave her a knowing grin. "Of course, Princess."

EVEN AFTER WHAT Ymvesi'ia had told him about Diwana Nkruuma and how the Buuekwenani felt about religion, Koruuksi was surprised at the lack of iconography of any sort in the councilor's chambers. Hers were more open than Duubaan's though just as plentiful in books filling stone shelves. What was even more shocking to Koruuksi, even after over a week in this city, was the oruu. All different kinds hung about the area, some floating, some sitting or standing on various surfaces. A few groups seemed to play with each other, while Koruuksi thought he even caught a pair of them fighting. Their shining forms, various shades, and hues of red and violet, gave the space an ethereal quality that seemed more akin with the stories Koruuksi had heard of the city.

It was also dark.

Nkruuma herself was younger than Koruuksi had imagined—younger than Duubaan by at least twenty years, or so—and very pretty. Her features were a bit softer than that of most Buuekwenani, with a face that was heart-shaped instead of tapering to a strong chin.

"Thank you for agreeing to see us on such short notice, Diwana," Ymvesi'ia said with a bow after she introduced them. Koruuksi and Uuchantuu did the same. Both of them now wore clothes of Buuekwenani fashion, and Koruuksi felt a bit more at home in the clothing now that he could take his mask off for a while.

Nkruuma smiled, returning the greeting.

"What can I do for you, Ymvesi'ia?" she asked as they sat. The woman met Koruuksi's eyes and looked him up and down, doing the same to Uuchantuu before looking back to Ymvesi'ia. "Afria's work?"

Ymvesi'ia smiled. "Yes, she said she appreciated the challenge. As for the reason we asked to see you, I believe Koruuksi will be able to explain better than I."

Koruuksi nodded his thanks to Ymvesi'ia, then thought for a moment as he studied Nkruuma. On the way over, Ymvesi'ia had explained to him and Uuchantuu that Nkruuma was E Kwekuue's head of religion and education in non-scientific studies.

She'd explained how E Kwekuue rejected the gods of ancient Atonga, the early Imaia and even Ynuukwidas and Kweshrima, believing them to be beings of great power, but not gods. According to her, the Buuekwenani believed that there was *some* god-like force at work, but that they can never know its agenda, citing their flight and loss with an arrival in paradise as a display of the contradictions in belief in a benevolent god.

Koruuksi gave Nkruuma a similar explanation to what he'd given Duubaan, touching on all the major points. Per Ymvesi'ia's advice, he did not mention Kweshrima, keeping from referencing her as much as he could despite touching on Yrmuunthal. He did, however, touch on Ynuukwidas—how far the God King had strayed from the role of a true deity, and how they believed him powerful enough to rip Boaathal from Efruumani when the Imaia left the world.

To Koruuksi's surprise, just as he stopped speaking, Uuchantuu started.

"I know that this may seem very outlandish, Diwana. And even if you believe us, it is a lot to ask. Though we would appreciate any help you can give us, we didn't come here to recruit any of your people or upset your way of life. We honestly didn't believe we would find a thriving city—we thought at most there would be a few hundred people holding out in hidden ruins." She paused for a moment.

"During the war, we thought we were on the right side of things. Some even believed we were fighting for a righteous and holy cause under Kweshrima."

Koruuksi tensed. The Diwana's face betrayed no emotion, however.

"I've since come to understand that there is rarely a 'right' side in war," Uuchantuu continued, "and that the side we fought on has a tenuous claim on that at best. We also know what it feels like to be betrayed by a god. Princess Ymvesi'ia has shared with us some of your history, and it seemed all too relatable the more she told us. If someone had offered to bring my people to a place of safety when we were forced to abandon our homes, I would have accepted their help, just as I imagine your people would have done so when they fled the Iron Empire. That time has come again. I beg you to help us bring your people to safety so that my friends and I can do something we *know* is good for once."

Koruuksi barely kept himself from flexing his fingers as Nkruuma considered their words in silence. He wanted to look to Ymvesi'ia and see her reaction, but didn't dare. Ymvesi'ia had specifically told them *not* to mention Kweshrima, and Uuchantuu hadn't said anything about speaking to the Diwana.

When Nkruuma smiled, Koruuksi's eyes bulged.

"I believe you are right, Uuchantuu. It pains me to think that we must soon leave this paradise that has so long been a sanctuary to our people, but your evidence seems sound, and only fools argue with science. I will agree to meet with His Majesty on this matter, provided you can get the rest of the Diwani to agree. If Diwana Warsama can corroborate your companion's evidence, I will work with her to push for immediate action."

Koruuksi looked to Ymvesi'ia just as the princess rose from her seat, smiling. She gave the Diwana a deep bow. "Thank you, Diwana."

Nkruuma smiled, returning the bow. "Of course, Princess. I will begin making preparations shortly, just to be safe."

They said their goodbyes, and Ymvesi'ia led them out of the building back onto one of the main boulevards.

"We did it," Koruuksi breathed, looking between Uuchantuu and Itese. "We actually did it."

The two women grinned. Koruuksi thought he could sense the tension between them growing a bit less nervous and transforming into something else.

"I have to admit," he said, looking to Uuchantuu, "you scared me when you mentioned Kweshrima."

Uuchantuu's cheeks colored, but she shrugged, "I know. It just felt right." She looked to Ymvesi'ia. "I'm—"

Ymvesi'ia shook her head, cutting Uuchantuu off. "Do not apologize. You two have already proved a few times that I am not always right."

"I could use a chuura after that," Uuchantuu suggested, smiling.

Koruuksi nodded. He wasn't too hungry, but those chuura were really—

Koruuksi stiffened, standing straight as he saw Luuhuuta jogging toward them.

The Natari woman barely broke a sweat. She was all lean muscle and almost as tall as Muuzuuri, with hips that had always made Koruuksi a bit jealous. She'd tied her crimped hair down into tight, thin braids. Bright blue beads at the ends complemented her warm, orange complexion and swung back and forth with her motions. Koruuksi sometimes thought of her as Uuchantuu's inverse in body-type, skin tone, and even their faces. Where Uuchantuu had a strong jaw and prominent, yet narrow nose, Luuhuuta's nose was twice as wide, and her slender face came to a point at her chin.

"Luuhuuta," he asked, "what is it?"

"We finally compiled all of the data from our observations," she said, handing Koruuksi a datapad. "Take a look."

Koruuksi frowned, taking the pad from Luuhuuta to study the display.

He noticed Ymvesi'ia peering at the device with interest out of the corner of his eye.

"What is that?"

Koruuksi tuned out Uuchantuu's explanation, briefly thinking about how excited Vise would be to see a datapad, as he read the display.

Once finished, he frowned, looking up at Luuhuuta, who nodded.

"Ymvesi'ia," he said, interrupting Uuchantuu, "are these figures correct?"

He stepped beside her and angled the datapad so they could both see it.

"Forty-seven thousand, six hundred and two acres of land with nineteen-thousand, five hundred and thirty-six of that used for livestock and farming, around thirty-four thousand inhabitants..."

Ymvesi'ia pulled back from the screen and blinked, looking between him and Uuchantuu, "Yes. Approximately, at least. I could have Vise verify the specifics, but...how did you—?"

"Observation is one of our specialties," Uuchantuu said. "Koruuksi's had the team walking around the city and gathering data so we would know exactly what we are in for if we get your father and the council to agree."

"And unfortunately," Koruuksi said, "we're either going to need to drastically move up our time-table, or come up with a way to make the distraction at Mjatafa Mwonga last long enough for us to land a capital ship on the beach or somewhere in the Vale, if that will even work."

Koruuksi sighed, meeting Ymvesi'ia's gaze. "Any ideas?"

Ymvesi'ia shook her head. "We can move up our meetings with the different councilors, but we will need to be careful. My father catching wind of what we are doing would be as bad as approaching him again to reconsider his decision. Keeping our society running does not allow for many loopholes." She frowned, raising a hand to her chin, then looked up. "I can have the Akjemasai help. They may not be able to speed things up, but I can let them know of the situation and have them compile supplies and take measures so that when we convince my father and the council, we can move immediately."

"Thank you," Koruuksi said. He still found himself unable to get rid of the tension, but that helped a bit. He looked Luuhuuta. "Have you been able to communicate with Remnant Base"

Luuhuuta shook her head. "Not from here. Our tech functions for the most part, but whatever protects this place interferes with our communications."

"We need to get out to the transports then," Koruuksi said, looking to Uuchantuu.

Ymvesi'ia smiled, "I will gather some Akjemasai and take you there."

21

Preparation

At first, E Kwekuue's leaders saw this connection to the rest of the world as a good thing that required needed accommodation. Despite how the Imaia and Iron Empire had preyed on their ancestors, they understood that much of the strength of those Empires came from their diversity of peoples and ideas. They soon came to realize, however, that too many people with too many different opinions meant no one would agree on anything, halting any meaningful progress in its tracks. This made tensions rise, and nearly led to E Kwekuue's demise.

Exodus countdown: 14 days, 22 hours, 26 minutes

Skadaatha returned home to find it filled with the scents of cooking—something that had become increasingly more common since Vysla had more time to spend at home. She picked out curry and paprik among the mix of spices, and the familiar scent of simmering beef and *vjazi* brought a smile to her lips.

Vysla stood over the kitchen's main countertop, ingredients set out all around him as he chopped. He had three different cutting boards out, two of them already used, as evidenced by stains on the wood and knives resting on them near the corners. One pot sat covered on the stove, while another filled low with water waited to be used. Near one of the cutting boards a bit farther away from Vysla sat a large bowl with a cloth placed over it.

Hanging up her coat—she'd done more official work today than usual, so she'd worn her uniform out—Skadaatha strode over to the kitchen and took her husband's hand. He squeezed it and glanced up at her with a smile.

"What are you making?" she asked. He raised an eyebrow. Skadaatha rolled her eyes. "What are you making besides njama?"

That scent was unmistakable.

Vysla grinned. He liked to make a large amount of food all at once and simply store whatever they didn't eat. It had often proved quite fruitful in their busy lives.

"Can you guess?"

"You've taken out all the ingredients?"

He nodded.

Skadaatha stepped away from her husband, undoing the buttons of her dress shirt as she looked around the kitchen.

Vysla had set out a large red njania fruit—he was currently cutting up another—a small icepepper, a large avoca and a choka, a green citrus fruit, all grouped together. When she lifted the cloth covering the bowl, she found sliced red kituun soaking. Closer to the waiting pot, he'd gotten out the maize flour and some salt and paprik.

"*Kachuumbrai* and uugala?" she asked.

He nodded, and Skadaatha grinned. "I'll change and be out in a moment to help."

Vysla moved over to the njama pot to tend to the simmering stew.

Skadaatha's smile deepened at that as she strode into their bedroom and divested herself of the rest of her dress uniform. She stepped over to the closet and picked through her clothing, looking for something that Vysla would appreciate that was also easy to clean. Or something she wouldn't mind getting dirty.

She decided on a bright, patterned shift dress, and quickly slipped it on before returning to the kitchen and grabbing an apron.

"How is the investigation going?" Vysla asked, turning on the burner for the pot of water as she took the choka and rolled it back and forth on the cutting board.

Skadaatha shrugged, then halved the choka, juicing one half into a small bowl Vysla had set out. "A lot of possible leads so far, but nothing solid. Aarnal saw the Lightforged adjunct doing something strange in Tower Six's control office, and he said that Kojatere spent a long time speaking with Jynos before poking around that hangar. They've seen her visiting other hangars as well, on the towers and in the city. There's also the matter of the long-term possible end to Kojatere's operation that Yndlova let slip, though she may have only told me that to distract me."

She took the bowl of soaking kituun and popped a slice into her mouth. The water had taken most of the bite from the raw, pungent vegetable, so she moved over to the sink and drained the bowl in the colander Vysla had set out.

"They're also trying to sideline me in as polite a way as possible," she continued, "so I've made almost no headway on any of the possible—Ah!"

Skadaatha almost dropped the bowl of rinsed kituun in surprise. She set it down, then looked down at her chest and then at Vysla.

He wore an insufferable grin, looking back and forth between her and the now-boiling pot of water, fingers dusted white with the same flour on her chest, neck and face.

"You were getting frustrated," he said when she gazed at him, wide-eyed, acting as though he hadn't just flung flour at her. "It sounds like you're getting impatient, which isn't like you."

Skadaatha searched for some sort of retort, then sighed and began combining all the ingredients for the kachuumbrai.

He has a point.

"I know. I'm not used to such stringent time frames, and now I have so many of them to juggle. Decades used to pass in the blink of an eye. Now, it seems like I have nothing but demands on my time." She sighed, adding a bit more salt to the salad. Skadaatha took a deep breath, then looked to Vysla. "Do you need me to help with anything else?"

He added a bit more flour to the growing mixture that would soon become their uugala and gestured toward the simmering pot of njama that he'd been stirring occasionally. "Watch that?"

Skadaatha nodded, moving around her husband and taking up the spatula to gently stir the simmering ingredients. "How long has it been going?"

"Forty-seven minutes. Should be ready soon."

Skadaatha nodded, breathing in deep to fill her nostrils with the wonderful aroma. Her mouth started to water.

"Should I expect this to have any surprises like our last few meals?"

More time to cook had led to Vysla experimenting with their food rather than just making it. Most of them had been enjoyable. They'd only had to find a restaurant to eat at twice.

Vysla grinned, but shook his head. "Not really. I want to make sure I get this right before I try anything new. I salted the water for the kituun, though. That should have drawn out the flavor a bit more. Oh, and add some extra paprik to the salad."

Skadaatha did so.

"How have the drills and tests for the reactors been going?" she asked, trying to distract herself. Normally, she would have enjoyed the comfortable silence with her husband. At the moment, however, Skadaatha knew that her mind would just wander back toward Kojatere and the issues with her investigation of the woman.

Vysla launched into a very technical explanation of the various calibrations and tests they'd performed to measure various output levels of the city's reactors and compare them to those installed in their capital ships and fighters. With the way Mjatafa Mwonga's thrusters had been placed far beneath the floor of the shallow sea, constructed and connected to the city structure through the use of undersea caves they'd bored out, they couldn't perform any true tests. Everything would come down to the day of Exodus. Ynuukwidas could help them hold together the city if anything went wrong, of course, but Skadaatha had plans for the city far beyond its function as a means of escape from Efruumani. Once that was complete, they could—

Skadaatha jumped as more flour hit her. She glared at her husband. He met her gaze with a flat look.

"You stopped paying attention."

Skadaatha just sighed, returning her attention to the stew. It would be ready in just a few minutes.

"I have something that should lift your mood," Vysla said. "Can you watch over both? The uugala should be ready to take out in three minutes."

Skadaatha nodded as her husband dusted the flour off his hands and walked off into their apartment. She leaned close to each dish, sniffing it. She thought for a moment, then added a bit of salt and paprik to the uugala mixture, and some more curry powder to the njama. She usually did that, but Vysla hadn't caught on yet. Maybe he finally would if they did this a few more times before Exodus.

Vysla's footsteps approached from behind a few moments later, and Skadaatha turned to find him carrying a polished, repaired version of the weapon she'd used against Kojatere.

"Here," he said, holding it out to her. "You'll need to find a way to test it as a siphon for innate investiture. The siphon works as expected on georaurals and gemcrests, but I didn't have a way to test beyond that."

Skadaatha took the weapon and looked it over, thinking. It was a bit thicker than the previous version with another section added on opposite the emitter. As she studied the weapon and the small, glowing georaurals set into its structure, an idea for how to test it and further her stalled progress with Kojatere began to blossom in her mind.

"You thought of something."

Skadaatha looked up at her husband and realized she was grinning. "I did."

"Do I want to know?"

"Probably not."

Vysla shook his head, but a smirk tugged at the corner of his mouth. Before he could turn back to the stove, Skadaatha pulled him into a deep kiss that made her blood run hot, brightening her clearnodes reflexively.

When she pulled back, she kept her hips pressed against Vysla's and gazed down at him, grinning.

He cleared his throat, straightening his glasses. "As much as I enjoyed that, I am quite hungry, and I spent a long time making this food."

Skadaatha laughed and kissed him again.

22

Make it Work

Just when it seemed the Buuekwenani would become like every other people and abandon the unique way of life that had sustained and protected them for so long, they banded together and demanded that the leadership find a way to make things right again without losing what they had gained from Uumgwefilo and the window they provided into the outside world.

Exodus countdown: 12 days, 22 hours, 41 minutes

"We're certain the Imaia's orbital ships won't pick up on this frequency?"

They'd left the city almost immediately after Luuhuuta had brought him the information and had been waiting for a reply for quite some time. The controls and blinking arrays of the transport's interior held a sense of familiarity yet seemed less wondrous than usual after so long in such an idyllic city. It also reminded them of what would come after they completed their task here.

Luuhuuta shook her head. "No one uses it anymore. The chatter we can pick up has gotten more and more scarce over the past few months due to their testing of new methods to use once off-world. We can still pick up a good amount from Mjatafa Mwonga, but not as much of the communications to their orbital ships or Myrskaan Station."

Koruuksi nodded, waiting for whoever was monitoring the communications array back at Remnant Base to reply.

Luuhuuta was lean, taller than Koruuksi, though not as tall as Muuzuuri or most of the Buuekwenani. She'd tied her hair back into tight, thin braids to help deal with the humidity, and had even donned a bit of the eye makeup Vise usually wore. Koruuksi smiled at that, nearly shaking his head at the wonders new clothing could work. And a sense of purpose, of course.

"So, this creates a shield around the entire ship?"

Koruuksi shared a grin with Luuhuuta at the wonder in Ymvesi'ia's voice, then glanced over at the princess and Uuchantuu at the back of the ship. They'd closed the doors so Koruuksi could have his mask off.

"Exactly," Uuchantuu said. "The georaural is still the only thing projecting and powering the actual shield—we haven't found a way around that, but the ship's computers allow us to switch it on and off and adjust the flow of power to it."

"Incredible."

Koruuksi smiled at that.

She's almost as fascinated as Vise seems to be.

Koruuksi wished she'd come with them, but Ymvesi'ia had said that Vise was busy with other duties at the time when she went to get the Akjemasai that had helped escort them out.

She'll be annoyed that we left her behind, anyway.

Koruuksi planned on showing her the datapads later, along with a few other pieces of equipment from the ship he'd thrown into his pack. Still... talking her through what he and Luuhuuta were doing while they waited for a response would have made him less nervous.

"We'll be able to make this work, right?"

Koruuksi blinked, looking back to Luuhuuta. She'd spoken so quietly he'd barely heard her. Her eyes begged him to confirm her question.

He put a hand on her shoulder. "It won't be easy, but we'll make it work. I promise. Ymvesi'ia told me that more of the Akjemasai and staff she and Vise had told have been warming up to the idea. And I think the way Angare and Kamili were talking with us on the way here is a good sign, too."

Luuhuuta gave him a tight smile, nodding. "You're right. Nothing worth doing is ever easy, is it?"

Koruuksi sighed, shaking his head. He looked to the transport's shaded windows. "No. No, it isn't. Try them again."

As Luuhuuta called out to Remnant Base again, Koruuksi took a deep breath, trying to calm his nerves. His eyes landed on Tshala and Kakengo talking with a few of the Akjemasai Ymvesi'ia had brought along, smiling and laughing.

Hopefully that will make things easier once everything falls into place.

From what Koruuksi had been able to gather, the Buuekwenani looked to the Akjemasai with a mix of respect and awe. They saw them as the first line of defense in keeping their Vale secret and safe from the outside.

Koruuksi eyed Ymvesi'ia at that thought, wondering if her decision to join the Akjemasai—or Kuula'ande's decision to let her—had been entirely emotional and out of respect and love for her late mother, or if that respect and the impact it had on how the people viewed her had calculated into that at all.

He looked back to Luuhuuta. "Anything?"

She shook her head.

Koruuksi blew out a puff of air. "Ugh. Try—"

"Hello? Icewing, this is Remnant One, over."

Koruuksi straightened at the familiar, crackly voice. He glanced to Uuchantuu to beckon her over, but she was already at his side.

"Naruuna, is that you?" Koruuksi asked, taking the comm.

"Koruuksi?" the voice asked, growing brighter. "I hope this is a good news call."

Koruuksi sighed. "Not exactly. How are things back there?"

"Busy, but good. We've managed to consolidate personnel, supplies and equipment from all of our different outposts to

Remnant One—not easy without attracting any attention, but we did it. We're still organizing everything and running drills and such, but people are getting a little antsy. Especially since it's so crowded."

"Rightfully so," Uuchantuu muttered.

Koruuksi nodded. "That's good to hear, Naruuna. Has Estingai's team returned?"

"Not yet."

Koruuksi sighed. She would know what to do in this situation. *But it would probably get very unpleasant very quickly.*

"What about transports?" he asked. "You should have some to spare now that you're done consolidating, right?"

"We do, but... per Commander Paiz's orders, the engineers have started either dismantling them to repair our fighters or armor and arm those in better condition as drop ships for getting to the capital ship. They're even taking apart what we had put together of the old cruiser. We can maybe spare one or two."

Koruuksi's grip tightened around the comm. The cruiser had been his last hope—it wasn't ready for non-atmospheric travel or a long voyage, but there could have been a way to make it work long enough to get to E Kwekuue and back with everyone on board and then hide on Darkside until—

Stop. Don't focus on what could *have happened.*

He had to take a few deep breaths before he could speak again.

"What about Kojatere? Any word from her? Or any way of getting word to her?"

"Sorry, Koruuksi."

He looked to Uuchantuu and Ymvesi'ia for an idea, then Luuhuuta. All three frowned, shrugging or shaking their heads.

He sighed. "See if you can get Paiz to send us one or two transports, and tell Marjatla to see if she can figure something out. Anything will help at this rate."

"Does that mean you found some help?"

Koruuksi glanced at Uuchantuu and Ymvesi'ia. "Some. Working on more. I'll tell you all about it when we get back. Over."

"Good luck, Koruuksi. Over."

Hanging the radio back up on its hook, Koruuksi looked to Luuhuuta. "Can you stay here and see what chatter you can pick up while waiting for the ships or Naruuna's reply?"

She nodded.

Koruuksi looked to Ymvesi'ia "Any chance you can spare a few—"

Ymvesi'ia nodded, smiling. "No problem."

She looked to Kamili, who nodded, then smiled at Luuhuuta.

Koruuksi smiled back at Ymvesi'ia.

"What do we do now?" Uuchantuu asked, brushing up against Ymvesi'ia. Koruuksi wasn't sure if either woman had done that consciously, or if they'd just done it.

"We go back to the city," Koruuksi said, "I need to think."

23

Healing

It took time and many failures, but eventually the king and the Diwani, E Kwekuue's new leading officials, found a way to integrate new technology and foreign ideas into their culture. It was a stricter, more harsh way of life than the Buuekwenani had grown used to since the accord with Uumgwefilo, but it worked. A part of this was the establishment of the Muukjebarat: those who would leave E Kwekuue to see the world and bring back new ideas for the Diwani to judge worthy of incorporation into society, and decide the best way to do so.

Exodus countdown: 14 days, 14 hours, 12 minutes

Estingai tried to keep from grinding her teeth as she made a few notations in her sketchbook. She'd trained for a whole day with Matsanga, and today, after exercising and trimming the short section of her hair, had tried for hours to find something new. So far, she'd come up with nothing.

Her powers were all stronger, of course, but that was simply an advantage—not something groundbreaking. Estingai had decided to try and look on the positive side of things, however. She'd started making notations in her sketchbook to help measure and internalize the differences between when she used a powermetal and when she did not.

Some were hard to measure—like how the latent power of her rednodes improved her reflexes, or to what degree she could manipulate chance with her yellownodes. She was down to about half her Auroralight now after consuming the light of an entire brace. She wanted to keep going but knew it would be better to stop and rest for a bit. There was still an entire day left before the next Auroraday.

And I'm exhausted.

Most Auroramantic abilities did not tax the body much beyond using up Auroralight. The mind was another issue entirely, however.

Finishing her notations, Estingai closed the book and sat back against the wall, eyes closed. She pressed the palms of her hands over her eyes, then scrubbed them upward, running her fingers through her hair.

I'm missing... something.

Glancing over at the powerstones she'd set her sketchbook next to, Estingai frowned. She wanted to keep going, but...

With a sigh, Estingai swept the powerstones up and deposited them in the small wash-leather sack before they could tempt her to start testing again.

She set the sack down on top of her sketch pad, then looked to the other small pile of silver-violet ore.

After a moment, Estingai picked one of them up and clasped both hands over it, closing her eyes again. She tried to figure out what exactly this one did. Matsanga had not given it a name, so she didn't even have that for reference.

She was more aware of the passing seconds and minutes without trying, but that didn't point her to anything. Some people simply had a better internal clock than others. Other than that...

She sighed, placing the stones back on the ground and trying to figure out a lack of anything like she felt when letting go of the powermetal.

After a few minutes of nothing, Estingai picked them up again. She was certain she could figure this out. She just needed—

Estingai frowned, opening her eyes for a moment. She peered at the stones, then set them down. Her frustration seemed to grow just a bit stronger.

But is that just because I'm giving up?

She picked them up again, and that certainty returned.

Are these giving more confidence?

Groaning, Estingai set the violet-tinted ore back down. A small boost in confidence was of no use to her if she had no direction. After a deep breath, she looked to the ore again, and remembered the workshop she'd once shared with Aiteperit and Uncle Suulehep.

We would have had so much fun figuring that out.

Estingai had always trained her hardest to push her Auroramantic abilities beyond what everyone else thought possible, but had discovered long ago that georaurals could make one just as dangerous as an Auroramancer with the right knowledge.

"Your practice is going well then, I take it?"

Estingai leapt to her feet, drawing her dagger even as she registered Matsanga and Ajida entering through the rough hole that had once been a doorway. Rather than roll his eyes at her or grunt, Matsanga met her eyes. They did not hold pity, but pain and understanding.

Estingai blinked as he turned toward her and engulfed her shoulder with one of his massive hands. Ajida padded over and licked the back of her hand.

"You're safe here, Estingai," he said. "Safe from anything that would attack you, at least."

A part of Estingai wanted to shrug off her mentor's hand. She didn't. Instead, she sank back down to the floor, crossing her legs. Ajida followed and curled up beside her. That made her feel a little better, but...

"I can't let myself think like that. Not until I'm finally safe, at least."

Matsanga sighed and began unburdening himself.

"And when will that be?" he asked. "When you escape? Or will you look for spies and traitors among you even then. Paranoia can be even worse than your bitterness, Estingai."

Estingai frowned, folding her arms over her chest. "It keeps me alive."

Matsanga grunted. "What use is being alive if you can't really live?"

Estingai didn't respond. The words were too similar to what Araana had said during their argument. Koruuksi had said similar things to her a few times.

"Did your practice go poorly?" Matsanga asked, "or were you just particularly frustrated?"

Estingai seethed for a moment at her failure, then sighed. "Both."

"Explain."

Of course.

"All I could do was sense and grow accustomed to the enhancement of the powermetal," Estingai said. "I made some notations about the exact magnitude of the magnification and if I could find any differences due to the power of the ore, but that didn't lead me to any revelations."

She waited for Matsanga to say something. He just met her gaze unblinking.

"With the violet metal..." she shrugged, "I became more aware of my internal clock and possibly more confident, but that was it. It didn't magnify my powers or allow me to change them to any degree. Nothing noticeable, at least."

Matsanga grunted.

Estingai frowned at that. "Are you going to wait for me to unravel some mystery about them, or just tell me? This directionless practice is a waste of time."

Matsanga ignored her question. The room fell into a relative silence as he rose and took out two of the sealed containers, then lit a fire and set them over it atop a metal grill. Estingai watched the flames dance, losing herself in their hypnotic movements for a while as Matsanga heated the food.

When he proffered her a bowl a while later, she hesitated.

"Eat," he insisted, pushing it toward her.

"So, you're not going to teach me anything else tonight?" she asked, reluctantly accepting the bowl, "even though what you did have me practice was a dead end?"

Matsanga shook his head. "You need to find something first with what I gave you—something that impresses me—before I teach you anything else. That should give you the motivation you need to accomplish it."

Estingai growled as she ate her stew, trying not to think about how good it was.

"Did you figure out what you can show me?" she asked between bites. "You had to have learned something over the centuries."

To Estingai's surprise, a slight grin tugged at the man's stony features.

"I was wondering how long it would take you to ask me that. There's one trick I can't explain, and something else I found that only an Iceborn can do."

Estingai just grunted, shoving another bite of stew into her mouth.

"Did you try scraping your knuckles on anything or giving yourself a shallow cut?"

Estingai frowned, hand stopping halfway to her mouth.

She studied Matsanga for a moment, brow raised, then set her bowl of stew down and gritted her teeth as she pounded her knuckles on the stone floor and dragged them a handspan before holding her hand up so Matsanga could see the broken and bruised skin. "Now I have."

Matsanga frowned, gazing at her for a moment, then shook his head.

"Take the powermetal and concentrate on your knuckles."

Estingai did as he said, shaking herself at the sudden influx of awareness, energy, and strength.

"Now imagine the skin re-knitting."

Estingai frowned, but did as he said, closing her eyes for a moment, then cracking one open to peek at her knuckles.

She sighed, dropping her hand. "Nothing—"

"Keep going."

"How long?"

"You'll see."

"I'm getting tired of all your half-answers, old man."

"It works better if you're quiet, brat."

Clamping her mouth shut, Estingai stared at her wounded knuckles, imaging them as they'd been before—the skin a flawless, icy blue, no brownish-blue discoloration or violet blood slowly rising above the raw skin.

Estingai did this for three minutes and forty-eight seconds, nearly afraid she'd strain something in her head, before she realized the discoloration was subdued.

"Keep going," Matsanga said at her gasp.

Estingai nodded, keeping her eyes and her mind fixed on her hand. It took two and a half more minutes, but her skin reknit just as she imagined, the bruising disappeared, and the cool air no longer stung her skin, though a bit of pain lingered.

Estingai gazed at her knuckles with wide-eyes, flexing her fingers, making fists—she even went as far as stretching the fingers back and forth before turning her gaze to Matsanga.

"That's incredible," she breathed. "Can it go faster?"

"Theoretically," he said, "though it probably takes practice and an understanding beyond what either of us possess. The body knows how to heal itself, and the larger the powermetal, the more effective and quicker it is, but it has its limits—to someone like me, at least. I imagine someone who has studied anatomy and medicine might be able to direct the energy to heal more complex wounds and do so more quickly."

Estingai blinked. "This is incredible! When did you figure it out? Why did you never share it with anyone?"

Matsanga pointed to the scars on his face. "I only look this good because of it. Call it an accident or desperation, but I didn't discover this until after I was too broken to care."

Estingai gritted her teeth. She wanted to yell at him for leaving her but held back. Information was more important than stupid feelings. To her and the entirety of the Remnant.

"Have you used it to heal anything more than that?"

Matsanga shrugged. "I try not to injure myself too often, so no—I haven't had too many opportunities. It does wonders for soreness, however. In small doses, at least, but so far, it's relatively inefficient."

Estingai frowned, then looked down at her gemcrest, tugging the neck of her shirt down a bit. She'd depleted at least a tenth of her remaining Auroralight.

All that just to heal some scrapes.

"I see," she said, whatever excitement she'd felt at the possibility of using Auroralight to be able to heal during battle now gone.

"Anything else?" she asked.

"Nothing that will make much difference in your time frame," he said, "but it may help you towards discovery. Did you notice during your testing that you had more direct control over your muscles? Enough practice with that and you could move with more efficiency and precision, strike with more force, check yourself over for small injuries you might not notice."

Estingai nodded, thinking, then looked down at her gemcrest again.

"What about moving Auroralight between gempairs?" she asked.

Matsanga nodded, seeming satisfied. "It helps with that, though Skadaatha taught me that without any aids, as I taught you."

Estingai nodded. That trick thad saved her life on many occasions. It might not make a difference against Kojatere, but had always come in useful when fighting lightforged and Auroraborn. Full Auroraborn like her could use all twelve abilities, but Auroralight usually only powered the nodes it filled. Where a greyarm or blackshadow would have an entire gemcrest to fuel their single ability, Auroraborn only had a single pair of gems to fuel each of their twelve abilities. Unless they learned to transfer the Auroralight to their other pairs of biogems like she and the other Knights had.

"That's good," she said. "Anything else?"

He shook his head. "Not right now. Finish your stew and give yourself some rest, catch a little sleep to help you think better when you continue practicing."

Estingai frowned, taking another bite of the stew. Even cold, it was good. Still, she brightened her violetnodes just enough to heat it up again.

"I don't have time for that," she grumbled.

"I know exactly how much time you have, Estingai," Matsanga said, voice firm. "Trust me."

Estingai sighed, but set about finishing her stew, putting a bit of heat into it to warm it.

Whatever problems she had with her former mentor, she could still trust him.

That gave her some comfort.

When Estingai finished her stew, she frowned at the empty bowl, then looked to where Matsanga had stacked the other leftovers.

She caught his gaze and held up the bowl.

"Any chance I could have some more?"

24

A King's Anger

For hundreds of years, this way of life sustained the Buuekwenani and Uumgwefilo, their sister city. Both lived in peace and prosperity despite the conflict that enveloped the rest of the world and the different powers that laid claim to Uumgwefilo. Until the ships arrived bearing the standard of the Scarlet Sun.

Exodus countdown: 11 days, 5 hours, 33 minutes

Koruuksi took another deep breath, trying to calm his nerves as the Akjemasai led him through the palace. He tried to distract himself from what he was about to do by looking at the artwork and trying to match it with what he'd learned so far about the history of the city and its people.

It didn't work.

He tried studying the Akjemasai's armor instead. No warrior seemed to have exactly the same kit, though all were colorful and ornate. Some had helmets styled after eagles, leopards, river beasts, or other forest creatures, with the feathers, pelts or skins adorning the helm and the rest of the body to continue the theme. Their armor was polished aluminum over padded cloth. Most wore bracers, muscled breastplates, scaled or segmented mantles and hip guards on the upper body, a brace of sidearms, daggers and tools at the waist, and aluminum shinguards. Most carried shields—either round or rectangular, but always with some sort of decoration hanging off the bottom—and either a long spear or one-handed sword, as well as a case on their back containing short spears, arrows, and a recurve bow. A strange blend of flamboyance, functionality, and personal style.

Suulehep would have loved it.

Koruuksi smiled at the thought of his uncle. Thinking of how incredible he would have found this place made Koruuksi feel a bit better.

By the time Koruuksi arrived in Kuula'ande's throne room, his teeth were clenched, and he'd begun to sweat more than usual.

"Ah, Koruuksi," Kuula'ande said, spreading his arms as he rose from his throne. His deep booming voice echoed through the chamber. "How are you and you people enjoying your time in my city? I see you have acquired some new clothing."

Koruuksi nodded, nerves making him glad for his mask, so he didn't need to attempt a smile.

We agreed this was the best play. Uuchantuu is supposed to stop me from doing stupid shit and she even agreed that I needed to do this. We don't have time to wait on the other Diwani.

Kuula'ande's warm welcome gave Koruuksi a bit more confidence that he was doing the right thing, despite Ymvesi'ia's warnings.

Kuula'ande is reasonable and intelligent. He seems a lot more accepting than Ymvesi'ia originally was. If we could convince her when she didn't even like us, at first, gaining Kuula'ande's help shouldn't be a problem.

He'd still made sure that Uuchantuu and their team had the way back to the ships memorized with everything packed before he came here.

I really hope it doesn't come to that.

"It is a paradise," Koruuksi said. "Even more incredible than most of the stories I'd heard when I thought it just a fable. And yes, your daughter was most gracious in acquiring more comfortable clothing for myself and my team. I'm still not entirely able to process how that exchange worked despite her and Vise explaining it to me, but I am grateful."

Kuula'ande laughed. "Yes, I heard my daughter seems to have warmed up a bit to you and your people since you first arrived. I had initially worried she might scare you off when I saw the way she stomped after you after our first meeting."

Koruuksi nodded. "She is very protective of her people, much like my own sister. I wasn't worried once I was given the opportunity to speak to her plainly."

"You should consider yourself honored that she changed her mind. She is very... prickly toward those who put themselves at odds with her, but just as loyal to those who can manage to get on her good side."

"I am very honored—because of Princess Ymvesi'ia and your hospitality."

He paused, looking around at the chamber, "I have not seen so many spirits in some time, and I've never seen them simply exist for so long without vanishing into their realm."

Koruuksi barely caught it, but Kuula'ande's warm demeanor slipped for a fraction of a second.

"Yes," he said, a smile returning to his face, "we don't know why, but we are honored that the oruu have chosen E Kwekuue to grace with their presence."

He gestured up toward a group of lightoruu near the windows.

Koruuksi blinked at the lie, but smoothed his features and continued, hoping he was being as tactful as he thought he was.

"I must admit, I'm amazed at your people's progress in science and economics," Koruuksi said. "I don't mean to offend, but for a self-sustaining, isolated society, even with the limited contact you used to have with Uumgwefilo, I must admit, I didn't expect this level and sophistication of technology. I doubt even the Imaia has thought to use georaurals in all the ways that you do."

Kuula'ande tensed slightly at the mention of the Imaia, but nodded. "Yes, we are very proud of our achievements."

"I can see why it would be—" Koruuksi paused as Ymvesi'ia strode into the room, her expression changing from one of purpose to one of alarm and apprehension for just a moment before she strode toward Koruuksi and her father. "—daunting to leave such a wonderful place behind."

Kuula'ande had looked to his daughter, but turned back to Koruuksi, the warmth gone from his expression, shoulders tense. "I believe I know where you are trying to lead this conversation, son of Kojatere. I would caution you not to do so. I informed you of my decision, and I have not changed my mind since."

"You must be mistaken, Father," Ymvesi'ia said, joining them. "When I heard of your decision, I made sure to inform Koruuksi of the consequences if he did not accept it. I have gotten to know him well over the past few days, and I can assure you he would not be so foolish."

Ymvesi'ia directed the last few words at him, face tense as she held his gaze.

Koruuksi's jaw bunched for a moment before he let out a sigh.

"Of course, forgive me."

Stop there. Just shut up and leave.

"I only wanted to make sure that you understood the science correctly, Your Highness, as there are likely areas your people have not explored that we have."

Ymvesi'ia's eyes widened as Kuula'ande's expression grew dark.

Stop. Stop it now.

His mouth wouldn't, though.

"If you had said yes, the timetable has moved up, but as Princess Ymvesi'ia said, I will not ask about that. However, I was also sent to ask about the power that protects E Kwekuue to see—"

"Silence!" Kuula'ande barked, his voice filling the chamber. What spirits remained in the room fled.

Fuck. Should have stopped.

"I extended you and your people hospitality," Kuula'ande said, "welcomed you to my city—my people's sanctuary. I refused your petition, yes, but since then I have been in talks with the council members trying to figure out a way to allow your people sanctuary in E Kwekuue without disrupting my people's way of life."

"Father—" Ymvesi'ia began.

Kuula'ande gestured for her to be silent.

Fuck.

"You asked carefully arranged questions rather than being direct. I have heard that your people are prone to such things, but I had hoped you would act otherwise. You do not accept my decision, and you ask of things you should not," Kuula'ande said, voice cold and steely. "This insult requires me to rescind my invitation of sanctuary and hospitality."

"Father, I—"

Kuula'ande ignored her, glaring at Koruuksi. "You and your people are hereby banished from the Vale of E Kwekuue. If you come to our forests again, our Akjemasai will not hesitate to do what they must to keep our people safe."

Koruuksi's heart sank.

I was wrong. Fuck, I was wrong.

"Akjemasai," Kuula'ande called. "Take this man and escort him and his people from our lands. Make sure they leave E Kwekuue far behind."

Koruuksi tensed as the warriors flanking the door moved toward him, then nearly jumped when a hand seized his wrist in a tight grip.

"I will take care of this personally, Father." Ymvesi'ia said. She turned her glare on Koruuksi. Her words came out as a growl. "This man deceived us both. I will see to it that he troubles E Kwekuue no longer."

Kuula'ande nodded, and after one last glare at Koruuksi, turned and walked off through another doorway deeper into the palace.

Koruuksi looked after and nearly fell over when Ymvesi'ia jerked him toward the exit. He barely had time to secure his mask before she dragged him out of the room.

"Ymvesi'ia, please," he hissed as she dragged him through the halls past armed Akjemasai who filed in behind them and wide-eyed staff that cleared out of the way. "I can—"

"Quiet," she snapped, not meeting his gaze.

Once they were outside the palace, she gestured to a few Akjemasai Koruuksi recognized—Angare, Kamili and Na'imbe—and pulled him slightly ahead of them and the others.

"You idiot!" she hissed, yanking him a bit closer to her as she kept up her brisk pace away from the palace. "I told you. I told you what would happen if you went to him with this again. What were you thinking?"

"Ymvesi'ia, I—"

"Was I not clear enough?" she continued, bulling over him. "It wouldn't have made a difference, would it? You were not direct with him. Maybe if you had been, he would have just ordered you out and been angry, but no. You had to try and—ugh! You idiot."

"Ymvesi'ia!" Koruuksi snapped, yanking his arm back hard enough to halt her.

She rounded on him. "What?"

"I'm sorry," he said. "Truly. I didn't know what else to do. We would barely be able to get all your people to our base in time as it is, much less any possessions they will want to bring or supplies we might need to sustain them." Koruuksi took a deep breath. "Your father seemed like a reasonable man. This seemed like the best option. I thought he would listen."

Ymvesi'ia glared at him a few seconds longer, then put her fingers to her forehead and closed her eyes.

"My father is a reasonable man," she sighed, "but his judgement can be clouded as easily as anyone else's. From his perspective, you asked leading questions in what started out as pleasant conversation, you were working behind his back, and took advantage of his generosity. And then you went and asked about our secret—" Ymvesi'ia cut off, taking a deep breath. "When you did all of that, the conversation was no longer about reason or logic, it was about emotion, principle and dignity."

"I'm sorry," Koruuksi said. "I'm just trying to help—"

"I know," Ymvesi'ia said, shoulders sagging for a moment. "You're still an idiot. Come on."

They hurried through the city, the Akjemasai around them wearing faces of stone. Koruuksi tried to take in the city one last time but frowned. E Kwekuue's splendor seemed dimmed with his failure. The city itself had been lost from the start, but now he'd failed to save the incredible people that had built and protected it.

Koruuksi spotted Uuchantuu dressed in full kit waiting by the door when the building came into view. A few moments later, the rest started filing out.

"You've got to be kidding me," Ymvesi'ia muttered under her breath.

She glared between him and Uuchantuu once they stopped before the building. "You two knew this would happen, and you did it anyway?" She looked to Uuchantuu. "You let him pull this stunt?"

Uuchantuu frowned. "Getting all the Diwani to agree would have taken too long. It was the only option we could think of."

Koruuksi shrugged. "We hoped it wouldn't turn out this way, but we're used to planning for the worst."

Ymvesi'ia shook her head.

"I'm guessing the fact that you're still alive means we aren't all slated for execution?"

Ymvesi'ia straightened, blinking. "Execution? We are not barbarians."

Koruuksi shrugged. "People can be even more 'civilized' than anyone here, yet be capable of things 'barbarians' would consider horrifying."

He looked to Uuchantuu. "We've just been banished. I need you to take everyone out to the ships and back to base and see if there is anything else we haven't thought of. If Estingai is back, tell her to come here."

Uuchantuu and Ymvesi'ia both frowned at him.

"I need to lead them back?" Uuchantuu said.

Koruuksi nodded, then turned to Ymvesi'ia. "Can you escort them back to their ships? Make sure they get there safely and as quickly as possible?"

"You are not going with them?" Ymvesi'ia asked. "What do you believe you can do from here? A city you have been banished from?"

Koruuksi shook his head. "Our plan with the council can still work. They don't have to know I'm still behind it."

"Bullshit," Uuchantuu said, stepping close to him. "I'm not leaving you here."

"Your presence in this city is not necessary to convince the council," Ymvesi'ia said. "I know the science well now, as does Vise, and I know how to approach each of them. After what happened today, your presence would only work against you."

"I was given a mission to complete," Koruuksi said firmly, looking between the two of them. "I didn't ask to lead it, but here I am."

He turned to Uuchantuu. "I need you and the others to go back and help everyone else. Either find a way to get more ships or some way of making the distraction at Mjatafa Mwonga even bigger than we planned so we can come here after evacuating Remnant Base." He looked to Ymvesi'ia. "I'm not in the habit of leaving friends behind."

Ymvesi'ia blinked at that. She opened her mouth a few times, as though to say something, but it took a few tries before anything came out.

"Fine," she said finally, voice tight. She turned to Angare. "Lead them back to their ships. I need you to send two of your number to go ask for volunteers to accompany Koruuksi's team back to their base. We will need to provide whatever help we can to save our people."

Angare looked between her and Koruuksi, expression grave, but nodded, "Of course, Princess."

"Oh, and make sure to send someone to get Vi—"

As if on cue, Vise pushed her way past a few of the Akjemasai to stand next to Ymvesi'ia. Koruuksi blinked as he took her in. She seemed somewhat out of breath, a light sheen of sweat on her forehead. Koruuksi felt his pulse quicken. The effect Vise's current state had on her chest was... hard not to look at.

Wait... did she run here?

"I came as soon as I heard," Vise said, looking between Ymvesi'ia, Koruuksi and Uuchantuu. She turned to the princess. "You go take Koruuksi's people to their ships, so you won't have just entirely lied to your father."

Ymvesi'ia frowned.

"I'll take care of him," Vise assured her.

A few of Koruuksi's team snickered behind him, and he shook his head before looking to Vise. "How did you know?"

Ymvesi'ia rolled her eyes. "Vise somehow always knows everything."

Vise grinned. "News like that, plus Kuula'ande actually shouting travels pretty fast in the palace."

"If you're staying, there's no way in hell I'm leaving," Uuchantuu said, locking eyes with Koruuksi.

"Uuchantuu—"

"If I come back without you and Estingai is there, she'll fly over here and raise hell, probably beat Kuula'ande and the council into submission, and then beat you half to death."

Koruuksi's objections died on his tongue.

She's right.

"This is the sister you said I remind you of?" Ymvesi'ia asked slowly.

Koruuksi shot her a sheepish grin.

Ymvesi'ia pursed her lips. "I am not sure whether to be offended or take that as a complement."

"Probably both," Uuchantuu said before looking back to Koruuksi. "I also want to be the one to do something stupid with you for once rather than being the one to clean up after you."

Koruuksi sighed. "Fine."

He turned to the rest of the team. "Muuzuuri, you're in charge. Ymvesi'ia and her Akjemasai are going to take you back out to the ships, and a few of them will be coming with you. You know what I need you to do?"

Muuzuuri and the rest of the team saluted. "Yes, sir. Good luck."

The Natari woman grinned. "And try to be quick about it. I'd rather not have to try restraining Commander Estingai either."

Koruuksi grinned, then turned back to the three women before him.

"Go," Vise told Ymvesi'ia, "before we attract too much attention."

She moved between Koruuksi and Uuchantuu, slinging an arm around each of their shoulders. "I've got these two."

Ymvesi'ia hesitated for a moment, then sighed, nodding. She looked toward Uuchantuu, and Koruuksi tried not to be too obvious as their faces colored, and they smiled at each other. They nodded and then Ymvesi'ia signaled for Koruuksi's team and the Akjemasai to follow her.

Koruuksi glanced at Vise and they shared a grin before she turned and ushered them back into the building.

"Alright, so how exactly do you plan on hiding us. Not in here, right?"

Vise shook her head. "Not for too long, at least." She looked to Uuchantuu. "Change out of those into some of the clothes we had made for you. But without the top. That will draw too much attention."

Koruuksi laughed as Uuchantuu's face lit up, earning him a punch in the arm.

Vise rolled her eyes. "Oh, get over it. No one will be looking at your chest."

Koruuksi grinned as Uuchantuu sighed and went deeper into the building to change.

Vise looked from her to Koruuksi, eyebrow raised, then sighed, shaking her head.

"What about me?" he asked.

Vise looked him over, lips pursed. Then she grinned.

"What?"

Instead of answering, Vise turned toward where Uuchantuu had gone. "Hurry up. I need your help finding a cart."

She looked Koruuksi up and down again, and Koruuksi followed her eyes all the way up to the tips of his antlers.

"A big one. Oh, and I forgot something else."

He cocked his head, then swore as her palm collided with his head.

"What in the light were you thinking?"

25

Sleepers

At first, Uumgwefilo fought them off. As the years passed, it seemed as though this Imaia would not return. The Muukjebarat brought back disturbing information, however. Tales of the Imaia's expansion and meddling throughout the world, and rumors. Some called the Imaia the conqueror of the Iron Empire. Others, it's successor.

Exodus countdown: 12 days, 29 hours, 54 minutes

Yndlova plucked another explosive from the case before her, inspecting it and handling it with care as she had the first eleven. The explosive wasn't live, but that didn't make Yndlova any more comfortable.

I should probably be handling these somewhere other than Othaashle's office.

It was the only place where secrecy could be assured, however, as only she, Itese and Othaashle herself had access.

The supreme commander's office in the High Command building was almost as large as Yndlova's entire apartment with all the walls knocked out, containing two massive ornate desks and a high-quality, if not exactly comfortable, chair between the two. The computer terminals and monitors on the rear desk were expensive, if not as rare as they had once been. A calculated amount of Imaia iconography decorated the wall behind her desk, with a flag of Atonga on one side, and of the Imaia on the other. The space kept organization an easy task, but she'd found herself going through more meetings ironing out minute details at the tables to either side than doing actual work. Here, however, her—or Othaashle's—personal office, everything in the room was oriented to allow for focus and finishing projects. The windows looked out on the Isle's main plaza, letting in the natural light, and a large round table with a hexagonal inlay dominated the room. Yndlova had appropriated that, with a few crates—the rest stacked on the desk that ran along two sides of the room, with utilitarian, yet comfortable chairs if she needed assistance. The only hint of luxury was against the wall near the door—a refrigerator, liquor cart, and a countertop with a machine that sped up the process of making tea or *kaffa*.

It held no ornaments or personal belongings of much value, as though no one else ever saw it. Othaashle had always preferred to exemplify the idea of what Redeemed should be in everything she did. That included holding on to belongings from one's past—even from after they had been Redeemed. The most attachment Yndlova had ever seen Othaashle show to something besides her armor, uniform or weaponry, had possibly been a favorite pen at one point.

Yndlova sighed at that thought. It didn't bode well for her research.

Shaking that from her head, beads clacking together as she did so, Yndlova held up the device, peering at the biogems that sparkled with Auroralight. If she looked close enough, she imagined that she could see the spirit that powered the georaural.

At first, Yndlova had been worried about using georaurals for explosives, as plastique was plenty powerful enough on its own, and the production of georaurals had been limited as they drew closer to Exodus. Djybuu, their explosives expert, had assured her, however, that the spirits within the explosives would not be destroyed in the blasts, as they were not physical.

Just the biogems, silver, and other rare materials.

They had the conservation ring and farms for harvesting biogems from plants and animals, and their various mines had carted as much raw metal as they could find back to Mjatafa Mwonga with the help of Skadaatha's railways.

Still...

Yndlova sighed. *I hope it doesn't take long to reach our new home.*

They were supposed to receive the data from the satellites they'd sent out some time today or tomorrow. Yndlova had decided to inspect the explosives to give herself something else to think about.

When the door opened, Yndlova started, nearly dropping her fifteenth explosive.

"Everything alright, Yndlova?"

Yndlova shook herself before turning to Othaashle and saluting. "Just lost in thought, Commander."

Othaashle nodded, closing the door behind her and joining Yndlova at the main table. She picked up one of the devices Yndlova had already inspected and held it up before her mask, cocking her head as she turned it about.

"How many did we get?"

"Ninety-six," Yndlova answered. "Sixteen for each location."

Othaashle nodded, then gestured to the second box that still sat on the floor. "Are those the ones you've already gone through?"

Yndlova shook her head. "Those are the caps—to hide the Auroralight and make them look less suspicious."

"And you are simply looking these over?"

Yndlova shrugged. "I want to check each of the components. Each has a receiver, detonator, fuel source, and then the georaural will direct the blast and make it more powerful."

"I see..."

Othaashle's tone made Yndlova look her up and down. She couldn't see Othaashle's face, of course, but the way her commander's shoulders sagged made her frown.

"Some help would speed up the process," Yndlova suggested.

Othaashle nodded, looking over one of the devices, then setting it aside before picking up another. "I don't want to leave anything up to chance with Skadaatha and her elites poking around."

Yndlova nodded, falling into silence as she worked with her commander.

"I'm worried about using so many of these," she said after a while. "I know that normally the spirits would just return to the Vale after these are destroyed, but after Exodus we will no longer be on Efruumani."

"Skadaatha believes we will find more oruu on whatever new world we settle," Othaashle assured her, "and the God King confirmed it. Even if we don't, once Lord Ynuukwidas is no longer required to constantly expend his power to hold Efruumani together, he will be able to split off pieces of his power for us to use."

Yndlova blinked. "But won't that weaken him?"

"No more than creating the Redeemed has. The power he gave us is a thimble of water from the seas. The spirits are mere drops of that same ocean."

Yndlova tried to reconcile that for a moment but found herself unable to do so.

"Have you begun leaking our intelligence reports about the Remnant?" Othaashle asked after a while.

Yndlova nodded. "I left out a few reports and papers, and made a few mentions when consulting about the explosives. It should work its way through our ranks in a few days, if not to the public." She paused, remembering her own unintended slip. "Have you made a decision on the operation's end-goal yet? I apologize again for letting that slip to Skadaatha."

Othaashle waved it off. "She would have found out somehow. It might even be better that she found out so early on—it won't seem like something we suspiciously kept from her until the last moment. As far as whether or not we will pursue that route..." She shrugged. "I want to wait until we get the satellite data before I decide. There wouldn't be much point in letting the Remnant flee to another world if we only find one that is habitable."

Yndlova nodded.

"I just came from a meeting with Itese and her team of Redeemed. They look quite promising," Othaashle continued. "It made me wonder about something similar for our longer-term end to this operation. Do you think you could put together a team of skilled spies that we could round up and throw into Makala as other Remnant spies we picked up in another sweep?"

Yndlova raised an eyebrow, but nodded. "What type of skill did you have in mind?"

"Technical skills. People who could help the Remnant build everything they need for an advanced, functioning colony with infrastructure that is well-planned and easily improved—especially long-range communication. They should be good instructors and leaders, as well, in case it takes us longer than a generation to arrive and annex the colony."

Yndlova nodded. "Of course, Commander." She paused, frowning. "How will they get out of Makala?"

"If we decide to go that route," Othaashle explained, "I will arrange for a quiet prisoner transfer to the bait ship. It should make them believe I really was on their side and quell any suspicions about spies in their midst."

Something in Othaashle's tone caught Yndlova's attention. She glanced at her commander again. Her shoulders sagged still, yet there was a tension to the woman's body, as though she was holding herself upright by force of will alone.

"Othaashle," Yndlova asked, setting down her current explosive—number thirty, she thought. "Did you have another vision recently?"

Othaashle sighed, setting down the device she'd been inspecting, then nodded.

"They're growing increasingly...difficult to deal with," she said, "especially since now I no longer know exactly what their purpose is. Knowing about the person I was is one thing, but remembering what she did, feeling the sense of conviction and righteousness she felt when performing such horrible deeds..."

She trailed off with a sigh.

"What—" Yndlova hesitated. "What do you see? I know you said you saw some of your former—of Kojatere's life and her time with Symuuna Team, but...is that it?"

Othaashle said nothing for a while. Not for the first time, Yndlova wished she could see through that mask to have some clue as to her commander's thoughts.

"Some things are still clouded," Othaashle said. "The visions clear up parts, but leave others just as foggy. I've seen more of my—of Kojatere's military history: her induction into the Knights Reborn, her training under Nevisi and Matsanga, her wins and losses in the field."

Othaashle paused, cocking her head. "She was much more... disagreeable than I expected. I... remember a time where Matsanga said that I—she was like Skadaatha. I think I resent that now even more than Kojatere did, but I can see the comparison. Then there are other things."

"What?" Yndlova asked, almost afraid to speak. She was experiencing something unheard of—something she had only dreamed of hearing from another Redeemed.

"A ball," Othaashle said, voice quiet. "Dancing on the ice in an exquisite gown, on a balcony high above the streets of the Nimikadeka capital. The thrill and joy of winning ice dancing competitions and travelling around Darkside. A brother who was also her best friend, and a husband she couldn't stand for a while when they first met."

Yndlova's throat grew tight. She had never thought of Othaashle or any other Redeemed as cold or unfeeling—she knew better than that—yet hearing such longing and tenderness in the woman's voice was so surreal, she almost couldn't believe it. It gave her hope.

"There was a lot more to Kojatere than being Kweshrima's champion," Othaashle said slowly, "The more I remember about her, the more I understand why the God King keeps us from remembering, and the more certain I am that I made the right choice in establishing our taboos. It's...I don't think many could handle it."

Yndlova gazed at the woman for a moment, thinking. The pain in Othaashle's voice made her stomach knot. Not for the first time, she wished she could see past the woman's mask.

How can I possibly soothe something like that?

"You know I was not born in the Imaia," she said slowly.

Othaashle nodded, "You were born in Aiduumba in 932 E.I.A, twenty-three before the Imaia conquered your home."

"And I was raised to oppose the Imaia," Yndlova said. "But by the time Imaia forces conquered Aiduumba, I was grateful for the stability it brought. I'd lived on the streets for most of my life before joining the military. I didn't even want to fight, but it was better than..."

Yndlova paused, looking up at Othaashle, the woman had turned toward her now. She could feel Othaashle's gaze on her through the draakon-like mask.

"Kweshrima and her followers did terrible things," she said, "but the God King wiped your slate clean when he remade you, and you have Redeemed yourself many times over by making the Imaia what it is today and eliminating the Union and now the Remnant."

Othaashle's posture relaxed somewhat, but Yndlova found herself wishing to say more.

Before she could do so, however, her datapad chimed. When she opened it, her eyes went wide.

"What is it?" Othaashle asked.

"The satellite data is in," Yndlova breathed. "They've been able to observe thirty-seven different star systems, five of which have worlds or moons in their respective habitable zones. Two even show signs of activity."

"Prepare a dossier on each of the systems," Othaashle commanded, straightening. "I want a brief summary and analysis on each as well as a threat assessment and monitoring proposal for the two with activity. We need to know which will be best for the Imaia to claim as its new home, and which would be best to send the Remnant off to."

"Won't the Ministry of Science be in charge of that?"

"I would like a military perspective in addition to their own analysis."

Yndlova nodded. "Of course, Commander. I'll go as soon as I'm done with these."

Othaashle shook her head. "I can handle these, I need something to clear my head and get my thoughts off the vision."

Yndlova hesitated, but saluted. "Yes, sir."

26

Exploring Scars

When the Imaia came once more, for the first time in their long partnership, Uumgwefilo asked E Kwekuue for help: troops to fight and protect both their people. With the information the Muukjebarat had brought back to E Kwekuue, the Akjemasai and many other Buuekwenani volunteered, eager to repay Uumgwefilo for connecting them to the outside world and keeping their secret all these years. They named themselves Ymbandi's Legion, and all reports told of their fierce defiance of the Imaia in battle. For though E Kwekuue had known peace for almost its entire history, powerful, skilled Auroramancers made up almost its entire population: something no other nation could boast.

Exodus countdown: 11 days, 3 hours, 45 minutes

Once Vise and Uuchantuu found a cart large enough to fit him inside, Koruuksi found himself doubled up under a pile of laundry for a journey across the city that seemed to stretch for hours. He struggled to keep his jaw clenched shut and his breathing regular in the cart's hot, stuffy air. Especially when it hit one of the few snags on E Kwekuue's streets or Vise and Uuchantuu turned the cart a bit too roughly.

When the cart finally halted and one of the women knocked on the side, Koruuksi straightened, digging through the laundry to his freedom. He gasped, taking in a deep breath of fresh air as he surfaced, then hurriedly climbed out of the cart.

He looked between Vise and Uuchantuu and pointed at the cart. "Not happening again. If I wasn't claustrophobic before, I sure am now."

Then Koruuksi took in his surroundings. There was just as much plant life and finely crafted stone as everywhere else in the city, but the abundance of aluminum inlay could have only meant one place.

He looked to Vise. "You're insane."

Vise just smirked at him, folding her arms beneath her generous chest.

She's doing that on purpose.

Not that he minded.

"I know the palace and the schedules of everyone inside it by heart, and happen to an expert at slipping in and out undetected from when Ymvesi'ia and I would do so as children. Kuula'ande also respects his daughter's privacy."

"We're hiding in Ymvesi'ia's chambers?" Uuchantuu asked, eyes wide, voice sounding a bit tight.

Koruuksi grinned, looking over at his friend. She still wore one of the *maopa* Ymvesi'ia had bought for her with nothing to cover her chest, as they'd stashed her and Koruuksi's packs with their extra clothing in the cart with him.

Uuchantuu met his gaze and narrowed her eyes. She didn't cover her chest, but her arms twitched. "Don't say anything."

"What? I think Ymvesi'ia will like that look on y—Ow!"

Vise shook her head as Koruuksi rubbed the spot on his arm where Uuchantuu had punched him.

"Get your things and come on," she said, gesturing for them to follow. Koruuksi fished both out of the cart and handed one to

Uuchantuu. "You didn't spend all that time sweating in a cart just for someone to come down here and find you."

"What about other servants finding us?" Koruuksi whispered as Vise led them through corridors lit with Auroralight rather than natural light from outside. They were narrower than the main hall, but still wide enough for Koruuksi and his companions to walk down side-by-side. "Is there somewhere in Ymvesi'ia's chambers we can hide?"

Vise snorted. "Yes, but they won't. Our cleaning staff went through the room two days ago, so they won't be by for another ten. They come through for a deep clean of the palace every two weeks, but Ymvesi'ia and I do most of the cleaning and upkeep on our chambers. As for laundry and plumbing, I think you'll find we're quite advanced in those areas. You're probably thinking of stories from your own histories if you think servants or staff would come through often enough to discover you. Uumgwefilo had those, but I always thought it strange that they needed armies of servants just to function."

Koruuksi shared a look with Vise.

"People in most places like to lord their power over others, even within the Remnant, unfortunately."

They continued through the palace, heads swiveling and stepping quietly, until Vise stopped before an ornate doorway and ushered them inside. From his experience in the palace and everywhere else he'd explored within E Kwekuue, Ymvesi'ia's chambers met Koruuksi's expectations. The basic construction—walls of blue, teal, and white marble with aluminum inlay—was similar to the quarters he and his team had stayed in, though more ornate, with more aluminum, the different colors forming various patterns. Thick, hexagonal columns stood at points of support throughout the room with aluminum inlay in various patterns similar to those Koruuksi had seen in other areas of the palace and the chambers he and Ymvesi'ia had met with the council members in. Shocks of white flowers spilled out from planters hanging from the ceiling in corners or near the columns, and through one of the doorless openings that were so common in this city, he spied what looked like a hexagonal bath or pool, lined with aluminum tiles, with a few intricate georaural devices worked into it.

And it was dark! Large curtains hung in the windows. Biogem lanterns gave the room a soft, dim lighting, but Koruuksi didn't have to worry about that burning him.

"That sort of thinking was bred and legislated out of our people long ago," Vise said, closing the door behind them. She immediately strode over to the windows. Thick curtains kept out light from various openings, and Koruuksi smiled, removing his helmet as Vise began drawing curtains and securing them with ties, dimming the light in the room. "My people fled here to escape the Iron Empire of Atonga, who took that to an extreme. We had no room for that within our society upon finding this paradise."

She gestured for them to follow as she strode through the main chamber toward another door.

"This is where you'll be sleeping," she said, grabbing some blankets from a cabinet before placing them on one of two long, plush lounge chairs before starting to spread them out. Koruuksi stepped forward to try and assist, but she swatted his hand away. "If you're hungry, I can get the two of you some food from the kitchens."

Koruuksi removed his mask and shared a confused look with Uuchantuu. "Won't that be suspicious?"

"Are the kitchens even open at this hour?" Uuchantuu asked.

Vise eyed the two of them. "I told you that our cooks here do so because they enjoy it, not because they are ordered to or must do so to feed their families. We have Siba, the morning chef, and Tuunde, the evening one. Tuunde and his team work when others sleep, preparing food and trying out recipes. They remain at their station in case anyone is working rather than sleeping and happens to desire a snack to help keep them awake. You must have noticed that some of the city is awake even when the rest is asleep."

Koruuksi nodded, "We do something similar. That way there's always someone on guard."

Vise's face grew tight at that.

Koruuksi looked to Uuchantuu to find that she'd set down and opened her pack, her mantle back over her shoulders, covering her chest. She pulled out two wraps and tossed one to Koruuksi. "I don't need any unless either of you want something from the kitchens."

Koruuksi pulled back the wrap, revealing a don keb, then raised an eyebrow at Uuchantuu. "Really?"

She shrugged. "What? I like them, and as far as I knew, we were leaving. I visited Muurad in the market and had him tell me how to make them, too."

Uuchantuu pulled a third one out of her pack and offered it to Vise, who smiled, but shook her head. "I'm fine. I'd just finished eating when I heard about your banishment."

Koruuksi swallowed a lump in his throat. The way Vise had eyed him when saying that implied he'd hear more about just how much of an idiot he'd been later.

"Ymvesi'ia told me about your ships and all the amazing technology in them," Vise said, walking back out of the smaller room. "I'm a little annoyed you didn't bring anything back for me."

Koruuksi glanced at his pack, where he'd stored a flashlight and audio player. He'd brought them back from the ship but hadn't had the chance to show them to Vise yet. He almost reached for his pack, but stopped when Uuchantuu yawned, eliciting a chuckle from Vise as she returned with pillows, setting them nicely on top of the couches rather than just tossing them.

"Sorry," he said, "I would have brought you something if we hadn't rushed off so quickly after Luuhuuta brought us the news."

"Would you like to wash?" Vise asked, rolling her eyes at Koruuksi before leaning against the door frame. "I could draw a bath or wet some towels for you to wipe yourselves off with." She eyed Koruuksi with an amused expression. "Especially you."

Koruuksi returned the look, hiding his concern. He couldn't tell if this was just how Vise was with Ymvesi'ia when performing her duties, or if she was busying herself as a distraction.

"I just need some sleep," Uuchantuu said. She walked back toward the couches and simply flopped down on the cushioned surface. Within moments, her figure relaxed.

Koruuksi looked to Vise to find her gazing at Uuchantuu with wide eyes.

"Did she—" Vise cut off, turning to him. She lowered her voice. "Did she really just do that?"

Koruuksi grinned. "Comes with needing to be able to grab some sleep whenever and wherever you can. I will take one of those wet towels, if you're still offering."

Vise smiled at him and went to fetch one. He looked after her for a few seconds, then glanced at Uuchantuu and shook his head before undoing his shirt. Rather than being able to shrug out of it as usual, he had to peel the sweat-drenched fabric off his torso.

He looked back to Vise just in time to see her stop and look at him with wide eyes, taking in his appearance. Koruuksi tracked her eyes and knew she was taking in the various scars his life had left on him.

"You can ask, if you want," he said. "Only if you give me the towel first, though."

Vise blinked and shook herself before doing so. Koruuksi brought the cool cloth to his face, wiping the sweat from his brow, then sniffed and looked to Vise. "Spicewood?"

She grinned, though it seemed a bit forced. "You need it."

Koruuksi snorted and rubbed at his neck with the cloth, reveling in the refreshing, cool wetness and the spicewood cutting through his body's own odor.

Vise didn't ask about his scars, and her grin faded. She didn't look at him but seemed to instead look through him for a moment before shaking herself.

"Would you mind coming with me?" she said, nodding away from the small room.

Koruuksi nodded and reached into his pack, pocketing the small flashlight and the audio player before he followed Vise through the main room and into one of the adjoining ones. She raced ahead of him, drawing the curtains as she had in the main room so that he wouldn't need to cover himself. He noted that it was more of an alcove than an actual separate, private space, similar to how the bedrooms in parts of the quarters he'd been given were laid out. At first glance, it seemed little different than the rest of the larger chamber. White plants with colorful flowers grew from various planters, some on the floor, some on shelves, some hanging from high up on the walls. Heavy, colorful curtains kept the room dark, and a bed big enough for two sat against the wall in the middle of the room. As Koruuksi studied the room further, however, he noted Vise's personal touches. A few georaurals, pieces of art, and some small, personal affects he made a note to ask her about at some point.

"This is your room," he said.

Vise smiled at that. This one wasn't forced, but it wasn't as big as usual.

"When I'm not sharing Ymvesi'ia's."

Koruuksi raised an eyebrow and Vise shrugged. "She has a big bed. Sometimes we just sit and talk and end up falling asleep together. Lately we've fallen asleep doing research."

Koruuksi nodded, continuing to towel himself off as Vise sat down on the bed. He allowed himself a slight smirk when he noticed her eyes on him again, this time looking more interested than they had before.

Still, she said nothing, however.

"You know, you were wrong about me not bringing you anything back from the ship," he said, reaching his free hand into his pocket as he set the cloth down on the edge of her nightstand.

Vise's face lit up as he handed her the flashlight and the audio player. He explained to her how both worked, then made her laugh with some shadow-puppets on the walls before they sat and listened to some music for a time. He'd hoped the distraction would lighten Vise's mood, but it didn't seem to work even after they'd listened through an entire playlist.

Eventually, Koruuksi took the audio player from Vise's hand and set it on the nearby table. He hesitated for a moment, then took her hand in his. The contact made the hairs on his arms stand on end and a shiver run down his spine despite the heat. Vise looked up at him with her large golden-brown eyes.

"You're not okay, are you?"

Vise shook her head.

"Do you want to talk about it?"

She dropped her gaze, voice small when she spoke. "No."

Koruuksi clenched his fists, a sudden anger at himself rising up. He and Uuchantuu had grown up with this burden, dealing with the overwhelming threat of being left stranded on a dying world every day. Vise had known about this for all of eight days, and they had a slim chance at best of getting her people out of here in time.

He needed to find some way to ease her burden for a while or distract her at the very least.

Koruuksi looked down at their hands. He picked the cloth back up and scrubbed at a few of his scars to make sure they were clean, then gently lifted her hand to one on his shoulder. She looked up, first at his scar and their hands, then at him, her gaze questioning.

"This was from getting shot during combat," he said. "We were raiding one of the Imaia's big railways that go to Darkside, for supplies. Before then, I'd always thought of myself as invincible in a weird way. I'm a full Auroraborn—we don't just get shot by a random enemy soldier. If we die, we go down doing something incredible, right? The adrenaline allowed me to keep on fighting once Uuchantuu patched me up, and I was able to use my Auroramancy to get us out of there in one piece, but when that wore off, it hurt so much. Uuchantuu gave me so much shit for it until she finally got shot in the leg one time."

Vise's eyes went wide.

Koruuksi grinned and pointed to his eyebrow, where a small scar turned the silver hairs white. "Any guess what this one was?"

Vise hesitated, then shook her head.

"I pissed off a cat when I was a kid and it scratched me."

Vise snorted, covering her mouth as her cheeks darkened. Koruuksi smiled back at her, and after a moment, she seemed a bit more at ease.

Vise took the wet cloth from his hand. A moment later, Koruuksi breathed in deep, closing his eyes at its cool touch on his back. Vise worked the cloth in small circles over his skin, her free hand resting on his shoulder, heat radiating out from it like a bonfire.

Can she feel my pulse getting faster?

"What about this one?" she asked, moving the cloth down to the left side of his back.

Koruuksi thought for a moment, then cleared his throat as his face grew hot. "That was one I got while in bed."

Vise snorted. "I know we come from different cultures, but I doubt you sleep on rocks."

"Well, I wasn't actually *in* bed when I got it. And I might have been a bit drunk."

"Jealous lover?"

Koruuksi met her gaze. "No—and don't listen to anything Uuchantuu says regarding that. She likes to make things up."

Vise grinned. "What happened, then?"

He shrugged. "I was blowing off some steam with a few friends, and I'd always thought that one of the guys, Toman, was very attractive—chiseled jaw, just the right amount of muscle, incredible dimples—"

"Nice backside?"

Koruuksi gave her a flat look, and she grinned.

"Just checking."

He rolled his eyes. "Anyway, after having a bit to drink, we went back to my room and started kissing and getting undressed, and I tried to roll us over so that he was on top—" He ignored Vise's smirk. "—and I accidentally rolled us both off the bed. I was on the bottom, and we'd just thrown most of our clothes on the ground when getting undressed, so I landed on a pile of gear, including the bottom edge of my helmet."

Vise's eyes went wide. "Were you...or was he...?"

Koruuksi shook his head. "We hadn't gotten that far yet. We didn't that night, unfortunately. I was too drunk for it to hurt at first, but it killed the mood when Toman realized I was bleeding from a big gash on my back."

"But you did sleep with him?"

Koruuksi grinned. "Two weeks later. I might have broken the stitches."

Vise rolled her eyes.

"What about this?" she moved her free hand down just below his right shoulder, the pad of her finger drawing a line of fire over his muscles.

It took a moment for Koruuksi to remember what was there—it wasn't a scar. He laughed. "I honestly forgot that was there."

"It looks like the symbols on your mask."

Koruuksi nodded. "It's kind of a stupid tattoo, but I've never regretted it. Uuchantuu and I got it with a few others in our unit back when things were really bad, just after Yrmuunthal. It lists our names and says that we're family, no matter what happens."

He left out that he and Uuchantuu were the only two of the five names on there that were still alive.

He could hear the smile when Vice spoke. "You two really are ridiculous, aren't you?"

Koruuksi smiled at that. "Just a bit."

"I think it's sweet."

Her hand moved between his shoulder blades, fingers tracing the lines of the tattoo he had there. "And this one?"

Koruuksi was surprised she hadn't asked about it sooner. "That one is for my brother, Svemakuu."

"Estingai's husband?"

Koruuksi nodded. "She has one, too. Not an exact copy, but something similar."

"What happened to him?" Vise asked, voice soft.

Koruuksi sighed. "He and Estingai attended a meeting of the disparate factions that had survived after Yrmuunthal was destroyed and the Union fractured. The point of the meeting was to forge the six groups into one in hopes of standing a chance against the Imaia. They thought they'd planned it well enough that it would be secure from any interference—Imaia or otherwise." He sighed, forcing the words out. "The Deathknight—the Imaia's champion—showed up. She killed everyone there."

"Except your sister."

Koruuksi nodded. "Except Estingai, though not for lack of trying. She had to dig herself out of an underground cave-in while lightless. That day, and what happened the following weeks—it changed her. Estingai had always been hard, but after that, she was just so angry. I don't think it helped that they never found Svemakuu's body."

"Why didn't that loss change you the same way?"

Koruuksi shrugged. "It almost did for a while. Uuchantuu helped. We tried for Estingai, but that seemed to only make it worse for her. Eventually, I decided that it would be best to remember what I loved about Svemakuu and try to keep him alive for everyone that knew him, especially Estingai"

Vise's arms had wrapped around his chest now, one hand still holding the damp cloth. It felt nice—the cold a welcome contrast against the heat from her arms over his chest, and the heat of her chest pressed against his back, her forehead resting at the nape of his neck.

"You've lost people, too. Haven't you?"

He felt her nod against his neck.

"We all have," she whispered. "Queen Asante didn't just take a contingent of the guards with her. Some went as an advanced force, but others who had served in the guard for a time underwent training along with volunteers. Though we kept ourselves as separate as possible to ensure our way of life continued, my people had a long, close relationship with Uumgwefilo at that point, and many either saw the threat the Imaia posed to them as a threat to us, or as something it was our duty to help fight against out of thanks for introducing us to the wonders of the outside world while keeping our secret. My brothers, Ashak and Zo'olo, and my sister, Nefe'erti, all went with my mother, Kanda, to follow Queen Asante and her children. My father stayed home to assist Kuula'ande, and Ymvesi'ia and I were too young. We tried sneaking out of the city to follow them, but Ma'ake, Ymvesi'ia's oldest sister caught us and took us back."

Koruuksi twisted around at the thickness in Vise's voice and found her looking down toward the sheets. He put a hand to her chin, gently tilting up her face so he could meet her eyes. They shimmered, unshed tears threatening to overflow.

"She convinced us not to try going after them again," Vise said, managing to keep her voice steady. "By telling us she had a very important job for us while she was gone. She told Ymvesi'ia that she needed to watch over E Kwekuue and protect it." Vise sniffed, forcing a smile. "You can see how she took that to heart."

Koruuksi nodded. "And what did she tell you?"

"To watch out for her sister. Ymvesi'ia would protect E Kwekuue, and I would protect her."

"It seems like you've both done a pretty good job."

Vise nodded, swallowing hard.

"What happened to your father?"

"He passed away. Shortly after he learned my mother wouldn't be coming back. He was so stricken with grief... one morning he just didn't wake up."

Koruuksi found himself at a loss for words. He turned around fully and pulled Vise to him, cradling her head against his chest. It just felt right. She gripped his shoulders and simply clung to him for a while, torso expanding and contracting with heavy, sometimes erratic breaths.

Koruuksi just held her.

Eventually, Vise pulled back and gazed up at him.

"I'm scared."

Koruuksi nodded. "So am I."

"I don't want to stay here and die. But I can't leave Ymvesi'ia, and—"

"Ymvesi'ia won't leave her people."

"I've known that, and I knew it would be hard to convince Kuula'ande, much less everyone in the city, but now it's all just—"

She clamped her mouth shut and closed her eyes, taking a deep breath.

Koruuksi cupped her face, stroking her cheek with his thumb until she looked at him. Then he smoothed a few loose locks of hair from her face, tucking them behind her ear.

"I told Ymvesi'ia that I would see this through. I don't leave friends behind. That applies to you, too."

Vise smiled at him, then raised an eyebrow, leaning in a bit closer. "Friends?"

Her tone made Koruuksi acutely aware of just how close they were, and their respective lack of clothing. He tried not to look down at her chest, but all of his practice since meeting her failed him. When he met her eyes again, his cheeks grew hot at the amusement on her face.

It was worth it to get her smiling again.

He cleared his throat. "I didn't want to assume. You seem to flirt with everyone, especially if you're nervous or don't want to talk about something, and I have a bad track record. I try not to be, but I can be a bit bitter at times, and I think Uuchantuu has a list of the people I've driven away."

Vise held his gaze, voice smooth as silk when she spoke. "I haven't seen any of that so far. You can be an ass, but you're no more bitter or cynical than you have a right to be, and rarely."

Koruuksi snorted. "Maybe spending the end of the world in paradise instead of a cave has just relaxed me a bit."

Vise laughed at that. The warm, wonderful sound encouraged him.

"You are also the first woman I've been interested in that's had her top off every time I've seen you."

"So, you are interested in me."

"I thought that was pretty obvious."

She grinned. "I didn't want to assume. And technically, I can't 'have my top off if I never wear one to begin with."

"I guess that's fair."

She reached out and brushed her fingers against his cheek. "You're the first man to catch my interest before I knew what your face looked like."

"And after seeing my face?"

Vise rolled her eyes. "You're also a bit of a bull-headed idiot at times, but I'm used to that from Ymvesi'ia."

Koruuksi laughed. "I hadn't noticed."

Vise raised an eyebrow. "You know you were an idiot with Kuula'ande, right?"

Koruuksi sighed. "Yes, trust me, I know. Ymvesi'ia made that quite clear. She nearly gave me a rash on my wrist."

"Oh, poor you."

Koruuksi found himself unable to pull his gaze from Vise's full, beautiful lips. His own were dry. His cheeks grew even warmer as he wet them and leaned in.

He jerked back as something wet and damp suddenly covered his face.

Koruuksi shook himself, pulling the cloth off before he raised an eyebrow at Vise, confused.

She smirked at him. "Not until you're clean."

He frowned, "I am—"

Vise looked down at his pants, then back at him. Fire darkened his face, and he had to restrain himself from shifting under her gaze.

Vise rolled her eyes. "Is that really something you want me to think you're embarrassed about?"

Koruuksi cleared his throat, straightening. "I'll go if you do."

"Nice try." Vise grinned, leaning in closer. "I want you nice and clean for where I want the night to go, not sweaty and smelly."

Koruuksi swallowed, pulse quickening as his pants grew more uncomfortable. He held up the cloth. "I think we'll need a new one of these, then."

Smiling, Vise rose and plucked the cloth from his fingers. "I'll be right back."

Koruuksi looked after her as she strode out of the room—*her room*—taking in her soft curves and the clothing that enhanced them even as it barely covered them. When she disappeared out of view, he glanced down between his legs. His pants were growing more uncomfortable by the minute.

Stop that. You can't be that obvious.

Koruuksi looked up at Vise's approaching footsteps just in time to catch the new dripping cloth she tossed to him. He caught it, then wiped his face with it, breathing in the scent. The cool helped him relax a bit.

"Sweetcitrus?" he asked.

Vise nodded. She leaned against the door frame, folding her arms beneath her breasts in a way that pressed them together and made Koruuksi's mouth dry. "One of my favorites."

"You're not a fan of subtlety, are you?"

She shook her head, "Not really. Not when I know what I want."

"Why the spicewood before, then?"

She shrugged. "It was closer, more of an evening scent."

Koruuksi grinned at that.

Vise raised an eyebrow. "What are you waiting for? Strip."

Koruuksi rose to his feet.

Why am I nervous?

It wasn't like he hadn't done this with dozens of other men or women.

They didn't make me smile and laugh the way Vise does.

Most of them had also been jealous of Uuchantuu. Koruuksi had never understood that.

Keeping his eyes locked on Vise's—it was hard not to drink in her entire figure—Koruuksi undid his belt and pushed his pants down to the floor, stepping out of them. He didn't try to be enticing, just quick.

Vise's eyes grew wide as she looked down, a smile tugging at her lips. Then she frowned. Frowned. Koruuksi followed her gaze down to his underclothes, which did absolutely nothing to hide his arousal.

He tried to keep the sudden, inexplicable insecurity from his voice. "Not up to your standards?"

Vise's eyes flickered back up to his, her frown deepening. "What?" Then her eyes widened. She snorted, covering her mouth. "Oh." She took a few steps closer. "No, don't worry. I don't think that will be a problem. I'm just confused. Why are you wearing two sets of pants?"

Koruuksi blinked at the absurdity of the question, then paused.

No one wears pants—they all wear maopa *wraps. The only people he'd seen wearing pants were the guards, and only those that went into the forest, not those who patrolled or stood vigil within the city itself.*

He shrugged. "They're more comfortable, I guess. They keep everything from moving around too much when running... I don't know—we just do?"

Vise smirked, eyes flickering back down to his hips as she nodded.

With a sigh, Koruuksi pulled those off as well, cheeks burning.

Vise's grin afterward made it a bit better.

Not really knowing what else to do, Koruuksi sat back down on the bed and started scrubbing his legs with the cloth.

Vise closed the distance between them and pulled the cloth from his fingers. "I can take care of that. Stand up."

Koruuksi did so and tried not to get too excited as Vise scrubbed down his lower half. She didn't make it easy, standing very close to him and shooting him the occasional smirk that made his blood rush.

She's being more handsy than she was on my back.

He supposed that wasn't something to complain about, given where Vise had implied she would like the night to head.

"Ymvesi'ia and Uuchantuu seem to like each other," she said as she bent down a bit to get his calf. Her fingers still found a way to trace lines of fire down his skin despite the damp cloth they followed. The scent of sweetcitrus began to fill the air around him.

Koruuksi laughed. "They haven't exactly been subtle, have they?"

Vise grinned up at him. "They're trying, at least. Do you think anything will actually come of it? Uuchantuu seems to forget how to talk around her half the time, and Ymvesi'ia..."

The cloth paused on his thigh as Vise sighed. "She has some baggage that I'm afraid keeps her timid."

Koruuksi frowned at that. He cupped Vise's cheek, tilting her head up so he could meet her gaze. Her eyes held... guilt?

"What kind of baggage?"

Vise bit her lip.

"Sorry," Koruuksi said. "That's not my place. You just seemed bothered. I—"

Vise squeezed his thigh over the cloth, smiling up at him. "It's alright. When we were younger and Ymvesi'ia first discovered she was interested in women, she pinned some of her hopes on me. I had to turn her down, and I don't think she's ever approached anyone else, since that inclination isn't common among Buuekwenani women. Even if it was, Ymvesi'ia has few peers, even among the Akjemasai. I hope Uuchantuu is at least able to help her be more confident in herself."

"Maybe we should encourage them. Give them some privacy and make sure they know they won't be interrupted."

Vise grinned up at him as she moved the cloth from his buttocks between his legs.

Koruuksi cleared his throat at that, hoping the noise covered up the moan that slipped out.

"You really love torturing people, don't you?"

Vise leaned in close. She met his eyes, glanced down between them, then met them again. "Seems like you enjoy being tortured." Koruuksi swallowed hard. "This is the most important place to clean, after all."

"Are you going to let me make sure you're all nice and clean once you're done?"

Vise grinned, leaning in a bit closer. "Fair's fair."

Koruuksi kissed her. He found it a bit strange that he was only now doing so, as Vise had already handled his manhood—and continued to do so, which usually came after the kissing—but enjoyed it nonetheless.

Vise melted into the kiss and the damp cloth fell to the floor as her hands roved about his torso. Her hips—still clothed for some annoying reason—pressed against his, making him gasp and eliciting a throaty laugh from Vise.

She looked about to say something, but Koruuksi wanted more. He took her face in his hands and kissed her again, pulling her to him, enjoying that she seemed just as desperate for his touch as he was for hers.

When she pulled back this time, Koruuksi found it hard to keep his eyes from her chest, rising and falling with her labored breathing. When he met her gaze, she grinned at him, eyes hazy.

She placed a hand on his chest, tracing shapes over his skin. "It's been a long time since someone kissed me like that."

Koruuksi grinned. "I highly doubt that."

Vise took a step back and looked him up and down. Koruuksi could feel her eyes drinking him in as her grin deepened.

"It's a shame you need to wear all that clothing when you're outside. You'd look very good in a *maopa*."

Koruuksi retrieved the cloth from the floor then raised an eyebrow at Vise. She rolled her eyes, though the grin never left her face as her hands traveled down to the edge of her *maopa*. Closing the distance between them, Koruuksi shook his head. "I get to do that."

"I didn't get to strip you of your clothes."

Koruuksi glanced to where he'd piled them on the floor. "They were sweaty and gross. I did you a favor."

Vise laughed and took a step back, glancing down at what little clothing she wore.

Grinning, Koruuksi placed a hand on Vise's flat stomach, enjoying the way she shivered at his touch, then hooked two fingers over the hem of her maopa wrap. He gave a gentle tug...

... and nothing happened.

Koruuksi frowned, tracing the hemline with his fingers as he looked for the right place to pull.

"You have no idea how to get this off of me, do you?"

Koruuksi glanced back up at Vise with a sheepish grin. "Not a clue."

Vise just laughed.

Koruuksi remembered something, and took the broad strip of cloth that hung down over the front of her thighs between his fingers. "Though if I remember correctly..." He began to lift it up. "... I don't necessarily need to remove this for us to have fun."

Vise swatted his hand away and shot him a pointed look. "That is considered very rude."

"Even when the woman in question has expressed a desire to be free of her clothes?"

"It's either rude or shows that the man is an idiot."

Koruuksi shrugged. "I could just rip it off. Though in my experience, women don't seem to enjoy that as much as men."

Vise shook her head, grinning, and pinched two parts of her *maopa*. She tugged, and then somehow tossed the fabric onto her bed a moment later.

Koruuksi blinked, looking back and forth between Vise and her discarded clothing, "That was all just one—"

His words died on his tongue as he drank in Vise's naked figure. Though the *maopa* hadn't covered much, seeing her naked made his throat dry and his blood rush. His pulse roared in his ears. In the absence of any clothing, her stripes outlined and enhanced the appearance of her figure, making it even more enticing.

"Wow."

Wow? Seriously?

Vise grinned.

"What?"

"Oh, nothing. I just tend to have that effect on people." Her fingers drifted down between his legs. "And that effect."

Koruuksi swallowed hard, his entire face burning as Vise plucked the cloth from his hands and took a step back, wiping herself down.

"I suppose I shouldn't bother telling you how beautiful you are, then?" Koruuksi said.

Vise smirked. "Not at all. I have no illusions about how I look but hearing it from others is always nice. Though be creative. I'm pretty sure I should have been just as beautiful before I took off my *maopa* as I am now."

"You are. I think the exact word the women on my team used to describe you was 'unfair'."

Vise laughed, "Only if looks are all men want, which is the case sometimes."

"I could say the same for women."

"Fair enough. There are times when all I've wanted is someone nice to look at, since I don't always have the time to discover much else." Her expression grew a bit guarded. "If you're looking for a woman that can fight, though, you'd be out of luck."

"I'm tired of fighting," Koruuksi said. "I'd rather have someone witty, warm, and annoyingly intelligent."

Vise's cheeks colored and she kissed him.

Koruuksi wrapped his arms around her. Both of them melted into the kiss, their hands exploring the planes and curves of each other's bodies.

When they finally parted, this time Vise only pulled back long enough to lean against him, pressing her head into his neck.

"It's been a very long time since anyone's kissed me like that," she said. "Or held me like this. I'm usually too focused on Ymvesi'ia or my duties to actively pursue anything."

"But you have done this before, right?"

Vise chuckled and flicked his chest. "Don't be an idiot. I'm pretty sure I'm older than you. I just don't usually have time for anything more than jumping in and out of bed, if we even make it to one. From what Uuchantuu said, you shouldn't have a problem with that, right?"

Koruuksi let his head fall back with a groan. "I'm going to kill her."

Vise giggled.

He looked back down at her. "Are you okay with that?"

"Depends on how good you are in bed. And if you're okay with my history."

Koruuksi hesitated, then decided to be honest. "I don't need to know. As long is it *is* history."

Vise's eyes widened, and for a moment, Koruuksi had worried he'd made a mistake. Then she smiled. "I think I can manage that."

Koruuksi returned the smile. He opened his mouth, then blinked as Vise placed a finger over it. "You need to stop talking, though. I have far too many other things I'd like your mouth to do."

Koruuksi held her gaze for a moment, then led her by her hand back to her bed. He sat her down on the edge, then leaned in and kissed where her shoulder met her neck.

"Like that?" he whispered.

"Mmm. Exactly."

She raised two fingers to where he'd kissed, then drew them down to her clavicle, just above her gemcrest. "And here."

"Watch out for my antlers."

Vise giggled, and he felt her nudge them out of the way as he kissed the spot on her chest. She directed his lips to different places on her body, filling his senses with the taste of her skin and the scents of the towels they'd used to clean themselves. When he looked up from kissing Vise's stomach, he found them laying on her bed with Vise studying his antlers. Her cheeks colored when he caught her.

"What?"

She bit her lip, cheeks growing a bit darker as her eyes flickered between his face and his antlers. "Can I hold them? Is that something people do?"

"Some people like it."

"Do you like it?"

Koruuksi's cheeks grew hot, and Vise giggled, pulling his face back up to hers by his antlers. She kissed him, then gripped both his antlers and pushed him back down until his face was between her legs. He grinned at her, and Vise crossed her ankles behind his neck.

27
Power Begets Conflict

When Ymbandi's Legion returned, E Kwekuue knew grief for the first time in centuries, and all the Buuekwenani mourned those who had given their lives in defense of their city. Uumgwefilo erected a monument of aluminum in thanks, unmarked save for the word "Ymbandi".

Exodus countdown: 12 days, 21 hours, 36 minutes

Matsanga was gone again when Estingai awoke. She relieved herself—Matsanga had chosen ruins with functioning plumbing, at least—then moved through a short routine of stretches and calisthenics, relieving joints stiff from sleeping on the floor. Once through with that, she took out the powermetal and the violet-tinged nuggets of metal, setting them on the ground before her, and started thinking.

After a while of sitting in the small chamber, thinking, and growing frustrated, Estingai decided she needed to move. She got up and looked around Matsanga's little storage area until she found what she was looking for. She took a handful of arrows and one of Matsanga's spare bows in one hand, then hefted the straw target with the other.

Once outside, she stuck the arrows into the dirt and chose a tree to hang the target on. A quick scan told her which one Matsanga likely used himself, and Estingai soon stood near the arrows with the bow in hand. She examined it, and frowned. It was much thicker than any bow she'd ever held, and had strange metal adornments. It was also Matsanga's height—about two heads taller than her.

When Estingai knocked an arrow and tried to draw, she blinked at the tension. Taking a deep breath, she set her stance and tried to draw again. The string barely budged.

Frowning, Estingai examined the bow again. Matsanga was a beast of a man, with arms as big as most Samjati weightlifters despite the Natari tendency toward slim, lean physiques. Even with that in mind, she should still be able to draw the bow herself...shouldn't she?

Estingai studied the bow a moment longer, wishing not for the first time that she had Samjati greynodes instead of Natari ones. She went and retrieved a less-intimidating bow and set up again before drawing. This time the string gave, the bow's limbs creaking as they flexed.

Estingai carefully let the tension go slack. She looked at the target, then the bow, then pulled the arrows from the ground and put more distance between herself and the tree.

When she drew again, Estingai pulled the arrow back to her cheek without straining, then let go of the string.

The arrow sank deep into the target, closer to the edge than the center, and Estingai frowned, taking another arrow from the ground.

She'd learned archery as a form of meditation and as an option for stealth missions. Firearms, railguns and silencers had all been in circulation when she'd started training with the Knights—despite, she'd later learned, Skadaatha's best efforts—but archers were silent, and a skilled one could take out several enemy soldiers or guards. Estingai had personally preferred Auroramancy to anything else when in combat, but she'd trained extensively to give Svemakuu someone to compete against. The last time she'd actually used a bow, however, had been around ten cycles ago, and it showed.

As Estingai nocked her next arrow, she took a deep breath and tried to center herself, aiming for the meditative state she'd once been able to achieve. Working with georaurals had once been able to transport her to that mindset without fail, but that was no longer an option.

It took several hours, but Estingai finally reached that state, switching back to the first bow at one point. She returned to reality only when crunching leaves alerted her to Ajida and Matsanga's approach. The icehound padded up to her and nuzzled its big fluffy head against her thigh, and Estingai couldn't help but smile as she reached down to scratch Ajida's head between his ears.

"I think I have something," she said as Matsanga walked over.

Her mentor raised an eyebrow. "Oh?"

"I figured out how you were able to pull on my Auroralight despite being Fireborn," Estingai said. "When I hold this, certain abilities—not those that have to do with fire—but some of them allow me a sort of push or pull to use one side of the ability or the other, though the equivalent Iceborn ability is much weaker."

Matsanga raised an eyebrow. "I don't think I realized I was doing that. I've had no one to practice on, however, so that would make sense."

Estingai brightened her blacknodes and pulled on the power, then brightened her violetnodes and created a flame at the tip of her finger. "Can you sense me using Auroramancy?"

Matsanga hesitated for a moment, then smiled. Estingai could feel herself returning the expression.

"I knew you'd be able to think of something, Estingai."

She beamed, energy bursting within her.

I figured out something he and Nevisi couldn't. They had centuries while I've had hours.

That encouraged her. She would find a way to stand against Kojatere.

"Do you realize what this means for georaurals?" Estingai said, smiling. "If this has the same mechanical functions as it does for Auroramancy, these metals could open completely new areas of study and engineering."

Estingai's fingers suddenly itched for tools and biogems. She hadn't experienced a craving to tinker like this in over seven years. She looked up, about to ask Matsanga if he had any tools or spare biogems, when she saw his frown.

"What is it?"

He gestured toward the broken down ruin that served as his home, "Let's go inside."

Estingai frowned, but collected her arrows and the target.

"What do you think of the bow?"

Estingai eyed her mentor. "Can you actually draw that thing? I had to that new trick with my greynodes."

He nodded. "I had to find something to keep me sane out here. A bow with that draw weight was an interesting project that kept me busy for a while. Once I made it, I had to work up to actually being able to wield it."

Estingai blinked, glancing at Matsanga's arms, but said nothing as she followed him inside. Once she put the bow back and they settled down in their usual spots, Estingai looked to Matsanga.

"Use your bluenodes on me. Flip them first, so you're trying to draw my power form me like an Iceborn."

Estingai blinked. Doing that to anyone other than an enemy on the battlefield or an opponent in an *imbe koa* match—when those had still mattered to anyone—was considered almost unthinkable.

Matsanga seemed to sense her thoughts and rolled his eyes. "It's just Auroralight, Estingai."

Estingai grimaced, scrubbing her fingers through her hair. "Right."

She closed her eyes, centering herself, then brightened her bluenodes. While Fireborn bluenodes could transfer Auroralight, those of Iceborn could draw Auroralight from others.

How did he take my power earlier though, if he didn't have any georaurals on him?

Estingai would ask about that later—maybe he'd even teach her about it with this.

Eyes open, she flipped the switch and brightened her bluenodes, pulling on the light within Matsanga's gemcrest. It resisted her pull most strongly at first, but Auroralight never simply let someone take it from its host. It was much easier with the powermetal, however, and within moments, Auroralight filled her.

Even as Matsanga slumped a bit before her, Estingai's body roared with energy, her gemcrest near to bursting, and the extra energy making her want to run or act.

"What now?" she asked, standing and shaking out her limbs to avoid the side effects of taking in more Auroralight than one's gemcrests could hold.

"Keep pulling," Matsanga said, voice a bit more tired than usual.

Estingai frowned. "But there's—"

"The powermetal should let you feel it," he said. "Keep pulling until I tell you to stop."

Estingai hesitated, then brightened her bluenodes again. She did feel something more within Matsanga. Not Auroralight exactly, but something similar.

Whatever this was, it resisted even more as she pulled, despite the powermetal. For what seemed like minutes, Estingai felt as though she was trying to pull down a mountain with her fingers. Then something slipped and power flooded into her.

"Stop."

Estingai gasped, stumbling back against the wall.

She looked down at her hands, at her chest, and threw off her overshirt so she could pull the collar of her undershirt below her gemcrest.

Estingai frowned. They didn't look brighter than before. And the extra energy—it was... not gone, but...

"What did I just do?" she asked.

Matsanga's eyes held a twinkle she hadn't seen in so long. "You drew out some of my innate power for yourself."

Estingai's eyes widened. "Explain that in a way that sounds less alarming, please?"

Matsanga snorted, settling down on the floor, one leg outstretched. "Certain individuals, myself included, are more... invested with power like that of Auroralight than others. We can't use that power for Auroramancy—not directly, at least, but it has other benefits."

Estingai closed her eyes for a moment, trying to detect something different within herself besides the feeling of extra power. She felt a bit stronger, a bit more positive than normal, her mind clear, but nothing aside from that.

Opening her eyes, she studied Matsanga.

"You didn't draw in enough to experience those benefits in a truly noticeable way," Matsanga said.

Estingai frowned, then blinked. "You're lightless."

Matsanga raised an eyebrow, gesturing to his chest. The shirt he wore was thin enough that earlier the glow of his gemcrest had been visible through it. "I thought that was pretty obvious."

Estingai rolled her eyes. "But you're not acting like it. Not unless you've spent far more time lightless and training yourself to push through it than I have."

Matsanga shook his head. "I have not."

"Then it buffers you against it?"

"Somewhat. The reason lightlessness makes one feel so powerless is because every creature on Efruumani experiences near constant investment due to the auroras. Even non-Auroramancers experience the latent gifts granted to them by their gemcrests. Lightlessness hits them so hard because they are suddenly without something they believed was constant."

He rolled his shoulders. "Having innate power the way I do is different. It doesn't get used up little by little, but there's also nothing I can actively do with it, save to bestow it on others or gather more of it. It does, however, grant me some passive benefits. The latent abilities granted by my gemcrest are bolstered even without Auroralight, as yours will be from now on—if not to so great a degree—and the amount of power I have seems to have given me more strength and energy than I should have, as well as the ability to use either side of certain Auroramantic abilities."

Estingai blinked. "Like how you took my Auroralight when you ambushed me?"

Matsanga nodded.

"Why don't you use this to suck in Auroralight and make yourself more powerful?" Estingai asked, mind reeling. "Couldn't you potentially make yourself as powerful as Ynuukwidas given enough time?"

"I think you underestimate exactly how much power a Throne grants one. That would take a *very* long time. Skadaatha told me that the power she once held was near-infinite, and that the power of a Throne is both greater and lesser than what she could call upon. Besides, it doesn't work that way—drawing in Auroralight, that is. Or bottling up that much power. Most souls can only hold so much."

"You obviously found a way past that."

Matsanga shook his head. "Only the second one."

Estingai thought to ask about that but waited. When Matsanga did not elaborate, she sighed. "What about acquiring the power then? If not from Auroralight, where did you get it?"

"Lightforged," Matsanga said, voice cold. "Their souls are... not exactly expanded, from what I can tell, but they have more innate power invested into them than most souls. It's what allows them to heal and makes them virtually immortal. It doesn't stop you from draining them of their power, however."

This, I could use.

"Permanently?"

Matsanga nodded.

Estingai considered that for a moment, then frowned.

Matsanga's words had implied that his trick with bluenodes could be done without the aid of the powerstone, but that she needed it to help make it possible. Did that mean she needed to pull more power into herself, or that with practice, she could eventually pull power from another unaided?

"How do you think I discovered the power-siphoning ability?"

Matsanga asked, not rising to her irritation. "I knew about the power-metal and their effects for centuries before I discovered that."

Estingai put her hands to her face.

Centuries?

"How the hell did you expect me to discover something after twenty-six hours of practice?"

"You were my most promising student, Estingai. If anyone can do it, it's you."

Estingai dropped her hands, peering at Matsanga. "What? I thought Kojatere was your most promising student?"

Anger started to smolder in Estingai's stomach at comparing herself to the woman.

"Kojatere was the most dedicated. She knew she was good, but wanted to be better than anyone else, so she pushed herself harder than most can. You were nearly as dedicated in your training, but you took to things so much quicker than anyone else. When you faced a problem, you figured out how to get through it with your Auroramancy, and you picked up my tricks and more advanced techniques almost instinctively. When you couldn't find a solution—"

"I would tinker with georaurals until I managed to puzzle something out from working with them."

Estingai wanted to smile at that. Her anger had died down mostly. Something else pricked at her, though.

"How am I supposed to move on after what she did?"

The words just slipped out.

Matsanga met her gaze.

"You heard the stories about me before you ever met me, Estingai. You didn't hold what I'd done against me."

"You weren't nearly as bad as she is."

"Aren't I?"

Estingai flinched at the sudden edge to his voice.

"I was there at the beginning of all this, Estingai," he grated. "Sure, Skadaatha likely would have found a way to create the Imaia without me —she had other pawns throughout Efruumani—but I gave it the momentum it needed to start as it did. I gave her creation a façade of honor and morality. I preached prosperity, tolerance and peace while she schemed and assassinated and worked from the shadows to make sure nothing stood in our way. And I did it all while of sound mind, believing I was doing the right thing. Even before that, I betrayed my people twice over, killed friends, and broke oaths I'd made to bind myself."

"Kojatere and I have both taken countless lives. She has her demons as I have mine. It's what happens in war—no one comes out unscathed, and no soldier or warrior is truly 'honorable'. You've forgiven us for that, or looked past it, at least. The hatred you hold is for Othaashle, not Kojatere. I know you're unsure of her allegiance, but either way, you need to let it go. Hatred never ends well for anyone involved."

"What should I do if I can't hate her?" Estingai scoffed. "Treat her like she is the woman that raised me, the mother I loved? Even if she might be Othaashle?"

Matsanga shook his head. "Pity her."

Estingai blinked.

"Pity the poor twisted woman she's become," Matsanga continued. "A woman denied the peace of death, robbed of who she was and twisted to serve a god who has become a more of single-minded vessel for his power than the man he once was. Pity the woman that was fed lies and told it was right to slaughter and murder, to rob others of death's peace so that her god could take even more life to eventually fight some unseen army, all while destroying the world he was charged to protect."

Estingai had no response to that.

Pity the woman that had left her for dead in a cave? Who had taken her husband from her? Her uncle? So many of her friends?

"She doesn't deserve it," Estingai spat.

Matsanga shrugged tired shoulders. "That may not be for you to determine. You don't deserve to let such hatred fester within you, however. If I'd done that... I'd be a much sorrier wretch than I am even now."

Estingai raised an eyebrow, but let the argument drop. She took a different route.

"Why did you disappear then? Why not just pick off Lightforged, draining their power until you were more powerful than Othaashle?"

"It's not that simple."

Estingai folded her arms. "I hear that a lot. It's usually bullshit."

"In this case, it's not."

Matsanga sat down again, and after a moment, Estingai followed.

"Power...changes a person, Estingai," he said. "It is part of why I believe Skadaatha was like she was, and part of why I believe Ynuukwidas thought it right to use the Imaia to conquer Efruumani. It is no accident that Natari are more outwardly emotional and Samjati more reserved. With the power constantly coursing through our bodies, whether or not we are able to consciously direct or control it, it affects us in a deeper way than just granting us abilities that help us to survive this world's harsh climates."

"And you believe that it could change you enough that you might not end up accomplishing the good you set out to do?" Estingai asked, Matsanga's words making more sense than she would have liked.

He nodded. "Or that my sense of what was good and right would change the more power I acquired. I would seek to do good yet leave only destruction in my wake. Even if I did not destroy, my perception would change too much. It isn't a new concept—it was why my people fled the Iron Empire long ago. Those in power often overlook or simply don't care about those they crush beneath their feet on the path of ambition. Anyone seeking to wield that much power does the same thing, just on a much larger scale."

"You believe Ynuukwidas was a good person, then? Before he ascended?"

"He likely was even for a time after that. Yet even that is not all of it."

"What do you mean?"

"The Imaia had a champion before Othaashle—one that fought against Kojatere when...well, when she was still Kojatere."

Estingai nodded. "I remember. I wasn't directly involved in many of those battles, though."

"I commanded from behind our lines rather than taking the field when the war first broke out," Matsanga said. "When I finally did take the field, my power was too great for most of their soldiers to match, so as I feared, they sent—or created—something that would match my power. Then Kweshrima made Kojatere her champion, and she defeated the Imaia's."

"And then Ynuukwidas took to the field," Estingai said, chest tight as she remembered that terrible, awful day.

Matsanga nodded. "And then Ynuukwidas took to the field. Power begets conflict, Estingai. It works the same with nations. One will brag of their armed forces and place them along their border. Even if they have no interest in attacking their neighbors, such an army so close to them will make them wary, and they will train their own forces to match their neighbor's should things come to it."

Estingai nodded, she'd heard the maxim before.

"Just as you come here seeking to match Kojatere's power, should you need to do so. And you've seen what happens when great powers come to a head."

Estingai sighed. She had. Most of Efruumani stood as a testament to that destruction.

Matsanga rose then, and Ajida rose with him.

"That should be enough of a lesson for today," he said, taking his bow and quiver from where he'd set them.

"Where are you going? I'll come with you."

Matsanga shook his head. "You need to practice."

He walked over to the cupboard and pulled out another wash-leather purse before tossing it to her.

Estingai caught it and emptied it into her palm. These silvery nuggets were almost icy-blue when they caught the light a certain way, yet had a violet cast to them, and they didn't have the same immediate effect as the other violet nuggets.

"What do these do?" she asked.

Matsanga met her gaze, then shrugged and started out of the

room. "Haven't figured that out yet, but I'm sure you can. It took Nevisi and I a while to figure out the trick with bluenodes. If anyone else can discover something, it's you. Kojatere figured out quite a few tricks on her own and you remind me of her, though more motivated."

"I'm nothing like her," Estingai said, the words leaving her mouth before she even registered them.

Matsanga held her gaze for a moment, then sighed. "Bitterness and anger don't suit you, Estingai. Whatever problem you have with Kojatere, I expect it should be directed more toward Othaashle than the woman who took you in and raised you as her own daughter."

Estingai should have just sat back down and kept silent, but she couldn't help herself.

"That's rich, coming from you. A bitter old man who ran away to live alone while others fought."

Matsanga shrugged. "I never said I wasn't. Maybe I just don't want you to turn out like I did."

Estingai wanted to punch the wall as Matsanga walked out.

First Koruuksi, then Matsanga. Half the family I have left, and my mentor.

Why did she have to be like this?

28

A City Asleep

With so many returning after years spent in the outside world—some with husbands and wives who had known nothing of E Kwekuue until stepping foot on its soil, the Buuekwenani way of life was challenged once more.

Exodus countdown: 11 days, 6 hours, 27 minutes

Ymvesi'ia gritted her teeth as she slipped back through the quiet, sleeping city toward the palace. She didn't want to be angry. She needed to be. It wasn't as easy as she'd hoped, however, and she didn't know how much longer she could keep this up.

Anger is better than fear. No matter how exhausting it is.

Anger at Koruuksi had been able to keep her distracted as she'd led her guards and Koruuksi's team through the forest back to their ships. When she'd said goodbye to the volunteers, however, many of whom were the closest things to friends that she could have as a princess—besides Vise, of course—a storm had overwhelmed that anger. She hoped she would see them again, but the uncertainty terrified her. When they'd asked her what this meant—if they were doing the right thing by leaving to help Koruuksi's people—she had barely managed to give them a convincing answer that yes, it was right. Thankfully, it seemed her blessing held great weight with them. Seeing those incredible transports rise into the air and fly out over the sea, though...wonder and sheer awe had overwhelmed everything else for a time, sustaining her for most of the trek back through the forest with Na'imbe and Kjate—those she'd brought along who had families to take care of, and so had not left. Muuzuuri and the others had left a single ship for Koruuksi and Uuchantuu to use to escape if things went poorly, and to use for communication if things went well. Ilona had made her promise to get the two of them to the ship if things went even more poorly than they already were. Ymvesi'ia had not hesitated. She didn't want either of her new friends to leave, but if she couldn't escape, she wanted them to have that chance, at least.

Koruuksi has good people. I should have seen that earlier.

Ymvesi'ia took the back entrance into the palace and passed through the halls without notice. She kept her eyes fixed on the white and silver carpet that covered the stone floor, not wanting to look up at the beautiful artwork that lined the halls. She would be forced to leave them far too soon. One way or another.

When she slipped in her room, Ymvesi'ia stiffened at the darkness, but relaxed in the next moment, smiling as her eyes adjusted. Uuchantuu poked around the room's main chamber looking at a few of the books Ymvesi'ia kept for herself. Ymvesi'ia rolled her eyes, though the smile did not leave her lips.

I should have known she'd bring them here.

Ymvesi'ia watched Uuchantuu move from her study of the books to a study of the cooling georaural set into the wall. Her face quickly grew hot, pulse racing. Uuchantuu looked beautiful in her wrap, even with the silly mantle. She wasn't made of luscious curves like Vise, instead sporting a lithe muscular physique like Ymvesi'ia's own, if a bit shorter. She'd taken out her braids, and Ymvesi'ia was surprised to see that her hair was curly, not crimped like most of the Natari refugees they'd taken in. The silver and white strands of her hair shimmered in the dim light, making the black seem even darker.

A gasp made Ymvesi'ia jump, and she realized Uuchantuu was gazing at her wide-eyed.

"Apologies," Ymvesi'ia said, turning to set her spear against the wall in an attempt to hide the heat in her cheeks. Then she remembered she was still wearing her face-covering and raised a hand to her head.

Maybe I'm more exhausted than I thought.

"I am tired," she said, turning back to Uuchantuu, "I must have gotten lost in my thoughts."

Uuchantuu nodded, gazing at her in silence.

The air between them grew thick, the silence deafening.

Ymvesi'ia swallowed.

Do something. Don't just stand here staring like an idiot.

Ymvesi'ia removed her hood and face covering, letting her frizzy, sweaty hair fall over her shoulders, hoping that would put Uuchantuu more at ease.

Uuchantuu blinked, then offered a nervous smile. "Did you watch the ships take off?"

Ymvesi'ia smiled, folding her hood up and hanging it up on the nearby hook. "It was incredible. I cannot believe that is commonplace for you."

Uuchantuu raised an eyebrow. "Honestly, it's somewhat hard to believe it isn't for you."

Ymvesi'ia cocked her head. "Why is that?"

"If people as smart as you and Vise are common here, I'd say you surely have enough people smart enough to figure out how to make something that flies."

Ymvesi'ia smiled at that. "True, but we don't have the infrastructure, and flying machines are a bit more conspicuous than we care to be."

"Fair point."

"Vise will probably be annoyed she did not see it," Ymvesi'ia commented, imagining her friend's chagrin when she told her about it.

She looked around the room, then frowned, looking back to

Uuchantuu. "Where is Vise? Did she go down to the kitchens for some food, or is she asleep?" She looked around the room again, "Where is Koruuksi?"

Uuchantuu's face colored, and she swallowed. "Uh...they're both in Vise's room, but they're not asleep. At least, they weren't when I woke up."

Frowning, Ymvesi'ia looked toward Vise's room. "Why—?" She cut off, eyes widening as she looked back to Uuchantuu. Her cheeks burned as Uuchantuu nodded, looking as uncomfortable as she felt.

Silence stretched between them again until Uuchantuu yawned, hurriedly raising a hand to cover her mouth.

"I should probably get a bit more rest," she said, turning toward one of the storage alcoves. Had Vise set up the pallets in there? "I'll leave you alone."

Ymvesi'ia bit her lip, hesitating.

Just do it.

"Wait," Ymvesi'ia said, taking a step toward Uuchantuu.

Uuchantuu stopped and looked to her.

Ymvesi'ia gestured to herself. "I need a bath after trekking back and forth through the forest in this, and I need some help getting out of these clothes. If you are tired, a hot bath might help, and bathing is always easier with a partner. Would you like to join me and wash off?"

Uuchantuu's eyes bulged, her face turning an even deeper red than usual. Ymvesi'ia frowned, confused, before remembering how outsiders, and Uuchantuu especially, thought about nudity.

Oh, Light, that must have sounded wrong.

Ymvesi'ia opened her mouth, searching for the right words. Before she could say anything, however, Uuchantuu smiled. "That sounds nice, actually."

Ymvesi'ia blinked at the woman for a moment, then smiled, trying to contain the giddy joy that arose within her.

Does that mean...?

Ymvesi'ia took a deep breath, steadying herself.

Don't assume anything. It's just a bath. That's what you offered, and she's probably trying to be accommodating. Don't make her feel uncomfortable.

Smiling, she turned toward the bathing chamber and gestured for Uuchantuu to follow her. When they entered the chamber, Uuchantuu gasped, her eyes wide as she took in the room.

"This is beautiful," she gasped, "and so big."

Ymvesi'ia studied her. "Was the one in your apartments not larger?"

Uuchantuu looked at her and nodded, "But that was for the entire complex. And this is just for you?"

Ymvesi'ia nodded, smiling at her bath. The aluminum edges reflected the light of the biogem lanterns, giving the room and the bath a near ethereal quality

"Vise and I share it. Most of the communities share a large bath or some of the public bath houses, but my father and I, and the Diwana, and their families, all have private chambers."

"That sounds like a lot of work if you don't have an army of servants."

"Did you not see how the baths at your apartments work?"

She walked over to the georaural panel and set the controls to start filling the tub with hot water. A few seconds later, water began to rise from the bottom of the tub.

Uuchantuu gazed wide-eyed at the mechanism. "Oh. That's why they were all so excited."

"You did not bathe with the rest of your friends?"

Ymvesi'ia held back a grin as Uuchantuu's cheeks darkened. "Showering with them back home is fine—everyone wants to just get clean as quickly as possible, and we're discouraged from wasting water. Just relaxing in a bath here, though…"

Ymvesi'ia peered at Uuchantuu as she trailed off.

Yet she feels comfortable bathing with me. Or maybe wants to in spite of not being comfortable.

Ymvesi'ia suddenly felt nervous.

What if I am misreading this? What if things go like they did last time? I—

She shook the thoughts from her head.

Do not treat it that way. Just take a bath and relax.

"You said you needed some help with your clothing?"

Ymvesi'ia blinked, her cheeks growing hot as she remembered saying that.

"Yes, but you do not—"

Uuchantuu waved her off. "It's fine—Koruuksi and I help each other in and out of our gear all the time. I expect this tunic and pants are worn over something else to help you blend in when in the forest?"

Ymvesi'ia nodded, turning away from Uuchantuu so she could watch the bath as it filled and let Uuchantuu see the ties at the back of her clothing. She nearly jumped when she felt Uuchantuu's fingers at the ties.

Relax. She's just taking off your uniform. Vise has done this for you thousands of times.

The issue was, Ymvesi'ia still got a little excited despite her best efforts whenever Vise helped her undress or massaged her. She chalked that up to never having been touched by another woman, but this was different.

"How did you build those ships?" Ymvesi'ia asked, trying to distract herself. "Koruuksi made it seem like your Remnant does not have much infrastructure of its own."

Ymvesi'ia shivered despite herself as Uuchantuu undid the last tie on her tunic. She rolled her shoulders forward and pulled it off as Uuchantuu went to work on the padded armor underneath, her knuckles brushing the exposed skin at the small of her back. Each touch erupted in sparks.

"Salvage and stealing, mostly," Uuchantuu said, "and a lot of trial and error. We have a lot of space to work in with one of the larger chambers that we hollowed out to make a hangar, but as far as producing circuitry or large sheets of metal, we don't have those capabilities—just enough to make and repair smaller weapons, georaurals or other pieces of tech."

Ymvesi'ia blinked, twisting around to meet Uuchantuu's gaze. "So it is true? You really live in caves?"

Uuchantuu held her gaze for a moment, then nodded, "For the last ten years or so."

Ymvesi'ia looked back to the bath and stopped the pump. She looked to the various bottles of salt and oil Vise used to make their baths even better but decided against trying—she'd never been able to draw a bath as well as Vise.

"What is that like?" she asked, hands going to the ties at her pants. The steamy heat rising from the water called to her.

"Very different than this," Uuchantuu said, a bit of mirth entering her voice. "We have some modern conveniences like datapads, communication, plumbing, and a relative amount of privacy, but there isn't a lot of time to just... be. Something always needs fixing or upkeep, and on the rare occasion there isn't, someone could always use some help. We have down-time, but that's used to blow off steam, exercise, and recover from work or missions more than it is to enjoy oneself."

Ymvesi'ia frowned as she let her pants fall to the floor and slipped out her armor, discarding it to the floor. She turned to Uuchantuu, wearing only her wraps and sandals. "That sounds like a hard life."

Ymvesi'ia had to hide a smile at the way Uuchantuu's eyes widened when she turned to face her, eyes roving over her body before locking on Ymvesi'ia's own.

Does she want more than just a bath?

The heat in Ymvesi'ia's cheeks seemed to match Uuchantuu's.

The woman shook herself, then shrugged, looking away. "You get used to it."

Ymvesi'ia slowly extended her hands toward Uuchantuu, looking to the other woman for permission. Uuchantuu swallowed, but gave a subtle nod, and Ymvesi'ia smiled in an attempt to put her at ease as she tugged at the right spots of Uuchantuu's wraps.

The beautiful clothing fell away, leaving Uuchantuu naked before her. Ymvesi'ia's throat went dry. The other woman's deep red skin was flawless, unblemished and unmarked save for a few faded white scars. She had legs Ymvesi'ia could only dream of. They seemed to go for leagues, and her petite torso only exaggerated the effect. She was lithe and muscular like Ymvesi'ia—not much fat anywhere beside her chest and at her hips—yet seemed sturdy despite her smaller bone-structure.

Ymvesi'ia wet her lips. She'd already seen most of Uuchantuu—simply seeing her breasts and hips wasn't what made Ymvesi'ia's heart race. It was that this woman who took her modesty so seriously, felt comfortable enough with Ymvesi'ia to shed her clothes and reveal what they hid.

Ymvesi'ia almost tugged at her own wraps, eager to enter the bath, but decided to be bold. She turned her back to Uuchantuu. "Can you help get these off me?"

Ymvesi'ia stifled a gasp as Uuchantuu's trembling fingers brushed the bare skin of her back just below the breast wraps, then started on those encasing her hips. Within a minute, both wraps fell to the stone floor.

Face burning, Ymvesi'ia looked back to Uuchantuu. "We do not want to let the water cool too much, right?"

She stepped into the bath, letting out a relaxed moan as the hot, steaming water enveloped her legs, then her hips. A few excitable heatoruu and wispy steamoruu floated into the room, coming to rest on the rim of the tub. They would likely sit there for a while, reaching down to make ripples in the water before moving onto somewhere else or settling down. Taking a deep breath, Ymvesi'ia dunked her head beneath the water, completely soaking her hair, then rose again, running her fingers through her hair before sinking back down to her shoulders. She turned around to find Uuchantuu standing at the edge of the bath, still wonderfully naked, eyes wide as she gazed at Ymvesi'ia.

Her pulse raced even faster.

No one has ever looked at me like that before.

Ymvesi'ia forced herself to relax, and smiled at Uuchantuu. "Come in."

The woman blinked, shaking herself as though her mind had

been elsewhere, then showed Ymvesi'ia a nervous smile as she stepped into the water. Ymvesi'ia grinned, stifling a laugh as Uuchantuu's nerves seemed to melt away as she stepped into the water, eyes fluttering closed.

"Oh, that's incredible," Uuchantuu breathed as her chest and shoulders submerged beneath the water. "If the others had told me a hot bath felt this good, I think I would have spent most of my time here in one."

Ymvesi'ia laughed, earning a smile from Uuchantuu as the other woman opened her eyes.

"Where did you live before the caves?" Ymvesi'ia asked.

Uuchantuu shook her head, then giggled as her hair splashed a bit of water around. "A few different places. I was born on Darkside, living in buildings made of stone and ice, and after I met Koruuksi, I moved around a lot with him and his family. For a while, we lived in a floating fortress made of ice."

Ymvesi'ia blinked at that as Uuchantuu rolled her eyes and made to tie up her hair. After biting her lip for a moment, Ymvesi'ia crossed the distance between them, rising out of the water until most of her torso was above the water.

Uuchantuu froze, eyes wide. Ymvesi'ia shivered at the way Uuchantuu's gaze lingered on her chest and stomach before meeting her gaze in a questioning look.

Ymvesi'ia knew she was the one who needed to be bathed after being in the jungle for so long, but it felt wrong asking Uuchantuu to help her with that.

Unless she is merely returning the favor.

A smile tugging at her lips, Ymvesi'ia stood to the side, gesturing for Uuchantuu to step a bit deeper into the bath. Uuchantuu hesitated, looking confused, but did so.

Ymvesi'ia took her seat and shook her head when Uuchantuu turned around to face her, "Either sit so only your head sticks out, or let yourself float on your back. I will wash your hair for you."

Ymvesi'ia worried she'd gone too far with that as Uuchantuu stiffened. She'd thought offering her the option of submerging herself would—

This time, Ymvesi'ia's spine went rigid as Uuchantuu lay back and let herself float in the water.

"Like this?"

Ymvesi'ia swallowed hard, pulse roaring in her ears. Uuchantuu's curves and the hard planes of her muscles rose out of the water like a red archipelago.

"Yes," Ymvesi'ia managed to force out, voice a bit thick as she tore her gaze from Uuchantuu's athletic body. "I am going to put your head in my lap so the water does not fill your ears, alright?"

Uuchantuu tried to nod, then made a face. "Yes. That sounds like a good idea."

Ymvesi'ia grinned at that and gently took the other woman's shoulders in her hands, guiding her floating body through the water until her shoulders rested just above her thighs. The contact sent a shiver through her.

Ymvesi'ia opened the nearby shampoo bottle and lathered it thick in her hands, then threaded her fingers through Uuchantuu's hair and lifted her head just enough to massage her scalp without letting the water wash the soap away.

"Do you know much about Darkside?"

Ymvesi'ia blinked at the question. "Not too much. We shared histories with the Uumgwefili, but their historians focused mostly on their own people and those they came into contact with. In the years leading up to their fall when printing had become so widespread and aluminum even more valuable, we told them we would trade well for as much information about the outside world as we could get. I think we maybe have three-dozen volumes on Darkside, however. I do not think my people truly believed a place like that could exist until those of our warriors who made it back told us about the Samjati they had met."

"Despite my skin tone and my abilities, I was raised among the Kysuuri," Uuchantuu said, "My people, the Banatuu, used to live in Lightside's deserts, but they were driven from their homeland hundreds of years ago and found refuge among the Kysuuri in the Wastes, adopting their way of life and becoming a sort of unofficial 'thirteenth tribe,' though they spread out and mixed in with all the different Kysuuri tribes."

Ymvesi'ia blinked. "The Wastes?"

"They cover most of Darkside. That half of our world is so cold that once it gets to a certain latitude, there is little difference between land and ocean. The ice is so thick, either way, that you could walk in a straight line come right back to where you started. Provided you're willing to walk over mountains, of course."

Ymvesi'ia smiled. "That sounds incredible. How does anything survive, though, if it is so cold?"

"Biogems help. The same way they do in deserts or caves on this half of the world, but the geothermal vents make it much easier. My people found them soon after wandering into the Wastes thousands of years ago. They built gardens and grand baths around the hot springs they found and traveled between different points to give the soil there a rest, so they didn't need to live purely off of hunting and foraging. The traditions that way of life gave birth to is why Koruuksi makes fun of me. When I still lived with my people, it was always so cold outside that we had to cover up as much as Koruuksi does here, though we needed thick, heavy clothing. In the baths, though, wearing clothing of any sort was pointless, since drying it would be a pain. The structures my people built did have a few private chambers, but most of the areas were common, social spaces, so in that context, nudity was okay. I know it's strange, but—"

"I do not think it is strange. It makes sense. We do not wear much clothing here because it is so hot, but I am certain our isolation played a big part in that, especially as the rest of the world modernized. Apparently, clothing with more coverage became the style for a short time after we first established relations with Uumgwefilo, but it never held. If I suddenly lived somewhere that was colder, though, or where everyone else covered up and gawked at someone wearing our clothing, I would probably cover up."

Ymvesi'ia blushed at Uuchantuu's small moan as she continued to massage the soap into her hair but smiled as she looked down at the other woman, her face so peaceful, full lips parted ever so slightly.

"Did you have any brothers and sisters growing up?" she asked.

Uuchantuu swallowed, clutching at her wrist just beneath a thin woven bracelet set with a few biogems.

"A sister. We lived in tribes and clans, so I had a lot of 'cousins' that I was close with as well. Some of them were almost as good as siblings, but I was closest with her. Now, though, Koruuksi is the closest thing I have to a brother."

The pain in her voice made Ymvesi'ia tense. "How did you meet him if you grew up among the Kysuuri? Those are not his people, I imagine."

"They're not," Uuchantuu said, smiling. "I met him through his parents and the Imaia's efforts, unfortunately. My people's way of life had been barely resisting change for some time, but Koruuksi's parents wanted him to know what he would be fighting to protect if he chose to fight the Imaia. We met when I was fifteen years old and spent a lot of time together. I liked to sneak off to watch him train, and his family didn't seem to have a problem with including me in his lessons. I got to meet his father, Aiteperit, and Estingai, and a few of the Knights as well, and they were always so nice to me. When he finally needed to leave for good, I just went with him."

"What made you go?"

Uuchantuu was silent for a while.

"While Koruuksi was training with us, one of the clans attacked mine. We found out that they'd been infiltrated and radicalized by the Imaia, and that was when I knew I had to do something. Our tribes would argue and have competitions, but none had outright attacked another for hundreds of years."

She sighed. "I thought about returning to help them at some point, especially when we started spending more time on Darkside, but... then Yrmuunthal happened. Lightside felt some effects, but Darkside was changed forever. For whatever reason, the destruction set off a massive amount of tectonic and volcanic activity. It shattered the thick ice that had covered the oceans to create the Ice Wastes and set off so many volcanoes we'd thought safe and dormant."

Ymvesi'ia tensed. "And the hotsprings your people lived near..."

Uuchantuu rose out of the water and turned to face Ymvesi'ia. The pain in her eyes made Ymvesi'ia's chest tighten.

"I only survived because I was away with Koruuksi and his family. My clan had already been mostly wiped out during the attack." She paused clutching at the bracelet at her wrist again. "I lost my sister and my parents in the attack. I lost everyone I knew. Koruuksi and his family took me in after that, but I still had some extended family in the Wastes. After Yrmuunthal...if there are any left, I don't know what happened to them."

Ymvesi'ia swallowed a lump in her throat. She wanted to hold Uuchantuu but didn't know how the woman would respond to it. Still, she couldn't look at those pained eyes anymore. She looked down and found the scars on Uuchantuu's body. She didn't have many, but each one hurt Ymvesi'ia to think of what had happened to Uuchantuu to leave a permanent mark.

"Can I try?"

Ymvesi'ia blinked, looking back to Uuchantuu.

"Washing your hair," she said. "I don't know if I'll be any good but..." Uuchantuu trailed off, her cheeks growing dark. "It felt really nice. I...want to make you feel that way."

Ymvesi'ia bit her lip as warmth flooded through her body. She nodded, holding Uuchantuu's gaze, then lowered herself into the water to float on her back. A wonderful shiver ran from her scalp to her toes when Uuchantuu cupped her head and gently pulled her across the bath's warm surface.

"Tell me about your family," Uuchantuu said. "Before everything happened. What were they like?"

Ymvesi'ia hesitated, trying to search for memories that were happy rather than bittersweet. The wonderful feeling of Uuchantuu's fingers on her scalp distracted her a bit. She started with her mother, telling Uuchantuu how she always managed to balance responsibility with humility, and how *she* had been the serious parent that would keep her father from indulging them. Then she moved on to her brother, Dimban. He'd been only a few years older than her and had been her closest friend other than Vise, who'd had a massive crush on him and decreed at least twice that she would grow up to marry him. Last, she spoke of her older sister, Ma'ake, who had always been so strong and confident, though she admitted that might have just been Ymvesi'ia's impression due to their twelve-year age difference. She'd always cherished the way Ma'ake had never treated her like a child, answering the more 'grown up' complex questions in a way she could understand at a younger age, but without treating her like a child.

"She is the main reason I had no need to ask my father about making love and where children came from," Ymvesi'ia said, grinning. "Even asking my mother to explain that would have just been so embarrassing. She would have been so serious and clinical, and my father would have tried to make too many jokes."

"How old were you when she told you?"

Ymvesi'ia's cheeks grew hot despite the current situation. "When I was twelve and walked in on her and her husband."

Uuchantuu barked a laugh, and Ymvesi'ia couldn't help but join in.

"That would definitely be embarrassing. It sounds a bit nicer than having it explained to you at eight while helping your father and a few of your cousins ease the birth of an elk."

Ymvesi'ia's eyes widened, and she looked up at Uuchantuu. "That sounds traumatizing."

Uuchantuu shrugged grinning down at her. "Only until you've helped about six or seven other animals give birth."

Ymvesi'ia shivered. "That makes me very glad that we have people who specialize in the care of livestock."

Uuchantuu chuckled. "Of course, it wasn't very helpful when I realized I wasn't interested in boys."

"When did you realize it?"

Uuchantuu shrugged. "I honestly don't know. I think that for a while, I really just didn't care that much. The first time I ever talked about it was when we took Koruuksi to one of the baths and it gave him a bit of sensory overload. I think he's probably repressed the experience, but he seemed amazed that I saw naked women all the time. We started talking about who was prettiest and mentioning certain parts of them that we liked, but another time when Koruuksi started talking about the other boys, I was confused about why he cared so much." She grinned. "For a while, I was actually disappointed that I didn't like boys, too, because I wanted to do everything like Koruuksi."

Ymvesi'ia laughed. "That is adorable."

She opened her eyes and looked up just in time to see Uuchantuu's cheeks turn a deep purple. Uuchantuu met her gaze, and for a long moment, neither of them moved. Ymvesi'ia felt as though she'd break the spell if she even breathed too deep.

Eventually, Uuchantuu looked down and her fingers started massaging Ymvesi'ia's scalp again.

"I imagine Koruuksi was very helpful in sharing his experiences with women and helping you find partners?" Ymvesi'ia asked.

"*Too* helpful. He always found very beautiful women to try and set me up with, but our lifestyle didn't really allow for more than a few fun nights. I wanted more."

Ymvesi'ia smiled at that, then bit her lip, thinking. She decided not to follow that train of thought for the moment.

"I tried to seduce Vise when I was younger," Ymvesi'ia blurted out. Her cheeks burned.

Uuchantuu's fingers stopped, then shook a bit.

Why the hell did I say that?

Ymvesi'ia looked up, then blinked when she realized that Uuchantuu was biting her lip, a strained smile on her lips.

"Are you laughing at me?"

"I'm trying really hard not to."

Ymvesi'ia realized she was smiling despite herself. "What iss so funny?"

"I was wondering if you'd admit to it."

Ymvesi'ia blinked, twisting to stand upright. "You knew?"

Uuchantuu gave her a flat look. "She's gorgeous, she likes to flirt, and she's your best friend. *Of course,* you came on to her."

Ymvesi'ia frowned. "I—"

"Was there alcohol involved?"

Ymvesi'ia snapped her mouth shut, cheeks heating "Yes."

"Were you and Vise both already in your bed, as you apparently often are?"

"Yes."

"Was she being her usual flirtatious, self?"

"Yes."

Uuchantuu grinned. "Then I'd be more worried if you somehow *hadn't* come on to her."

Ymvesi'ia rolled her eyes but couldn't help the smile that tugged at her lips as Uuchantuu grinned at her.

"How did she react?"

"Better than anyone else probably would have. She let me down easily, telling me she loved me, but not in that way. Later, when I was less fragile, she said she had suspected I had a crush on her, and that a part of her wished she was be attracted to women so she wouldn't need to let me down. She said that when I kissed her and she felt nothing, that she knew she was definitely not attracted to women."

Uuchantuu snorted. "So, not only is she beautiful, but she's incredibly kind and gracious?"

Ymvesi'ia nodded.

"At least we don't need to compete with her."

Ymvesi'ia laughed so hard she almost fell into the water. Uuchantuu steadied her, and when Ymvesi'ia met the other woman's gaze, the heat of Uuchantuu's desire rushed through her body. Her breathing suddenly felt too shallow.

"You probably need to wash more than just your hair, right?" Uuchantuu asked.

They stood close. Very close. The water barely covered their hips.

Ymvesi'ia felt her hand rise out of the water toward Uuchantuu and stopped it, suddenly very afraid. The air in the room seemed too thick, too hot.

This is too much. What if—?

Ymvesi'ia nearly jumped as Uuchantuu held a sponge out toward her. Ymvesi'ia looked from her hand to her face. Uuchantuu's smile made some of her tension melt away, but what put Ymvesi'ia at ease was the woman's golden eyes. They reflected Ymvesi'ia's own mixture of trepidation, eagerness, and arousal.

"You first, or me?" Uuchantuu asked.

Ymvesi'ia forced a smile. It wasn't as hard as she'd thought. "You."

She took the sponge, closing the distance between them, and Uuchantuu turned around, presenting her back to Ymvesi'ia.

Ymvesi'ia rested one hand on Uuchantuu's shoulder and brought the sponge to her back. As she worked it in slow, firm circles, she found her eyes drawn to Uuchantuu's scars again. She didn't ask about them, though. That still seemed too personal.

More personal than this?

Ymvesi'ia tried to tell herself that this was just bathing, getting each other clean—something she'd done with Vise thousands of times, and with other members of the guard on occasion back when she'd first joined their number.

She knew it was a lie. Vise's touch would occasionally send shivers through Ymvesi'ia or make her heart beat a bit faster, but those moments were nothing compared to the way her body felt now.

"I am supposed to be strong for my people," Ymvesi'ia said. The words just slipped out. She didn't know what had made her say them, but she couldn't stop them. "But I am just as scared as I would expect any of them to be if they really knew what was going on. How are you and Koruuksi so strong?"

Uuchantuu was silent for a moment, then shrugged. "I don't think 'strong' is the right word. When you've lived the life that he and I have, the end of the world looming over you isn't as bad as you'd think. It's just something else to deal with."

She paused. A moment later, her hand covered the one Ymvesi'ia rested on her shoulder, squeezing it. Rather than sending shivers through her or making her chest tighten, that simple touch spread a wonderful, comforting warmth up Ymvesi'ia's arm and through the rest of her body. She smiled.

This is right. This is what I've been looking for.

Ymvesi'ia swallowed. This was no longer just a bath. She didn't stop scrubbing Uuchantuu's back, however.

"Koruuksi meant what he said," Uuchantuu continued. "He doesn't leave his friends behind. He also has an annoying habit of figuring out impossible situations. It's what makes him so annoyingly arrogant, at times."

Ymvesi'ia chuckled at that, relaxing a bit as she traced a fingertip over a long scar on Uuchantuu's lower back. "He does seem like the type."

"You can ask, you know."

Ymvesi'ia bit her lip, "How?"

Uuchantuu shrugged. "We were ambushed during a raid on one of the Imaia's trans-hemispheric railways. We'd been relying on the same tactics despite Estingai's objections, and the Imaia proved her right that time. They saw us coming and caught us off guard. That was part bayonet, part sharp rocks that I fell onto during the fight. The one above it was a bullet wound that made it through my armor. It was superficial, thankfully, but it still took far too long to heal."

Ymvesi'ia shook her head, taking Uuchantuu's fingers before she could move on to the next scar. She met Uuchantuu's gaze and held it, though her eyes kept wanting to look down to Uuchantuu's lips.

So close.

"How did you keep going back?" Ymvesi'ia asked.

Uuchantuu shrugged, taking the sponge from Ymvesi'ia and starting on her. Ymvesi'ia held in a gasp at the contact.

"These aren't the worst," Uuchantuu said. "They're just stories—a record of the engagements I've been in that I can pull out if I've had enough to drink to start comparing sizes with the boys. Not being able to go out and fight right away was harder than getting hurt in the first place. Koruuksi and I have both chewed each other out for trying to go out and do something before we were done recovering. Other soldiers had to do that sometimes, if no one else could, but we were considered too valuable as Auroramancers."

Ymvesi'ia blinked, glancing down at the crest of rednodes adorning Uuchantuu's clavicle. "I did not realize you were an Auroramancer."

Uuchantuu nodded, a smile tugging at her lips. A disc of shining, golden light appeared between them, spinning around a few times before winking out of existence.

"You? I mean, I assumed so, but—"

Ymvesi'ia nodded. She brightened her pair of violetnodes and directed the heat into the water. A moment later, steam rose from the surface.

"I think it is part of what finally convinced my father to let me join the guard. He knew I could handle myself."

Uuchantuu nodded, and Ymvesi'ia bit her lip as the other woman's eyes and fingers found the scar at her hip, usually hidden by her wrap. Ymvesi'ia shivered at the touch, eyes fluttering closed for a moment.

"Does this have anything to do with the other part? Or is it something you received after?"

Ymvesi'ia opened her eyes and found Uuchantuu gazing at her. Those golden eyes told Ymvesi'ia that Uuchantuu's pulse raced just as fast as her own.

Ymvesi'ia looked down to where Uuchantuu held her hip and brought her own hand down to trace the thin white line with her fingertips.

"It is what earned me the respect of the Akjemasai," Ymvesi'ia said, "though I was not trying to do anything like that at the time."

She almost whimpered when Uuchantuu let go of her hip, but relaxed when the woman moved behind her, the sponge never leaving her skin, and continued to sponge the sweat of a hot day in the jungle from her skin.

"It was after the survivors returned from the expedition my mother led against the Imaia," Ymvesi'ia continued, shivering as Uuchantuu's fingertips brushed her shoulders. "After I recovered from the shock of finding out that those of my and Vise's families were not among them, I interviewed every one of them I could for stories, so that Vise and I could have something more of our families to hold on to."

She stifled a gasp as Uuchantuu's knuckles grazed the small of her back, sending her pulse racing.

"There was one man who seemed a bit off, though. We took in some refugees and survivors from Uumgwefilo, so the fact that he was not Bueekwenani was not enough to go on. It bothered me enough that I tailed him for a while, trying to see who his friends were and where he went. One day, I followed him out of the Vale and into the forest when the guards happened to be conveniently absent. I wasn't as stealthy as I thought, however, so he learned I was following him and tricked me, forcing a confrontation. I took a chance asking him why he would betray our secret. Instead of denying it or answering, he attacked me."

Ymvesi'ia felt Uuchantuu hesitate for a moment.

"He caught me off-guard and gave me that scar with his knife. I was stupid and had not brought along any weapons, but my Auroramantic training kicked in, saving me."

She paused for a moment, shuddering at the memory. She could almost smell the ozone, the cooked flesh and singed hair. Ymvesi'ia realized she'd clenched her fists so tight that her nails dug into her palms. She tried to relax but couldn't. She–

A hand touched her shoulder.

Ymvesi'ia started, whirling around toward Uuchantuu.

"He was the first man I ever killed. I managed to hide myself until I heard a patrol coming and they took me back here to stitch me up. My father was furious, but he told me he was proud of me for doing something so brave." Ymvesi'ia laughed. "He also told me that if I was going to be an idiot, he at least wanted me to be one with proper training and equipment."

Uuchantuu laughed at that, the sound filling Ymvesi'ia with that same comforting warmth as before.

"You were pretty intimidating when you ambushed us in the

forest," Uuchantuu said, "And when you came out to stand next to your father in the palace.

Ymvesi'ia turned around to face her, pulse racing at the sight. She smirked at Uuchantuu. "You did not exactly look intimidated in my father's throne room."

Uuchantuu's eyes widened, her cheeks coloring, and Ymvesi'ia laughed.

"I was hoping you'd forgotten about that," she said.

Ymvesi'ia shook her head, "Never. Normally, Vise is there beside me to absorb all of that kind of attention."

Uuchantuu rolled her eyes. "It's unfair how gorgeous that woman is."

Ymvesi'ia's smirk slipped. She looked down at the water.

"But she's not my type."

Ymvesi'ia met Uuchantuu's gaze. "She is not?"

Uuchantuu shook her head, smiling. She moved a bit closer in the water and cupped Ymvesi'ia's cheek. Ymvesi'ia's eyes fluttered at the touch, air rushing out of her in a gasp.

"I like more athletic women. Someone who can handle herself in a fight. Someone who looks out for those close to her."

Ymvesi'ia felt herself drawing closer to Uuchantuu, as though something were pulling her. Uuchantuu's breath warmed her lips.

Their lips brushed. Ymvesi'ia's eyes closed as a thrill rolled through her. It felt almost unreal. At that thought, she opened her eyes and remembered where she was and what she was doing.

"Ymvesi'ia?" Uuchantuu asked, looking confused as Ymvesi'ia stepped back. Her hand had fallen from Ymvesi'ia's cheek. Her eyes held pain and fear, her cheeks bright red. "I'm sorry. I thought—"

Ymvesi'ia shook her head. "Do not apologize. I am just—I..." She trailed off with a sigh, covering her face with her hands, "I am such an idiot. I knew I would mess this up."

Ymvesi'ia froze at a hand on her shoulder and slowly looked to Uuchantuu.

"So, the kiss wasn't a problem?"

Ymvesi'ia swallowed and shook her head. "Not at all. Iam the problem. I am sorry for freaking out. No one has ever..."

Uuchantuu raised an eyebrow, cheeks coloring even further. "That was your first kiss. Other than Vise?"

Ymvesi'ia swallowed. "It was the first time anyone has ever kissed me. Buuekwenani women are not usually attracted to other women, so I did not expect..."

She trailed off, then smiled at Uuchantuu. "I hoped, though."

Uuchantuu smirked, closing the distance between them. "I can kiss you again, then?"

Ymvesi'ia bit her lip, then nodded.

Uuchantuu leaned in. This time the kiss was more than just their lips brushing. That same thrill ran through Ymvesi'ia, causing her hair to stand on end. She gasped, then laughed when Uuchantuu placed a hand on the small of her back and pulled her closer so that their bodies pressed against one another. Ymvesi'ia couldn't stop smiling as she took Uuchantuu's face in her hands and deepened the kiss.

When they finally pulled back for air, it was just enough to breathe. Ymvesi'ia rested her head against Uuchantuu's, their chests rising and falling heavily as they drew in ragged breaths.

"I can see why people like doing that so much."

Uuchantuu laughed. "Do they usually do it naked like this? Where I come from, kissing usually comes at least a little bit before the clothes come off."

Ymvesi'ia shrugged, grinning at her. "I told you I am an idiot."

Uuchantuu smirked, her free hand tracing the muscles on Ymvesi'ia's back, sending shivers through her.

Ymvesi'ia bit her lip. "I have never done this before."

Uuchantuu raised an eyebrow. "I would hope so, given no one had ever kissed you before."

"Vise gave me some advice for myself, but most of it was about men, so—"

Ymvesi'ia blinked as Uuchantuu pressed a finger to her lips.

"That's fine with me."

Ymvesi'ia shivered as Uuchantuu looked her up and down. The other woman's gaze caressed her body like a thousand gentle fingers.

"You said you're familiar with yourself?"

Ymvesi'ia blushed. "Painfully."

Uuchantuu laughed. "I've been there."

She raised dripping fingers and brushed her knuckles across Ymvesi'ia's cheek, "We don't need to do anything you don't want to, alright? Just tell me what you like or what feels good."

Ymvesi'ia nodded slowly, hands trembling in anticipation. "What about you?"

Uuchantuu laughed as she kissed her. "I like that you think that way. Do what feels natural, and I'll guide you. There's no pressure to do anything you don't want to, alright?"

Ymvesi'ia shook her head. "I do not want to let a chance like this slip away."

"The whole city is asleep right now, right?"

Ymvesi'ia nodded. "Most of it. For the next eleven hours or so."

Uuchantuu nodded. "Then we have at least that long to just relax. Provided the bath doesn't get too cold and we don't get too pruney."

For a while they simply held each other. Ymvesi'ia didn't think she'd ever felt so comfortable in another's presence. Maybe Vise, but not in this way.

"Uuchantuu?"

"Yes?"

"Is this just the prelude to a few hours of fun?"

"I'd like it to be more than that."

Ymvesi'ia smiled.

"Good."

29

Personal Research

Scholars and philosophers will debate whether we overcame that challenge, failed, or simply adapted as was necessary in the following years.

Exodus countdown: 10 days, 22 hours, 38 minutes

Yndlova scanned the data on the various screens and papers before her in a secluded corner of the archives, a frown pulling at her features. While the Imaia's records were extensive, and growing more so every day, the information Yndlova sought was from before the Imaia had begun keeping such detailed records. Few had kept digital records at that point, and so much had been lost following Yrmuunthal's destruction. Paper burned, disintegrated, and tore all too easily.

It didn't help, of course, that she couldn't search directly. Yndlova had tested her avenues with a few Redeemed she knew the former identities of because she'd been there when Othaashle chose them. All records on them ended in the same statement: killed in action. Just like Aada's. Just like those of countless other soldiers. Her body hadn't been recovered, but the reports Yndlova had looked up on Suumosalmi and Tolvajaari had shown Aada had not been alone in that respect.

Yndlova sighed, stretching as she leaned back in her chair.

Even worse than that, she didn't have any records of 'rebirth' for the Redeemed to compare with. Just her own memory. Itese would know, as a Redeemed, but for that same reason, Yndlova didn't want to make her uncomfortable.

"Something wrong, Adjunct?"

Yndlova started, nearly tipping over her chair as Othaashle approached.

"Commander," she gasped, half-rising before Othaashle put up a hand to stop her.

"I wanted to commend you on the group you picked for our operation," Othaashle said, stopping at the opposite end of the desk Yndlova had chosen, "They seem to be taking to the training quite well."

Yndlova smiled, trying to keep the nervousness from her features.

She can't see what you're looking over. The monitors block the papers from her line of sight.

"Thank you, Othaashle."

Othaashle nodded, continuing. "I interviewed each of them and I believe one of them is ready to be thrown into Makala."

Yndlova blinked. "That's fantastic."

Spacing out their entry had been one of Yndlova's main concerns. Even if Othaashle was able to use the rescue of the prisoners as a smokescreen to distract the Remnant, a group of unknown prisoners all thrown in just before their successful escape would seem far too convenient to anyone who looked too closely.

"What did you think of the reports on the new systems?" she asked.

"Fishing for compliments, Yndlova?"

"I meant the content. And whatever the Ministry of Science prepared."

Othaashle chuckled. "Your work was impeccable as always—reading those reports made it easy to pick out the salient details from the Ministry of Science's lengthier ones. I made a few adjustments to the plan for monitoring the habitable planets before handing it off."

"Which planets did you recommend?"

"Habitable worlds five and six. With Mjatafa Mwonga as a base of operations, all we really need is a terrestrial world somewhere between the beginning of a star's habitable zone and its frost line, but five's climate is the closest to what the majority of the Imaia is used to. It and most of the other worlds we found seem to rotate on their axes, so I believe the conditions will prove suitable for our Samjati citizens as well."

Yndlova grinned. She'd thought the same.

"Itese told me that you've stopped by her training sessions with her team of Redeemed a few times."

Yndlova swallowed, tense, hoping Othaashle wouldn't notice how off-guard the question had caught her.

"She said you showed some interest in one of the women in particular," Othaashle continued. "Nakina, I believe."

Yndlova opened her mouth, yet found she had nothing to say. She did not want to lie to Othaashle—not after she'd betrayed her trust with Skadaatha.

But can I risk her putting a stop to my work? Can I risk never knowing? Never seeing Aada again?

She couldn't decide. Instead, she met Othaashle's gaze through her mask and awaited her superior's judgement.

"I've noticed lately that there are times where you seem very withdrawn or close-mouthed," Othaashle continued, stepping around the desk until she stood beside the monitors. "Especially since I told you about my visions. Is there something bothering you, Yndlova? Something to do with the taboos of the Redeemed?"

Yndlova sighed, tucking a few braids behind her ear. "You know the... friend I told you about? The one I lost?"

Othaashle nodded.

"I believe she is a Redeemed. Nakina, specifically."

When Othaashle said nothing, Yndlova continued.

"I had no idea who she might be until I heard her voice the other day when I stopped by Itese and her team. It—" She paused, taking a deep breath. "It is part of why I originally sought a position as your adjunct, and why I refused promotion the first few times. Now, I have other reasons to stay, but that has always been in the back of my head."

Yndlova kept her back straight, despite wanting to shrink into her chair.

There. I said it.

Othaashle stood, tone neutral as she spoke. "Clean this up and meet me back in my office. We need to discuss this in private."

A short while later, Yndlova stood in Othaashle's office, its windows overlooking the Village of Light. She waited for Othaashle to dismiss her or tell her she was to be reassigned.

Instead, Othaashle poured them both some lightliquor—a special drink made with microscopic pieces of biogems suspended within the liquid that could hold Auroralight.

Yndlova took hers with uncertainty. "Commander?"

"What was your goal in looking up information on your friend, Yndlova?"

There was no bite to Othaashle's tone, but its neutrality unsettled Yndlova just as much.

"I never really thought that far ahead," Yndlova admitted. "I just wanted to know that my friend was alright, maybe... try to be her friend once more."

"And when I started having my visions, then realized they were memories, you hoped she might remember you?"

Yndlova nodded, taking a sip from her drink.

"I don't believe that will happen," Othaashle said. "Not naturally, at least. I do want to make absolutely certain, however, that the rest of the Redeemed are not susceptible to the return of their memories and former selves."

Yndlova blinked, peering up at Othaashle. "I thought you were certain this is only due to the Aathal."

"I am. We know very little about the Aathal or how their power works, however. I want to make sure the Remnant or the Enemy, or whatever other forces we may face after Exodus won't be able to find a way to do this to our most powerful weapons. Especially now that the Remnant knows it has happened to me."

"Because of how vulnerable the visions leave you?"

"Not just that. As I told you, simply knowing who I was is difficult enough. Experiencing it is even harder. If the others will have to go through this, I want to be prepared to help them through it or prevent it from happening in the first place."

She paused, lifting her mask just enough to take a sip of lightliquor, then looked back to Yndlova. "I would ask for your help with this. In return, I will help you confirm if Nakina truly is your friend remade. If not, I will help you uncover who she is."

Yndlova's chest grew tight. "But your rules—"

"Not everything can remain as it is," Othaashle said, "And you have always been a friend to the Redeemed. Those of us you've chosen to befriend and take the time to engage with seem more comfortable when they venture off the Isle into the rest of the city. I would be a fool to discourage something that has such an effect on my people."

Yndlova nodded, smiling. "Thank you, Othaashle."

"It is no less than you deserve, Yndlova." Othaashle downed the rest of her drink. "I will let you know how I wish to proceed. In the meantime, I want additional shield georaurals placed covertly around the Vale in combination with explosives. I want the shields to direct the explosive energy up and away from Boaathal so that the Remnant believes they destroyed or at least damaged it, making them more confident."

"And giving our people more reason to fight."

"Exactly."

"I will see it done, Commander."

Othaashle nodded, then headed for the door. She stopped in the doorway and looked back toward Yndlova. "Did Itese assist you at all with your... personal research?"

Yndlova shook her head. "It would have made things easier, but I figured it would have made her uncomfortable."

Othaashle seemed to think about that for a moment, then nodded. "Thank you again, Yndlova."

She left Yndlova sitting with the rest of her drink. She downed it, then shook herself.

Finally. Finally, I have a solid lead.

Yndlova would find a way to truly show Othaashle her gratitude. Helping her with protecting her people was not nearly enough to thank her.

Battle of Tolvajaari
Location and Intent:
The Juusan plan was to encircle the Imaia division with two pincer-attacks over the frozen lakes of Jyrvasjaari and Tolvajaari. The northern attack over Jyvasjaari was to begin at 06:00 and the second would start when the first had brought results. This was later changed and both attacks were to begin simultaneously.

The Imaia main effort was to make a frontal assault with two battalions (606 and 124) over the Tolvajaari lake to the Juusan positions near Tolvajaari village, while Imaia battalion 366 executed a flanking maneuver from the north to the Juusan rear across thick, wooded areas.

A single narrow, old muddy road toward the village that wound among a dozen smaller lakes. Just before the battle a snowstorm brought nearly half-a-meter of snow, complicating the terrain further. Due to the thick fog, there was no aerial contingent to this battle. Due to mud, many tanks were stuck and unable to actively participate during the battle. Many were also lost even after the Juusan withdrawal.

Itese sighed, stretching her head to either side before she looked down at her notepad. So far, she'd looked through reports of three major engagements between Othaashle's first appearance on the battlefield and the first battle Itese remembered participating in. She'd accumulated a list of fifty-four Auroraborn across both sides so far, with many more to go. Once she finished that list—as much as it could truly be finished—she would need to compare that with casualty lists.

After I compile those.

Taking a deep breath, Itese returned to her reading. The Isle's archive building was much more modern than the Military Archive building, and much less crowded. She had an alcove all to herself next to a window without being entirely secluded from other Redeemed doing their own research.

She scanned through the composition and details of the battle, complete with diagrams and photographs, before getting to the aftermath.

Aftermath:

Juusan losses were over 100 dead and 250 wounded, with Imaia losses of over 2000 dead and heavy equipment losses due to the terrain. Heavy Imaia losses can be attributed to Juusan tenacity and the late arrival of the Mestari, whose presence quickly turned the tide of the battle. This battle was one of several early displays of the effect the Redeemed have on the morale on both sides of a battlefield.

Names and Status of Recorded Casualties:

"Itese, there you are."

Itese stiffened at Othaashle's voice. She tried to look up slowly as the woman approached, to act like she wasn't attempting to break the taboo the Redeemed held most dear.

"Mestari," Itese said, saluting as she rose from her seat.

Othaashle waved her back down, standing straight-backed across the terminal desk from Itese. "How is your team's training progressing?"

Itese blinked, then relaxed, thankful for her mask. "I believe they will do our people proud."

Othaashle nodded. "Good. Let them know their main task will be funneling the Redeemed to the ship. I have decided that we will be allowing the Remnant to escape with a team of spies in their midst. I would ask your team to accompany them, but unfortunately, that wouldn't work too well."

Itese nodded. It was their people's biggest weakness as a weapon. They could sneak when needed, but they were relatively useless for most forms of espionage.

Though if Skadaatha is to be believed, that will not be needed when we face the Enemy.

Itese glanced at Othaashle again and frowned, noticing a bit of tension to the woman's posture.

"Did you have another vi—memory, Mestari?" Itese asked, her voice low. Not that there was anyone in this corner of the archives to overhear.

Othaashle cocked her head. "Yes, but it's not that."

She folded her hands behind her back. "Why are you so interested in my visions, Itese?"

Itese bit her lip. She'd tried to keep her interest contained since she'd learned of the visions, directing what questions she couldn't hold in toward Yndlova, but it seemed she hadn't been as successful as she'd hoped.

I need to be honest with her. She didn't think she could trust me with the visions and that burdened her and Yndlova. I need to ensure that she is able to trust me with whatever is bothering her now.

"I know who all the Redeemed were," she said. "I was there when you chose almost every one of them, and for those that I wasn't, it wasn't hard to connect the dots when looking over intelligence reports and the like. For some time, only your former identity, my own, and a handful of others were unknown to me. Epekora and those Redeemed before me are dead, now, and I know that you were once Kojatere, Champion of the Knights Reborn. Now the only identity I remain in the dark on is my own."

She sighed, gesturing to the screens between them and the few papers she'd printed out. "I've been looking through battlefield reports, casualty lists, intelligence reports regarding Auroraborn, and anything else I could think of to try and gain some hint of who I was before the God King remade me. I know we're not supposed to think this way, and I've tried not to, but I can't stop. There's an emptiness within me."

Itese paused again, wondering if she should continue.

"This has led me to think more and more that our taboos will soon become unsustainable. Within our own ranks, at least, especially if we wish to expand our number after Exodus, as planned."

Itese snapped her mouth shut once the words left her mouth.

I said it.

Silence spread between them. Itese sat under Othaashle's masked gaze. She nearly jumped out of her chair when the woman finally spoke.

"I agree."

Itese blinked, eyes growing wide, "You do?"

Othaashle nodded. "I'm not yet sure how we would handle it, but it needs to be done. I wanted to ask your help on something related to that actually—I want to make sure that the Aathal is the only power than can return memories to a Redeemed, and if it is not, I want to prepare for it. Now that the Remnant know I have had some of my memories restored, I don't doubt that some of them have thought about trying to do the same to other Redeemed in hopes of gaining their sympathy. If you help me in this, I will help you discover who you were—something more than just a name on a report somewhere. Do I have your aid?"

Itese blinked, barely able to think straight after what Othaashle had just told her. "Of course, Mestari."

Othaashle stepped closer and put a hand on Itese's shoulder. "Thank you, Adjunct."

She stepped back, then gestured to the papers and the monitors. "I would appreciate if you put this on hold for now. I don't want you accidentally discovering anything that could interfere with the tests I have planned or risk one of the others discovering your work. I will let you know when I need your help."

With that, she left.

Itese remained nearly slumped in her chair, overwhelmed by the swirl of emotions. She'd been found out, yet she was not in trouble for it. Instead, Othaashle offered her a chance to fulfill the desperate need within her in a way that served her people.

It seemed almost too good to be true, but Othaashle had never let her down before.

30

Among the Stars

E Kwekuue became more insular, cutting down contact with Uumgwefilo and recalling most of their Muukjebarat for fear of capture and torture by the Imaia. They still honored Uumgwefilo, and both peoples helped the other prepare in case of an attack by the Imaia.

Exodus countdown: 9 days, 28 hours, 19 minutes

Ymvesi'ia paused to catch her breath and look out over the Vale as she neared the observatory. Her legs burned and her heart pounded from the effort of climbing for so long—even with her greynodes brightened—but the view was worth it.

The large dome loomed before Ymvesi'ia as she reached the top of what had seemed an endless supply of stone-carved stairs, aluminum inlay at either end distinguishing them from the rock and plants around her. It was not perfectly round—not on the outside, at least—or even symmetrical. The Heart of the Vale protected them from the outside world, but none of them knew for certain exactly how far that protection stretched. The dome was the only part of the structure not built into the mountainside, so its façade had been designed to look like an extension of the rocky summit from above and to anyone looking at the Vale from without.

For a moment, Ymvesi'ia frowned, wishing she could have brought Uuchantuu here to share this with her. Her lips tingled, remembering the kisses they'd shared. Even just thinking about it made Ymvesi'ia's pulse quicken—something she didn't need after climbing a mountainside.

She shook herself.

That would have been too risky.

It also would have slowed her down and distracted her. As tired as she was from the past two days, she would have been too susceptible to such a distraction.

Glancing back up at the observatory, Ymvesi'ia clenched her fists.

This needs to go well.

She wasn't too worried about convincing Diwana Warsama that there was a problem—she'd been able to convince all the others, save Duubaan. All of them had given her the bare minimum, however. They would support her if called to meet, but none of them would initiate a session unless they knew they would be able to do so unanimously.

Taking a few deep breaths to reign in her heartbeat, Ymvesi'ia started on her last stretch toward the observatory complex and rehearsed how she would appeal to Warsama.

She knows the science better than any of the others, and observing the outside world is her duty, as is defending us from it.

Ymvesi'ia glanced up at the dome again and frowned.

I should have asked Koruuksi if there was anything in the stars that could aid my argument.

She would just have to do without that.

When Ymvesi'ia reached the observatory entrance, Diwana Warsama and two of her aides waited for her.

Diwana Warsama bowed to Ymvesi'ia, a smile on her full lips. The older woman had her hair tied back in a tight braid, held with ornaments that glowed with Auroralight. She was shorter than Ymvesi'ia, barely taller than Vise, but meeting her eyes had always made Ymvesi'ia feel like she was the shorter one. She and her aides all wore longer, thicker wraps that covered more of their bodies to keep them warm despite the chill of the thinner air at this altitude. Ymvesi'ia's violetnodes negated any need for her to do the same.

"Thank you for meeting me, Diwana," Ymvesi'ia said, returning the woman's bow and dimming her greynodes.

Warsama grinned. "Thank you for climbing all the way up here."

She gestured toward the observatory. "Shall we?"

"Mbada'andi said you had something of great importance to speak about, Princess."

Ymvesi'ia nodded. "You have heard of the man, Koruuksi, that came to the city ten days ago, I assume?"

"The one who petitioned His Majesty twice and was thrown out the second time?"

"Yes. I believe my father was wrong to do so."

Warsama raised an eyebrow, and Ymvesi'ia explained her reasoning to the Diwana. She was practiced at it by now after drilling with Koruuksi and Vise and providing similar explanations to three of the other councilors, yet the gravity of the situation made her clench and unclench her hands. This time, she only had to go with the facts, at least, rather than needing to appeal to an agenda.

When she was done, Warsama studied her in silence for a moment. Ymvesi'ia caught her two aides sharing a wide-eyed look.

"Come with me," Warsama said, quickening her pace toward the observatory. "There is something you need to see."

Inside the observatory, the ceiling rose almost impossibly high, the perfect dome inlaid with images of their people's history—their flight from the Iron Empire, their loss of almost half their number during that flight, their arrival in this sanctuary, and their partnership with Uumgwefilo that had led to this observatory's construction. Shelves of books lined the walls for several stories, with research assistants climbing up tall, mobile ladders to reach the higher texts. And of course, massive telescopes dominated the large space within.

Warsama led Ymvesi'ia to the largest telescope, then said something to the pair of researchers stationed next to it. They hurried over to the controls, and Ymvesi'ia blinked when a seam in the dome began to part, flooding the chamber with light, and the massive telescope began to move.

When both stopped, Warsama stepped up to the great mechanism's eyepiece and looked into it. Her mouth drew to a thin line.

"What is it?" Ymvesi'ia asked, drawing closer.

Warsama sighed as she pulled back, giving Ymvesi'ia room. "See for yourself."

Wary, Ymvesi'ia stepped up to the device and looked through it.

At first, she frowned, unsure of what she was supposed to see.

Then ice entered her veins.

She stepped back from the device, trying not to shake as she looked to Warsama. "How long have those been there?"

"A few years," Warsama said. "Not in the same place, of course, but... we've kept a careful watch, recording everything."

"How have they not found us?" Ymvesi'ia asked, more to herself than the Diwana. "If we have the technology to observe them, surely they have the same?"

Warsama sighed. "I'm not sure. The only answer we've been able to come up with is that the Heart must do something to protect us from their technology—an illusion, confusing their sensors, or simply shrouding us in some manner."

Ymvesi'ia bit her lip. "Then... do you believe it can protect us? Even after the Imaia leave Efruumani?"

Warsama was silent for a while, then shook her head. "I cannot be certain one way or the other, but I do not believe the Heart has that kind of power."

Ymvesi'ia frowned, then blinked when Warsama placed a hand on her shoulder. "What I offer, however, is corroboration of your friend's claims. Those about Efruumani's precarious situation, and that there are worlds that exist out among the stars."

∽

YMVESI'IA KEPT her breathing steady and her expression pleasant as she laid down on the couch across from her father in their private dining chamber. It was larger than necessary for just the two of them, but her father hadn't been able to move to a smaller room. She didn't think she could either.

"Ymvesi'ia," he said with a smile, "it's been a while since we've been able to share a meal together."

Dembe and Ka'abe, two of Chef Tuunde's assistants, strode into the room carrying trays of food. The smell made Ymvesi'ia's mouth water.

"What did Tuunde make for us?" she asked, though she was already certain of it.

Her father grinned. "Chicken *muuambe* with sliced mango."

Ymvesi'ia smiled and waited for Dembe and Ka'abe to set up their food on the raised dining platform between her and her father, thanking both of them.

She waited until they were out of earshot and took a few bites of one of the mango slices before speaking again.

"I have been busy since you banished Koruuksi and his people," she said, taking a sip of thibara.

Her father rolled his eyes and waved the question away.

"We don't need to talk about that."

"Yes, we do, Father."

Ymvesi'ia tried to keep her voice level.

She wished they didn't. Warsama agreed that they needed to take action, and soon. She'd shown Ymvesi'ia all sorts of data they'd collected and observations they'd made that supported Koruuksi's claims. Unfortunately, the Diwana declined to call a meeting of the Diwani, saying it would only complicate matters if she did so. Her tone had kept Ymvesi'ia from objecting or pleading further.

Just a calm conversation over dinner—nothing to get emotional about.

"Not about your decision to banish him," she continued as her father frowned. "I agree Koruuksi overstepped."

Her father nodded, seeming satisfied by that.

"But that should not have a bearing on his claims or his argument for them."

The king sighed.

Ymvesi'ia continued before he could say anything.

"You saw how skeptical I was at first, so I spent the next three days after he arrived researching the possibility of his claims."

"As did I," he said. "The research was too inconclusive—the same conclusion I believe you reached."

Ymvesi'ia nodded. "But did you ask Koruuksi for clarification once your research hit a dead-end? To clarify the science beyond our understanding?"

Her father shook his head. "I know you wish to see the best in people, Ymvesi'ia, but asking him such questions would have given the young man leave to spin whatever answers suited his needs."

Ymvesi'ia shook her head. "I spoke with him when I grew frustrated with my research. Vise and I did more research after that, and just to be safe, we asked Diwana Warsama and her researchers if they could validate Koruuksi's claims."

Her father raised an eyebrow.

"They were able to," she said. "I believe him, Father, and it terrifies me."

She shivered, forcing the memory of what Warsama had shown her through the telescope out of her mind. The Diwana had insisted E Kwekuue remained unseen, but it still made Ymvesi'ia's stomach turn.

Her father's gaze grew contemplative, mouth drawing to a thin line, and for a moment, Ymvesi'ia thought she'd gotten through to him.

Then he shook his head. "Even if all their science is correct, there is no way the Imaia could have found a way to separate Boaathal from the world. It is a World Tree, after all. Even if they did, the Heart of the Vale would protect us as it always has. Did Koruuksi explain how the Imaia plans on removing Boaathal?"

Ymvesi'ia frowned.

He does not want to believe. He knows that there is a possibility this could all be true, but he does not want to acknowledge it.

Ymvesi'ia had never thought of her father as a man who could be frightened—even when the guard had brought her back to the city, wounded and exhausted, she'd only seen him relieved, never scared.

But who would not be scared of the end of the world?

Ymvesi'ia shivered, taking a bite of her chicken to give herself a moment to think.

"They did not," she admitted. "But Father, Koruuksi and his team were terrified. They hid it well, but..." She paused, taking a deep breath. "They did not explain how the Imaia plans to take Boaathal from the world, but Diwana Warsama confirmed that it seems they have a way of controlling the auroras."

"That proves nothing," her father said, a slight edge to his voice. "The auroras are a part of Efruumani. A god might be able to control them, but that does not mean he has the power to rip a World Tree from its world. The Vale will protect us, Ymvesi'ia. It always has. Have faith in that."

Ymvesi'ia hid her sigh behind her cup of thibara.

A part of her wanted to stop here and change topics so that they could simply have a nice, delicious dinner together. It had been a while since they'd done so.

But is my comfort worth it? Even if it was not the fate of my people at stake, should I back down from confronting my father just because I do not feel like it?

Ymvesi'ia took a generous sip of thibara, followed with a deep breath.

"I have seen their flying ships, Father. They know of people who have been to Atjakuu and back. Diwana Warsama let me look through her telescope and see the ships the Imaia has out among the stars."

Her father's face darkened. That was getting to him, but she needed to press further.

"When Tombara started rumbling," she continued, "those who

fled survived. Those who did not listen to them or thought they knew better perished. I believe this situation is the same. We cannot discount such warnings—" She pointed to a group of lightoruu and heatoruu that danced around the room. "—especially when even the oruu are acting—"

"Enough, Ymvesi'ia!" her father snapped, face hard.

Ymvesi'ia held his gaze and did not wilt beneath it.

"That young man and his soldiers—*soldiers*, Ymvesi'ia, not refugees—came here for the Heart. I don't know what they want with it, but they would not leave it to us if we revealed it."

Ymvesi'ia narrowed her eyes. "First you say that there is no way the Imaia can take Boaathal with them when they leave, then you say we should not listen to Koruuksi because you think he wanted to take the Heart from us?"

"I did not say I thought they would take it," Kuula'ande shot back. "The goddess they followed destroyed Yrmuunthal. Maybe they cannot take it from us, but this new successor might be able to drain it of the power that protects us, if they do not simply destroy it."

"They were here to help us," Ymvesi'ia protested

Her father held her gaze for a long moment, then sighed. "He asked you about it, didn't he? The Heart."

Ymvesi'ia's jaw bunched. Koruuksi may not have asked about the Heart by name but differentiating that from him asking about the Vale's 'secret' would just be splitting hairs.

"See?" Her father said, his voice more saddened than angry, now. "I'm sorry, Ymvesi'ia. I know he attempted to befriend you. Can we just stop talking about this and finish our dinner together?"

Ymvesi'ia wanted to, but she knew she wouldn't be able to keep herself from broaching the subject, and she knew there would be no talking to her father about it in a constructive way when he was like this.

What else do I have to talk about, anyway? All I have done since Koruuksi arrived is work with or against him. With Uuchantuu banished, I cannot even talk to him about her.

"Enjoy the rest of your dinner, Father," she said, rising. She paused halfway and snatched up the rest of her meal, then turned and strode out of the dining chamber toward her chambers.

The defeated sigh from her father as she exited the room made her stomach twist in knots.

31

Music of Aioa

E Kwekuue's offer of sanctuary remained open, and the Buuekwenani gave Uumgwefilo instruction for what their people would need to give up should that day come.

Exodus countdown: 10 days, 26 hours, 40 minutes

Matsanga had managed to sneak out again without waking Estingai, though Ajida had stayed behind for some reason. Instead of waiting for him in the dwelling, Estingai tried distracting herself with calisthenics and some of the acrobatic practice forms Matsanga had taught her a lifetime ago.

It was a bit unnerving at first, as Ajida followed her out and watched the display, inquisitive eyes tracking her, but Estingai got over it once she reached the level of concentration necessary for the more complex forms.

The practice made her miss Svemakuu and Koruuksi, however, and eventually she had to stop, both to rest her body and clear her head.

When Matsanga appeared from the tree line, Estingai wasted no time.

"Will you teach me the second lesson, now?" she asked, jogging up to him.

Matsanga held her gaze for a long moment, then nodded. He led her back to his shelter, Ajida falling in alongside him, then emptied the pack at his shoulder into a few different jars and containers before sitting down.

Estingai grinned, taking a seat across from him.

"Your second lesson is about music," Matsanga said.

Estingai frowned but didn't question him—as absurd as that seemed.

That seemed to satisfy him, and he pulled over one of the bags he'd worn out, fishing through it as he spoke.

"It is the key to everything—Auroramancy, Aathal, the laws of our reality—everything."

He fished out a small wooden flute and handed it to Estingai. She accepted it, but frowned, looking at it before glancing back toward Matsanga.

"What do you think I've been doing this whole time?" Matsanga asked, a rare hint of a grin on his face. "Hunting and foraging doesn't take that long, Estingai."

She blushed.

"If you listen close enough when brightening your blacknodes, you'll notice that each Auroramantic ability has a unique...melody to it."

"Melody?"

Matsanga shrugged. "Or rhythm. Though, neither term fits quite right. The sensation of someone brightening their violetnodes is different than someone brightening their aquanodes. If you take a Samjati Auroramancer and a Natari, and have them both brighten the same pair of biogems, you'll hear the interference between the different signals they give off. Hold a nugget of the powermetal and brighten your blacknodes and clearnodes, and that signal might become even more clear—something you could think of as a rhythm, or even a melody. If you were to stand along the twilight band in utter silence with Atjakuu overhead, with enough power, you'd be able to hear its melody, too. According to Nevisi, every part of Aioa has its own unique melody. Learn your own and find the right ways of combining it with the melodies of the world around you, and the possibilities are limitless."

"Is that why Nevisi always has her violin with her?"

Matsanga nodded. "She's not the best at explaining, unfortunately, and everyone's... unique melody that is required to do anything is... well, unique."

"Have you had any success with this?"

Matsanga shook his head. "You need to hear the melody yourself. Nevisi could hear mine, and played it for me, but I could do nothing with it. About three weeks ago, I thought I heard something, but..." He shook his head. "Anyway, from what she said, the possibilities are potentially limitless, though doing anything takes quite a bit of Auroralight." He pointed to the flute. "Take that and go outside. Play around with it a bit, but don't compose—listen for the melodies of the world around you and try to imitate them."

Estingai raised an eyebrow. "Should I also find some iceweed to smoke to make sure I'm in the right state of mind?"

Her eyes bulged when Matsanga raised a hand to his chin. "I actually never thought of that. It probably couldn't hurt."

"You're telling me to go smoke," Estingai said in disbelief. "You?"

Matsanga shrugged. "You're not a rebellious teenager looking to cause trouble or escape from life. And it's not like iceweed is addictive."

Estingai gave him a flat look.

Matsanga rolled his eyes. "I know it sounds... well, stupid. I told Nevisi as much."

"What did she do?"

"She played something on her violin and opened a portal to the cognitive plane that took us from Saanad to Uumgwefilo in seven minutes."

Eyes bulging, Estingai looked at the flute, then rushed out the door.

32

Secrets

After a few decades, Uumgwefilo called for aid once more, and E Kwekuue answered.

Exodus countdown: 9 days, 19 hours, 52 minutes

"Are you joking?" Uuchantuu hissed. "You cheated!"

"You're just bad at this game," Koruuksi laughed. "You only ever win when we play teams."

Ymvesi'ia's stress from the conversation with her father began to melt away at the sound of Uuchantuu's voice.

And Koruuksi's, she realized. He had come to have just as much of a positive effect on her as Uuchantuu did, if not in quite the same way.

As she entered her quarters' main room, Uuchantuu looked up, and Ymvesi'ia shared a smile with her. Koruuksi grinned at them. A knowing grin that, despite the heat in Ymvesi'ia's cheeks, lightened her mood further. The room was dark as usual since Vise had hidden Koruuksi and Uuchantuu here, allowing Koruuksi to wear just the bottom half of his wrap. He and Uuchantuu sat across from each other on the floor, playing some sort of card game.

I'll have to ask Uuchantuu to teach me to play. That way we can beat Koruuksi.

"Where is Vise?" she asked, shooting Koruuksi a pointed look.

Koruuksi nodded toward Vise's room. "In bed."

Ymvesi'ia sat down next to Uuchantuu. "I would have expected you to be with her."

Koruuksi's grin widened. "I was. She's asleep now. Resting."

Ymvesi'ia's cheeks grew hot, even though she was the one who had made the joke in the first place.

"I *was* asleep."

Ymvesi'ia looked up as Vise, looking stunning, as always, took a seat beside Koruuksi, stifling a yawn.

"I just woke up."

Ymvesi'ia blushed, then smiled when Uuchantuu laid a hand over hers.

Ymvesi'ia looked to her—

What are we, exactly?

None of the labels she knew of seemed to fit someone she had only known a few days, yet cultivated such intense feelings for.

Does it matter?

Ymvesi'ia decided it didn't.

"How did things go with your father?" Uuchantuu asked.

Ymvesi'ia gave her a tight smile, then sighed, looking to the other two. "I may have made things worse."

Their faces fell.

"I can try to convince the Diwani to call for a session to discuss it rather than having my father to do so, but that will mean either convincing Duubaan that they can be in agreement, or the rest of the Diwani to break precedent. It will take time."

"Time we don't have," Koruuksi muttered, rising from his seat next to Vise. He sighed, running his hands through his hair. "I'm such an idiot. If I had just listened to you, Kuula'ande might be more—"

"Stop."

Ymvesi'ia raised an eyebrow at Uuchantuu and Vise's simultaneous reprimand, then had to hold in her laughter at the look the two women shared.

"You were an idiot, as usual," Uuchantuu said, looking back to Koruuksi, "but I told you to be an idiot that time, so I'm as much to blame as you are."

"We'll be happy to berate you later," Vise added, "but right now, all we can do is keep trying."

Koruuksi frowned at the two of them, then sighed and turned to Ymvesi'ia.

"Is there anything else you can think of?" she asked.

Koruuksi raised a hand to his chin, eyes growing distant. After a short while, he looked to Uuchantuu. She nodded slowly.

Ymvesi'ia frowned, looking between the two of them. "What?"

Koruuksi sighed, looking between her and Vise. "When we first spoke, I asked you about whatever it is that protects E Kwekuue."

Ymvesi'ia tensed.

"You deflected, so I didn't ask about it again, figuring I would just need to wait until later. Since we won't be able to get the evacuation started as early as it needs, we need to know what it is that keeps you safe here—to see if it can help save you. It's the only option we have left."

Ymvesi'ia frowned, holding Koruuksi's gaze.

That young man and his soldiers came here for the Heart. I don't know what they want with it, but they would not leave it to us if we reveal it to them.

She swallowed, looking between Koruuksi and Uuchantuu.

No. I trust them.

She could.

Right?

"How do you think it will help you?" she asked slowly. "You do not even know what it is."

Koruuksi shrugged. "I don't know. My mother told us that there was something here that would help us escape—make finding a new home easier. Maybe an Aathal? That's the only thing I've been able to think of that could shield you from the Imaia and Ynuukwidas for so long. Maybe it could—"

"Koruuksi."

Ymvesi'ia blinked as she turned toward Vise, surprised at her friend's tight, harsh tone. She couldn't remember Vise ever speaking that way. She glared at Koruuksi now, suspicion replacing the previous affection in her eyes, body tense. It made Ymvesi'ia tense in response, despite Uuchantuu's hand still holding hers.

"I thought you said your mother was Kojatere," Vise said slowly. "Even we know that she died many years ago."

Koruuksi sighed. "It's more complicated than that."

"Since when is death complicated? Either someone is dead, or they are alive."

Koruuksi narrowed his eyes, a hardness entering them. "Surely you've heard of the Lightforged—the 'Redeemed,' as the Imaia refer to them."

Ymvesi'ia swallowed hard. She had. The warriors that had returned to them—and even some of the Uumgwefili refugees—had spoken of them in hushed, quivering voices, making them out to be unstoppable demons.

"Your mother is one of them?" Ymvesi'ia asked.

"She was their leader."

Pain laced Koruuksi's voice, though it did not waver.

"Was?" Ymvesi'ia asked, cautiously.

Koruuksi sighed, but nodded. "I have to believe she's really returned. She—who she was, Othaashle—almost killed me two weeks ago, four days before Uuchantuu and I left with the others to come here."

Ymvesi'ia found herself rapt as Koruuksi explained what happened, despite how unbelievable it all seemed.

"She's the one that sent us here to save you," he finished.

Ymvesi'ia considered for a moment. Koruuksi had spoken with such hope and affection, yet...

"You are not entirely sure that you can trust her," she said. "Are you?"

Koruuksi shook his head. "I want to trust her, but we're preparing for the worst. Even if this ends up being a trap and she betrays us, we're doing all we can to get a capital ship and get off this world. That's part of why I want your people ready to go, or gathered at our base, ideally. I don't want them to board a ship that is under attack, and I don't want the Imaia to find this place, even if they do so as they leave this world. They don't deserve to be here."

Ymvesi'ia sighed, looking down.

She could understand now why he hadn't explained everything to them at the beginning—he still seemed not to want to fully acknowledge the situation.

But can I still trust him with the fate of my people? With the Heart? Is that what is—

"Why didn't you tell me?"

Ymvesi'ia looked up.

Vise was on her feet now, glaring at Koruuksi with a mix of anger and pain.

"You could have trusted me with this."

"I didn't think it needed explaining," Koruuksi said, frowning. "I'd already dumped the end of the world onto your shoulders. You didn't need to deal with that and my problems at the same time."

Vise's voice grew a bit louder, more strained.

"I will decide what I can deal with, not you."

"I didn't mean that—"

"And that isn't just your problem—not if the fate of my people hangs on whether or not your trust is misplaced."

"I told you, either way—"

Ymvesi'ia tuned them out, rising from her seat. She strode toward the balcony and slipped between the curtains, careful not to let in too much light.

Once out on her balcony, she took a deep breath, trying to relax as she looked out over her city. When had her heart started pounding so fast?

My city. My responsibility.

Her mother's words came back to her.

"This is your city while I am gone. Your father is a wonderful man and a good ruler, but even he needs help sometimes. Our city and its people are too precious a burden to refuse help when it is offered."

The shuffling of cloth behind her signaled Uuchantuu's entry. The woman stood on the balcony next to her a moment later, leaning on the stone railing.

Ymvesi'ia said nothing, but after a moment, moved a bit closer to Uuchantuu so that their arms touched, a comforting warmth spreading through her.

For a while, they stood there in silence—save for Koruuksi and Vise's argument in the background, at least—gazing out at the city together. The streets and canals formed a beautiful maze that stretched out before them, interrupted by errant figures of the forest that surrounded the city and filled most of the Vale, climbing up the slopes of the Vale's mountains. To the south on the opposite end of the Vale, where one of the rivers flowed down from the mountains, terraced fields spread out from the banks, creating a wide gap in the trees framing the rushing water.

Uuchantuu toucher her hand—just the edges brushing against one another, but it sent wonderful shivers down Ymvesi'ia's spine.

"It's beautiful," Uuchantuu breathed, finally breaking the silence.

Ymvesi'ia looked to her. As if sensing her gaze, Uuchantuu met her eyes.

"One of the most beautiful sights I know," Ymvesi'ia said.

Uuchantuu smiled.

"I do not want to leave it."

Uuchantuu took her hand.

"Neither do I."

Ymvesi'ia sighed but held Uuchantuu's gaze for a while. Running her thumb over the back of Uuchantuu's hand, Ymvesi'ia glanced toward the city's eastern edge. The trees rose high above the buildings and the rest of the Vale there, continuing toward the center of the basin before cutting over to the west, obscuring the Heart and the way to it.

Taking a deep breath, she met Uuchantuu's eyes once more.

"My father warned me you and Koruuksi would ask about it," she said. "He thinks you came here to take the Heart of the Vale from us."

Uuchantuu nodded. "And what do you think?"

Ymvesi'ia frowned, squeezing Uuchantuu's hand. "I do not know what to think. I want to trust you—both of you. The past few days have been some of the most wonderful of my life, but I cannot let that cloud my judgement when it comes to my people. Neither of you told me about Koruuksi's mother."

"It wasn't my place to say anything about that," Uuchantuu said, looking back out over the city. "And it's a sore subject that he's barely even spoken to me about. I want to believe—Kojatere was a mother to me, too, for a while—but I know there's a chance that all of this is just some elaborate trap."

"Then why are you going through with this?"

Uuchantuu looked back to her, eyes intense. "Because it's the only chance we have. Either Kojatere helps us steal the ship, or we steal it despite her."

"And the Heart?" Ymvesi'ia asked. "How does that help?"

Uuchantuu shrugged. "I wish I knew. Kojatere apparently said that it would help hide us from the Imaia and find a new world among the stars. If it's supposed to make finding a new home easier, maybe we can use it to escape and come back here for you once we find a new home. Maybe the Vale will protect your people long enough for us to come and get you once the Imaia are gone. I imagine they'd be more motivated to listen to us by then."

Ymvesi'ia sighed, remembering what Warsama had told her.

"Sorry," Uuchantuu said. "The dark humor comes with the lifestyle."

Ymvesi'ia shook her head. "It is not that. What you're asking of me is just... it is a lot."

"I understand. Whatever you decide, Koruuksi and I will make sure we get as many of you and your people on that ship as we can."

Ymvesi'ia nodded.

Something is definitely wrong with the oruu and the rest of the world, but is that worth risking the Heart? Or am I putting too much faith in something I can't understand, just like my ancestors did?

"You know the raid I told you about," Uuchantuu said, "the one where I got my scar?"

Ymvesi'ia nodded.

"It turned out that the Imaia had been given a bit of inside help from one of the other factions that had persisted before we became the Remnant. We learned that a small portion of their leadership was working with the Imaia, though their people didn't realize it. We didn't know what their motives were, but they needed to be dealt with. We couldn't simply kill them, or we would have risked playing into the Imaia's hands, and possibly incited the people against us even without the Imaia directing them. Estingai...she and her husband had thrown themselves into uniting the factions willing to work with us. This was just before Svemakuu—her husband, Koruuksi''s brother—and all the leadership died. With them occupied, Koruuksi volunteered and led the mission by himself. He turned the people against their leaders without even realizing it, showing them how they'd been played. Our faction had a lot of skilled warriors in it, but we weren't that great with people. Most people knew of Koruuksi, and he had maintained friendships throughout most factions, including that one. Without his charisma and connections and just his natural ability to put people at ease, the mission would have failed.

"After..." Uuchantuu trailed off with a sigh. "He was shaken up. He hated that it seemed so easy to him. He hadn't needed to learn any special skills or really try at all except when training and guiding his team. He said it terrified him when he realized that he'd just slipped into maneuvering people and acting with the mission's agenda without even thinking about it. Estingai and I put in a lot of work to snap him out of it and get it back to normal. Especially after his brother died and we found out that we hadn't completely eliminated the threat from within."

Ymvesi'ia blinked, glancing back toward her room, "Koruuksi?"

Uuchantuu nodded.

"That is... hard to believe. Everything just seems to roll off of him."

"It's what he had to become," Uuchantuu said. "He thinks it's best if people don't see how much he is affected by that which threatens to grind everyone else to dust, and he has a point. Even if he's an asshole sometimes, he's a charming one, and people either try to emulate his good mood, or try to upstage him and let it affect them even less." Uuchantuu sighed, looking back to Ymvesi'ia. "Either way... the whole point of telling you that was to show you that Koruuksi does not want to cause any trouble among your people. He just wants to save them."

"And you both are willing to risk your lives and those of your comrades to save us?"

Uuchantuu shrugged, smiling, though Ymvesi'ia caught the flicker of pain in her eyes.

"People like Koruuksi and I—and most of the Remnant, to be honest—haven't earned a happy ending, Ymvesi'ia. We're hoping that saving you all might be enough to get us that."

Ymvesi'ia took Uuchantuu's hand in hers.

"Is that the only reason you are doing this?"

Uuchantuu smiled. "We may have found a few other reasons along the way."

Ymvesi'ia kissed her. She'd meant it as just a quick, affectionate gesture, but once her lips met Uuchantuu's, Ymvesi'ia found herself unable to pull away. As the kiss deepened, her mind began to fog, pulse racing. It was only when her hands started wandering over Uuchantuu—and Uuchantuu's over her—that Ymvesi'ia remembered where they were, and why she'd come out here.

Reluctantly, she pulled back from Uuchantuu, but didn't release her. She needed Uuchantuu to steady herself.

"You alright?" Uuchantuu asked.

Ymvesi'ia gazed at her for a moment, then her city. She nodded. "I think so."

Leading Uuchantuu in with her, Ymvesi'ia strode back inside.

They found Koruuksi and Vise staring at each other, the room rife with tension, though she couldn't tell what kind. They stood very close to each other and didn't appear standoffish... Ymvesi'ia almost felt like she was intruding until Koruuksi looked up, meeting her gaze.

"What would you do with the Heart?" she asked. "If I agreed to take you to it?"

"Specifically?" he shrugged. "No clue without knowing exactly what it is."

Vise glared at him and Ymvesi'ia blinked as a low growl came from Uuchantuu.

Koruuksi rubbed at his temples. "Sorry." He drew in a deep breath, then met Ymvesi'ia's gaze. "I would do whatever I could to save both our peoples, Ymvesi'ia. Is it an Aathal? A World Tree?"

Ymvesi'ia hesitated, then nodded.

Koruuksi snorted. "I don't know what you and your father are so worried about, then. We would need the Imaia's technology to actually take it from you, provided what they're doing with Boaathal works. That took them decades to construct."

Ymvesi'ia frowned. "Then how would it help you or my people?"

Koruuksi shrugged. "Don't you have stories about that? Most stories about Yrmuunthal and Boaathal—before the Imaia claimed it, at least—end with the Aathal granting gifts or wisdom to those worthy or in great need who visit them."

Ymvesi'ia exchanged a look with Vise.

"Not exactly," Vise said. "Though it is tradition for our royalty and Diwani to meditate in the Heart for a full day every year. Ymvesi'ia pulled some strings to let me accompany her a few times. Though we have not done any studies to provide empirical evidence, it is believed that meditating within the Heart provides one with wisdom, clarity of mind and a longer life. I haven't heard anything about physical gifts, however."

Koruuksi looked to Ymvesi'ia and shook her head. "Neither have I. No royal secrets about that, unfortunately."

"We won't know if we don't try," Uuchantuu said. "According to Kojatere, it was Boaathal that started her on the path toward remembering who she was."

Koruuksi stepped toward Ymvesi'ia, meeting her gaze. "You can trust me. I swear it."

Ymvesi'ia looked to Vise again. Her friend glanced at Koruuksi, still not seeming too happy, but nodded.

This is right, Ymvesi'ia assured herself, looking between Uuchantuu and Koruuksi, *and if it is not... the Heart will be the first to judge us.*

She looked to Koruuksi. "Get changed. If we are doing this, we should do it now, while most of the city is still asleep."

Koruuksi's eyes widened. "You mean you'll do it?"

Ymvesi'ia nodded. "I will take you to the Heart of the Vale."

33

Coward

This time, the fighting dragged on far longer.

Exodus countdown: 9 days, 17 hours, 10 minutes

Estingai, it turned out, was not as bad with a flute as she would have thought. She'd taken lessons in music before meeting Svemakuu, and the simple, six-holed flute Matsanga had given her wasn't exactly hard to play with a decent tone, but she hadn't touched an instrument in decades. Not since she'd started fighting.

And I never stopped.

Rubbing her forehead with her fingers, Estingai set down the flute with care.

Matsanga had told her to try and find the 'natural melodies' of the world, so she'd spent most of her day outdoors sitting atop one of the sturdier upper levels—what was left of them, anyway.

She'd fooled around with it, learning the relationships between the different pitches, and had managed to imitate a few bird calls and mimic a few of the songs she heard others sing when working or just bored, but nothing had just come to her—not like she expected Matsanga meant, at least.

Taking a deep breath, Estingai took out her sketchbook and started with a landscape for a warm-up, focusing on the forest that stretched out before her like a sea of rich browns and near-blacks. Her mind began to relax as she worked—just as Estingai had hoped. She needed to think about the 'music' Matsanga had spoken of differently.

As she sketched, however, moving on to a few more imaginative pieces of herself playing the flute, and then a few caricatures of Matsanga's icehound where she tried to capture the animal's too-inquisitive eyes and emotive expressions, nothing jumped out at her. She kept her ears open, sparing some Auroralight to enhance not only her hearing, but her sense of pitch and tone color, but that didn't seem to work, either.

Estingai found herself frowning, teeth gritted in frustration by the time she finished a sketch of Matsanga—not as he was now, but as she'd seen him back when she was his student. He'd been scarred back then, eyes ancient and pained, but he hadn't looked so old.

So tired.

Estingai realized she'd hoped for that man when she'd come searching for him. She could understand what he'd become, though, which troubled her.

She was furious at him for leaving, yet how many times had she wished to just hop in one of their ships and fly away, leaving everything and everyone she knew and loved behind?

And she was just so tired. That, she could understand.

Maybe...

Estingai looked down at her sketch again.

Maybe I could talk with him.

Instead of yelling at him, trying to guilt or bait him into helping, she could relate to him—show him that it was possible to keep going even when you just wanted to run away.

Estingai gathered up her things, then leapt down off the ledge, breaking her fall with a bit of Auroralight to ease the burden on her knees.

She looked inside the main room and found it empty, so she decided to explore the rest of the ruins and look for him.

Her *mshauuri's* home seemed somehow much smaller from the outside. It had been built into a hillside, and despite the damages of time, war and scavengers, remnants of what at once would have been a beautiful villa remained. The steep, pointed rooftops, balconies and tall, pointed windows indicated that the maps she had of this area showing old Kaleva borders were correct. Though faded, she picked out hints of the soft, pastel colors that people had favored. Though she and Matsanga spent most of their time on the main floor, the building had once held at least three floors, maybe more. Around the back she found an aquifer connecting the structure to a nearby lake that bore signs of Matsanga's handiwork, as well as what looked like a small workshop and forge.

Finally, Estingai returned to the main room and set her things down, leaning back against the wall. Estingai had seen homes like this before they were taken by the ravages of time and war—places with far more space and luxury than anyone could need while children like her had gone without knowing where their next meal or bed would be. She'd fought in places like this when noble families had transformed them into fortresses to protect their own wealth and power rather than those who depended on them.

Estingai took a deep, shaky breath, trying to clear the tightness in her chest. She tried to relax for a few minutes, but she'd never been very good at that, even before training to become a soldier. She either needed to sleep or do something. Svemakuu had been the only one that could get her to truly relax and do nothing.

Estingai took a deep breath, fighting back that pain.

Her husband was gone. She couldn't do anything about that—the most she could do was make sure he hadn't died for nothing.

Estingai's restlessness soon turned to curiosity, and she walked over to Mwyndobir, studying the great, imposing sword that was almost as famous—or infamous—as Matsanga, nearly synonymous with her mentor. She'd done a few sketches of it since coming here, though she had better ones in her quarters back at Remnant Base from when she'd seen Matsanga fighting and practicing with it. The blade itself was long and thick, with intricate georaurals worked into the hilt and handle. She didn't recognize any of the designs, but knew that Matsanga had built the weapon long before modern georaural designs. She almost reached out to grasp it—the weapon had always seemed too large and unwieldy even for a man as strong as Matsanga.

As Estingai went to sit back down, the dresser that Matsanga had taken the powermetal out of—the one with the false bottom in one of the drawers—caught her eye. She bit her lip, knowing she shouldn't, but after a quick look around, Estingai stepped over to the drawer and took out the false bottom.

Her throat tightened as she carefully picked up an old portrait—one that had been crumpled up, then smoothed out, cracking some of the acrylics. A content family of five gazed back at her, dressed in clothing centuries old. A handsome man with a deep red complexion, full lips, a strong chin, and shoulders like an ox stood beside a beautiful woman with prominent cheekbones, a slender face, and black spots painting her red-orange skin. Before them stood three children, their resemblance unmistakable. Two sons and one daughter. It took Estingai a while to pull her gaze from the portrait and back to the drawer. Her eyes were hot with tears when she finally did. A collection of journals lay stacked inside. She took the one on top. Its leather cover was unadorned, yet oiled and smooth. Cared for.

Soft footsteps behind Estingai formed a knot in her stomach. She stood and turned to face Matsanga, holding onto the journal and its contents.

Her former *mshauuri's* face was unreadable, and the icehound looked between the two of them, expression almost concerned.

"What is this?" Estingai asked, holding up the journal and portrait.

"I think you know." His voice was level, still gravelly, but without emotion.

"You rarely ever mentioned your family."

"They died hundreds of years ago. Why would I bring them up?"

Estingai held up the book, flipping through a few pages. "This is the book you used to write in, isn't it? You held on to it, even in your exile."

"And you should have realized I had a reason for keeping it tucked away."

Estingai raised an eyebrow at the sliver of emotion that entered his voice.

I'm getting to him.

Despite being as Natari as one got in every other sense, Matsanga had never displayed—not to Estingai, at least—the fiery temper that even she had inherited. She didn't know why, but she felt a need to see him let that take over.

"Why is the portrait in such bad shape?" she asked. "Did you have to recover it quickly? Or did you crumple it out of anger?"

Matsanga said nothing, eyes growing hard as he stared at her.

Estingai turned around the portrait so that the picture faced him. "I've been trying to figure out which one is which. This one is you, obviously, and this one is your wife, Moremi, right? And this is—"

"Stop!"

Estingai flinched at the raw pain and anger in Matsanga's voice. She looked him over and realized the man was trembling, fists clenched.

"Don't you think I had a reason for never discussing my family?" he grated. "In all the time we've known each other—in all the time since they passed—don't you think that if I could talk about them, I would? To keep them alive in the heart and mind of someone other than myself?"

Estingai swallowed, knowing she should just drop it, but she couldn't.

"What happened to them?"

Matsanga's eyes widened, and the man took a few deep, almost strained breaths before he spoke.

"Shykaan, my oldest, died in combat against the Iron Empire."

Estingai flinched. She'd known Matsanga was old, but the Iron Empire had fallen almost a thousand years ago.

"He believed it was his duty to take up arms against such a force of tyranny. Sometimes I find myself glad that he didn't survive to see what became of the nation he fought for. Or his family."

"I'm sorry," Estingai breathed, not knowing what else to say. "I know how that feels. I—"

"Do you?"

The words hit Estingai like a greyarm slap. Rage burned in Matsanga's eyes.

"You are a child, Estingai," Matsanga grated. "You lost your family and your husband. Now you don't know if you can trust your adoptive mother. I lost everything."

Estingai shrank back.

"My son, Taketa, died by assassination," Matsanga continued. "Not even one of Skadaatha's, but one sent by those he'd tried to strengthen against the Imaia. Moremi died of old age. Watching her waste away while time barely touched me broke something within me. Somehow, I think her death hurt even more than my daughter's. I tell myself sometimes that it was Skadaatha that killed my Klaaora—that the assassin I put down simply wore her face."

Matsanga drew in a sharp breath, knuckles white.

"My people lost their home, and what remained of us was not simply lost to me but twisted by Skadaatha. I lost every family I tried to be a part of. I was betrayed by every god that I put my faith in. Every time I failed, I tried to do better, to prove that I deserved life, but everything I touched crumbled until the burden finally crushed me. Even after Kojatere died, I thought we could make it work, but then when I saw what she'd become and she told me what Kweshrima had done, I just couldn't—"

"When you saw what she'd become?" Estingai demanded, cutting through Matsanga's raw, gravelly tone with a ragged snap of her own.

Matsanga said nothing, but she could see the answer in his eyes.

"You knew," she breathed, not entirely able to believe it. "You knew who Othaashle was, what Kweshrima had done, and you didn't warn us."

"Estingai, I—"

"No!" she shrieked, "You do not get to speak. Not after what you said to me. You knew. You could have warned us—about both Kweshrima and Othaashle. Instead, you just abandoned us. Everyone thought I was crazy for so long!"

"Estingai," he said, voice soft. "It wouldn't have—"

"You can't know that! She made it look like we were covering up Kweshrima's sins. She timed it just right to shatter the Union and any support we had. She—"

Estingai had to pause to breathe through gritted teeth.

"She killed them both, Matsanga. She killed my uncle—the man that was almost as much a father to me as you or Aiteperit. Then she murdered my husband and left me to die. Except when you ran, I did not. I dug myself out of the rubble, and I kept on fighting. I forged the Remnant out of the disparate factions Othaashle had sought to shatter by murdering their leadership. I'm the reason we even exist to have a chance at escape. You—"

Estingai cut off, grinding her teeth, heart pounding. She was so angry she could barely think straight.

"You think you're a monster?" she said, throwing the journal and its contents to the floor. "You're not. You're something far worse. You're the coward that runs and hides while everyone else fights to survive when the monster has them cornered."

Estingai pushed past him toward the exit, tears burning her eyes. She walked out of the small room and toward the forest, unsure where she needed to go, but knowing that she needed to be far, far away from Matsanga.

She barely made it to the tree line before the pain grew too great and she started sobbing, tears running down her cheeks.

34

Something Incredibly Stupid

The people of E Kwekuue had never felt more alone.

Exodus countdown: 9 days, 19 hours, 24 minutes

The hairs on Koruuksi's neck stood on end as he crept through E Kwekuue. That most of the city's people were in their homes asleep didn't bring him much comfort when light bathed the city, as it always did on Lightside. Most of those awake were working outside of the city, but not all.

Rather than dress him in the new clothing she'd had made for him, however, Ymvesi'ia had found some Akjemasai whites for him to wear over his mask, gloves, and foot-wraps. Anyone who looked too closely would realize that something was off, but at a distance, he would likely just appear to be one of the guards.

If they're too tired to notice my antlers...

That would be a big 'if'.

Koruuksi glanced to his side, then Ymvesi'ia's.

We'd be less conspicuous if it was just Ymvesi'ia and a guard walking the city while everyone slept.

Uuchantuu and Vise had insisted, however. He and Ymvesi'ia had both stressed that they didn't need the other two women, but Uuchantuu said she needed to make sure nothing bad happened to him, and Vise had laughed, saying there was nothing he could do to make her stay behind, and she would come in handy as a distraction if they needed it. Koruuksi hadn't protested much, and neither had Ymvesi'ia. Their company wasn't necessary, but he still wanted them to come along.

Uuchantuu's presence meant she wore nothing over her chest, however, as doing so would make her even more conspicuous than Koruuksi from a distance.

She handled it well for the most part, though every time Ymvesi'ia turned to her, she flexed her hands and a bit of color entered her cheeks and neck.

Ymvesi'ia led them through deeper parts of the city Koruuksi assumed were more residential. They still passed by plazas and shops and larger buildings he could only guess the functions of, and the bright stone and aluminum inlay continued throughout this district, but they kept to narrower streets and stepped quietly. The canals made their journey wind about rather than following any semblance of a straight path, but Ymvesi'ia and Vise seemed confident in their path. Koruuksi clenched his fists and focused on his breathing when the canals forced them to cross bridges in full visibility of the nearby streets and buildings, but tried his best to keep calm.

Until Ymvesi'ia and Vise yanked him them into an alley and held fingers to their lips.

Hushed voices reached Koruuksi a few seconds later. He almost brightened his clearnodes and blacknodes by reflex—one to hear, the other to conceal use of his Auroramancy—but decided against it. His blood was pounding in his ears so hard that enhancing his hearing would only make him more nervous. Koruuksi crouched down as much as he could, flattening himself against the wall as they waited. His heart started to race, but he took deep breaths to reign it in.

Vise's hand clasping his undid his work. Though now his blood pounded for a different reason

He met her gaze and held back a frown at the nervousness in her eyes. After thinking for a moment, he leaned in close. "You told Uuchantuu to go topless just to mess with her, didn't you? My antlers would give me away long before anyone noticed she had her chest covered."

Vise's breath was hot on his ear as she let out a soft laugh. "What, you never mess with her?"

Koruuksi rolled his eyes. "Not like that."

"You should try. It's very fun. Especially with Ymvesi'ia around."

They cut off as the approaching footsteps and voices grew louder. They spoke in Buuekwenani, so Koruuksi couldn't understand much of it. Koruuksi took Vise's hand in his and pulled back enough to meet her gaze, trying to convey confidence and reassurance through his touch and posture since she couldn't see his eyes. He hoped she didn't sense how much of a bluff it was.

Vise smiled, squeezing his hand back.

Koruuksi tensed as the footsteps grew louder and stayed that way even as they faded. Only when Uuchantuu tapped him on the shoulder did he relax and get back to his feet.

Ymvesi'ia led them through shaded alleys and outer streets to a part of the city that was familiar to Koruuksi, though only in passing.

They came to a large wall overgrown with vines and other foliage. The trees here rose impossibly high above the city—higher than most of the trees in the Vale. Koruuksi stopped as soon as he came within a pace of it, looking to Uuchantuu. He found her already starting wide-eyed at him.

"Koruuksi?" Vise asked in a hushed voice, resting a hand on his arm.

He looked to the wall, then to her. "There's something different here. A...calmness I can't quite place. I remember it from my first few days here, but thought nothing of it, then.

Vise looked to Uuchantuu, then Ymvesi'ia and grinned. "Told you they'd be able to sense it."

Ymvesi'ia rolled her eyes. "Come on—we're too exposed here."

Koruuksi frowned. Then his eyes widened as Ymvesi'ia stepped through the wall of white. He tensed, looking to Vise for an explanation. She just grabbed him and Uuchantuu each by the arm and pulled them toward the wall. Koruuksi waited for stone to block his way, but instead he found only a thick, but malleable layer of foliage between him. He pushed through it after Uuchantuu and Vise—his antlers getting stuck three times—and found himself in a long corridor between high walls covered in bright, white leaves and colorful flowers with a carpet of spongey white grass at his feet.

Koruuksi glanced back at the wall of plants, then to Uuchantuu, who looked just as confused as he did. He looked between Vise and Ymvesi'ia for an explanation.

"The Heart of the Vale is sacred to us," Ymvesi'ia explained. "We want it accessible for our people, but hidden from most of the city. Just in case. Now, come. This leads deeper into the Vale."

Koruuksi nodded slowly, then followed, the spongey grass strange beneath his feet after so long walking on stone.

They walked for some time, their surroundings growing lusher and more beautiful with every step. Unlike the too-bright forest that surrounded E Kwekuue, this living corridor Ymvesi'ia led them down seemed almost otherworldly to Koruuksi. There was white, but it shone somehow with its own light rather than that of the sun. As the corridor widened, twisting and turning, the lush walls around them seemed to grow higher. Lush, blooming flowers painted the walls with splashes of color, filling the air with their sweet, vibrant aromas. As they ventured deeper, Koruuksi noticed a few animals that seemed far too comfortable around humans—little firefoxes with their six tails, birds, and small monkeys all went about their business, paying Koruuksi and his companions no more than a few glances.

It wasn't just their surroundings, however. That nebulous feeling that had tugged at Koruuksi back at the entrance to this long, hidden corridor grew stronger and more tangible. He felt more relaxed—not tired or sleepy, his muscles seemed alive with energy—as though the very air of this place extracted all tension from his body and mind.

Koruuksi smiled as he noticed Ymvesi'ia and Uuchantuu up ahead, holding hands and leaning against each other as they walked forward. Looking to Vise, Koruuksi realized they were doing the same.

"It really is an Aathal," he breathed.

Vise looked up at him with an almost lazy expression. "We already told you it was. Why so surprised?"

Koruuksi thought for a moment. "I'm surprised that the stories are true. I've always heard that merely being around an Aathal puts even the most violent and troubled souls at peace. I was lucky enough not to have to worry about that sort of thing when I visited Yrmuunthal."

Vise nodded. "That is part of why we value it so highly."

"I can imagine."

Koruuksi peered at Vise. When she looked up at him, he grinned. "What?"

"It's nice to know that this is what happens when you feel relaxed around me, even after I was an asshole earlier."

Vise shrugged. "I may not have been the most understanding, either." She grinned at him, leaning closer. "If you like me 'relaxed' like this, you should try getting a few drinks in me some time."

Koruuksi cleared his throat as his cheeks grew hot. Vise just laughed.

Koruuksi had no idea how long they walked for—he didn't mind, really, due to the sense of peace and contentment the Aathal brought to him. When they finally reached the Aathal, however, the Heart of the Vale, he found himself speechless.

The trunk, a pillar as smooth as polished redstone, rose at least twelve times Koruuksi's height into the air before branches exploded outward forming a thick, lush canopy that would have plunged the entire clearing into darkness had the tree itself not shone with its own light. As Koruuksi followed the branches outward, he saw they turned down toward the ground after a certain point. At first, he thought they just hung downward, then he blinked, taking a step back.

They grow down into the wall. Is this entire maze formed from the branches of a single tree?

That was impressive even for something out of legend.

"I can see why Kuula'ande is so against showing this to outsiders," Koruuksi breathed, "or leaving it behind."

"Some have theorized that our proximity to the Aathal and its influence on us is what makes our society possible," Vise explained. "Not just the abundance of life and energy that infuses the Vale or whatever helps keep us concealed from the eyes and technology of the outside world, but how it affects everyone's demeanor. The effects out in the city and the other populated parts of the Vale are more subtle, but after living here for so long, they believe it has infused us just as it does everything else, leading to less strife and conflict among our people. We're also certain it is the cause for our abundance of auroramancers."

Koruuksi nodded, seeing the logic in that.

I should send Estingai here before the attack, if possible. This would be good for her.

Koruuksi glanced over at Uuchantuu to see what she thought of the idea, and found her openly weeping, no longer trying to cover up.

Uuchantuu looked to Koruuksi as he approached her, putting a hand on her shoulder, a mix of awe, pain, and confusion in her eyes.

"How?" she choked out, "How could Kweshrima have brought herself to destroy something so incredible?"

Koruuksi pulled her into a hug and glanced back at the World Tree. A shiver ran down his spine. Yrmuunthal had been even more incredible.

Koruuksi found it difficult to pull his gaze away from the Tree.

"I don't know," he said, looking back to Uuchantuu, "but we can't think about that now."

"What do we do?" Ymvesi'ia asked. "Now that we are here, I mean?"

Koruuksi looked back to the tree and mulled that question over. All the stories he'd heard had one thing in common.

He took a step toward the tree.

His foot had barely touched the spongey grass beneath when two sets of hands grabbed his arms.

"Koruuksi, no," Uuchantuu gasped. "You've heard the stories."

"I have."

"Then you know not to go too close," Vise said. "Even we know that."

Koruuksi hesitated, looking between the Tree and the two women holding him back.

"I need to," he said, meeting both their gazes. "If it helped my mother, then it should help me."

I need to believe that it helped her—that my mother really is alive again.

Uuchantuu sighed, releasing his arm. "I guess I can't really hold you back from doing something stupid—your idiocy has gotten us this far, after all."

Koruuksi grinned. "*My* idiocy?"

He ignored Uuchantuu's glare and looked to Vise. Her fingers tensed around his arm, eyes hard. "You really believe this will work?"

He nodded. "I need to."

Vise bit her lip, then released his arm.

Koruuksi leaned in and kissed her. He found it hard to pull away. When he did, he looked to Ymvesi'ia and nodded toward the Aathal. "Do I have your permission?"

She nodded. "Find something that will—"

The princess cut off, eyes widening. She looked back the way they'd come, and Koruuksi followed her gaze. It took him a moment, but he heard it: footsteps. Marching.

Ymvesi'ia looked back to Koruuksi. "Someone must have seen us. Go. Go, now."

Koruuksi hesitated for only a moment before facing the Aathal. He did not run toward it—that seemed too idiotic even for him—but strode forward with purpose, teeth gritted.

He felt something change as he approached after crossing a certain point. The ground rumbled, roots creaking—some even poked through the grass.

Fuck.

Fear warred with the Tree's relaxing aura.

He stopped for a moment, then forced himself forward.

One of the women gasped, calling out for him.

"I'm alright," he called, continuing forward. "Stay back."

Fuck, fuck, fuck, fuck.

Koruuksi soon came close enough to touch the Aathal. He raised a shaking hand and froze as roots ripped from the ground around him, and the bark of the trunk before him shifted and split, opening like the cavernous maw of some ancient beast.

Koruuksi clenched his teeth and continued toward the opening, closing his eyes as the sound grew louder, flakes and chips of bark falling over him.

Then, nothing.

The creaking and shifting, the rumbling beneath his feet, all of it had stopped.

Koruuksi opened one eye, then the other, unclenching.

Koruuksi found himself in a chamber of indeterminate size, with a ceiling of unfamiliar stars and walls that seemed natural wood one moment, and carved, polished stone the next. The stars were not the source of the chamber's ambient light, they just... were. No entryway stood behind him, yet before him, at the other end of the chamber, a way opened to a room beyond, one that seemed just a hint brighter despite a floor black as the starry sky above. He'd never seen such a dark sky, even on Darkside.

"Hello, Koruuksi."

Koruuksi jumped, whirling toward the voice, then stumbled back.

Golden eyes gazed at him from above a dimpled smile. A trim silver beard outlined a strong jawline, complementing a deep blue complexion, and wicked antlers towered above a head of messy silver hair.

"Svemakuu?" Koruuksi breathed in disbelief. "How?"

His brother frowned. "I must apologize. This was merely a familiar form I took in an effort to put you at ease. I can see that has failed."

The figure started to shift.

"Wait!"

It stopped.

Koruuksi took a deep breath. "You don't need to change. I was just surprised."

The figure's features shifted back to a perfect copy of Svemakuu.

"Who are you really, then?" Koruuksi asked. "Or...what are you?"

The figure grinned. "The name I once bore was Tiopo Kuushan. What I am is a much more complicated matter, and I don't believe you came here to discuss that, did you?"

Koruuksi shook his head, "I did not."

"What did you come here in search of, Koruuksi?"

Koruuksi raised an eyebrow. "You don't know?"

The figure shrugged. "That is another more complicated matter."

Light, this thing even has his mannerisms down.

It was unnerving, yet at the same time...

Light, I miss you, Svemakuu.

"I came seeking a way off this world," Koruuksi said.

"For you alone?"

The genuine interest in the being's gaze transported Koruuksi back in time. Svemakuu had looked at him the exact same way when Koruuksi had asked him and Estingai if there was any difference between getting girls or boys to pay attention to him.

Koruuksi shook himself, bringing his mind back to the present. "I want to make sure that my friends and my people get off this world safely and find a new home. I was told you—the Aathal, I mean—could help with that."

The figure nodded. "The first—a way for you to escape this world, I can guarantee. The second...that I can only offer you a chance at."

"Why?"

"There are too many moving factors," the figure said simply. "Whereas if you wish to leave Efruumani for another world..."

The figure trailed off and stepped to the side, gesturing to the hallway behind him. Koruuksi blinked. He hadn't noticed that before.

He took a step forward, then stopped.

No... I can't do this—not just me.

Koruuksi looked back to the figure. "What about my friends? The ones waiting outside for me. Can they come with me?"

The figure seemed to think for a moment—the same serious expression Svemakuu had worn when considering tactics. Koruuksi shivered.

"I would allow them to accompany you, and for them to enter safely, if that is what you wish." The figure held out a hand to him, "Then I will lead you to a new world where you can live in peace. All you need to do is come with me."

Koruuksi gazed at that hand for a moment, then up at the face that looked so much like his brother's. It made thinking hard. He wanted to be with his brother again, but that wasn't what would happen, right?

I could be with Vise and Uuchantuu and Ymvesi'ia, somewhere we don't need to worry about war or rules or the end of the world.

"Would we be able to go to a world with other people on it?" he asked. "People who could help us?"

The figure nodded. "There are many worlds in Aioa where you would find individuals sympathetic to your cause, though some may be more primitive than others."

He could escape, just like Estingai had always wanted to. Start over. It would be hard, but it would be a sure thing. They could find other peoples and nations to help them, people they could guide rather than having to start over from scratch.

Estingai.

She wouldn't be able to come with him.

"No."

Koruuksi looked up at the figure and took a step back.

The figure cocked its head, looking almost hurt for a moment in a way that sent a lance through Koruuksi's heart.

"I can't," he forced out. "I haven't earned an escape for myself. Not if doing so leaves others to die."

And I don't leave friends behind.

That didn't just include the three women waiting for him out in the Vale. It included his team, all his friends back at Remnant Base. Estingai.

My mother.

"Is it a trap?"

The figure blinked at him.

"Is all of this just a trap?" Koruuksi demanded. "Did Boaathal really help bring back my mother? Or is this just an elaborate way for the Imaia to round up and get rid of us once and for all and snatch up E Kwekuue in the process?"

"I cannot say."

Koruuksi clenched his teeth, balled his hands into fists, squeezed his eyes shut. He wanted to roar in frustration, to beat this figure into submission until it gave him the answers he needed.

Dammit!

He took a deep breath, trying not to shake as he forced the words out. "I need to try to save the rest of them. Even if it means I don't make it out. That's the ending I deserve if I can't save the rest of them."

Koruuksi blinked as the figure smiled at that, seeming... satisfied?

The figure held out its hand, palm-up. It held what looked like a large seed, half the size of Koruuksi's fist. It glowed almost impossibly green.

Koruuksi reached toward it, then hesitated. "What is it?"

"It is what I can offer you in aid. You will know what to do with it when the time comes."

Burying his frustration at the cryptic answer, Koruuksi took hold of the seed, flinching when it pulsed in his hand. He peered at it for a moment, drinking in the power that seemed to radiate from it, then looked back to the figure.

"Remember the decision you made just now, Koruuksi," the figure said. "You will face a similar moment in the near future. It will serve you well to act with the same character you have just now."

The figure stepped back, and before Koruuksi could say or do anything, everything went black.

A moment later, he found himself on his back, gasping for air, the majestic World Tree looming over him.

Koruuksi looked at his hand. He still had the seed, still pulsing with energy and shining impossibly green.

Tucking it away, he rose to his feet and found the three women looking not at him, but back the way they'd come. Beyond them, a group of guards approached, weaving through some of the roots that made up the edge of the clearing. Koruuksi could just pick out a more ornately dressed figure that he assumed to be Kuula'ande at their head.

Koruuksi walked up behind the women. All three jumped and turned to face him, wearing mixtures of relief, curiosity, and worry on their faces.

Koruuksi met each of their gazes, then looked to the guards.

He stepped toward Vise and pulled her close, kissing her deeply. He found it even harder to part from her than last time. When he did pull back, he met her gaze again and brushed her cheek with his knuckles.

"I really hope that wasn't the last time I get to do that," he said, smiling.

He turned to Uuchantuu. She gazed at him for a moment, then looked to the guards. When she met his gaze again, her eyes told Koruuksi she was ready to fight.

And that she doesn't want to.

"We can take them," she said.

She was right. Neither of them had brought weapons, but they didn't need any.

Koruuksi shook his head. "I said no violence, and I meant it. Even if they were enemies... fighting here doesn't seem right."

Uuchantuu nodded, and Koruuksi turned to Ymvesi'ia. He stepped close and took her hands, tucking the seed between them. She glanced down, then eyed him curiously.

"Look after this for me," he said. "I trust you to do what is right for both our people. If you need to, use the ship near the beach to get this to my people, no matter what happens to me. It's far more important than my life."

Ymvesi'ia held his gaze, swallowing.

"Promise me."

She nodded.

Koruuksi smiled and squeezed her hands, then turned to Uuchantuu.

She took a deep breath. "We're about to do something incredibly stupid, aren't we?"

Koruuksi nodded.

Uuchantuu rolled her eyes, then crossed over to Ymvesi'ia and kissed her. When they pulled back, the princess whispered something to Uuchantuu too soft for Koruuksi to hear. Uuchantuu smiled, then turned to Koruuksi.

"What's your idiotic plan this time?"

Koruuksi nodded for her to follow him toward the approaching king and guards. He pulled off the white hood revealing his mask to leave no doubt as to his identity, then raised his hands over his head and met Kuula'ande's disbelieving look with a smile.

35

Understanding

When Uumgwefilo fell to the Imaia, the Buuekwenani took in as many as they could, but the Vale grew rife with fear and panic as the fighting raged on outside E Kwekuue and both peoples mourned and feared discovery.

Exodus countdown: 6 days, 4 hours, 13 minutes

"Alright, moving on to test number three," Yndlova said, crossing off the second test as failed on her notepad. She planned to type it up later. So far, there wasn't much to type, "An opal-enhanced orangemind georaural."

As she spoke, Othaashle handed the device to Itese. It was small, easily held in one hand. Each of the seven biogems—six small sunstones at the points of the hexagonal structure, and one larger opal in the center—shone bright with Auroralight. As far as Yndlova could tell, this one wasn't much different from the last one they'd tried, except for the opal and the configuration of the sunstones. Apparently, the configuration alone could make the power of a georaural or the rate at which it used its Auroralight vary wildly.

Yndlova found herself staring at it in amazement at the intricate metalwork required to both contain the gems and allow for the integration of the electrical wiring that allowed one to activate the device with a mere push of the button on its underside.

This one, and the others they had tried, were specifically used to improve memory for those involved in judicial trials, scientists working on particularly difficult projects, and those experiencing cognitive decline. Theoretically, it would allow Itese to remember beyond when she'd been remade, if that was even possible.

Yndlova glanced at Othaashle.

Under normal circumstances, at least.

Yndlova didn't believe any of this would work. She agreed that they needed to try in order to be absolutely sure, but Othaashle had remembered her former life because of Boaathal's involvement. Most seemed to agree that the power of a World Tree was far beyond anything their georaural science could achieve.

Yndlova shook herself, realizing that Othaashle and Itese were waiting on her.

"Ready?" she asked.

Itese nodded.

"Proceed."

Itese tensed and pressed the button, holding it down. The geoaural's gems flashed, nearly blinding Yndlova. Itese gasped and went to one knee, a hand on the floor beside her.

Othaashle crouched beside her. "Itese?"

Itese straightened, still on one knee, chest heaving with each breath as she raised a hand to her head.

"It didn't work," she forced out through gritted teeth, fingers twitching around the now dim georaural.

"What did happen, though?" Yndlova asked.

Itese let out a heavy sigh. Instead of standing, she sat on the floor with legs crossed.

They'd decided on Othaashle's quarters for their tests due to the privacy it lent them. They stood—except Itese—in the main room. Like every other room save the office, it did not look lived-in. The sparse, stock furniture, and amount of Imaia iconography felt somewhat staged and impersonal. Yndlova saw it as the sign of a good, active leader who had little time to do anything but work or sleep when she returned to her quarters. As she looked around the room, Yndlova realized she couldn't remember a time that the three of them had been able to take a break like this.

With everything ready for Exodus except the Ministry of Science's tests, there isn't much for us to do unless they decide to launch early.

"I was able to reach back to my first memories as a Redeemed," Itese said, "but when I tried to go further, it felt like I was trying to use my skull to break through a wall."

Othaashle snorted at that.

"Everything was so vivid," Itese continued, turning her head toward Othaashle. "I think I understand now how your visions can have such an effect on you. It was more of an experience than a memory." She shook her head. "I'm still a bit disoriented from 'waking up' as a Redeemed."

Othaashle nodded, "It will fade."

Yndlova frowned, a bit lost. She knew that *she* wanted Itese to succeed, but...

Itese shouldn't want this, right?

She turned to her friend. "Why do you sound so disappointed? Isn't it a good thing that this isn't working? It means the Redeemed are safe in this respect."

Itese and Othaashle shared a look, then turned to Yndlova.

"Itese and I have been discussing some of the Redeemed taboos," she said slowly. "We've come to the decision that things like concealing one's former identity will cease to be sustainable if we begin expanding our number after Exodus, as planned."

"Within our own ranks," Itese clarified. "We still believe it necessary to conceal our former identities from everyone else, but among the Redeemed, it will be difficult to do so. Without the Remnant, we will be choosing from the people of the Imaia or any other capable races we may encounter after Exodus. Even now, the difference between Samjati and Natari is quite obvious."

Yndlova took in a deep breath at that. Skadaatha had assured them they would encounter other peoples as they visited new worlds. Before, she'd been skeptical, but the reports of a planet with intelligent activity proved her point.

"I already know the former identities of most of the other Redeemed," Itese continued, "or at least which side they were on. I came before them and was there when Othaashle chose most of them."

Yndlova held back a curse. Of course, Itese would have known.

But would she have told me?

It didn't matter. Yndlova never would have put Itese in that position. She liked to think that was part of why they worked so well together.

"I agreed to help Itese find out who she was," Othaashle told Yndlova, "even if these experiments don't work."

Yndlova nodded slowly, looking between the two. "Why don't you just look it up?"

"It's not the same," Itese snapped.

Yndlova blinked as Othaashle put a hand on the other woman's shoulder. "She's right. I've told both of you about my visions—how seeing them is more like reliving that life than simply remembering or knowing about it. However..." Othaashle trailed off, looking to Yndlova, then back to Itese. "Are you sure that is what you want, Itese? The more visions I've had, the harder the emotions that come with them are to process. You may not like the person you were."

Something in Othaashle's voice caught Yndlova's attention.

She seems even more drawn out than before. She must have had another vision.

"Do you know?"

The urgency in Itese's voice made Yndlova blink.

Othaashle, however, shook her head. "I have holes in my memory from around the time of my death and rebirth. One of those is when I chose you, unfortunately. Many of the early Redeemed like us, however, came from the Union side."

Itese sighed, shoulders slumping, then looked between Yndlova and Othaashle. "That was the last georaural, right?"

Yndlova shrugged. "There are more we could try, but that one was our best shot without working directly with a georaural scientist. Unless you want to try grinding up some infused orangenodes and snorting the dust like people supposedly used to."

Itese barked a laugh. "I think we can skip that. It sounds a bit too painful, and from what I remember reading, the investment isn't absorbed correctly. The intended effects are minor at best, and they sometimes have... strange side-effects."

Yndlova grinned. "Well, 'strange' is what we're looking for, isn't it?"

"Before anyone starts snorting anything," Othaashle cut in, "I thought of something. When Skadaatha attacked me in the remnant base, she used a weapon that was far more powerful than it had any right to be. The way she was using it should have depleted the Auroralight far sooner than it did." She looked to Yndlova. "Do you think you can find a way to ask Skadaatha about it? Something about giving a bit of extra power to the explosives? I'm certain Vysla had a part in making it for her."

Yndlova sighed, rolling her eyes. "Yes, sir."

She glared at Itese when the woman cackled, then looked back to Othaashle. "Why do I always have to deal with Skadaatha?"

"You know she likes you," Itese said. "In some very strange way."

"And you know she hates me," Othaashle pointed out.

Yndlova closed her eyes, rubbing at her temples, then sighed as she set down her notepad and took her uniform coat off the hook near Othaashle's door.

"You owe me for this," Yndlova said, giving both pointed glances.

"I'll be back in a bit."

36

Arrogance

Trade with the outside world through Uumgwefilo slowed to a trickle, and though the people of E Kwekuue felt safe within their secret borders and the unique protection they offered, their insular way of life gained a claustrophobic element.

Exodus countdown: 6 days, 3 hours, 52 minutes

> *System 14: Habitable World 1*
> *Class: Terrestrial*
> *Star: F-Class*
> *Orbital Position: 5*
> *Orbital Period: 433 Standard days, 721 local days (given a rotation period of 25 Standard hours)*
> *Moons: 2 (terrestrial)*
> *Diameter: 15928 km*
> *Gravity: 210 percent*
> *Primary Terrain: Shallow ocean with large, forested islands, some points of major continual storms. Foliage mostly yellow and orange in color with some blue.*
> *Occupation: Signs of primitive, but widespread civilization.*

> *Little urban coverage, few artificial lights visible when the planet is not in direct sunlight.*
> *Atmosphere: Breathable*
> *Climate: Tropical, similar to Lightside's polar band.*
> *Ideal for colonization, but not initial habitation due to current occupants.*

Skadaatha glanced over the report again as she considered it, then set the printout on the stack of those she considered viable for exploration and possible exploitation of resources, but not large-scale habitation. Though the research teams had already taken the liberty of classifying terrestrial planets with liquid water already present as 'habitable,' Skadaatha knew that those planets were simply those where life would occur naturally. With Mjatafa Mwonga, the Imaia could sustain itself long enough to terraform at least one desert planet or moon with little effort.

Overhead lights illuminated the stark room. Behind her, at the back of the room, the skulls of Draakon, one from Lightside, one from Darkside sat on display—a reminder of her age and power. Three neat stacks of paper sat on her wide, arched desk, her display screen in the inactive position next to the datapad she kept here. Music from speakers at the room's corners provided a pleasant backdrop as she sat back and took in the space. A stand holding an ancient helmet from the Iron Empire decorated one side of her room, while a titansteel blade rested upon a stand across from it. One of Matsanga's works. She no longer saw his fall from the Imaia as a betrayal. He had simply been too weak to do what was necessary. Too concerned with the now rather than what was to come. Picking up her datapad with one hand, Skadaatha used the other to light the solitary candle that adorned the right side of her desk, filling the room with a mixture of nutmeg, cinnamon, and pepper.

The stack of unread reports on her desk had shrunk considerably since she began her reading, but the stack of potential candidates was still thin. The tallest stack—those of systems with potential for mining or relay stations—would prove useful at some point, but not for many years. The Imaia had to establish a new homeworld first.

> *System 17: Habitable World 2*
> *Class: Terrestrial*
> *Star: Binary System*
> *Orbital Position: 3*
> *Orbital Period: 182 Standard days, 304 local days (given a rotation period of 24 Standard hours)*
> *Moons: 3 (terrestrial)*
> *Diameter: 10465 km*
> *Gravity: 150 percent*
> *Primary Terrain: Desert. Arid, rocky, sand dunes, crags and canyons, mountains. Small signs of surface water, maybe 1-2 percent.*
> *Occupation: Scans detected life and signs of civilization. Unknown if the civilization is active or if we have detected only remains.*
> *Atmosphere: Breathable*
> *Climate: Hot and arid*
> *Suitable for habitation, but not ideal. Possible presence of an Aathal. Terraforming and regular exchange with Mjatafa Mwonga would be required.*

Skadaatha frowned at that. One habitable but occupied, the other unoccupied but barely habitable as it was.

> *System 22: Habitable World 3*
> *Class: Terrestrial*
> *Star: Class unclear*
> *Orbital Position: 2*
> *Orbital Period: 289 Standard days, 462 Local days (given a rotation period of 25 Standard hours)*
> *Moons: 1, terrestrial*
> *Diameter: 11080 km*

Gravity: 190%
Primary Terrain: Glaciers and massive underground caves, similar to Darkside beyond the twilight band.
Occupation: No signs of life or civilization detected.
Atmosphere: Breathable.
Climate: Frigid, similar to the Ice Wastes of Darkside before the Destruction
Candidate for terraforming or gathering resources. Not suitable for habitation otherwise.

That report went into the tallest pile. She skimmed through the rest, finding a few barely habitable systems and a few that could be good candidates for terraforming, but the rest had few planets in the star's habitable zone. That, at least, seemed to match the fragments she could remembered from the time before she'd arrived on Efruumani. Much of Aioa was empty and lifeless, filled with gas and rocks that for all their beauty possessed no life or hope of sustaining it. When she tried to grasp any more than that, however, the thoughts slipped away like everything else from that time.

Skadaatha sighed, rubbing her temples, and decided to save the few remaining planetary reports for later. She'd already decided on a few good candidates, and as Vizier and head of the Ministry of Science, her decision mattered far more than the approval of the Senti and Mkuutana. Those formalities would simply make the decision official and known to the public.

As Skadaatha shuffled through a few more items—technical reports of the recall of forces and of all the raw materials they'd managed to pack into the city's lower levels—Skadaatha wondered how long it would take for the seed she'd planted during her test to bear fruit. She couldn't pin all of her hopes on that, of course, but at the very least, it would put Kojatere on edge and make her easier to manipulate and distract.

The thought made Skadaatha grin as she tapped the weapon hanging from her belt. Vysla had truly outdone himself this time.

She closed her eyes, reveling in the extra innate power she now held. It wasn't much, not when compared to what she had once held, but it was proof that Vysla's weapon worked exactly as she had hoped.

It performed far better than I had imagined.

This technology proved promising for whatever other uses Vysla had in mind for zidanio.

I need to make sure to thank him when he gets home tonight.

She had a few ideas in mind that would be quite enjoyable for both of them. Those would come later, however. For now, she needed to finish her reports.

Skadaatha's smirk turned to a thin line as she came to the reports about the Fingers of Atonga. Teams had recovered as many train sections, georaurals and valuable materials as they could. All of those at the Darkside stations she'd visited had finally come in, bringing everything they could with them. Only a skeleton crew at Outpost One remained outside Mjatafa Mwonga now, with their own attachment of transports and fighters, if needed. Her grand project would die with Efruumani in little more than a week. Other than that, everything was in order. They could have left the world behind them today if it wasn't for the public's need for reassurance. She had traveled through Aathalspace herself to reach this world, and they'd already sent satellites through to explore Aioa.

But my word, even Ynuukwidas's word, is not enough to assure the common citizen of travel to distant stars without testing.

The city itself had been stockpiled with enough resources to manufacture more starships and build out the city however they wished, as well as ample resources for terraforming, though that plan was not widely known outside the Ministry of Science.

She briefly scanned those reports, knowing her subordinates would comb through all the minutiae, and stopped when she came to an update on the progress of the various projects Yndlova had sought her help with concerning the Samjati and other refugees.

Skadaatha let out a sigh at the thought of Kojatere's adjunct, hoping the woman would be open to continued work together even after Skadaatha took care of Kojatere.

Once through those reports, the rest was purely bureaucratic—

Skadaatha flipped back a page, eyes narrowing as she lifted the sheet from the pile, eyes combing over the words.

Prisoner transfer confirmation. Initiated by Bykome Kotaane, logistics. Lieutenant Natsoje Mbaa assisting. Occupants will be moved to Rim Hangar Ten for labor.

Authorized by Supreme Commander Othaashle Mestari.

Skadaatha grinned.

This is wonderful.

It would take barely any effort on her part to spin this in her favor and make Kojatere's betrayal even more damning than she'd planned.

The woman was clever, but her arrogance would be her downfall, just as it had been before.

You are making this too easy, Kojatere.

37

Professor Modibodjara

It was not long after Uumgwefilo's fall before Queen Asante left to fight with the majority of E Kwekuue's remaining battle-trained Auroramancers. Few of the warriors they had sent years ago had returned, and she sought not only to aid in the fight against the Imaia, but to find all the Buuekwenani and Uumgwefili warriors she could and bring them home.

Exodus countdown: 6 days, 3 hours, 44 minutes

Yndlova took a deep breath as she stepped off the lift onto the House of Innovation's top floor, preparing herself to deal with Skadaatha. Unlike Othaashle, Skadaatha seemed to prefer working out of her home.

She also has a husband. Can't exactly blame her for that.

Yndlova knocked on the doorframe and waited. She knew that she was the best choice if they needed someone to work with Skadaatha. That didn't make dealing with the woman any easier.

The door opened a few minutes later to reveal Skadaatha's husband rather than the woman herself. Vysla Modibodjara was a tall, lanky man with short, crimped black hair, a slim, yet fit build, deep red-orange skin and golden-brown eyes. As before, when she'd met the man at government and military functions, his warm smile seemed far more genuine than any she'd seen Skadaatha give. "Adjunct Yndlova, to what do I owe this visit?"

The greeting was so antithetical to what Yndlova had prepared herself for that it took her a moment to get her bearings and return the smile. "I was looking for the Vizier, Professor Modibodjara, is she home?"

"You missed her by just a few minutes."

Yndlova held in a sigh of relief despite knowing she would still need to deal with Skadaatha later. She almost bid Vysla farewell and turned away but stopped.

He definitely had a hand in making that weapon.

Vysla likely knew more about the mechanics of what Othaashle and Itese needed than Skadaatha. He would also be far easier and more pleasant to deal with.

"Actually," Yndlova said, "you might be able to assist me more than the Vizier. May I come in?"

Vysla raised an eyebrow at that, but smiled again a moment later, stepping aside to allow her into his home. She'd expected something like Othaashle's quarters—barely lived in and uninviting—yet found the apartment surprisingly cozy, with a sense of personal care everywhere she looked.

"Would you like some tea?"

Yndlova blinked, but smiled. "Yes, please."

"My wife has always spoken very highly of you despite the... tension between herself and Commander Othaashle," Vysla said, getting out two mugs and individual strainers. "What can I help you with?"

Yndlova barely kept herself from gaping.

Skadaatha speaks highly of me?

She was surprised the woman spoke about her at all, much less that it wasn't all complaining.

"I—" Yndlova began, then paused, unsure how best to broach the subject. "Commander Othaashle mentioned that the Vizier... demonstrated an unusual new weaponized georaural for her—one that seemed to consume Auroralight at a far lower rate than it should have for the energy it output. I assume you had a hand in making it?"

"Your assumption is correct."

Yndlova almost missed it. The slight hesitation as Vysla washed off the small spoon he'd used to fill the strainers with the dried herbs and spices for the tea.

He knows Skadaatha attacked Othaashle. Does he suspect I know?

He probably did. The man was renowned throughout the Imaia as one of its most brilliant minds, rather than simply being brilliant in a single field.

"I'd wondered if that same technology could be applied toward memory recovery," she said, recalling the story she'd made up for Skadaatha. "Something that could either break through traumatic blocks on something an individual might not want to remember, or something that could allow one to view another's memories along with them."

Vysla turned to her wearing a contemplative expression, two fingers at his chin. "That's an interesting idea. The technology is relatively new, so its only applications so far have been in energy and arms, as usual, but I don't see why that wouldn't work." He met her eyes and smiled. "I think that would make quite the interesting project."

He turned around and took the steaming mug of tea and lifted the dripping filter from it, setting it in the sink before walking it over to Yndlova. The spicy aroma reached her before he'd covered half the distance.

"Thank you," Yndlova said, taking the mug carefully by the handle. "I'm surprised you're not down at one of the universities, helping with the testing."

Vysla smiled. "I have a public appearance tomorrow, but those I left in charge are more than capable of handling things themselves.

We could be leaving now, but you know how the Council and the legislature like their redundancies."

Yndlova couldn't help but grin at that. "Yes, they make that quite clear in the amount of paperwork I have to review and fill out."

Vysla laughed, then gestured to the kitchen table. "Care to provide me with more specifics on your project?"

38

The Gift of the Vale

When Queen Asante's contingent returned, she was not among them.

Exodus countdown: 8 days, 27 hours, 58 minutes

Ymvesi'ia took a deep breath as her father entered the council chamber, steadying herself and trying to project the poise and confidence of a queen that her mother and sisters had tutored her in when she was younger. Years had passed since she'd last been here, and the space seemed smaller, somehow, yet more intimidating. Even more so now that her father had arrived.

As her father approached his seat, the last of the eight aluminum seats that remained unoccupied, Ymvesi'ia's fingers closed around the seed in the pouch at her hip, flexing. Its pulsing energy calmed her a bit, but not as much as she would have hoped.

Remember the plan.

Vise's incredible memory and thirst for knowledge had saved her when her father had brought the Akjemasai to the Heart to arrest Koruuksi and Uuchantuu, and she and Ymvesi'ia had spent almost the entirety of the time that had passed between then and this meeting researching the laws and precedents that governed E Kwekuue's ruling bodies.

She still wished Vise could have been here.

No one else was allowed in this meeting, however, leaving the two tiered rows of seats along the walls, normally occupied by aides and specialists, empty. Ymvesi'ia, her father, and the six councilors met alone under the sun. No roof covered the chamber, which sat atop one of E Kwekuue's many tiered, pyramid structures, with only an overhang to offer some shade to those in the benches when occupied. Patches of white hung over from the planters atop those overhangs, and from various shelves and planters around the chamber. Lightoruu and a few timeoruu—those that appeared whenever someone was waiting, patiently or impatiently—hung about the councilors. Aluminum spread throughout the chamber like intricate lace, the lines meeting in the chamber's center where they thinned to outline a map of the Vale.

Looking at that map—at her home—made Ymvesi'ia wish even more desperately for her friend's presence.

Instead, Vise waited with a few of the Akjemasai that Ymvesi'ia trusted most, ready to spring Koruuksi and Uuchantuu and get them to their ship if things went poorly.

Ymvesi'ia winced at the thought of being unable to see Uuchantuu again before she left, then shook herself, drawing in another deep breath.

"Which one of you called this meeting?" Ymvesi'ia's father said uncertainly, eyeing each of the seated council members. He frowned when his gaze landed on Ymvesi'ia, sitting in her mother's chair.

"I did, Father."

His frown deepened. "You don't have that authority, Daughter."

Ymvesi'ia swallowed the lump in her throat and tried her best not to sound petulant.

"Per chapter thirteen of *The Gift of the Vale*, I do. E Kwekuue must always have both king and queen to rule—or king and king, or queen and queen, should circumstances of marriage run that way. In the absence of a married co-ruler, the vacant responsibility falls to a child, other family, or a ward specifically appointed to the purpose."

Ymvesi'ia paused, looking around at the Diwani. "Though I was never officially named to this role, I have effectively held and wielded that power for some time. That code also states that if the two rulers are divided on an issue of state, they are obliged to bring that issue to the council to reach a decision."

Ymvesi'ia looked again to Diwana Warsama, who smiled at her before turning her attention toward Kuula'ande.

"I do not think any of us can deny that Ymvesi'ia has filled the role of queen for some time now, Highness, and you have allowed and even encouraged her to do so on certain occasions." She paused, looking around to meet the eyes of the other councilors. "By gathering here at her request, each of us councilors have recognized her authority, whether we did so knowingly or not."

Warsama glanced back at Ymvesi'ia and they shared a small smile before Ymvesi'ia turned her attention back to her father.

Ymvesi'ia's father looked between the two of them for a moment, then sighed, taking his seat.

"I expect this is regarding the fate of the two trespassers?" he asked.

Ymvesi'ia shook her head. "Not directly, though it should decide their fate."

Kuula'ande groaned. "So it is about that, then."

Ymvesi'ia nodded. "I do not believe you gave Koruuksi's petition the proper consideration for such grave claims, and you made the decision alone, without consulting myself or the council. I have met with each councilor, and most of them support my decision to assist Koruuksi and the Remnant and begin evacuating the city."

Ymvesi'ia eyed Diwana Duubaan at that last part.

"While we originally agreed with you, Princess," Diwana Nkruuma said, "that was before Koruuksi's banishment and his subsequent disregard of that banishment, followed by his trespassing in the Heart."

Legessa and Kenjata murmured in agreement.

"That is irrelevant," Ymvesi'ia said, trying to keep her frustration under control, "I exercised my powers to detain Koruuksi and Uuchantuu on their way out of E Kwekuue, and I had every right to take them to the Heart of the Vale."

"Technically, Princess," Duubaan said, "though you are right on the second point if it stands alone, you should have brought the matter of Koruuksi's banishment to the council to decide upon it instead of taking action in opposition to your father's expressed will."

Ymvesi'ia narrowed her eyes. "So I was supposed to do nothing and exile a man from our lands before we could determine if his banishment was just?"

"Might I suggest we stop wasting time and discuss the issue at hand?" Warsama said. "I must insist the princess is correct in the urgency she gives it."

"How can we believe any of the supposed evidence presented to us?" Diwana Mandel asked. "At the moment, it looks like Koruuksi and this team deceived us to get to the Heart."

"I agree," Legessa said. "We cannot take anything they said at—"

"I must stop you there, Diwana," Warsama said. "My scientists have corroborated Ymvesi'ia's conclusions and the arguments the young man presented to Their Majesties."

That silenced them for a moment. Duubaan and Legessa in particular appeared troubled.

"What about Boaathal?" Kuula'ande asked. "Have you discovered a way for a World Tree to be separated from its world?"

Ymvesi'ia had found herself with no answer to that a few days ago. This time, she was better prepared.

"That is irrelevant," Ymvesi'ia said calmly, even as her father turned his disapproving gaze upon her. "Until Kweshrima destroyed Yrmuunthal, we did not believe it was possible to destroy an Aathal. Until I saw the Remnant ships fly away from our beaches and the Imaia ships in orbit, a part of me did not entirely believe such things were possible, either. The Imaia has Ynuukwidas at their head. We may no longer worship him as a god, but that does not diminish his power. With their ability to travel to the stars and the power of a god at their disposal—one more powerful than she who destroyed Yrmuunthal, by all accounts—who are we to challenge the belief that they could take Boaathal with them when they leave?" Ymvesi'ia let her words ring in the air for a moment before regarding a darker conclusion she'd come to since Koruuksi's arrest. "If the Imaia is overconfident in their ability to remove Boaathal from Efruumani," she added in a softer voice, "they might end up destroying it in the process of leaving."

The faces of the Diwani—even Warsama—darkened, and their shoulders slumped.

"The Heart will protect us," Legessa said. "It always has."

Nkruuma cleared her throat. "I must caution against such beliefs. Just because the Heart does not claim to be a god does not assure against misplaced faith. I originally agreed to a meeting because I knew we could not place such faith in an idol again, no matter its power. I believe that Warsama will agree with me when I say that the Heart's protection cannot be assured."

"Fine."

Ymvesi'ia blinked, looking to her father at the single, grating word.

"Majesty?" Nkruuma asked.

The king looked around the circle. "Let's say Koruuksi's claims are true. Either the Imaia leaves and takes Boaathal with them or destroys it in the process, leaving Efruumani to be destroyed as it falls into Myrskaan or the sun. What can we possibly do about it?"

Ymvesi'ia swallowed, chest growing tight at the slight waver in her father's voice.

Light, he really is terrified.

She couldn't blame him—she'd been terrified since Koruuksi had told her and she had accepted that reality. Knowing that her father felt the same, however, shook her. Confronting him was one thing, but...

How am I supposed to be strong when he is not?

Ymvesi'ia felt at the seed again and straightened her back.

Mother was able to do it. I can do it, too.

"We cannot make war upon the world to keep it from ending," Ymvesi'ia's father continued, "and we cannot hope to stand against the Imaia. We failed at that once already, and our people do not know war."

"Our people barely knew war when my mother led them against the Imaia," Ymvesi'ia said, "yet they followed her anyway because it was what needed to be done." She paused, looking around the chamber. "Thankfully, we need not fight in this situation. Only those who wish to do so will be needed, at least. We have been in this situation before. When the Iron Empire threatened our people, we fled, knowing it would be death to stay. We were rewarded with this paradise. We must hope that doing so now will work out just as favorably."

"We lost half our people to the sea on our journey here," Kenjata pointed out.

Ymvesi'ia leveled a glare at her. "We already risk that by deliberating over this. We needed to act days ago."

"Even if we did, Daughter," her father said, "the word of king and council only goes so far in situations such as this."

"Our people are unaware of this threat," Duubaan elaborated. "They will be slow to act if we tell them they must leave and abandon all they know to escape a threat they cannot see."

Ymvesi'ia clenched her teeth, trying not to grind them.

Look at the positives.

"But you agree that something needs to be done?" she asked, looking to her father and the councilors.

They each nodded, though some reluctantly.

Silence stretched through the chamber as they thought.

"Princess Ymvesi'ia could give the order," Warsama said, breaking the silence so suddenly Ymvesi'ia nearly jumped out of her seat.

"Me?"

Warsama nodded, looking around at everyone.

"The people know her. Even those who don't love her and respect her for nearly giving her life to keep our home a secret from the Imaia. They respect the Akjemasai, and respect her even more for being a part of it. By extension, everyone knows and respects Vise, and most of the workers she oversees will come running at her call, and they would be the most important in an evacuation."

Ymvesi'ia blinked at that, thinking of how Vise had taken a bit longer with her duties the past few days than she normally did, even when Koruuksi had been waiting in her rooms for her.

Kenjata snorted. "That woman is so damn gorgeous that half the men in the city would follow her out if she asked it."

Ymvesi'ia rolled her eyes. She couldn't really argue with that.

Warsama cleared her throat as a few of the others—including Ymvesi'ia's father—laughed at that.

"My point, is that if Princess Ymvesi'ia makes this announcement to the people in concert with the Akjemasai and my scientists, it could work."

Ymvesi'ia rose from her seat. "Then we must act immediately. How fast can we gather everyone in Patakytifuu Square? Once Koruuksi and Uuchantuu are released, I can have them assist Vise and myself with the Akjemasai and the workers."

The chamber went silent, and the king frowned at her. "You think your friends are getting out of this unscathed? They broke the law and defied my orders."

Ymvesi'ia's eyes bulged. "Unscathed? Do you know what they planned on doing the moment they confirmed we would be ready to evacuate? They would call their people to assist us while Koruuksi and Uuchantuu left with their warriors and our own to attack the Imaia's stronghold. They plan to face death to save us. You can either release them so they can help us—even though they owe us *nothing*—or you can lock me up with them for knowingly disobeying your orders as well."

Her father held her gaze. "That must be discussed at a later time."

Ymvesi'ia sighed inwardly, mouth drawing to a thin line. She would protect Koruuksi and Uuchantuu, but she needed to protect her people first.

The king looked to the others. "The matter of evacuation is not as simple as we would like. We should take this slowly—spread word through the Akjemasai and the workforce and let them start talking so that when you make your announcement, it does not come out of nowhere."

Ymvesi'ia clenched her fists. She knew that they were trying to find the best way to execute this, but there simply wasn't time. It made her want to scream!

Her balled-up fist brushed against her pouch and the seed within.

Ymvesi'ia's eyes widened. She retrieved the seed, cupping it in both hands before her. It pulsed as she gazed at it, almost glowing a green no dye could achieve.

"Ymvesi'ia?"

Ymvesi'ia looked up at Warsama's question.

"What is that?"

Ymvesi'ia held forth the seed so that everyone could see it.

"The Heart accepted Koruuksi. My father can verify it."

The councilors, all wide-eyed at her words, looked to her father. He was silent, saying nothing until he noticed Ymvesi'ia's glare. "I saw him exit the Heart as I arrived."

Silence.

Duubaan broke the silence, speaking slowly, "That affords him leniency, then. We must trust the Heart's judgement."

"It affords him more than that," Ymvesi'ia said, thrusting the seed forward. "He came out of the Heart with this. Rather than fight his way out or try to hide it, he gave it to me."

"This can work," Warsama said.

All eyes turned to her.

"She and the young man can address the people together," she elaborated, "with the heart's gift. They will see it as a blessing upon what we ask of them. We must leave our paradise, but the Heart has given them something to guide us on our way."

Ymvesi'ia struggled to reign in her hope as one by one, each of the councilors nodded—even Duubaan—until finally it came to her father.

39

Failure

The survivors brought word of war raging across the entire world and the devastation left in its wake. Their fantastical tales of the foreign, mysterious Darkside were tempered by their descriptions of the destruction there, and of the friends and family lost.

Exodus countdown: 9 days, 10 hours, 57 minutes

Estingai sat huddled under one of the forest's larger trees by the time Matsanga found her. She assumed he was trying to be heard, as the crunch of leaves beneath his feet reached her ears long before the toes of his boots came into view.

Estingai didn't look up, letting the silence stretch as she tightened her arms around her knees a bit further.

After a short while of standing, Matsanga sat before her, legs crossed. A flash of red and black at the edge of her vision told her that Ajida had come with him, and now sat next to him.

"I'm sorry, Estingai," her former mentor said. "I know it probably doesn't mean much now, but I am deeply, truly sorry."

He was silent for a while, as though waiting for her to respond, before he continued.

"I tried to tell you I was broken," his voice was still gravelly, but sounded almost strained somehow. "Every time I try to do something good, I fail. I thought that maybe with you it could be different—that I could actually help for once without mucking things up, but I..." He trailed off with a sigh. "I should have known better by now. That is why I came here, Estingai, why I can't go with you. This exile, my isolation and suffering, is my penance for all the horrible things I have done. All the death I have left in my wake. I tried redemption, but you've seen how that worked out."

She glared at him. "The world is about to fall into the *sun*, Matsanga. I won't let you just die like that."

"That's my choice, not yours."

Estingai tilted her head up just enough to meet Matsanga's eyes, then glanced at Ajida.

"And her? Does she need redemption, too? Does she need to suffer?"

Matsanga exchanged a look with his white-furred companion.

"We are bound together," he said. "She does not experience the same pain I do, yet she understands my need for penance. Neither of us would lay down and let the Imaia kill us if they came, but... living for hundreds of years takes a toll, Estingai. We've made our peace with this."

Estingai frowned at that, Matsanga's explanation tugging at a memory. Then she lowered her gaze again, saying nothing. After a while, Matsanga rose to his feet, dusting off the leaves.

"I truly am sorry, Estingai," he said. "I wish I could have done better by you."

Estingai thought about encouraging him—telling him he could have a chance at least if he came back with her. She thought about snapping at him, too. But what would be the point?

I never expected to get out of this alive, anyway. I was just an idiot that let myself hope against my better judgement that things could be different.

Matsanga let something fall to the ground before her, making a soft thump in concert with the crunching of the leaves.

"I packed up your things for you, and threw in some extra

supplies," he said, "I'll stay away from the main room of the ruins until I see your ship come and go if you want to wait there, but there should be enough for you to set up camp out here until your way home comes to get you. Ajida is the most dangerous thing left in this forest, so you'll be safe."

He waited again for a few minutes before finally turning to go.

"Wait," Estingai said, looking up after the first few steps.

Matsanga stopped and turned enough to look over his shoulder.

"You said there were three lessons," she said. "You never told me the third."

Matsanga held her gaze, then sighed, looking down.

"The third lesson," he said, barely loud enough for her to hear, "is in combining the first two."

He looked at her a moment more, then turned away again and started back toward the ruins.

She barely heard his last few words over the crunching of leaves as he walked away.

"I failed at that, too."

40

I Hope You Remember

If Queen Asante's loss hadn't been enough to force King Kuula'ande's hand, when the survivors told him of how the gods took sides, and that one of them had destroyed Yrmuunthal, a sacred World Tree, causing a cataclysm that had effected every corner of Efruumani except E Kwekuue, he decreed that the Buuekwenani would close themselves off from the world entirely. No one objected, and only the Akjemasai were allowed beyond the pass. They would keep watch, and eliminate anyone who came looking for our sanctuary and the secrets it holds.

Exodus countdown: 6 days, 2 hours, 25 minutes

> *System 32: Habitable World 4*
> *Class: Terrestrial*
> *Star: K-Class, estimated to be around 3,000 degrees warmer than our own star.*
> *Orbital Position: 4 (Last within the frost line)*
> *Orbital Period: 99 Standard days, 220 local days (given a rotation period of 18 Standard hours)*
> *Moons: 1 (terrestrial)*

> *Gravity: 140%*
> *Primary Terrain: Forests, snow fields and oceans.*
> *Occupation: Scans indicate signs of life, but no civilization or urbanization detected.*
> *Atmosphere: Breathable*
> *Climate: Frigid, not unlike Darkside. Average cover and temperature of the planet seems to fluctuate over the orbital period.*
> *Suitable for habitation, but not ideal. No presence of Aathal detected.*

Itese popped another chocolate-covered laiaberry into her mouth, suppressing a yawn as she chewed the sweet, yet bitter snack, mask tipped up just enough to eat. She scanned the next few lines before turning to the next file—the rest of the data was much more detailed, but far too dense for her purposes. She expected most of the Imaia's citizens, used to warm temperatures, would have a hard time adapting to life on such a frigid planet, anyway.

> System 35: Habitable world 5
> Class Terrestrial
> Star: G-Class, estimated to be at least 3,000-4,000 degrees hotter than our own.
> Orbital Position: 5
> Orbital Period: 160.5 Standard Days, 207 local days (given a rotation period of 31 Standard hours)
> Moons: 5
> Diameter 21,600 km
> Gravity: 200%
> Primary terrain: Lakes, canyons, plateaus, grasslands, and forests. Grasslands and forests are primarily bright green in color, rather than the various darker shades of foliage on Efruumani.
> Occupation: Scans indicate signs of life, but no civilization or urbanization detected.

> Atmosphere: Breathable
>
> Climate: Temperate. Same fluctuations of temperature and cover over the orbital period that has been observed on other habitable worlds.
>
> An ideal choice for habitation. No presence of Aathal detected.

Itese glanced up from the file as Othaashle came out of her office, holding a drive in one hand.

Itese frowned. She didn't have that with her when she went to her office.

Othaashle walked over to Itese and held it out to her.

Itese looked between Othaashle and the drive. "What is this?"

Othaashle lowered the drive. "Yndlova might take a while, and even then, she won't have a solution ready for us, if Skadaatha even agrees to help at all."

Itese nodded. "I know."

"I had another idea," Othaashle said, holding up the drive again. "What if reading about who you are triggers those memories? It seemed to happen a few times with my visions." She pushed the drive toward Itese. "This is who you were. All I could manage to find."

Itese's chest tightened, eyes growing hot. She searched for the right words but couldn't find them. She stared at the drive for a moment, then took it.

"You don't need to read it here," Othaashle said, "but I wanted to be here for you. Just in case."

Itese held the drive in both hands. She stared at it for some time before finally thinking of something to say.

"Did you know me?"

Othaashle nodded.

But as Othaashle, or Kojatere?

"Which—" Itese began, then bit her lip. She had to take a few deep breaths before she could continue. Her hands felt like they should be shaking. "Did I fight for the Union?"

"Like I told you," Othaashle said, "many of our earlier number were chosen from the Union. It was my job to seek out enemy Auroraborn. At first, to eliminate them, then to bring them to Ynuukwidas for Redemption." She pointed to the drive. "That will tell you everything you need to know."

Itese picked up her datapad. She almost inserted the drive, but her hand shook too much. Her chest tightened even further around her pounding heart. Her mask seemed tighter than usual, hotter.

She stood, dropping the drive and her datapad as she headed for Othaashle's restroom. "I need a moment."

Itese ripped her mask off the moment she was inside, unbuttoning her shirt a bit further as she closed the door behind her.

Her blood rushed, breaths coming in shallow gasps.

Itese turned on the water and splashed some on her face. The cool water was exactly what she needed. It washed away the hot sting of her building tears and seemed to help shock her out of whatever had come over her, if only a little.

Gripping the edge of the sink, Itese closed her eyes. She took deep, long breaths, trying to slow her pulse.

Finally, Itese opened her eyes and looked in the mirror.

Silver eyes with hints of gold in them gazed back at her above broad, high cheekbones and a round face. Full lips rested between a small, rounded nose and a strong chin. For a moment, she saw a pale blue-violet complexion instead of the grey-white of the Redeemed.

She sighed. It had been a long time since she'd looked at her own face. Itese could remember doing so a few times after her Redemption and when she'd begun seriously considering looking into her former identity.

Am I ready for this? Can I take the final step?

Itese took another deep breath and patted her face dry before looking in the mirror again.

I can do this.

The questions surrounding who she had been had made Itese aware of an emptiness within her. She wanted to fill that void. It would allow her to be someone Othaashle could talk to about her memories.

She's always been there for me and the other Redeemed. She deserves someone who will be there for her.

Resolved to her decision, Itese donned her mask once more and stepped into the hallway. As she closed the door behind her, she noticed something she'd overlooked on her way in—what looked like a spare boot sticking out of Othaashle's hall closet.

"Othaashle," she called, "I think some of your armor toppled over in the closet. I'll get it."

As Itese reached for the handle, however, she frowned.

That's a standard issue boot. Not one of Othaashle's.

They were similar, but every piece of Othaashle's armor and uniform had been crafted to make her stand out from the rest of the Redeemed.

Has she kept her old armor, maybe? From when she was the only Redeemed?

Itese opened the door, then gasped and stumbled back, falling to the floor in horror as she tried to back away from what she'd found.

A Redeemed sat crumpled in Othaashle's closet, but its uniform and mask were too loose. What she could see of the limbs looked pale and withered, as though only bone and sinew lay beneath the skin. No light came from its gemcrest or the eyeholes of its mask. She'd seen only a handful of the Redeemed look like this before, after they'd had their power drained completely.

Itese's blood pounded in her ears, air coming in shallow breaths again.

Footfalls from behind made her whirl around, and Itese found Othaashle looking between her and the withered husk of the Redeemed—*Auroras, who is that? They're dead, aren't they? Actually dead*—with wide eyes.

Itese scrambled to her feet.

"What is this?" she demanded.

Othaashle said nothing.

"Tell me!"

Othaashle thrust a hand to her side and Itese froze where she stood. Six seconds later, Ilkwalerva formed from mist and motes of fire. Othaashle's fingers closed around the hilt as she leveled it at Itese.

No.

"This wasn't me, Itese," Othaashle said, voice wavering.

Itese wanted to believe her, but—

"Then explain this!" she demanded.

Othaashle shook her head, voice strained when she spoke. "There's no time."

Itese primed her biogems, dropping into a fighting stance. Before she could even move, Othaashle stood over her. Itese felt too hot and too cold at once. Ilkwalerva cut through her stomach; the tip of the blade protruded from her back. Its edge cut her with every breath.

Itese looked up just in time to see the glow of Auroralight beneath Othaashle's mask.

"I'm sorry, Itese."

Itese slumped to her knees, causing pain to lance through her even as her senses began to dull. Something tugged on her Auroralight, then went even deeper.

"There's too much at stake."

Itese's thoughts started to slow.

"Auroras, it's too early."

Itese gasped as Ilkwalerva left her body, taking the last of her Auroralight with it. The world fuzzed around her.

"I always considered you a friend, Itese. I hoped we could be again. I hope you remember."

Something hard hit Itese in the side of the head with a loud crack. Darkness consumed her world.

Epilogue 1
Bykome

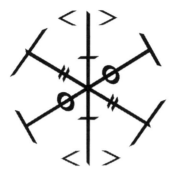

Exodus countdown: 6 days, 3 hours, 5 minutes

Not for the first time this night, Bykome flexed his fingers—switching his drink back and forth between hands—trying to rid himself of some of the stress he'd built up since Kojatere's surprise visit a week past. The idea of actually participating in an operation for the army once more was bad enough, but working with an officer in the Imaia police force that his family had a personal relationship with? What were the chances?

Is the danger to my family really worth this? Did I make a mistake?

Bykome pushed the doubt from his mind—something he'd become quite good at over the years. The time for questions like that was past. He'd committed, knowing very well that he couldn't ignore Kojatere's charge, especially if she was lying about being Kojatere and not Othaashle. He still had a hard time wrapping his head around that. Even if he never told Kanika about it, he wouldn't be able to look her in the eye. If he fought carefully to change the Imaia from within, how could he ignore an opportunity to free those the Imaia had treated with such cruelty? He would have become a hypocrite, something he despised even more than the Imaia's authoritarian rule.

Still, questions bit at him even now. Had Kojatere put him and

Natsoje together purposefully? Had she thought their connection something he would appreciate? Or had it simply been coincidence?

From his position near the window, Bykome glanced around the officer's apartment, taking a sip from his lakka—an element of Samjati culture the Imaia had no problem appropriating. The furnishings were modest, but fine, as expected for one of Natsoje's rank and pay grade, with decorations displaying the family's pride in and service to the Imaia. All Bykome could see was a home filled with propaganda. He and his wife had similar decorations of course, but only out of necessity.

He caught movement on the edge of his vision and turned back to his study of the garden and its shades of black contrasted with the colorful blossoms of different flowers.

"I feel I need to thank you again for accepting my invitation."

Bykome forced a pleasant expression and smiled as he looked to Natsoje, affecting that he had just noticed her coming over. The woman came to stand beside him, taking a sip from her glass. "Myndir loves it when the kids help him cook, but he rarely has such skilled and willing help with preparing the food as Dalile and your wife."

Bykome glanced over at the women in question, then back to Natsoje, smiling. "I doubt they've had anyone as creative as Myndir to work with. That meal was delicious."

Natsoje glanced back at her husband. "He got the idea as soon as Kanika showed him the peppers growing in your garden. I wanted to have you two over to thank you for letting us invade your home, but everything else about tonight was Myndir's idea."

"It was nothing. My nephew was ecstatic when he heard Anar would be visiting."

Natsoje chuckled. "I could tell."

"Any news on when they'll be able to return?" Bykome asked, voice lowered. "Kanika and I try not to bring it up—Aiana and the others are shaken enough as it is."

Natsoje frowned. "They're doing quick work, as usual. Most of the rubble has been cleared away but patching up that part of the building without making it appear like a patch will take time. We can take the kids for a night or two if any of you need a break. And don't worry—I'll keep an eye on Hovase and Anar."

Bykome laughed and had to hold back a frown. Despite the uniform Natsoje wore and the pride she took in it, Bykome found he genuinely liked this woman.

"You seem a bit tense," she remarked. "Is everything going well with the transfer?"

Bykome sighed, nodding. "Yes. The final transfer should go through tomorrow. The Imaia is nothing if not efficient."

Natsoje nodded. "You would know more than most. It's because of people like you that the city is able to relax while the scientists run all the tests they want before Exodus."

He gestured out the window to the large garden all the apartments on this floor of the quadrant looked out on. "This just makes me think about the days when the world still looked like this. How beautiful it was."

Natsoje nodded, eyes going to the cultivated foliage, though her expression seemed to harden. "If the rumors I've heard are correct, Othaashle will soon see that the Remnant answers for Efruumani's destruction and all the other crimes that can be laid at their feet."

Bykome was about to agree out of habit, then hesitated, studying Natsoje. She obviously believed the Imaia's propaganda where the Remnant and the Union were concerned. She wouldn't have risen as far as she had if she didn't. Yet, she was an intelligent woman who, though accepting of what the Imaia fed her, did not seem the type to shovel down anything and everything without question. Could this be why Kojatere had chosen her to work with him?

Glancing at his nephew and Anar, Bykome set his jaw, nodding to himself. Amadika and Tinotembo already shared some of the views he and Kanika pushed. Considering their son's infatuation with Anar, there might be more meetings like this in the future. Whether or not those included himself and Kanika, if not handled properly, that could go poorly, becoming quite dangerous for the family he had married into.

"When we spoke of them last, you said you pitied those who still follow the Night Mother's cause, correct, as well as the prisoners we helped transport?"

Natsoje raised an eyebrow at Bykome, but nodded. "I did."

"Do you truly blame them for everything you would lay at their feet?" he asked, voice low.

Natsoje blinked, stiffening.

"Not the leadership of the Night Mother herself," Bykome specified, "but the common soldier. What the Night Mother did was unforgivable—we saw how many from that side fled to the Imaia after she destroyed the Aathal. Yet, I don't think we can truly lay all the blame for the state of the world at her feet."

Bykome waited a moment, meeting Natsoje's eyes. She remained silent, stern, but her eyes held a glimmer of curiosity. Bykome continued.

"In my line of work, I was out in the field quite a bit when I first started out, mapping the best supply routes and ensuring the food that we sent out actually made it to our people on time."

Doing so had also given him a steady flow of useful intel to feed to the Remnant, as well as the ability to ensure that a negligible portion of rations and supplies always went 'missing' in transit. Before the Imaia had entirely retreated into Mjatafa Mwonga at least.

"While I was out there, however," he continued, "visiting farms and mines and traveling along the supply routes, I noticed exactly how much we taxed the land in our hunger for resources."

He paused, taking a sip of his lakka. He'd almost forgotten about it, but it would help prevent him from going hoarse.

"Our goal is to not only defeat the Enemy but recruit other worlds and peoples to help us in our cause and prepare them for it—if they truly are out there as Skadaatha says. To accomplish that—for the way the leadership wishes us to go about it, at least—we will consume more and more resources every year. Thus, we will need to expand and harvest resources without end. That is not sustainable for a single world and may not even be sustainable for multiple worlds with the Imaia's projected goals."

He glanced to the garden again, then back to Natsoje. "Even before the Night Mother set us on the path to abandon Efruumani, we were consuming its resources at an alarming rate, scouring the land of beautiful sights like this. Most of it was simply digging up the land for all the fire and ice metal we use, but every time I rode out with the supply lines, I saw more and more acres of forest cleared and hills flattened, transformed into farmland to ship back here. Even with the vertical farms we developed here, we will likely need to press hard for whatever resources we can on our journey, whether it be energy, metals, stone and soil, or even water."

He looked back to Natsoje and affected an embarrassed sigh. "Forgive me for rambling. Kanika usually chides me before I grow too philosophical. My point was merely that as much as we would like to hold the Imaia up as something shining and perfect, it is not, and we need to remember that so when mistakes and oversights occur, we can learn from them and improve. Otherwise, we will likely become just as deserving of your pity as the prisoners and those fools that attack us rather than seeking peace among us."

Bykome took another sip from his drink to make the stop seem less abrupt, turning his gaze back to the garden, but keeping Natsoje's expression within his periphery.

Had he overstepped? He was practiced at this, but usually he dealt with people much less involved in the actual structure of the Imaia.

His tension fled when Natsoje finally nodded, expression thoughtful, though he held in the sigh.

"I'll admit," Natsoje said slowly, "I did not expect such... perspective from someone whose line of work seems so..."

"Uninteresting?" Bykome supplied with a grin. Natsoje colored, taking a sip of her drink, and he chuckled. "Don't worry. It can be a monotonous job at times—I think that might be part of *why* I get so philosophical. Something to keep me energized."

Natsoje smiled, though some of the color remained in her cheeks. "Regardless, you've given me some things to think about in my own line of work. I'm not sure I agree entirely with your theory that we would have in time scoured Efruumani as thoroughly as the Night Mother did, but I agree that we need to keep our opinions of the Imaia from growing too immaculate. Realism will allow us to progress toward the ideal we would have the Imaia become."

Bykome smiled in agreement, then drained the rest of his lakka and took one last look at the gardens, remembering a similar patch of plants behind his old home from what seemed ages ago, before going to refill his glass and using that as an excuse to segue into a conversation with Mynidr and Amadika about the food he'd prepared. As they spoke, he glanced over at Natsoje, hoping his words had planted seeds of contemplation rather than dissension. He watched as she pulled out her commdisk, holding it up to her ear for a moment before getting her uniform coat from where it hung near the door. She kissed her husband and son before telling them she'd be right back—one of her colleagues needed her in the city.

Bykome looked after her for a moment once she was gone, then forced himself to take a deep breath and unclench. He just had to make it through this transfer, and after that, she would have little reason to suspect him of any disloyalty to the Imaia.

Epilogue 2
Alajos

Exodus countdown: 6 days, 30 hours, 47 minutes

Alajos tapped his foot to the rhythm of the song's lilting beat as it played over the low hum of his miner's engines and the various systems that allowed the thing to operate and keep him breathing in the dark space between worlds.

Thank the Imaia for inventing these blessed things, he thought, glancing at the audio player mounted on his cockpit's display, *And thank Bykata for making a version that works without Auroralight.*

The scientist had been a nobody at the time, just a tinkerer, but millions benefitted from his work these days.

Alajos had piloted this same mining vessel, which he'd named *Hanuuko*, for six years now. The first few months had been daunting, and he didn't think he *could* have focused on much besides piloting the craft and mining the gas once inside Myrskaan's atmosphere. Now, the entire affair was just as boring and routine as any other mundane job like farming or sailing. Sometimes he forgot why he'd even volunteered for this posting in the first place. Not for the first time, he wished he could have been some sort of artist. Even a mechanic. There was an art to the latter, and he had some skill in it, where he had none in painting or playing instruments. He could carry a tune, lock into a rhythm, and sing well enough, but so could everyone else. The freedom of flying still provided a bit of a rush whenever he left the station's hangar or traveled in and out of Myrskaan's atmosphere, navigating the impossibly fast winds. Making the same trip every day dimmed a bit of the luster, however.

As his miner sped through the vacuum—not at top speed, but as fast as he could go without truly pushing the old craft—it, like all the other miners, had gone through various updates and overhauls over the years as the tech available to them improved, yet these craft were meant for hauling power rather than speed. Myrskaan Station came into view, growing larger with every passing klick.

Myrskaan Station, or just 'The Station," as most of its inhabitants referred to it, had originally been conceived as a test run for Mjatafa Mwonga as well as a gas mining station: a prime example of the Imaia's efficiency in everything, save bureaucracy. Large solar panels created a massive border around the ever-rotating gravity rings, which generated enough artificial gravity to keep everyone on their feet and strong enough to journey back to Efruumani with ease, if needed. The main dome-like structure faced the sun, while a long needle extended down toward Myrskaan. That was where they stored most of the gas, and where the engines lay for when they one day left orbit to follow after Mjatafa Mwonga.

The large cruiser tethered near the station's main hangar bay, however, was new.

Must've come up while I was out.

As Alajos neared the hangar bay, he flipped the necessary switches and dials to enable autopilot almost unconsciously, then shifted in his seat, leaning back a bit as the station's computers connected with *Hanuuko* and did the last bit of work for him, guiding the ship in. The song ended, switching to one that brought a smile to Alajos's lips. Natari music was recorded over that of the Samjati peoples in an intentionally disproportionate manner—just one more subtle and quite ingenious variety of Imaia propaganda—but Alajos had the necessary connections. That, combined with the audio player, let him listen to the music of his people whenever he pleased.

As he passed through the hangar's magnetic forcefield, Alajos raised an eyebrow at the number of people milling about and offloading supplies from transports that must have come from the cruiser. Some wore engineer's uniforms, but most were soldiers. Alajos frowned at that. Technically, he was part of the Imaia's naval research and supply arm, yet he had chosen this posting originally in part because of the low number of *actual* soldiers that lived on the station. He had to force himself to relax as *Hanuuko* finally came to a halt, locking into her station.

After taking a moment to collect himself and pocketing his audio player—Alajos didn't want to show any discomfort around the soldiers—he released the cockpit hatch and climbed out onto the wing. He unzipped his jumpsuit down to the waist, shrugging out of it and welcoming the cool, clean air—well, cooler and cleaner than the cockpit—before stretching muscles just on the verge of cramping from prolonged inactivity. Glancing around as he stretched, Alajos found himself surprised at how small the transport ships were in comparison to his miner. They were shiny and new and of a sleeker design, and had more room to move around, of course, as most of his ship's bulk went to storing the raw gas he collected. Still, the transports looked like toddlers compared to his own craft.

Once he was done stretching, Alajos climbed down from his miner and walked over to the rear to start unloading the large canisters. He hadn't even made it to the first one before some of the hangar workers joined him.

It was their job to unload all the miners and other ships that came in, but Alajos needed the hard labor after a day of what essentially amounted to sitting on his ass for six hours while he pressed various buttons. He was proud of his physique, and the labor helped keep him in shape, which both he and his wife, Karale, appreciated. He'd also learned that insisting on offloading his own ship rather than leaving it all to the hangar workers won their favor. Out of all the miner pilots, he had to buy his own drinks the least.

"What's the cruiser doing here, Obasa?" he asked, taking out his audio player and setting it on one of the low ledges. He turned up the volume a bit and altered the settings to play a Natari song. Though he was sure most would think nothing of it, Alajos did not want to play Samjati music where it might draw the wrong kind of attention to him.

The tall, dark-skinned Samjati woman shrugged, unfastening the locks on the first cylinder before moving onto the tubes that connected it to the main intake valve. "Some last-minute Exodus prep from what I can tell." She grinned at him, setting her cylinder down on the loading cart she and the others hard brought over. "You gonna just head off today? If not, get to work. The sooner we're done, the sooner your smelly ass can shower and clean that jumpsuit."

Alajos grunted, returning the grin and picking one of the fifty cylinders to offload as the others laughed.

"Anyway," Obasa continued, unfastening another cylinder, "looks like the *Awuusi'i*—the cruiser—and its crew are here to help us monitor Efruumani after everyone leaves on Mjatafa Mwonga. If our tests determine that it might be habitable again, they'll help us establish a base down there. If not, they're going to take all of us along after the city, towing the station and as much gas as we can carry."

Alajos nodded to himself as he set his cylinder down next to Obasa's and Kakrono's before moving onto the next one. That—the Imaia's activities after Exodus—was his true purpose on this station. He and his few companions were isolated, but they would do what they could.

"They bring anything besides the ship and all the soldiers?" he asked.

"A few georaurals they want us to test in zero-gravity, the vacuum and Myrskaan's atmosphere," Kakrono said, raking a gloved hand through his thick reddish mane. "A bunch of copies of the non-georaural tech we sent down to them, and a few new fighter and miner models." He grinned at Alajos, "Maybe you can find a way to test one of those fighters."

Alajos chuckled. "That'd be nice. I'm assuming they already sent some pilots along for that, though."

Njake, a light-orange skinned, striped Natari, shrugged. "Who knows, maybe you can convince them you'll offer a different perspective or some crap like that."

Alajos laughed at that.

"They also brought along a few more support personnel," Obasa added. "Some good-looking men and *very* good-looking women."

Alajos snorted. His wife had been one of those very good-looking men and women brought up as 'support personnel.' They all had actual jobs, but they were up here to provide new faces and companionship for those who remained unattached.

"I hope there'll still be enough room on the station and the cruiser by the time we figure out if we're leaving or going back down, " Alajos commented.

A few nods answered.

"They also brought along a couple of Redeemed," Njake added, thumbing over his shoulder. "Only seen those two so far, but I bet there are at least two more still on the cruiser."

Alajos stiffened as he followed the man's gesture across the hangar, taking only a moment to look at the two ornately armored figures up and down. His fists tightened, pulse quickening a bit despite his best efforts to keep calm. Those two had once been Samjati by their antlers, though their masks would keep Alajos from recognizing them.

"Doesn't really make sense to me," Kakrono said. "Don't they need Auroralight to survive?"

"Probably some volunteers for an experiment now that we're leaving Efruumani. I'd refrain from asking them about it," Obasa commented. "Hopefully they'll keep to themselves,"

The others—Alajos included—nodded in agreement. He'd always found the discomfort those up here regarded the Lightforged with strange, yet that regard could be a valuable tool, especially now that some of them were here. He just hoped the elites *did* keep to themselves so that they didn't become too familiar.

"That reminds me," Kakrono said, climbing up to release one of the higher tubes, "supposedly the Mestari and the Vizier have found a way to destroy the Army of the Night—or the 'Remnant,' as they apparently call themselves, now—for good."

"It's about time," Obasa said.

Alajos murmured something noncommittal in agreement, keeping his breathing steady and trying to force the sudden tension from his shoulders.

Destroy the Remnant for good?

Alajos no longer felt cool, but cold. As though spikes of ice had been rammed into his insides.

I need to warn the others. Or do they already know?

Gritting his teeth, Alajos continued with his work and tried his best to keep up the atmosphere of camaraderie. He and the others would do what they had come here for regardless, yet they needed to discuss what would happen should they be the last remaining members of the Army of the Night among the Imaia. As he worked, he found his eyes drawn more and more frequently to the Lightforged. They paid him no mind, yet a strange dread washed over Alajos.

Once he and the others finally finished unloading all the filled cylinders and refitting empty ones, he headed out of the hangar to wash off, then find Santer or one of the others, thinking of what excuses he could use to meet with them. He couldn't do anything out of the ordinary, yet as Alajos headed toward his quarters within the station, it was all he could do not to sprint away from those Lightforged and straight toward his compatriots.

Epilogue 3

Araana

Exodus countdown: 6 days, 38 hours, 14 minutes

As the hatch to the transport's main compartment opened, Araana glanced back over her shoulder, though she knew what she would see. Only one figure had waited atop the stone outcrop as she brought the transport down carefully onto the uneven ground.

Estingai glanced around the hold as she walked in, then met Araana's gaze. The commander's eyes were downcast and contemplative. She carried a small bundle aside from her own pack of supplies, but that was it.

Estingai nodded, and Araana closed the hatch. No words needed to be exchanged to relay their mutual failures.

Yet Araana couldn't bear that strained silence. "Were you waiting long?"

Estingai shrugged as she settled into her seat across from Obnjoka and Nainasa. They had failed, too.

"A while," she sighed, "but I had... things to think about."

Her tone said she didn't want to speak any more, and Araana reluctantly let her. Just a look at the woman told how much Estingai had on her mind.

Araana, Obnjoka, and Nainasa had all failed in recruiting the former champions of the army assigned to them by Kojatere. Araana had hoped Estingai would be the one of them that succeeded. Yet now that she knew their commander shared in their failure, Araana doubted if anyone else would succeed. She didn't think any less of Obnjoka, Nainasa, or any of the others, but Estingai was the best of them, the most determined.

How can any of us think to succeed where she failed?

Araana had tried telling herself that none of them had failed. The former champions had already made their decisions.

Still, there was a small part of her that kept insisting she would have succeeded if they'd had just one more day. Just one more day, and maybe they could have convinced these fallen, broken heroes to fight one last time.

Yet Araana knew that months would have made no difference.

"What's in the bundles?"

Araana blinked at the question. She twisted around to see Estingai looking at the small bundle strapped to the floor in the corner. Araana glanced at the bundle Estingai carried, then at the warrior herself. "Mementos. Looks like all of them had something they wanted us to carry on for them."

Taivetti had given Araana love letters of all things. Not her own, but ones passed down her family line. They would likely be useless in helping the army against the Imaia, yet Araana had been honest when telling Taivetti that she would guard the letters and their contents with her life. She'd read them in between attempts to try and convince the woman to come with her. Many had brought Araana to tears with the raw emotion and sad, yet beautiful story they told. She would do everything she could to make sure the love in those letters and the people that had written them were not forgotten.

As Estingai added her own bundle to the pile, securing it beneath the netting, her eyes took on a determined cast that startled Araana.

"Estingai?" she asked, "did you learn anything, at least?"

Estingai looked over at her, frowning. "Maybe." She walked into the cockpit to rest a hand on Araana's shoulder. "We hadn't planned for their assistance in our original plan. If we do fail, it won't be because of this. If the others succeed where we failed, then that will be wonderful, but for now, let's focus on picking them up so we can get back and prepare for our attack."

Araana swallowed, stunned at her commander's words, and even more so at the faint smile Estingai offered her before buckling into the seat next to her.

"Do you want to fly?" Araana asked.

Estingai hesitated a moment, then shook her head. "I need some time to think. Would you mind?"

Araana nearly gaped. She couldn't think of a single other occasion when Estingai had refused to pilot an aircraft of any kind.

"Of course not," she managed to stammer after a moment.

Araana collected herself and lifted the transport into the air. Before she headed off toward where Aindama would be waiting, she glanced back at Estingai, and found the commander's eyes closed, her posture seeming strangely relaxed. Was she meditating?

Whatever you found, Estingai, Araana thought, turning back to the view before her and moving the transport forward over the dark, rocky landscape, *I hope you can share some of it with us before we strike at the Imaia.*

Epilogue 4
Matsanga

Exodus countdown: 6 days, 23 hours, 8 minutes

Matsanga thought of Estingai as his legs carried him back toward his cave, Ajida padding along silently at his side. He rolled heavy shoulders, adjusting the string of hornhares hanging over them. Those, along with the sack of roots and tubers, should be enough food for a few days. For him at least.

Not for the first time, he tried to convince himself that Estingai and the Remnant truly would be better off without him. He hadn't been entirely truthful with her when telling her that he'd given up.

He did not believe he had much fight left in him—not enough to go out and seek combat, at least—yet he wanted to be ready should one come to him. Matsanga spent much of his time hunting, yet he spent almost as much conditioning himself, mainlining his physique and meditating on the powers he wielded. He knew he might simply die with Efruumani's last breath soon after the Imaia left. Yet he knew how useful the Imaia would find his skill, especially if they could manage to turn him into a Lightforged. He shivered at the thought.

If Efruumani took him with it, there was nothing Matsanga could do to stop it. He would accept the world's judgement. Yet if the Imaia came for him, he would be ready, and he would take as many as he could with him.

Why, then, would you not go with Estingai? Even if it is just to sacrifice yourself for the chance that she and some of her comrades may escape this broken world.

Matsanga sighed at the thought. Was it because that offered too much hope? For both himself and Estingai? Was it—

Ajida stopped beside him, nose up, testing the air, and Matsanga stiffened, looking up at the cave entrance just a few paces ahead. His blade lay in the cave. Even without that or his Auroramancy, he could put up a decent fight, yet—

Matsanga gave himself a shake, collecting his thoughts. He wasn't that out of touch, was he? Centering himself, Matsanga reached out with his mind, tuning into the music of this world, of the souls of the very stones that resided on it. He found a familiar melody and relaxed, stroking Ajida's furry head.

"C'mon," he grunted, continuing forward. "We've got a visitor."

But what in Efruumani's name is she doing here?

Once they reached the cave's outer chamber, Ajida darted through the narrow passage, tail wagging. Matsanga rolled his eyes, following after.

Nevisi, sitting by a low fire, laughing as Ajida licked at her face, looked exactly as Matsanga remembered. Thin, elegant antlers rose from her hairline, her long black hair shone in the moonlight. She'd stopped aging well before he had, so despite being centuries older than him, Nevisi barely looked thirty. Her silver eyes, sharp as ever, flickered to Matsanga as he walked in, appraising him immediately.

"Rumor has it you're dead," he said, dropping the pouch of roots and tubers near his other supplies. He glared at Ajida.

Really?

Matsanga's companion turned around at his question and shot him an overly-wolfish grin.

"There's a rumor mill all the way out here?" She asked with a smirk, straightening.

Matsanga grunted, retrieving the stands for his spit. "I guess I deserved that."

He set up the stands, then sat down across the fire from Nevisi, setting down the string of hornhares over crossed legs. "Though I could ask what you're doing all the way out here."

"I've been busy," she scratched behind Ajida's ear, sending her tail into a frenzy—Matsanga didn't understand why she kept the ruse up around Nevisi, "doing what needs to be done to win against the Enemy rather than simply against the Imaia. I've done what I can, but now I need your help."

Matsanga barked a bitter laugh, setting the last hornhare in a row on the stone floor with the others. "Did you and Estingai plan this? She comes to soften me up, then you come in for the kill?"

"Not exactly, though I'm a bit hurt you think of me in such predatory terms. I thought we were old friends."

Matsanga sighed, digging the point of his skinning knife into the hornhare's flesh, "We are."

Nevisi smiled. "Good. Anyway, Estingai knows I'm still alive, but not that I'm involved. I evaded the man she sent to try and recruit me, though he was very thorough in his search. I am the one that told them where to find you and the others, however, if indirectly."

"Why would you do that?" Matsanga growled, annoyed at Nevisi's smile and her revelation. "All you did was get their hopes up for no good reason. You know we're just a bunch of broken old souls."

Nevisi raised an eyebrow. "Don't blame me for your cowardice, Matsanga. What you and the others have chosen isn't merely a life of exile. It's a slow, agonizing method of suicide that allows you to punish yourselves every day until this world dies." The woman's voice was infuriatingly cool, almost perky, even. "You've merely convinced yourselves it's something else because you don't have to hold the knife that opens your veins."

"Is there really a difference when death is assured either way?" Matsanga grated, ignoring the insult and attempting to rein in his temper.

"You know you don't believe that," she said, expression showing neither reprimand nor judgement, just her customary amused serenity. "You're broken, Matsanga—you and all the rest. But it's not death or battle that you fear. It's the idea of a second chance, of putting yourself back together. The idea that you might get the chance to live on, that people might see you as heroes once more."

"You're wrong," Matsanga said, voice thick. He set the hornhare's pelt to the side, setting the freshly skinned carcass in a bowl, then moved onto the next one and cleared his throat. "Maybe you're right about the others, but not me."

He paused, fingers flexing around the knife handle and the hornhare, then set them down and met Nevisi's silver eyes. Darkness, but he hated how those eyes always seemed to read him and everyone else so easily.

Looking to Ajida, he arched an eyebrow.

You're not going to say anything?

She shrugged.

I will follow you, as always, but this is a conversation between you two.

Matsanga sighed.

"How would you feel," he said, holding her gaze, keeping a tight rein on his tone, "if you devoted your life to a cause, then found out that it was twisted into something monstrous, turning you into a monster by association? If you then took the opposing side, hoping to atone for all the terrible things you'd done, only to discover that this new cause was just as bad? What would you do, Nevisi? How would you reconcile that?"

A dangerous light entered Nevisi's eyes. "Do you truly believe Estingai and Koruuksi are monstrous? That they are even remotely similar to Skadaatha or any of the Imaia's fanatical elites? Do you believe that the Knights and the others you trained and mentored in the Union are no different from those you trained so long ago in the Imaia? As indoctrinated or fanatical as you yourself once were?"

"No," Matsanga forced out between gritted teeth. Why did she have to bring up that part of his past? "You know I meant Kweshrima, not them. Ynuukwidas and Skadaatha and their Imaia are cruel and calculating in what they do, but how is a goddess that simply decides to destroy an Aathal and the world itself any better? The Imaia has reasoning behind their actions at least, even if they have twisted them beyond recognition."

"And you assume Kweshrima had no reasoning for her actions?"

"None that she deemed good enough to share with any of us," Matsanga snapped.

Ajida grumbled at the outburst, and Matsanga frowned as Nevisi scratched his furry companion behind the ears. The thread of emotion he felt from Ajida—along with her pointed look—made him sigh and reign himself in.

Nevisi studied him for a while before she spoke again. "And what if she had a reason? What if what she did had to be done? As she saw it, at least. You know what power can do to a person."

Matsanga blinked. What was the woman getting at?

"I expected you, of all people, to see the bigger picture, as I did," she said, finally sighing and showing some real emotion. "We're not ascended, but close enough."

Matsanga frowned. "What does that have to do with anything?"

Nevisi narrowed her eyes, and Matsanga started.

"With the power like ours comes responsibility, Matsanga. I know you didn't ask for this—neither did I. I know Kweshrima did not ask for it either. The fight against the Enemy is bigger than our wants, bigger than hers or Ynuukwidas's, greater even than our struggle against the Imaia. At some point, you, the Remnant, and the Imaia all need to realize that. Skadaatha's way of going about things is twisted and too out of balance, but she's right that we are the only ones who know of the threat. The Imaia—what it has become—will be needed against the Enemy. I hope and pray that when the Imaia and the Enemy finally face each other that they will wipe each other from Aioa—if the Imaia has not changed by that point, at least—yet its existence and what spurred it to become what it has, is painfully necessary."

Matsanga stared at Nevisi, eyes wide. She was serious.

"If the Imaia is what's needed to fight the enemy, then why am I needed as well? You can't think I will rejoin the Imaia or that they would even accept me without turning me into one of their Lightforged."

"Don't be ridiculous," Nevisi said curtly. "While the Imaia is needed, so is the Army of the Night—not the Remnant, but the force they need to become once more. Both to fight the Enemy and prepare other worlds against both it and the Imaia. We can make sure what happened here does not happen to other worlds and peoples." Her eyes took on an unfamiliar intensity as they bored into him, tone dropping to a whisper barely audible over the fire's crackling. "If there is even the smallest chance for us to survive and escape this place, to warn other worlds of the Enemy and the Imaia and the threats they pose, then we need to take it. Then we can all deal with our own personal issues and seek some form of closure."

Nevisi stood suddenly, and Matsanga did so by reflex. Ajida rose to her feet, eyes darting back and forth between them, curious. She stepped closer, stopping mere inches from the fire. Its flickering light made her glowing eyes seem the molten rock that boiled beneath Efruumani's surface.

"I can give you one last chance, Matsanga," she said, "to strike at the Imaia, and to be more than a broken wretch that hides, waiting for death." She extended a hand over the flames. "Will you take it?"

Matsanga stared at that outstretched hand, then down at his own, half-raised. It trembled. He trembled. He looked to Ajida. His long-time companion met his gaze with fierce, knowing eyes, and nodded.

He looked back to Nevisi, meeting those intense, silver eyes, and rolled his shoulders.

THE END

Want more of this world? Get the Cozy Fantasy Novella FREE!

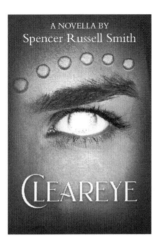

To sign up for my author newsletter and get your free copy of *Cleareye*, visit www.spencerrussellsmith.com/freenovella or Scan the QR code below!

Set over 1000 years before *Awakening the Lightforged*, *Cleareye* tells the story of Kaalev, a deaf musician with the power to enhance all his senses except one, as he searches for acceptance and meaning in his life.

THANK YOU SO MUCH! PLEASE KEEP READING!

After years of writing, rewriting, learning about story, creating fictional languages, worlds, and cultures, drawing maps, and more rewriting, *Awakening the Lightforged* is finally here. Your journey into Aioa has begun.

I can't properly express how much it means to me that you read this book. Without readers, stories cannot truly live. I can write all this out, wrap it in a beautiful package, and put it out into the world, but only when someone picks it up and starts reading, do these characters and this world come alive. Thank you so much for supporting me and making it possible for me and other writers like myself to practice this craft that we love so much.

If you're looking for more to read, I highly recommend picking up *The Last Knight* before you continue onto *The Shattering*, Book III of *Awakening the Lightforged*. Where *The Shattering* races to the end of our story, picking up immediately after the final epilogue, *The Last Knight* begins immediately after the prologue of *Throne of Darkness*, and gives a bit more insight into the Remnant, and Estingai, Koruuksi, and Uuchantuu specifically.

If you enjoyed this book, please consider rating and reviewing it on Amazon and/or talking about it on other platforms. It makes such a huge difference. Hundreds of thousands of authors fight for a place in your heart, in your eReader, or on your bookshelf every day. Leaving a review for an author you love is one of the single most powerful things you can do as a reader to help readers find their books, and authors find their readers. Reviews are what help our books stand out from the sea of millions of books that grows larger every day.

This is my passion. I am going to keep doing it until the day I die, and I want to be able to spend as much time as I possibly can writing and working on creating wonderful stories for you to read. I would love it if you could help make that dream a reality.

I solemnly promise to make sure that this is the worst book of mine you ever read, because I will never stop writing, learning and nerding out about prose and story, and improving my craft. The stories will only get better from here.

Spencer Russell Smith

The Shattering is now available!

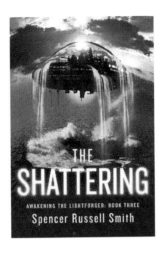

The first book of *Awakening the Lightforged* is now available on Amazon.
Koruuksi's fate is uncertain, Estingai has failed, and Othaashle just turned on her second after finding a dead Redeemed in her home. And all with a week left until the world's end! Will the Remnant pull everything together and escape their dying world? Or will the Imaia wipe them out once and for all?
Go to: https://amzn.to/3PRbcOk to read the series' thrilling conclusion!
She defeated a fallen goddess and recovered her stolen memories. But one mighty foe may still be her downfall...

ABOUT THE AUTHOR

Spencer Russell Smith is an author of Space Opera and Epic Fantasy. He also makes his own suits of armor, composes music, and dives deep into the rabitholes of history during his free time. He loves to create immersive, magical worlds, explore the theoretical relationship between magic and technology, balancing the massive scope of his genre with small, intimate moments that tug at the hearts of his readers.

He makes his online home at www.spencerrussellsmith.com. You can connect with Spencer on Facebook, Instagram, or Tiktok, find his music at https://soundcloud.com/spencersmithcomposer, and you should send him an email at mail@spencerrussellsmith.com if the mood strikes you!

facebook.com/spencerrussellsmithauthor
instagram.com/spencerrussellsmithauthor
tiktok.com/@spencersmithauthor

Acknowledgements

There are a lot of people who helped me on this journey, either directly or indirectly.

Kyle Fitzharris gave me a published author I could talk to, some realistic advice about the industry, and the motivation to get this done.

James Blatch, Mark Dawson, and the SPF Community provided me with a window into the indie author world, and gave me the confidence to publish these books myself rather than waiting for lightning to strike and grab a traditional deal.

Jonothan Oliver provided me with professional feedback and criticism of my novel, as well as some much-needed confidence and insight into the industry.

Stuart Bache and Felix Ortiz crafted the incredible cover for this book, making it feel more real.

I owe a lot to my mother and father and the rest of my friends and family for supporting me and believing me since I started this journey in high school.

Brandon Sanderson is a godsend for posting his lectures online, showing me Fantasy that breaks from tradition and encompasses incredible, expansive worlds, and reminding me to enjoy the journey rather than focusing on the destination.

Daniel Greene's YouTube channel provided invaluable knowledge and insight, and the man himself was an inspiration for having the courage to self-publish his own works.

I also owe a lot to Christopher Paolini for inspiring me and showing me the reality of a teenager who could be a published author.

My wonderful wife, Marissa Botticelli-Smith, put up with my constant ramblings and questions and gave me such detailed feedback on my book that I believe she is a large reason why Mr. Oliver found editing my work so enjoyable.

I have to thank my best friend Keshav Dasu for telling me to stop procrastinating and focus, for letting me call him up whenever to talk about story and magic and characters, for pushing me to have a better grasp on my craft, and for the incredible chapter header illustrations he provided.

Lastly, I owe more to J. R. R. Tolkien creating Middle Earth, and to Peter Jackson and his team for creating the films of the Lord of the Rings Trilogy, than they can ever imagine. Watching those films changed my life, and revealed to me exactly what I wanted to do with my life—something I have come to learn more and more is incredibly rare—at age twelve. I actually wrote my college essay on that subject.

Thank you all so much. Even though you may not know it, you helped this book come to life, and it means the world to me.

Notes on Pronunciation

This note is intended to clarify the pronunciation of names in the different languages of Efruumani.

Consonants

C: though not often used for names in this book, always has the value of *k*, never *s*
J: always has the value of *y* as in your, or yell
G: always has the sound of English *g* in get.
The apostrophe marks a glottal stop, which can be pronounced like an English double-consonant:
n'n for example, would be pronounced as the *nn* in *unnamed*, as opposed to *unaimed*.

Vowels

A: always has the value of *a* in *mark* or *kart*
AA: always has the value of *a* in *cake* or *tame*
AI: always has the value of *y* in *sky* or of *i* in *kite*
E: always has the value of *e* in *let* or *ten*
I: always has the value of e in *free* or *preen*
Y: always has the value of *i* in *kick* or *bid*
O: always has the value of *o* as in *okay* or *omen*
UU: always has the value of the *oo* or *ew* sounds as in *pool* or *stew*

INTRODUCTION TO AIKWE ARNA'S HISTORY OF THE BUUEKWENANI

Introduction to Aikwe Arna's History of the Buuekwenani

Though culturally, our people were of the Nambaatuu, being ruled by the Atonga made no difference. When Ezanga defeated Ketshande in the duel and our lands were suddenly under their yoke, others fled, but we stayed and welcomed the tax man. We were allowed to continue worshiping Oshuunta as long as we made the proper offerings to Anyawuu and acknowledged him as a powerful deity. Our Auroramancers, however, we kept secret from the budding empire, sending only those who wished to see new lands and serve as offerings to make the Atonga believe Auroramancers uncommon among us, and so consider us unimportant.

Because we kept our Auroramancers hidden and trained them differently than the monks of Atonga, we knew of the danger of Tombara long before anyone else. We prepared our ships, and our families and tried to warn our neighbors. Some listened. Others accused us of heresy and went to the Atonga. That was the first time we had to fight and defend ourselves. If the mountain's eruption had not covered our flight to the sea, our people likely would have been captured and persecuted for hiding our Auroramancers and worshipping the god that saved us, rather than those that destroyed their worshipers.

∽

The seas were hostile in the days following the mountain's eruption. Massive waves buried groups of ships beneath the waves, and dark clouds blotted out the sky, hiding the auroras. Every one of our people became lightless, and for a while, all hope seemed lost. When we found land, however, though the sky had not cleared and the seas were still troubled, our people flourished in an untouched paradise. When the auroras returned, we celebrated for an entire week. From then on, Auroradays became holy. Times for celebration and hope for the future, and remembrance of the past and pain of lightlessness.

∽

It was not to last, however, as others fled in the aftermath of Tombara's eruption and the devastation left in its wake. They came looking for succor, and some were grateful when we gave it. Others were jealous and angry of our prosperity in the wake of the dark times. Some were simply covetous and driven by greed. Once again, our Auroramancers were driven to violence. Our people were safe, but our peaceful way of life was disrupted, and our people lived in fear for the first time in memory.

∽

When the Iron Empire came and offered protection in exchange for wood from our forests, iron from our mountains, and a shipyard in one of our sheltered bays, our people rejoiced. We wanted nothing more than to resume lives of peace, living off the sea and the coast, with our Auroramancers serving their people instead of giving their lives to protect them. The Empire was so impressed by our Auroramancers, they allowed them to do as they wished, and ask only that our Auroramancers teach their own.

Our joy did not last. We had exchanged a handful of hyenas nipping at our haunches for an Iron Draakon that loomed over us. Game became scarce as the forests were turned into ships. Fish fled as the increasing ships in the bay disrupted their patterns. The iron mines led to sickness for anyone who ventured too close, attracted rough, foreign workers, and stole many of our own people. In time, even our Auroramancers were drafted into the Iron Empire's service. They had trained their own oppressors. When currency came and enslaved our people it bore the hammer of the Iron Empire on one side, and the sun of Atonga on the other.

Yet our gods of sea and storm had not abandoned us. When it seemed as though our people might fade into obscurity, lost to history, a savior emerged wielding the hammer and flame of a blacksmith of the Empire. In secret, he armed our people and secured ships for flight. He was betrayed by an unknown ally, yet he led us from bondage, and dealt a great blow to the Empire with the theft of their ships.

Some wanted to let the sea guide us, as it had given us our salvation. Others wanted to travel as far from the Empire as possible, even suggesting the supposed sunless lands, where Auroras alone lit the skies.

∼

Before we could make a decision, an Iron Fleet found us. Though our people had made these ships with their own hands and knew them well, we were too heavily laden to outrun the warships, and we had few weapons or warriors, while they had the Iron Marines. Then came the storm.

∼

At first, we thought it a sign of wrath and disapproval. Though the storm smashed the Iron ships and bore us far from them, it had also taken half our people with it—the blacksmith among them—and left us drifting for days.

∼

Then an unsettled coast came in sight, thick with forests at the foot of great mountains that climbed toward the clouds. Some believed we should settle the coast. Others wished to return to the seas and search for those lost in the storm. In the end, we decided to venture inland toward the mountains and hide from the Empire, should they come searching again. There, we found a pass through the mountains and the paradise within. Upon seeing it, all agreed that this would be our new home. Our Sanctuary.

∼

We burned a single ship as an offering to sea and storm for leading us to this place, and as a farewell to the lives we had once known, and those we had lost. The rest, we took apart and carried into the mountains to build our new homes. Though things were peaceful at first, as all groups do, we found grievances to bicker about and came to disagreements about how to live our new lives in secrecy without fear, and comfort without excess. The struggle nearly broke us, but what emerged were the Buuekwenani.

As we settled into our new home, we found a strange, silvery metal that those of us familiar with metalwork could not identify. Some had heard myths of a silvery metal that came from the sky, yet in our valley it was as plentiful as fish on a reef. We discovered its strength and its ability to disrupt Auroramancy, and used it in many things from construction, to jewelry, to armoring our warriors. Though even our own people had trouble finding the pass if they ventured outside our borders, we had learned to be prepared. After a generation spent in this new home, we learned of another gift of this new sanctuary: every child born within the Vale became an Auroramancer.

Despite this, as our people grew, some wished to expand our borders. Longing for the sea, we built settlements on the coast where our people could live as we once did and bring back fish to feast upon. When they did, we realized that many of our children had never tasted the sea's bounty before that, and our conviction to keep a strand of the coast for ourselves grew.

As we had feared, outsiders soon found that settlement, and attacked. The ships that came did not bear the Iron Hammer, yet we could not risk word of our people's location spreading. Our warriors fought off the attackers, yet we knew more would come searching. A brave group of volunteers feigned flight when the invaders came again, vowing to never return to our sanctuary. They protected not only our safety, but that which we hid from the world: the gift we had discovered at the Heart of the Vale of E Kwekuue.

We never learned what became of them, but after that we withdrew into the mountains. Only our Akjemasai warriors ever ventured out into the forests beyond, keeping watch for any who grew too curious, and ensuring none ever found the pass. For a time, our people lived in peace and isolation, and likely would have forgotten about the world beyond our mountain walls if not for our time of remembrance every Auroraday.

Until one day when our Akjemasai encountered a party from a neighboring peoples, and instead of frightening them away or killing them all, they let one live: a young woman one of the Akjemasai judged deserving of mercy, and brought back into the city. The young woman and the Akjemasai who brought her to E Kwekuue survived only because the latter was the daughter of our king, and loved by many.

Though both were almost executed anyway, Princess Ymbandi used her influence with her father and the Buuekwenani to sway opinion and judgement in her favor. Princess Ymbandi worked with the foreigner, Taatuube Rabesala, an influential woman among her own people, the Uumgwefili, to reach an accord between our two people. The Uumgwefili would keep our secret and help protect our interests in addition to supplying us with information of the outside world. All in exchange for aluminum and sanctuary, should they ever need it.

Despite some initial back and forth, the arrangement resulted in prosperity for both peoples. The Uumgwefili helped create the illusion that the mountains and forest surrounding E Kwekuue were undesirable land and hid the caravans that flowed between the two people, running everything out of their nearby city, Uumgwefilo. Taatuube's family ensured that the rulers of that city saw guarding E Kwekuue's secret as a near-holy cause, and made sure everyone privileged to such information understood that the relationship with E Kwekuue was Uumgwefilo's lifeblood.

Eventually, however, problems arose. There were initial border disputes between nearby farmers and wanderers with the Akjemasai, but those were the least of our worries. With finite space and resources, the Buuekwenani had adapted to a very specific way of life. The influx of new ideas, luxuries, and materials not just from Uumgwefilo, but every people our allies came in contact with, challenged that way of life.

At first, E Kwekuue's leaders saw this connection to the rest of the world as a good thing that required needed accommodation. Despite how the Imaia and Iron Empire had preyed on their ancestors, they understood that much of the strength of those Empires came from their diversity of peoples and ideas. They soon came to realize, however, that too many people with too many different opinions meant no one would agree on anything, halting any meaningful progress in its tracks. This made tensions rise, and nearly led to E Kwekuue's demise.

Just when it seemed the Buuekwenani would become like every other people and abandon the unique way of life that had sustained and protected them for so long, they banded together and demanded that the leadership find a way to make things right again without losing what they had gained from Uumgwefilo and the window they provided into the outside world.

It took time and many failures, but eventually the king and the Diwani, E Kwekuue's new leading officials, found a way to integrate new technology and foreign ideas into their culture. It was a stricter, more harsh way of life than the Buuekwenani had grown used to since the accord with Uumgwefilo, but it worked. A part of this was the establishment of the Muukjebarat: those who would leave E Kwekuue to see the world and bring back new ideas for the Diwani to judge worthy of incorporation into society, and decide the best way to do so.

For hundreds of years, this way of life sustained the Buuekwenani and Uumgwefilo, their sister city. Both lived in peace and prosperity despite the conflict that enveloped the rest of the world and the different powers that laid claim to Uumgwefilo. Until the ships arrived bearing the standard of the Scarlet Sun.

At first, Uumgwefilo fought them off. As the years passed, it seemed as though this Imaia would not return. The Muukjebarat brought back disturbing information, however. Tales of the Imaia's expansion and meddling throughout the world, and rumors. Some called the Imaia the conqueror of the Iron Empire. Others, it's successor.

When the Imaia came once more, for the first time in their long partnership, Uumgwefilo asked E Kwekuue for help: troops to fight and protect both their people. With the information the Muukjebarat had brought back to E Kwekuue, the Akjemasai and many other Buuekwenani volunteered, eager to repay Uumgwefilo for connecting them to the outside world and keeping their secret all these years. They named themselves Ymbandi's Legion, and all reports told of their fierce defiance of the Imaia in battle. For though E Kwekuue had known peace for almost its entire history, powerful, skilled Auroramancers made up almost its entire population: something no other nation could boast.

When Ymbandi's Legion returned, E Kwekuue knew grief for the first time in centuries, and all the Buuekwenani mourned those who had given their lives in defense of their city. Uumgwefilo erected a monument of aluminum in thanks, unmarked save for the word "Ymbandi".

With so many returning after years spent in the outside world—some with husbands and wives who had known nothing of E Kwekuue until stepping foot on its soil, the Buuekwenani way of life was challenged once more.

Scholars and philosophers will debate whether we overcame that challenge, failed, or simply adapted as was necessary in the following years.

E Kwekuue became more insular, cutting down contact with Uumgwefilo and recalling most of their Muukjebarat for fear of capture and torture by the Imaia. They still honored Uumgwefilo, and both peoples helped the other prepare in case of an attack by the Imaia.

∾

E Kwekuue's offer of sanctuary remained open, and the Buuekwenani gave Uumgwefilo instruction for what their people would need to give up should that day come.

∾

After a few decades, Uumgwefilo called for aid once more, and E Kwekuue answered.

∾

This time, the fighting dragged on far longer.

∾

The people of E Kwekuue had never felt more alone.

∾

When Uumgwefilo fell to the Imaia, the Buuekwenani took in as many as they could, but the Vale grew rife with fear and panic as the fighting raged on outside E Kwekuue and both peoples mourned and feared discovery.

∾

Trade with the outside world through Uumgwefilo slowed to a trickle, and though the people of E Kwekuue felt safe within their secret borders and the unique protection they offered, their insular way of life gained a claustrophobic element.

It was not long after Uumgwefilo's fall before Queen Asante left to fight with the majority of E Kwekuue's remaining battle-trained Auroramancers. Few of the warriors they had sent years ago had returned, and she sought not only to aid in the fight against the Imaia, but to find all the Buuekwenani and Uumgwefili warriors she could and bring them home.

When Queen Asante's contingent returned, she was not among them.

The survivors brought word of war raging across the entire world and the devastation left in its wake. Their fantastical tales of the foreign, mysterious Darkside were tempered by their descriptions of the destruction there, and of the friends and family lost.

If Queen Asante's loss hadn't been enough to force King Kuula'ande's hand, when the survivors told him of how the gods took sides, and that one of them had destroyed Yrmuunthal, a sacred World Tree, causing a cataclysm that had effected every corner of Efruumani except E Kwekuue, he decreed that the Buuekwenani would close themselves off from the world entirely. No one objected, and only the Akjemasai were allowed beyond the pass. They would keep watch, and eliminate anyone who came looking for our sanctuary and the secrets it holds.

THE FIDDLER IN THE NIGHT

Modern Lyrics

High in halls of ice that hang among the stars,
Kept aloft by dancing lights.
Memories arise of ages long past.
When the fiddler plays to the night.

She plays for her friends, for family and love,
For the ancient days of her youth
For those gone so long that without the dancing lights
Their names would have vanished, too

But in song, their memories live on.
In her songs, their souls dance again,
When the Fiddler plays to the night,
Their souls shine bright again.

She plays when the storms howl and shriek,
And when the moon shines bright on high.
From the frozen coasts, to the high mountain peaks,

Her songs raise spirits and bring a tear to the eye.

And in song, their memories live on.
In her songs, their souls dance again,
When the Fiddler plays to the night,
Their souls shine bright again.

And in song, their memories live on.
In her songs, their souls dance again,
When the Fiddler plays to the night,
Their souls shine bright once again.

High in halls of ice that hang among the stars,
Kept aloft by dancing lights.
Memories arise of ages long past.
When the fiddler plays to the night."

∼

Ancient Lyrics

Under the light of Myrskaan and star and moon
When the fiddler's songs fill the night
The dancing lights travel o'er icy dune
Grant us life, and let us shine bright.

She plays for her friends, for family and love,
For the ancient days of her youth
For those gone so long that without the dancing lights
Their names would have vanished, too

But in song, their memories live on.
In her songs, their souls dance again,
When the Fiddler plays to the night,
Their souls shine bright again.

She plays when the moon shines high in the sky,
And when stormclouds gather like a shroud
From the frozen coasts, to the top of the world,
Her songs raise spirits and warmth.

And in song, their memories live on.
In her songs, their souls dance again,
When the Fiddler plays to the night,
Their souls shine bright again.

And in song, their memories live on.
In her songs, their souls dance again,
When the Fiddler plays to the night,
Their souls shine bright again.

Under the light of Myrskaan and star and moon
When the fiddler's songs fill the night
The dancing lights travel o'er icy dune
Grant us life, and let us shine bright.

CONTINUE READING FOR AN EXCLUSIVE LOOK AT "THE LAST KNIGHT"

1

THE LAST DAY

Exodus countdown: 6 days, 2 hours, 13 minutes

It took every shred of her deteriorating will for Kojatere not to sprint through Mjatafa Mwonga's inner ring. That would be far too conspicuous considering what she'd just done, and whoever had framed her.

All that work with the Lightforged and nothing to show for it!

She'd had one more idea, but no time left to look into it.

Her right hand twitched as she headed toward the nearest railway stop. Once she boarded the public transport, she could ride it out of the populated areas, then use Auroramancy to propel her toward the outer ring and the hangar that held the ships she'd prepared for the Remnant's escape.

They're all supplied and ready, the last prisoner transfer should go through later today. I just need to wait until then.

Once the last of the prisoners were on the cruisers, she could take out the Lightforged stationed aboard, then blow the explosives she'd planted to cover her escape. She would signal the Remnant to come get the other two cruisers if they needed them. They could use the transport ships on the cruiser to go get Koruuksi and Estingai and their respective teams if they hadn't completed their missions yet, though they were supposed to return today.

An errant thought broke Kojatere's focus. She wondered if E Kwekuue really did exist; if Koruuksi had found any people or an Aathal there, as she suspected was the case. That led her mind to Boaathal and the potential method of saving the Lightforged she was leaving behind. That brought back the image of Itese, unconscious and wounded, and the husk of the other Lightforged someone had planted in her quarters.

Kojatere took a deep breath at that, trying to steady herself and not startle anyone around her more than her appearance already did.

She'd shed her iconic armor, cloaking herself in typical Samjati clothing along with a mask to hide the majority of her Lightforged features. Yet she could not keep herself from tensing whenever she passed a person in uniform. It didn't help that the clothing made her sweat profusely. Her violetnodes alleviated some of the day's heat, but they did nothing to distract the way her sweat soaked her clothing and made it cling to her skin. The hairs at the nape of her neck prickled. She swore she could feel the gazes of any who looked at her. Hopefully, no one would notice the color or lack of grain of her antlers.

Just get out of the main city and you'll be fine.

It didn't work.

Auroras! Who had left that husk there? *How* had they drained that Lightforged of its investment in the first place?

Kojatere tried to focus on that rather than what she'd done to Itese.

I hope I didn't kill her.

The woman should still be alive. Kojatere had knocked her out and used Ilkwalerva to drain enough of the woman's investment that she wouldn't be chasing after her any time soon. The guilt still sat like a lump of lead in her stomach.

Does freedom for the Remnant justify what I did?

She hadn't merely struck Itese. Not in the other woman's eyes, at least. No. Itese would believe Kojatere—or Othaashle, rather—had betrayed her and the rest of the Lightforged. Their family.

Kojatere gritted her teeth, trying to shake those thoughts from her head. All of the Lightforged—Itese included—were the Imaia's most feared weapons. She shouldn't feel bad about harming one to save her children and the rest of the Remnant. Should she?

They're the enemy...but what if they're also like me—not given a choice in the matter?

Kojatere knew that some of the Lightforged had been made from Imaia Auroramancers on the cusp of death, giving them another chance to fight for their nation. Others, however, had been like her— killed in battle, their souls kept from passing through the Gates of Dearth by the power of Ilkwalerva and Ynuukwidas. They were given no choice in their service to the Imaia.

Kojatere's own memory of how she'd been taken...

She shivered, then tensed, fearing another vision. Those hadn't stopped with Kweshrima's sacrifice and the subsequent flood of knowledge. Some of what the goddess had shown her had faded from memory almost immediately or blurred, slipping out of her thoughts every time she tried to focus on it. Over the past two weeks, many of those memories had sharpened. Memories of both Othaashle and Kojatere had hit her the same way they had before, incapacitating her. She'd been able to play that off to Yndlova and Itese when they had asked—both the incapacitation and the emotional trauma the memories returned to her—yet if she had one here, now...

Kojatere swallowed, heart beating faster, louder. For a moment she panicked, scanning the moving crowd around her for anyone with clearnodes, afraid they would be able to hear how loud her pulse roared and know that something was off.

But I'm Othaashle, their Champion. If anyone notices, I can just tell them they need to keep quiet and act normal—for the safety of the Imaia.

She took a deep breath, calming somewhat.

Yes, she was Othaashle—their Champion, their hero—no one would look at her in suspicion. Othaashle knew of only one person who would, and she suspected that was the same person that had somehow drained and killed a Redeemed and left her in Othaashle's quarters to frame her. But how—

No! I'm Kojatere. Kojatere, hero. Not Othaashle. Othaashle is a monster.

Kojatere shuddered. The balance between her two selves was getting worse. It wasn't as though she had another person inhabiting her mind, but Othaashle's impulses and way of thinking—the compulsions Ynuukwidas had programmed into her mind when he denied her death and twisted her into a weapon—were strong whenever they arose. It was getting harder to tell if the impulses were her own or Othaashle's. Balancing them had been hard enough before she'd started receiving memories from her early days as Othaashle.

Even now, that part of her considered Itese a friend, and rebelled at what Kojatere had done. Yet she knew that Itese had done terrible things in the name of the Imaia.

So did I.

No. No! She hadn't. That had been Othaashle. Not Kojatere—not *her*.

With a grunt as the railway station came in sight, a small crowd waiting to board, Kojatere forced her mind to focus on the task at hand. She flexed her hands open and closed beneath her large sleeves, hoping no one noticed. It helped, if only a little.

Kojatere had the detonators with her just in case. She didn't want to start things off earlier than planned, but she might have no other choice if Skadaatha was truly behind that body. No doubt she'd found Itese by now.

When Kojatere reached the rail stop, she looked both ways down the track. She spotted the train, but it was far—at least three stops away. About seven minutes depending on the operator's promptness and how many people waited to get on and off at each stop.

Returning her attention to the crowd around her, she saw a few people glance at her, but none stared or tried to make conversation. That should have relaxed her.

It didn't.

Keeping her breathing and heart rate under control grew more and more difficult with every passing minute it took the train to approach.

Kojatere scanned her surroundings, trying not to be too conspicuous, then froze when she noticed a familiar face across the street. It took her a moment to remember the face.

Natsoje. The woman I told Bykome would assist with the prisoner transfers to the hangars.

What was she doing here? The woman seemed to be looking for something or someone. When her gaze passed over Kojatere, Kojatere flexed her hand open, reflexively trying to summon Ilkwalerva, before she remembered that she was in disguise and that summoning the monstrous blade in the middle of a small crowd would definitely give her away.

Still, something felt off. Natsoje hadn't noticed her, but—

"Commander Othaashle!"

Kojatere jumped at the voice, both sides of her immediately on edge, hand opening and summoning Ilkwalerva. She stopped it, though for once, she was thankful for Othaashle's instincts—neither part of her had ever liked or trusted Skadaatha.

She could have tried to hide, but Kojatere suspected it would do no good. With the knowledge she'd received from Kweshrima—most of which she still didn't fully comprehend—she suspected Skadaatha had located her with a method that would see right through her disguise.

As those around her looked around—either toward Skadaatha or for their hero whose name she'd called—Othaashle turned toward Skadaatha. The brown-and-grey-skinned woman strode toward the rail stop, fully armored, long white braid hanging over her shoulder. A weapon not unlike the one she'd used against Kojatere in the Remnant base, hung at her side.

The Vizier had come after Kojatere less than three weeks ago, yet it felt like ages.

The hiss of released air and the loud hum of the railcars signaled that the transport had finally arrived at the stop behind her. Those around her rushed into the car, and few rushed out past Kojatere. She considered jumping in for just a moment, trying to blend in, but Skadaatha would know, and the railway—while better than walking—couldn't outrun Skadaatha or the powers she wielded.

Instead, Kojatere shed her Samjati hood and cloak, leaving her in plain white, yet functional clothing, and stepped forward to face Skadaatha.

The Vizier wasted no time.

"One of the Redeemed has gone missing, Supreme Commander," Skadaatha said, hand dropping to the weapon at her side as she closed the distance between them, stopping only a few paces away. "As have some very dangerous prisoners, from a site few are allowed to even know of."

Kojatere resisted Othaashle's—and her own—impulse to summon Ilkwalerva and strike Skadaatha. As much as she would have liked to do so, she needed to get to the hangar and signal the Remnant. Fighting Skadaatha would do no good.

"I will look into it, Vizier," Kojatere said, assuming Othaashle's mannerisms and tone. "Though I fail to see why you thought it necessary to air such sensitive information in the middle of the street."

Skadaatha laughed, and Kojatere gritted her teeth. She lowered a hand to her side. Not to summon Ilkwalerva. Making it to the hangar might not be an option anymore, but she still had one way to signal the Remnant from here.

If they're watching the city.

"Oh, it is quite necessary, Commander," Skadaatha said, fingers closing around the weapon at her side. "The people of the Imaia deserve to know of a secret prison maintained by their supposed 'hero.' They also deserve to know that the missing Redeemed was last seen visiting your apartments. He hasn't been seen since."

Kojatere narrowed her eyes, stepping closer, lowering her voice. "Does this Redeemed have a name, Skadaatha? Did you bother to learn it before you killed him and left him in my apartment to frame me?"

Skadaatha tensed for a moment. Then she flicked the fingers of her free hand, and Kojatere tensed.

A loose crowd had gathered around them on the street. Kojatere had been too focused on Skadaatha before. She hadn't noticed the woman's elites creeping through the crowd.

They're respected heroes of the Imaia in their own right.

Normally, Kojatere's word would win out if it was just her and Skadaatha, but with her elites...

"You can come quietly," Skadaatha said, lowering her voice.

Kojatere snorted. "You're joking."

Skadaatha shrugged. "It would have been easier that way."

The Vizier raised her voice again, then pointed into the crowd.

Kojatere followed her gesture and blinked. *Natsoje.*

"Lieutenant Natsoje," Skadaatha said, "as a member of the Mjatafa Mwonga Urban Corp., I ask for your assistance in arresting the traitor Othaashle Mestari for crimes against the Imaia. She has abused her power and station as Champion and Supreme Commander of the Imaia to round up undesirables and turn them into her own personal army of Redeemed. When one of the Redeemed discovered this plot and decided to be a patriot and attempt to turn her in, she murdered him."

Kojatere sighed. "Clever, Skadaatha. Very clever."

She slipped her hand into her pocket and grasped the detonator, placing her thumb on the plunger even as she primed her violet and opalnodes, using some of the knowledge Kweshrima had given her that she could comprehend.

I really hope I don't have another vision any time soon. Please be watching.

Kojatere pressed down on the plunger.

Everyone around her crouched or dropped to the ground as the city shook around them.

Even as explosions erupted from the guard towers, from the hangars and shipyards in the military-industrial district just outside the inner city, from cleared tenements and storage houses nearby, Kojatere flared her violet and opalnodes.

Ilkwalerva coalesced from motes and mist into her hand, and through it, pulling on the extra power it granted her, and the well of power she'd taken from the Throne, Kojatere sent a massive bolt of lightning into the sky. It spread, forking out and crackling as it flashed over the sky, creating a miniature electrical storm that would be seen from all over the Mjatafa Mwonga. And hopefully, beyond.

Efruumani's final day had come.

2

MOVE OUT

Exodus countdown: 6 days, 2 hours, 30 minutes

Despite herself, Estingai hesitated as the transport's doors hissed open before her. It was only for a moment, but it was still a sign of the weakness within her. She couldn't afford that. Not a thread of it. Not anymore.

Her team had failed. *She* had failed. Through no fault of their own, of course, but that didn't matter. What mattered was they had been unable to retrieve the help they so desperately needed.

Estingai needed to be strong, so she did not allow herself to linger or paused as she strode off the transport into Remnant Base's main hangar. She headed straight for the command station. Once she had an assessment of how things had gone here, of how Koruuksi had done with his mission, she could cement a plan of action.

Two plans. One ideal, one in case Kojatere betrays us.

As Estingai glanced around the hangar, she noticed an incredible number of fighters and other transports. That made her smile, a shiver running down her spine.

It's happening. It's actually, finally happening.

And they had a chance this time. A slim one, yes, but still a chance.

Estingai looked from the ships to the faces of those running between them or tuning them up. The confusion on their faces when they glanced toward Estingai and her team made Estingai stop, jaw tight, fists clenched.

She whirled around and found Araana and the rest of her team trudging behind her. It took them a few seconds to realize she'd stopped, but when they did, each of them stood straight and saluted Estingai, giving her their attention.

They need this.

So do you.

So did everyone in the hangar.

Estingai raised her voice just a bit louder than necessary, knowing the rock walls of the hangar would carry her words to those who needed to hear it.

"We failed."

A few members of her team, including Araana, flinched as if struck.

"It doesn't matter."

They blinked at that.

"We did what we could," Estingai continued. "This was not the sort of mission we are used to. We find and eliminate targets. We stay hidden. We steal what we need to survive. We avoid surveillance. In those situations, we can do much to control our success. That was not the case with what we just attempted.

"We were sent to save broken souls whose help would have been an incredible boon to us. Yet they did not want to be saved. Some people are simply broken beyond repair. Even Knights."

Estingai paused, stepping toward them.

"But not you. Not *us*. We are strong. We've decided to fight despite everything that's been thrown at us. We've been broken, but we still choose to fight."

Araana and the others met Estingai's gaze. She saw more resolve in their eyes this time, and she nodded, allowing herself a tight smile.

"Their help would have made things a whole lot easier on us," she said, "but that isn't how we do things, is it?"

They shook their heads.

"No, it isn't," Araana said.

Estingai nodded. "Everything here looks orderly, but I want to make sure we're ready when the time comes."

She scanned the hangar again. From what she could tell, they had more than enough supplies to last them for a while once they left, and again, seeing so many fighters and ships assembled sent shivers down her spine. Her fingers twitched, itching for controls to close around as she soared through the sky.

Later.

When her eyes passed over a familiar ship, Estingai looked to Araana. She put her hand on the woman's shoulder. "Can you go find Koruuksi for me? Tell him to meet me in the command room. We need to know what he found."

Araana nodded, looking encouraged.

"Then," Estingai said, "take everything we were given and make sure it is somewhere safe. It's the least we can do."

Araana gave her a tight smile. "Thank you, Estingai."

As Estingai walked out of the hangar and through the base's winding halls and tunnels, her step quickened at just how many people she passed, all with a sense of purpose. When she neared one of the main chambers, she glimpsed a few unfamiliar Natari in strange armor. The sudden burst of color in these otherwise dark, earth-toned halls nearly made Estingai stop. Instead, she continued on, encouraged.

At least Koruuksi succeeded.

She knew that the average soldier—even one of a mythical city like E Kwekuue—likely didn't measure up to Matsanga or the others her team had searched for. Yet all seven of that group had been warriors. She imagined Koruuksi had found far more than just that handful.

When Estingai reached the command room, mechanical doors hissing open to admit her, she found Uuldina, Paiz, Miek'ka, and Marjatla gathered in quiet discussion. They looked up at the hiss and their expressions lifted. Estingai had to conceal a frown at that, knowing she would disappoint them.

"Estingai," Uuldina said. "Did you succeed in your mission?"

Sighing, Estingai shook her head, forcing herself not to look away as their expressions fell.

"My team and I failed, unfortunately," she admitted. "Matsanga and the other Knights have no fight left in them, so we will need to do without their help."

The four nodded gravely.

"That is...unfortunate," Paiz said.

"Do we have any updates from Kojatere?" Estingai asked. "Everything in the hangar looks in order. I assume everyone is here?"

Marjatla nodded. "We have consolidated personnel, supplies and equipment from all bases to Remnant base. Everyone and everything is ready to go once we get the signal from Kojatere. At the moment, we have most either triple-checking weapons and equipment or running drills to streamline our evacuation. We haven't had any update from Kojatere yet, but she told us to be ready tomorrow at the earliest."

Estingai sighed. She'd hoped for at least a status update from the woman—something she could analyze for any sign or threat or duplicity.

She was about to ask for more specifics when the doors hissed behind her. Araana entered the room with Muuzuuri and one of the colorfully dressed Natari soldiers she'd seen earlier. The man's deep red skin, shining silver armor and white underclothing would have been enough to catch the eye by themselves, but the colorful adornments of feathers and tightly wound cloth on the spear the man held, as well as the hem of his clothing and edges of his armor, nearly made him an eyesore.

Ilona and Araana's grave expressions set Estingai on edge.

"What happened?" she demanded, voice low, but firm. "Where is Koruuksi? Where is Uuchantuu?"

Muuzuuri hesitated, sharing a look with Araana.

"He stayed behind," she said. "After we failed. Both of them did."

Estingai clenched her fists, a growl rising in her throat. "Explain."

"It wasn't just a group of refugees surviving in ruins, Estingai," Muuzuuri began.

"I can see that," Estingai said, gesturing toward the warrior.

Muuzuuri blushed, cheeks turning violet. "Yes, well—there is an entire city we need to save. Koruuksi angered their king, unfortunately, and couldn't convince him or their ruling council to flee the city or send a large force with us, so Dembana and seventeen more of the guard came with us in secret with the help of their princess."

Estingai blinked, trying to get her emotions under control as she digested Muuzuuri's information.

It didn't work.

"You. Left. Them. Behind," she hissed, taking a step toward them. "My brother. My sister. You left them behind to try and salvage a hopeless cause, and brought only eighteen warriors to help?"

She drew in a deep breath, and shook as she let it out.

"Araana, prepare a team to go rescue Uuchantuu and my idiot brother. I will be going to handle this personally."

The woman nodded and practically sprinted out of the room.

Estingai met the gaze of the Natari. That she had to look up to do so only fueled her anger.

"What kind of king doesn't accept help offered when the world is ending? Are you people blind?"

The warrior's eyes narrowed, full lips somehow drawing to a thin line. Estingai clenched her fists. They shook as she restrained herself from breaking the man's jaw.

A loud, blaring alarm cut through whatever either of them had been about to say.

Estingai whirled toward the generals, then the displays.

"What is happening?" she asked as Meik'ka rushed to one of the aids monitoring those displays.

Meik'ka's eyes went wide as she looked back toward Estingai.

"Well?"

"It's Mjatafa Mwonga," the woman breathed. "Our remaining spies broke comm silence. They are reporting multiple explosions within the city, plus a sudden lightning storm near the center. Our scouts and relays near the coast are reporting the same."

"That must be the signal," Paiz said.

All of them looked to Estingai. Somehow, everything went quiet despite the alarms. The hair on her arms stood on end.

They're all looking to me.

It was too early. The base was ready, but...

Koruuksi. Uuchantuu. I can't leave them behind. Not them.

Especially not after the way they'd left things.

She turned to Araana, Muuzuuri, and the Natari warrior.

"Koruuksi and Uuchantuu can take care of themselves, Estingai," Muuzuuri said. "They know what they're doing. Koruuksi told me to make sure you went forward with the plan whatever happened to him."

The Natari warrior nodded, catching Estingai's attention.

"Koruuksi is a good man," he said in heavily accented Atongo. "A clever one, too, as is our princess. Together, I believe they can convince His Majesty to send more help and save our city."

Estingai flexed her hands, anger and guilt rising at even the thought of choosing Kojatere over Koruuksi.

But it's what he'd want me to do.

She let out her frustration in a half-scream, half-grunt, slamming her fist against the wall, then looked to the generals. "Tell everyone to move out. Ready the fighters and transports for the drop team. We leave Efruumani today."

A shiver ran down her spine as the words left her mouth, and she could see they had the same effect on the others.

"We make for Mjatafa Mwonga," she continued. "But I want a few transports held back ready to leave for E Kwekuue the moment we have an opening."

She rounded on the Natari warrior.

"Leave two of your people behind to go with that team. Whether or not Koruuksi and your princess succeed in convincing your king to evacuate, we're going to get him, and your people to safety. The rest of you are with me."

3

TO KNOW EACH OTHER AGAIN

Exodus countdown: 6 days, 1 hour, 39 minutes

Yndlova had to steady herself as she stepped off the lift onto Othaashle's floor. Her mind was still trying to make sense of the amicable conversation she'd had with Vysla. On her walk back, she'd analyzed it over and over again, trying to find some sort of guile in the way he presented information or asked for specifics, but she couldn't find any. She'd simply enjoyed talking with him.

Can the man really just be that different from his wife?

As she came to Othaashle's door, dialing in the passcode known to only herself, Othaashle, Itese and a few others, Yndlova took a deep breath and reigned in her expression.

Regardless of the confusing circumstances surrounding it, she'd secured Vysla's help.

Hopefully, it will actually work.

Yndlova had to admit that the man was a genius—likely one of the reasons Skadaatha married him. If anyone could find a way to restore Itese's memories, it would likely be him.

As the door opened before her, however, Yndlova frowned at an empty apartment.

"Othaashle?" she called, stepping inside. "Itese?"

No answer.

Narrowing her eyes, Yndlova stepped deeper into the main room.

She looked toward the balcony, but the door was closed, and no figures stood on the part she could see. The drinks and stacks of papers still sat on the main table.

Did they get called away?

Yndlova likely would have been called as well, unless it was an internal affair of the Redeemed.

She almost turned to go back to the lift and look for them elsewhere, maybe try their comms, when a shuddering croak reached her ears, sending shivers down her spine.

Yndlova tensed, falling into a crouch.

With careful steps, she approached the hallway, rounding the corner.

She froze, ice flooding her veins.

Two Redeemed lay in the hall, still in their armor. The one further away made bile rise in Yndlova's throat. It looked even more bereft of life than a corpse—more like a husk. The one closest to her...

"Itese."

For a moment, Yndlova assumed the worst, wondering what had happened to Othaashle.

Then she remembered herself and dropped to Itese's side, fighting back the panic as she looked over the wound. She ripped off Itese's breastplate and clenched her jaw. The woman's gemcrest was dim.

When Itese moved, drawing in a shuddering breath, Yndlova nearly screamed.

She's alive. Thank the God King.

Grabbing her friend under the shoulders, Yndlova pulled Itese toward the balcony, wrenching the door open in her haste. She laid Itese down, then started taking off her armor and throwing it back into the hallway.

Itese drew in a ragged breath, gemcrest filling with Auroralight.

"It's not fatal," Yndlova said, taking care as she pulled Itese's shirt up to get a better look. Even as she did, muscle and skin started to knit together before her eyes.

Oh, right.

It was slow and would likely take a couple of hours to fully heal, or for the pain to go away, but Itese would be alright.

She sighed as relief washed over her.

"Yndlova."

Yndlova looked to Itese, the hoarseness of her friend's voice pained her.

"My mask," Itese said. "Can you take it off?"

Yndlova hesitated. "Are you having trouble breathing?"

"Technically, I don't need to." Her voice was less hoarse this time. "It's just claustrophobic."

Yndlova bit her lip but did as Itese asked.

I've seen Othaashle without her mask, and I've been trying to find my friend. Why should this—

Yndlova froze. Her chest tightened and a lump formed in her throat as the mask fell from her fingers.

Shining silver eyes stared up at her from a face of pale grey. Yndlova imagined she could see the miniscule hints of the woman's former blue-violet complexion. She teased out a familiar jawline and cheekbones and wonderfully full lips from under shining golden markings.

"Aada," she breathed.

It was her.

She was alive. All this time!

Yndlova reigned herself in, schooling her expression. It was one of the most difficult things she'd ever done, but she couldn't dump everything on Aada in this state.

Itese, not Aada. For now, she has to be Itese. As much as I wish it didn't need to be.

She realized Aada—Itese—was staring back at her, and had probably seen all the emotions play over her unguarded face.

Yndlova swallowed, rising. "Your friend. I need to—"

Itese's hand closing around her wrist cut Yndlova off, sending a shiver through her.

"I don't know who that is," Itese said, still out of breath despite her healing. "Drained like that, I can't recognize them but..." She trailed off, squeezing her eyes shut. "They're gone. They were dead when I found them after you left."

Yndlova blinked, looking between Itese and the husk. "Who—?"

"Othaashle."

Yndlova went cold. "No. You must have—"

"Yndlova." Itese's voice was firm, those familiar eyes hard. "It was Othaashle. I don't know if she killed that Redeemed, but she knocked me out and drained me of my Auroralight. I don't know if she left me alive on purpose or tried to kill me and was simply careless, but it was her."

"No," Yndlova breathed, falling back against the balcony wall. "No. It couldn't have been. She would never do that. She must not have wanted you dead. If Othaashle wants someone dead, they're—"

Her words died on her tongue as a low boom rumbled across the inner district. Followed by another, and another. Yndlova looked out just as fire flashed into the sky, smoke rising into the air after.

Then a massive bolt of lightning shot into the sky. It passed high above all the buildings, above even the Vale, then forked out in every direction, creating a miniature lightning storm that sent shocks of blue throughout Mjatafa Mwonga's orange sky.

Yndlova gasped, looking to Itese. Her friend wore the same shock on her face. Then Yndlova went cold. "No."

Itese cocked her head.

"The explosives we made. That's what this is," she breathed, putting the pieces together. Othaashle *had* betrayed them. In a way that ran so much deeper than attacking a friend.

"But those were all dummy targets," Itese said. "Ships and equipment that needed to be replaced, tenements that should be torn down, empty warehouses."

Yndlova shook her head. "You don't understand. Othaashle requisitioned more for the Vale's perimeter. Shields to direct blasts away from the Vale should the Remnant try to approach it or cut the city off from its energy. She worked on them herself."

Itese's eyes widened. Yndlova swallowed the lump in her throat.

"With just a few tweaks to the shielding mechanism..." Itese began.

"She could direct the energy of the blasts inward at the Vale itself," Yndlova finished, "at Boaathal."

Silence reigned over the balcony for a long moment. Then Itese squeezed Yndlova's hand.

"Go," she said. "Save Boaathal and the Vale. Even if the blasts wouldn't destroy it, that could be a devastating blow to the city's infrastructure and to Exodus. And stay away from Othaashle. She may have betrayed us, but we're no match for her."

Yndlova gritted her teeth, but nodded. "What about you?"

Itese let go of Yndlova's wrist. She tried to push herself up but gritted her teeth and groaned with pain before falling back onto the balcony floor.

"I'm out of this for now," she said. "Find Taizak and put him in charge of the Redeemed until I can take over. He'll know what to do in a situation like this. Tell them to stay away from Othaashle as well. I don't know if they would believe her betrayal. Even if they did, I don't know if they could bring themselves to strike her down if they managed to gain the upper hand in a fight."

Yndlova took Itese's hand again despite herself. "Are you sure you're okay? Do you need me to send a few Redeemed? I can—"

Itese closed her other hand over Yndlova's. "I'll be okay, Yndlova. You need to make sure things stay that way. Go save the city."

Yndlova hesitated. This was all happening so fast. Othaashle's betrayal, the bombs going off, the threat to Boaathal, finding Aada again.

At that thought, Yndlova looked down at Itese, her friend, who had once been so much more.

She needs me.

Yndlova's strength returned to her and she rose to her feet, still gazing at Itese.

I found her. After all this time, I have my friend back. Even if she doesn't know.

Yndlova had to make sure that it wasn't all for nothing. That both of them survived to see what could happen now that they had found each other. To make sure they could know each other again as they once had.

I won't fail. Not this time.

GLOSSARY

GEMCRESTS

Every living creature on Efruumani, both flora and fauna, is born with a gemcrest of biogems, or "nodes" as they are often referred to in conjunction with their specific color, but other than the legendary Draakon, which have unfortunately passed into extinction, only the sentient races of the Natari and Samjati are able to use those gemcrests as a focus for the abilities commonly known as Auroramancy. On plants and animals, the placements of these gemcrests vary widely, but they are more consistent on the sentient races, forming over the brow on Samjati, and at the clavicle on Natari. Each gemcrest is made up of twenty-four individual biogems that are smooth and rounded to the touch, capable of holding brilliant auroralight for up to nine days if the individual uses no auroramantic abilities during that time. If these biogems are cracked, they will still function, but will leak auroralight, depleting the individuals store of auroralight at a faster rate.

THE AURORAS AND LIGHTLESSNESS

Efruumani is defined by its auroras. The tidally locked world would contain no life on either side if not for the strong magnetic field that gives life to these magical auroras, and the power they give all life on Efruumani to adapt to its otherwise harsh environments. Though solar flares constantly and erratically hit the habitable moon's magnetosphere, the auroras dance constantly at both the anti-solar and sub-solar poles, and every six days, they spread out over the skies, dancing through the atmosphere like a massive net and showering Efruumani with their light, converging on the twilight band, where they linger before returning to the poles. When these auroras light the skies, every biogem, whether in a living creature's gemcrest, or harvested from one, fills with auroralight. Though the gemcrests vary by size, all hold enough auroralight to last from six to nine days on Efruumani, during which they experience the latent benefits of those gemcrests. Auroramancers are the exception to this, as their abilities use up auroralight at a faster rate. If they use up their reserves and are unable to replenish their auroralight from a harvested biogem, they will become lightless.

∼

Lightlessness is the absence of auroralight in one's system. It manifests differently depending on the color of an individual's gemcrest, but in general it is a sort of physical and mental depression brought on by a lack of auroralight flowing through one's body. To deprive someone—even an animal—of auroralight intentionally is considered torture, and those with auroralight to spare will offer it to someone who is lightless or on the verge of being so without a second thought. Long-term effects of lightlessness have rarely been studied, and though there do not appear to be any permanent effects, recovery after an extended period of lightlessness is a long and arduous process. There have been individuals able to function with some sense of normalcy while lightless, but those individuals exhibit a strength of will far beyond that of the average person.

AURORABORN, FIREBORN, ICEBORN, AND GENETICS

Auroramancy is a genetic ability, and at the same time, not. Two auroramancers, or even one auroramancer and a non-auroramancer will have a better chance at producing an auroramancer child than two non-auroramancers, yet it is not an exact science. It is estimated that at any given time, twelve percent of the world's population are auroramancers, and of that fraction, one twenty-fourth are full auroraborn, with access to all twelve auroramantic abilities. It is estimated that another twenty-fourth have opalescent gemcrests, which are effectively useless both in Auroramancy and in any latent abilities they pass on, and that the other eleven auroramantic abilities are divided equally among the remaining auroramancer population.

There are two sides to every auroramantic ability, reflecting both the climate and Throne of the side of the world that each race inhabits the majority of. Natari auroramancers can use one set of abilities, for which they are often referred to as "fireborn" or sometimes "lightborn", and Samjati auroramancers are similarly referred to as "iceborn" or "shadowborn" for their abilities. When the two mix, and the union produces an auroramancer, that auroramancer either has one set of abilities or the other, never one of each. For the most part, Samjati and Natari experience the same latent effects of a given gemcrest, with the exception of grey and violet gemcrests.

ORIGINS OF THE POWERS AND LEGENDS

Gemcrests and Auroramancy have been around as long as Efruumani itself, with the Draakon likely earning their places as the original auroramancers. It is speculated that at one point, there were only six auroramantic abilities for either race, with this perspective pushed by those who have engaged in the study of history and the study of the mystical Thrones of power, but there is little evidence to corroborate sub arguments.

INDIVIDUAL ABILITIES BASIC MECHANICS

All life on Efruumani is constantly using auroralight. This is coloquially referred to as "burning" auroralight, likening it to a candle or oil lantern. To use one's abilities, an auroramancer can "brighten" their gemcrests or "nodes", "flare" them for bursts of power, and "dim" them to stop using their abilities or even suppress the latent effects they receive from their gemcrests. Very skilled auroramancers can even brighten and dim their gemcrests node-by-node. This is part of the trade-off that full auroraborn experience when using their powers, as they must learn to control their abilities by individual node, or at least by each pair of colored nodes.

Through great discipline and concentration, non-auroramancers can slightly dim or brighten their gemcrests to achieve augmented or diminished latent effects. The benefit is often not considered worth the intense training, but for those with moonstone or emerald gemcrests, the difference could be between winning or losing a fight or athletic event, or even between life and death.

Because auroramancers use up their auroralight at a faster pace more often than not, they experience a compounding effect of the latent abilities, especially while using their abilities.

Violet or Amethyst

Those with an amethyst gemcrest have the latent ability of temperature regulation inverse to their auroramantic ability. Samjati are able to produce cold sensations or even ice if there is enough water in the air around them, while they tend to run warm to better adapt to their native environment. Natari can produce heat and fire, while they tend to run cool, giving them a break from the humidity and constant heat of their environment.

Since cold is merely the absence of heat, the Samjati amethyst ability is not as straightforward as its Natari counterpart. While the Natari can heat objects with a touch, or even the air around them, as well as produce directional fire or even lightning if they flare their abilities, heating up that air until it becomes fire or plasma, the Samjati instead siphon the heat from the air around them or the object they are holding. As such, while Natari can "shoot" and direct fire or lightning from a starting point to an end point, Samjati, more often than not must choose an endpoint or space in the air. They can freeze the air around someone, but cannot imitate Natari by throwing columns of ice or darts, unless they form those darts and then physically throw them. The one exception is when Samjati flare this ability. A flare can power freezing the air far away from the auroramancer, or it can power what is colloquially referred to as an "ice beam" or "cold shock". This connects the auroramancer to a point in the distance and supercools the air in a thin line from one point to the other, leaving whatever is on the receiving ends supercooled and flash frozen. It also creates a flash of light and a screech due to the sudden localized drop in temperature.

Aqua or Aquamarine

Those with an aquamarine gemcrest sleep more soundly anyone else, yet wake more easily and are either more refreshed or alert when they do so. They also tend to be more alert and focused in general when awake. The auroramantic ability allows manipulation of the races' respective elements. Natari are able to manipulate fire, lightning or energy, and molten lava up to a certain distance and volume. They are also able to cool lava, but that requires a flare of their powers. Samjati are able to manipulate ice, water and mist up to a certain volume and distance, though changing phases requires them to flare their powers. Each race is able to shape its respective element and move it through space. The more they manipulate and the farther the distance from them, the more difficult it is, and the more auroralight it uses up.

∼

Green or Emerald

Those with an emerald gemcrest tend to have better constitutions than anyone else. They are more resistant to disease, muscle aches, stomach aches, never have allergies, and heal at a noticeably faster rate than anyone else. Emerald gemcrests grant the ability to push and pull on the races' respective elements with the focal point as one's center of gravity. This does not allow for the same freedom of movement that those with aquamarine gemcrests command, but it does have its advantages. Samjati are able to push and pull on ice and water, and can form a bubble around themselves with great practice, while Natari can do the same with molten lava or volcanic rock. The greatest advantage both hold is a semblance of flight and fast movement. Both can hover over either element and push themselves in great arcs to travel large distances at a great speed. One observation made by Samjati that have ventured to lightside is that the warmer the water, the more effort and auroralight it takes to push or pull.

Those particularly skilled in balancing their pushes and pulls are able to achieve incredibly graceful, almost dance-like movements in the air.

~

Grey or Moonstone

Those with moonstone gemcrests have their latent abilities split by race. Those of Natari heritage tend to move faster and be more agile with incredible balance, stamina and flexibility, while those of Samjati heritage tend to be stronger, have stronger bones and ligaments, have an easier time building muscle, are harder to cut or scrape, and have more control over and awareness of their individual muscles. The auroramantic abilities are similarly divided. Samjati auroramancers can brighten their gemcrests to achieve greater strength and durability, as well as bursts of it, and the Natari can do the same with physical speed and endurance. Both can achieve a semblance of the other's ability to a certain degree. Natari can move their limbs faster to harness more power in certain movements, and Samjati can use their strength to run faster or control their muscles to move faster in short bursts. Moonstone nodes use up auroralight at a faster rate than most other colors

~

Clear, White, or Diamond

Those with diamond gemcrests have more acute senses than those around them, are more sensitive to touch, can distinguish color and tone quality and flavor a bit better, and experience greater and more frequent arousal, both sexual and flight or fight, so they tend to be more perceived as more passionate, erratic, or emotional. The auroramantic ability allows for senses that are enhanced even further. Flaring their abilities can give great temporary bursts of pain and clarity depending on the sensory input. All senses are enhanced at once and though the auroramancer cannot pick and choose, those who are especially skilled can tune out the other senses.

∼

Multicolored or Opal

An opal gemcrest is often considered the most useless gemcrest. To this day, it has no known latent effects, and its auroramantic ability is only useful in conjunction with other abilities. An auroramancer with opal biogems can flare their auroramantic abilities far beyond that of a normal flare, to the point where it will deplete anywhere from an entire biogem to a pair.

The only way in which the opal gemcrest has been deemed useful by itself is that those with one who have experienced lightlessness seem to feel less of a depression, as though by not losing access to any latent abilities, the effects of lightlessness are muted.

∼

Orange or Sunstone

Individuals with a sunstone gemcrest have extremely good memories. Often, they have some sort of eidetic memory of some sort, whether it is visual, audio, or some other sort of mnemonic assisting. The ability it grants is that to see into the past. The more auroralight expended, the father into the past one can see, and the longer an expanse of time they can view. This sort of past-sight is localized, however. A person on one side of the world would not be able to view the past of someone sitting on the other side of the world, or even down the street from them. Some have reported occasionally being able to touch a person or object and see their past beyond the current location, but that is an area requiring further study.

Yellow or Topaz

Those born with a topaz gemcrest are either born lucky or unlucky. The degree of that good or bad luck varies, but the distribution tends to lilt toward moderately lucky, though that luck does not always manifest in the ways one would expect. Some believe that these individuals have a greater connection to Fortune rather than simply being lucky, or are maybe more aware of their place in events.

As such, auroramancers with a topaz gemcrest are able to manipulate luck, chance, and coincidence in a localized manner. They can further manipulate their own luck, or do so for everyone or a few individuals in a room they occupy. Theoretically, an unlucky topaz auroramancer could constantly expend auroralight reversing their luck, but this would require many spare biogems, as topaz biogems use up auroralight even more quickly than moonstone biogems.

Red or Ruby

Ruby gemcrests bestow quicker and more deft reflexes on individuals. The auroramantic abilities they bestow are again similar, yet divided between the races. Natari have the ability to create and manipulate hardlight, while Samjati have the ability to create and manipulate darklight. Both of these can act as solid constructs, though while hardlight is more angular and solid, darklight tends to form in more rounded or circular constructs with wispy edges. While auroralight is necessary to maintain both, one's will is what defines the shape. Ruby auroramancers are often seen as masters of their thoughts due to the control they must exert to keep their constructs in a given shape. Recent study has discovered that both hardlight and darklight are a sort of magnetic forcefield capable of keeping air and pressure in or out of a given area. Though hardlight and darklight are often used as armor, shields, or blunt weapons, it is almost impossible to use either to create an edged weapon due to how fine that edge would need to be in order to cut as well as a metal or even wood edge.

~

Blue or Sapphire

Those with sapphire gemcrests will age slower than others and in general look younger once reaching maturity. This includes their skin aging less easily, and Samjati with sapphire gemcrests experience sunburns less frequently to a point. All with sapphire gemcrests have younger, more child-like features in general even after maturity.

The sapphire gemcrest offers auroramancers the ability to transfer power. Samjati can take auroralight from others, while Natari can give their auroralight to others. This is easier to do with animals or non-auroramancers, but even then, if the person is aware and resisting, it can be difficult. Though this can be done without touching the target, it is extremely difficult. If one's gemcrest is full, the recipient gains a burst of energy that can affect them in strange ways, and experiences a concentrated, sustained boost of the corresponding latent ability of the gemcrest they have taken their energy from.

For auroramancers, many believe that they can only steal enough to fuel a single pair of biogems, and while this is easiest, it is not impossible to use auroralight from another single-color gemcrest to fuel an entire auroramancer's gemcrest.

Samjati are stigmatized for this while Natari are praised, and most Samjati with sapphire gemcrests have an unspoken rule that they will never steal enough to make another lightless, and try to only do it in dire situations.

~

Amber

Amber gemcrests give individuals a certain amount of foresight. The feeling is like a premonition or gut-feeling, but more solid. Auroramancers can use an extension of this that allows them to see a short time into the future, and speeds up their mental processing in order to act on this information in a timely manner. This ability burns through auroralight more quickly than any other and makes these individuals particularly dangerous, as one on a battlefield or in a fight could take down countless opponents even without much skill.

Though gifts of foretelling and prophecy are rare, they do occur almost exclusively in full auroraborn and those with amber gemcrests.

∼

Black or Onyx

Onyx gemcrests make an individual more aware of the Auroramancy being used around them, and interfere to a small degree with others' abilities to detect power being used in their immediate vicinity. They allow Samjati auroramancers to hide their own use of power or create a fog around them, and allow Natari to detect uses of power. Skilled onyx Natari auroramancers are able to pick out exactly what auroramantic abilities are being used, and even sense auroralight being burned at a resting rate. They say there is a certain music that defines each one, but nothing they can latch onto enough to replicate.

∼

Full Auroraborn

Full auroraborn have twelve pairs of each color biogem. Their ability to use all twelve powers of a given set makes them extremely dangerous. There have been no recorded instances of individuals with a full gemcrest who were not auroramancers, but auroraborn do experience a mix of those same latent effects, just to a lesser degree. Similarly, the tradeoff for their abilities is economy of auroralight. While some skilled auroraborn have figured out how to transfer auroralight between their different pairs of biogems, they can only burn two biogems's worth of one color at a given time—though this can be offset by their opal flares—and they must choose which abilities to expend their auroralight on. Due to this, auroraborn often use up their auroralight faster than any other auroramancers, and they cannot always be burning at faster rate like many single-color auroramancers do.

SUBSTANCES OF INTEREST

Silver

Silver has demonstrated the ability to pierce pure investment, such as aurora or Efruumani's spirits, the oruu. Some primitive cultures who feared the oruu used to capture and pierce the spirits in rituals. While many of these old practices were barbaric, their study led to our modern, far more ethical methods of corralling the oruu and manipulating them for our purposes. Though there have never been tests to confirm, it has been theorized by Vizier Skadaatha that if a god such as Lord Ynuukwidas, or his avatar, at least, is made of pure investment, silver could potentially harm a god in ways that other materials cannot. Though no credible evidence has been found, it is rumored that Lord Ynuukwidas created a weapon of silver for Othaashle Mestari to use against Kweshrima if necessary, though that point is now moot. It has been theorized that Type-Two Lightforged, the Unbound Redeemed, are more affected by silver than other metals, but Othaashle Mestari has not allowed tests to confirm. She did, however, confirm the rumors that all Redeemed armor is plated or lined with silver depending on the function. She would not elaborate on why.

Aluminum

Aluminum possesses the remarkable ability to disrupt abilities fueled by investment (auroralight), so far including both georaural technology and Auroramancy. Tests are still being run to measure the exact parameters of this disruption, but it has proven invaluable in military use, engineering, and integration into georaural technology. In georaural technology, aluminum plating and wire can be used to direct the effect of a given georaural, or even one of its smaller components. Its most common application is shielding. The lightweight metal can disrupt the fire conjured by a violet-crest Fireborn, but it will not do anything special or unusual against fire or magma manipulated and directed by a Fireborn. If someone uses Auroramancy within a room lined with aluminum, a black-crest Fireborn will be unable to sense the activity. Similarly, a black-crest Fireborn inside an aluminum-lined room will be unable to sense any Auroramantic activity outside the room.

Iron

For whatever reason, iron causes severe injuries and illness to both Natari and Samjati. While other metals will simply cut and lacerate, iron burns to the touch. This does not apply to any other species on Efruumani, however. Any animals or plants cut with an iron blade experience the same effects as when cut with any other edge, metal or otherwise.

 Causes harm to Natari and Samjati

Zidanio

Zidanio somehow increases the power, strength or potency of whatever it touches exponentially. This extends to physical strength, latent biogem abilities, and use of Auroramancy, though not to georaural technology. The metal itself cannot be used as a battery, but can be used in concert with one to great effect in increasing output. Measurements are still being recorded to test the effects of greater and lesser quantities of metal with a given device or auroramancer. The Redeemed would be perfect test subjects, but for political reasons, that could cause unneeded issues. Tests such as heat treatment and the creation of alloys are forthcoming pending the discovery and mining of greater quantities of this ore, as the current supply is too low and too precious to accidentally waste. Studies of myths and folk heroes on both lightside and darkside suggest that Zidanio has been used in the past without knowledge of its exact properties to create supposedly holy talismans and arms of great power that granted their owners incredible abilities, physical strength most common among them.

When applied to georaural technology, the metals do not impart power to the device, but instead act as a power converter, an even greater breakthrough. This allows georaural technology, previously only capable of being powered by auroralight, to be powered by other forms of energy such as electricity. It was this breakthrough that allowed the Imaia's scientists and engineers to make such incredible breakthroughs in spacefaring technology so quickly, and is largely what will allow project Exodus to work as planned. While the widespread application of such technology could be revolutionary, catapulting even the most average citizens of the Imaia years into the future, the limited supply of the material has led to its existence being classified, as its applications must be carefully weighed and applied where they will most benefit the Imaia as a whole.

∽

Aikanuum

Aikanuum somehow increases the physical speed of whatever it touches, or rather, increases the capacity for physical speed. Reactions and reflexes are most uniformly affected, while the act of walking or running or conscious movement seems more easily regulated. Its touch seems to grant a sense of what is going to happen, but this is hard to measure, especially in comparison to the increased speed. Myths and folklore imply that like Zidanio, this metal may have been unknowingly used in the past, allowing for individuals to move and react at great speeds, as well as premonitions. Other folktales of impossibly lucky individuals, even when compared to yellowcrests, fortune tellers, and prophecies suggest that this metal may have more properties, but how to test and quantify these properties remains a mystery.

When used with georaural technology, Aikanuum increases the "battery-life" so to speak, of a given device. It both takes longer for the device to use up its stored power, and seems to almost entirely eliminate decay when not in use. Flares and functions that take increasing amounts of energy still use more energy than the base functions, but at a proportional rate.

THE REDEEMED

The Redeemed, or "Lightforged," as they are referred to by enemies of the Imaia or those uncomfortable with the Redeemed, are the Imaia's elite warriors, led by their champion Othaashle, the first of the Redeemed. Not much is known about the Redeemed outside of their own numbers and the leaders of the Imaia's priesthood and armed forces. The public is told that the Redeemed are warriors that fell in battle on one side or the other, who Ynuukwidas, Lord of the Imaia, judged worthy of Redemption and a second chance at life to fight for the Imaia. They are supposedly immortal warriors who always wear masks to hide the identity of those they once were from themselves and others. They have no memory of their past lives, and are seen as a symbol or Ynuukwidas' power and the might of the Imaia. They fight the battles of the Imaia so that fewer of the Imaia's citizens need give their lives in service of their neighbors.

∽

Though "Redeemed" is the official term used to refer to these soldiers, in scientific terms, they are referred to as lightforged invested entities, either Type-One or Type-Two. The type-one entities are what are most commonly referred to as Redeemed, whereas type-two are often referred to as "Unbound Redeemed." Though the preferred term refers to their physical state, type refers to the manner of their creation.

All Redeemed are created by snatching a soul before it passes on through the Gates of Death. That soul can be held for a thus-far indeterminate amount of time, though it is theorized that the soul will start to deteriorate after a certain point. Upon "resurrection," the soul is restored to the physical realm by tying it to something physical with power, and then using that same power to fill any cracks or wounds the soul sustained at the time of death or during its previous life. It has not been conclusively proven, but theorized, that the more a soul suffered in life, and the more traumatic its death, the greater power it would wield as a Redeemed, or at the very least it would possess a greater affinity for the use of its powers. Upon resurrection, the soul is granted the abilities of a Natari Auroraborn in addition to their previous Auroramantic abilities.

Type-One entities are resurrected by re-attaching their soul to a physical body, usually the soul's original body. When this happens, the body's skin turns a pale white-grey, and markings of shining, solid gold that feel like metal to the touch form over its body. These do not appear to form any sort of uniform markings, though they close over open wounds in stylized manners, and there is at least one grouping on either side of the torso, each limb, and the face. The irises turn a silver, gold-flecked color and glow. If the body is Samjati, the antlers turn silver and become as hard as steel, forming sharp edges and points. If the body is Natari, any markings such as stripes or spots turn gold. They also grow a second gemcrest. If Natari, they grow it out of their brow, and if Samjati, out of their clavicle. The newer gemcrest seems to have tiny gold flecks at the edge of each individual biogem on the gemcrest, but since these are usually covered by a mask or armor, little formal study has been performed. Most Redeemed also experience some sort of growth in height or musculature upon resurrection. This is theorized to happen because their primary duty is that of intimidating warriors.

∽

Type-Two entities are souls whose physical bodies could not be retrieved, either because they were lost on the battlefield or too far gone upon death to be restored. These souls are given bodies constructed of hardlight, with accents of the same gold that the Type-One entities receive. Though their bodies are slightly transparent, they appear to function normally, though somehow, these individuals seem to grow back the gemcrest their old soul maintained. Something fascinating, but not properly researched at this point.

∽

The cost of this resurrection for both types of Redeemed is the lost of who they once were. When they awaken, they have no memory of the person they once were. It is assumed they somehow retain certain general knowledge incongruous with true amnesia, as well as honed reflexes and skills, as though the lightforged train, the only sort of "basic training" they are known to receive is a formal education in Auroramantic abilities and the use and application of newer technologies. Lord Ynuukwidas has explained that he scours the Redeemed of who they once were, so that their loyalties to the Imaia will not be tested, and they will not need to worry about discrimination based on who they were before their redemption. Because of this, all type-one entities wear masks to hide their faces, and most wear either a uniform or full armor at all times. Type-two entities have facial features that move like a normal face when they speak or look around, but the features emulate that of the masks of the Redeemed, and betray very little emotion.

Though it is not known exactly how Lord Ynuukwidas catches these souls before they pass through the Gates of Death, it is believed that the sword, Ilkwalerva, wielded by Othaashle, is the mechanism through which this is performed, as in battle, she often sought out the most dangerous enemy Auroramancers, and reports have confirmed that the other Redeemed did not begin to appear until after Othaashle began using Ilkwalerva in battle much more frequently rather than simply relying on her Auroramantic prowess.

Made in the USA
Middletown, DE
24 October 2023

41227633R00307